THE ALL-NEW, ALL-ORIGINAL ANTHOLOGY OF THE SCIENCE FICTION THAT IS CHANGING SCIENCE FICTION!

THE BERKLEY SHOWCASE

"BILLY BIG-EYES"	HOWARD WALDROP
"THE GODS OF REORTH"	ELIZABETH A. LYNN
"SERGEANT PEPPER"	KARL HANSEN
"THE PRINCESS AND THE BEAR"	ORSON SCOTT CARD
"RAISING THE GREEN LION"	JANET E. MORRIS
"LAST THINGS"	JOHN KESSEL
"THE ADVENTURES OF LANCE THE LIZARD"	RONALD ANTHONY CROSS
"STEPFATHER BANK"	DAVID ANDREISSEN

New Writings in Science Fiction
Edited by Victoria Schochet and John Silbersack

The Berkley showcase

Vol. 1

Edited by Victoria Schochet & John Silbersack

NEW WRITINGS IN SCIENCE FICTION AND FANTASY

BERKLEY BOOKS, NEW YORK

THE BERKLEY SHOWCASE:
NEW WRITINGS IN SCIENCE FICTION

A Berkley Book / published by arrangement with
the authors

PRINTING HISTORY
Berkley edition / April 1980

ISBN: 0-425-04446-7

A BERKLEY BOOK® TM 757,375
PRINTED IN THE UNITED STATES OF AMERICA

CONTENTS

INTRODUCTION

In the publishing trade, what you now hold in your hands is referred to as a "house" anthology. That means that THE BERKLEY SHOWCASE is edited by the science fiction editors of a mass-market paperback house, editors responsible for, among other things, the editing and publishing of five science fiction titles every month. Those titles add up to a great many words passed to press, covers commissioned, blurbs written, books bought and sold. A great many books by a great many authors—over 120 authors make up Berkley's science fiction list. Fortunately, among them are Robert A Heinlein, Frank Herbert, and T.H. White. The tremendous success of authors such as these allows us the freedom to experiment, to take risks, to invest in new writers and try to make them as successful as possible. To a great extent, this is what THE BERKLEY SHOWCASE is all about: a nonprofit-oriented house anthology which will allow us to search out and publish new talent.

Of course, the anthology is about other things as well. It gives its editors the satisfaction of reading short story as well as novel submissions. It gives us the chance to add to the wealth of talent in the science fiction field in a way that Berkley has not been able to before. We are absolutely delighted to become a new market for short story writers and readers alike, especially since the short story remains the cornerstone of science fiction literature. But the most important thing this anthology can do is the same thing all collections should do: bring to the reader excellent, provocative stories written by authors whose publishing histories may run the gamut from nonexistent to beyond the call of duty.

Undoubtedly, the anthology will not remain merely a collection of stories. As we put this issue together, we realized that it didn't do everything we wanted it to. In the future we intend to include interviews with Berkley authors, excerpts from novels in progress or upcoming, articles on various aspects of science fiction publishing, and so on. We may have had a sense of what we wanted this book to be, but it really has found its own life, despite our preconceptions. And in choosing what stories to buy from the hundreds of submissions we have received, we learned a great deal about our own tastes. We can only hope now that our tastes and yours coincide, and that you find these stories, all of which we feel are fresh, exciting speculative works, to be as enjoyable as we did.

—Victoria Schochet
—John Silbersack

BILLY BIG-EYES

by Howard Waldrop

A love story, we believe, to be rightly told must be more daringly executed than any cops-and-robbers chaser. Shakespeare knew this instinctively, and his various Montagues and Capulets conduct their private lives as though planning the great train robbery. Lately though, mass culture has opted for passion pablum served with a spoon. The result: Love Story *and its ilk rule the fray. Fortunately Howard Waldrop, a true Elizabethan at heart, has succeeded where Lonelyhearts and Hallmark sap have too long held sway. "Billy Big-Eyes" is skillful narrative, rousing adventure, and a passionate love story, all coursing the spaceways in a world that must be perceived to be believed.*

"To hear the sun—
What a thing to believe.
But it's all around
If we could but perceive.
To know ultraviolet,
Infrared, X rays,
Beauty to find
In so many ways."
—"Om"
Mike Pinder
The Moody Blues

The technician turned away from the plotboard.

"Very good," said the man down in the middle of the room. "Now could you please light it in something I can see? Ultraviolet, infrared?"

The plot analyst looked sheepish. He switched his console to a higher mode. "Sorry, sir."

"Forget it," said Maxwell Big-Eyes from the floor. He put one arm under the other elbow. With the fingers of the supported arm he tapped his teeth, studying the board.

Maxwell Big-Eyes was Chief of Scouts Emeritus. He had given thirty years of active duty to the Service and had distinguished himself.

He was retired and kept in consultant capacity, called only to handle special problems. His other duties were largely ceremonial in nature.

Beneath the well-known masked face was still the mind of a Scout, the same which had charted unnumbered sectors, led rescue missions, advised and questioned the leadership of the Systems for three decades.

All the bureaucracy, speeches, ceremonies and dinners in the worlds had not dimmed his enthusiasm for the jobs at hand. His first was to make the Systems of worlds a safer and better place in which to live. The second, and most important to him, was the welfare of each and every Scout in the Service.

Maxwell Big-Eyes was stocky of build. He was dressed in red tight trousers, a vest of purplish satin, a russet cape. A leather and plastic mask covered his face from nose to forehead, leaving mouth and hairline exposed. The straps of the maskpiece extended over the back of his head. Where the eyes on his face should be were two opaque lenses the size of grapefruit.

"This was the last position?" he asked.

"Positive." said the plotter.

Maxwell turned to the man in the white smock behind him. "Snorkel, I'd like you to get my niece Dierdre up here, and readings on the conditions of the missions of the other Scouts. But . . . "—he put up his hand—"I'd like to talk to Billy myself."

"You think it wise to let him know? His mission is on critical status right now."

The two men were of the same age though Doctor Snorkel was much taller, had a mustache, carried himself more erectly and was not Sighted. His hair was solid iron-gray; that of the shorter man was peppered.

Maxwell turned to the plotboard which to the two others in the room was dark.

"We'll wait and see what he finds before we contact him, then."

Snorkel put his hand on Maxwell's shoulder. "Max," said the scientist, "mightn't it be better if we didn't let him know?"

The old Scout turned to face his friend. There was no expression on the blank, large-orbed mask, but the mouth below was a tight line. The tight line opened and closed.

"I know why you're saying that, Otto, so I'll let it pass." Then the short old man sighed. His mouth grinned, relaxed. "I'll do it when the time comes. He's my great-nephew. If anybody has to be upset, let it be me."

From his ship *The Argus*, Billy Big-Eyes had been watching the suspicious plasma cloud for some hours.

To normal human eyes the night around him would have been black, broken by points of stars, a smudge of dust cloud, perhaps the solitary dot of a comet rounding a sun nearby.

Billy was not watching with normal human eyes, and he was not looking at darkness. He scanned the cloud in several spectra, ultraviolet, infrared, long radio, X ray, those further above and below.

The night in infrared was a dull glow like heated metal, pulsing in the light of interstellar hydrogen. There were tight points, like holes punched in paper, where certain stars gave off no IR radiation. There were others with streamers and long flares like painted brushstrokes. The whole of space around him was covered with the light, as if a colored scene from one of Dante's hells.

In the ultraviolet, the stars and space became draped velvet curtains and the light itself was frozen and black. Stars were dull balls of fur, gas clouds became scrim curtains behind which the suns beat coldly. With a few seconds concentration, Billy could see through all the other gases around him.

The plasma cloud ahead was different, though; still opaque.

X ray held the strangest view of all; sleeting points of light flew in every direction, away, toward, tangent to him. Some appeared just before his eyes and receded forward, cosmic rays which had passed through the ship and his head. The space around him roared in that spectrum. The sleet moved like an aurora, a shimmering wave through which at first he could see only a few kilometers.

The stars slowly took form through these garbage hazes. In the X ray they were hollow, like glass ornaments or fishbowls, and they spun slowly as he neared them. Then they hove to on the sides and receded as if they were crystals pulled on wires away from him. Gas clouds were in view only a few seconds before he looked through them to others beyond.

And so on, up and down the spectra, each view having its own problems and wonders and needs.

There was one range in which Billy could not see.

Visible light.

To normal humans, Billy Big-Eyes was blind as a bat.

Using the Scout Relay, the people in Control sent out the last known position of the *Nightwatch*, its probable course, the possible dangers in the sector it had been assigned.

The Scout Relay was a remnant of the old Snapshot system. It had once been used to connect widely separated points by means of Kerr black holes. Scanners from orbiting relays sliced across the Planck lengths of these rotating blackbodies every 10^{-33} seconds, finding the minute wormholes which opened and closed in those frequencies. Messages sent into these vortices came out somewhere else; that somewhere was inside a Scout ship.

The Snapshot system had been built by the first of the great old solid state intelligences, when man had lived on Earth. It had worked then, and continued to work. Communication across light-years was instantaneous and unerring. It was like talking to someone in the next room.

The Scout Relay was one of the two frequencies using the network. The other was for Systems communications which held together the web of worlds.

The Control people received the acknowledgments from the other Scouts about the missing *Nightwatch*, and then they waited.

"According to Billy's last transmission, he was nearing the probable. His estimate was four hours to RP," said Doctor Snorkel.

Maxwell Big-Eyes scanned the plot of the as-yet uncontacted ship of his great-nephew. Then he sat still, turning his head to study the other sector wherein the *Nightwatch* was lost. He envisaged the growing cone of search needed to find the missing ship. It would expand geometrically with every arithmetic expansion in time.

The place where the ship could be found was at first a funnel with a point at one end, extending outward and widening, .001, .003, .09, .27 light-years across. It would continue to widen and lengthen with the passage of time.

The job of the rescuers was to reach the area, cut it into small sectors and begin their search for the ship or some trace of it.

When the ships came out of their High Acceleration ftl modes, they would drop immediately to the speeds at which the *Nightwatch* disappeared.

There would be a long and tedious search if they did not find it within the first few days. The sectors they covered would be quickly dwarfed by the growing probability cone. At the end of the first day's time it would cover three times the original area. It was widening with every passing hour.

This did not mean that the *Nightwatch* could not be found, only that the probabilities were against it. The ship *could* be only a few thousand kilometers from its last position, at a relative standstill. The Scout could be repairing whatever trouble there was, or be on the way back toward its original course, under radio silence. Some way could be found to signal the searchers. All these things were possible.

Meanwhile the cone of search continued to grow like a chambered nautilus adding room after room to its shell.

Snorkel watched his stocky friend. "You think he'll join the search," he asked, "when we tell him? Even though his position's wrong, his vector's too far off? Even if we don't give him permission?"

"Hmmm?" Max came out of his thoughts. "Yes."

"Here comes Dierdre," said Otto Snorkel, rising.

"She always cheers me up," said Maxwell Big-Eyes. He too rose to meet his great-grandniece.

Billy Big-Eyes was a Scout, one of the Sighted whose job it was to search, to map the stars, reconnoiter space and find usable black bodies. The Systems, the government of mankind's planets, tapped these black holes, harnessing their energies to meet the needs of the worlds. The Scouts, in their great crystal ships, used their visual gifts like interstellar mountain men on Old Earth.

Billy was of the family Big-Eyes, whose honor and fame stretched back to the Secondary Worlds. The name had been bestowed on them by Council for the trait they held in common. The eyes were their fortune and fame, their reason for life, their albatross.

The Big-Eyes had chosen long before to breed for the trait and had submitted themselves and their offspring to operations, changes, mutations. These brought about the enlargement, the expansion of sight into other spectra. It set them apart from the rest of mankind forever.

The mutations had been worked on their eyes for generations. The size was a product of that. The operations, performed from puberty of the individual onward, allowed sight in other spectra while they were being trained for Scouthood. These changes further separated the Sighted from the rest of mankind. The mutations worked on the eyes of the Sighted from generation to generation gradually lost them normal vision; rather, they left eyesight behind. To all the Sighted, there was a gap between the high infrared and the low ultraviolet. This was the only spectra in which the Scout could see nothing.

The Scouts flew great crystal ships between the stars, leaving jets of radiation half a light-year long. The ships were engineering miracles for their simplicity. They could have been built with systems for the detection of black bodies; complicated equipment with backups, warnings and scanners, but they had not been. They were simple reflector dishes seventeen kilometers across, powered by engines which pushed them around the starways.

In High Mode, they carried the Scouts faster than light toward the sectors they had been assigned. On station, they could drift leisurely for months, correcting course, barely pushing the great curved mirrors through space. They sailed the night like windows, and not much in the electromagnetic spectrum got by them.

Each dish was made of a crystal tracework, like a perfectly formed spiderweb. Within the limits of the dish were sets of smaller reflectors, and smaller inside these, a reverse Eltonian pyramid of mirrors and accumulators. Their focii were in the control room of the ships, set above the center of the dish. It was here the Scout sat and watched the Universe for signs and portents.

"Hello, Uncle Max." said Dierdre. She was slim of build but gave no hint of fragility. She was in her early teens and had undergone the first two of the operations which would give her complete Sight. She wore the great protective opaque helmet all Scouts wore outside the confines of their Ships or homes. It was transparent to all but visible light. The chrome helmet made her look like an egg atop a doll figure. Maxwell hugged her, and she touched her helmet to the side of her great-granduncle's face.

Only Maxwell Big-Eyes, some of the retired Watchmosts and the men and women who had foregone Scouthood wore only the light protective masks. Some Scouts considered them ostentatious and a sop to the rest of humanity. Maxwell wore his now because he had never been able to let his hair grow in the years he had been a Scout. The idea of a full head of hair had always attracted him.

"Hello, Dierdre," said Doctor Snorkel. "How are the eyes?"

"Just fine," she said, sitting in a small chair in the near center of the room. She looked up at the softly glowing plotboard above them.

"Could you give me the positions of the others?" she asked the technician.

He looked to Snorkel.

"Give her every assistance," said Snorkel. "Act on her requests as you would mine or Max's."

"Very good, sir."

* * *

The human eye detects nothing which subtends less than thirteen minutes of arc. The eyes of the Scouts had been altered far beyond the human. At the focus of their ships, the waves moving through the night were shunted and reflected into the Scout's eyes. The Scouts were the human lenses of the gigantic telescopes which were the ships.

In their lives, and in their crystal ships, their work, their mutations, the Sighted were set apart from mankind. They were also honored among them, respected and proud.

The Families of the Systems were not limited to the Sighted; there were many others. Some had varying talents and skills, others had no useful skills at all. These latter had been in the service of the Systems for tremendously long times, and performed about as well as could be expected. They received their name and station among the honored families by longevity.

The Pilemongers, the Dimsdales and the Pierceys could be found in every part of the government.

There were also the three *pongoides* families, the Gumps, the Kongs and the Youngs, whose anthropoid talents were suited to many jobs true humans would find dangerous, difficult or tedious.

It was the Talented Families who were the mainstays of the Systems: the Sighteds, the Naturals, the Speakers, the Quick, the Sleepers, the Unseen and the Aware. Each had some special genetically or somatically produced skill needed in mankind's habitation of the galaxy.

The Naturals came in touch with any planets which bore life. They read the worlds, discerned the relations between living things and the planet, proscribed the limits of mankind's growth there.

The Sleepers oversaw and controlled those processes for which the human lifetime was not long enough. Their wakings and walkings, measured in decades and centuries, were as days and weeks to them. Some third- and fourth-generation Sleepers were still in the service of the government.

And on through each of the skills needed; for the settlement of worlds, the transfer of materials, the running of the Systems. For each of the talents needed there was a Family or Families. There had been for centuries, there would be for ages.

Most important among these were the Sighted families: the Ocullis, the Watchmosts, the Big-Eyes, the Lemur-Pottis and the Scoutmakers.

The family Big-Eyes was the oldest of them, and the toughest. Maxwell Big-Eyes thought himself the best Scout who had ever served a career. He was now retired. He thought Billy would be a better Scout than he, and that his great-grandniece would be better still.

Dierdre watched the changes on the great screen. It gave three-dimensional overviews of the original path of the *Nightwatch*, the location of the other Scout Ships, their courses and probable search patterns.

She turned her head toward Max. "It doesn't look very good, does it?"

"You can tell that? Then it's worse than I thought," he said. Snorkel, standing behind him, looked toward Dierdre and raised his copious gray eyebrows.

"Well, there's Abraham Watchmost, there." Dierdre pointed toward the diagrams. "He's closest, but he's in deceleration mode already, and it'll take him longer to get back up to speed than it will for..."—she checked a readout on a side display—"than for Yvonne Oculli to reach the point of last contact." She looked past the display to the ceiling. "That will be sometime day after tomorrow. *Then* the search can start."

Max leaned on one elbow, propping his uncovered chin.

Dierdre turned to him. "Does Billy know yet?"

"No. He's at a critical mission phase, he thinks. I'll let him know as soon as he reports back."

She looked at the plotboard. "He doesn't even show on that sector."

"He's not. He's much too far away to be of any help. And he's on the mission we've been planning for some time, one we don't want aborted."

Dierdre pulled her feet up into the chair, hugged her knees. "He loved her, you know." she said.

"Yes," said Maxwell Big-Eyes.

Black holes do certain things in one spectra and others in another. Once within visual range, a Scout can spot one within a few hours. Black bodies themselves have no appearance, but there are associated electromagnetic phenomena which mark them to the trained observer. Most are formed from the remnants of stars. Not all the exploding shells and chromospheres manage to escape the intense gravitational tides which the singularities form.

It is for these signs a Scout looks. The plasma cloud ahead of Billy was a probable in many ways, not in others. It was still opaque in ranges where it should have been translucent. His gravity sensors within the ship still gave indefinite readings, even so close. This made him think there were very unstable conditions inside the cloud. That it surrounded a black hole.

Billy watched in the infrared, then shifted his mind up to the ultraviolet. The cloud did not resolve, it simply became opaque in other interesting ways.

He broadcast on the Scout Relay frequency. As he did, he watched his own message speed away like a giant forked cactus. That was always disconcerting, no matter how many times he did it.

"I'm punching in readings," he said. "The shipboard pickups can't do much more than approximate what's going on."

Billy studied the console. It glowed softly in the UV and IR. Warning lights in the ship were visible in seven spectra; should an emergency occur, the Scout would have warning no matter what frequency he happened to be looking at. None of the trouble lights were on now. The ship was quietly doing its job of transporting its lone human occupant on his mission.

Behind and above Billy lay another great spattered gas cloud, a few solitary young stars, all the apparatus of creation. He kept glancing to the burnt old stars spread to the sides. They looked like tarnished fishbowls hung in a room full of moss.

The plasma ahead intrigued him. Its shape and size were like nothing he had seen. It should have already been transparent in the X ray, but showed detail in small depth. Billy sometimes wished for the ability to see through a light-year of lead. Scouting would be much simpler if he could. His vision in the X ray depended on the amount of radiation leakage in that form. Something bright enough for him to see through in that depth would have crystallized all the metal in the *Argus* and left him a dead man.

He set a tangential course for the heavy edge of the cloud. It would be like slipping through the wall of a hurricane except that chances were small for a calm windless eye inside. It would be like sailing into the target end of a cyclotron as big as a sun.

* * *

"He's not still in love with her, is he?" asked Max.

"He says he isn't." Dierdre scratched at her knees with her short-clipped fingernails. She wore shorts, boots and a red halter. Her great chrome helmet bent toward her knee.

"You'd better have that checked by the medic this afternoon," said Doctor Snorkel, reentering the room.

"What is it?"

"A rash. Side effect of some of the drugs we used in the last operation. Billy had it for months. Mostly nerves, not much we can do except give tranquilizers."

"I don't want any more tranquilizers," said Dierdre to Snorkel. "I'm wonky enough anyway, early in the mornings, and I feel *blah* by nighttime. *And* I get edgy."

"That's the way it's always been," said Snorkel. "Except for Wilhelmina Scoutmaker. She became hyperactive. So we had to give her stimulants; then she showed the same tensions as everyone else."

"Is there *anything* about me you don't already know?" asked Dierdre.

Snorkel smiled. "Tell me something, and I'll let you know if we know it or not."

Maxwell Big-Eyes had been listening, his hands cupped together in a cone, teeth touching fingertips. He sat slumped in his chair. He always slumped. He'd had to sit upright in the focus rooms of ships for many years, and was in rebellion against all parts of his past.

"Dierdre, they knew everything about *me* when I was going through the operations and training. I think on their deathbeds the directors tell *everyone* about us. It's passed down like shamanlore. A secret cabal of personal information."

"Not quite that bad," said Snorkel, drawing himself to his full height. "The more we know, the better we can gauge your progress, the smoother we can make the treatments, the sooner you'll get away from us."

"You're talking a little like we're cattle again." said Dierdre.

Snorkel winced. "This is an inexact science. The development of unknown quantities such as yourself. Some of the nomenclature from earlier times has carried over. I'm terribly sorry."

"Oh, fuck it all! I'm sorry, Otto. All this boredom, all these tests, I just don't feel like..."

"You're also growing," said Snorkel. "One of the problems is that we have to wait until puberty before we begin the larger alterations. It would be better if we developed a technique for genetic manipulation for the Sighted. We've tried and failed, so far. Puberty is the worst time to undergo a major change. You haven't learned to live with your body, the one you grew up with, and we change it."

"In my time..." began Maxwell Big-Eyes.

"We know," said his great-grandniece, "you walked twelve kilometers a day through a photon accelerator, just to keep in shape."

Maxwell smiled. "You're right. I'm getting old. I'd like to move back into the past and live there, instead of worrying about the future.

"Dierdre, a Scout spends all the adult life worrying about the present and future. From adolescence on is the training, then the work of looking out for the rest of mankind. All too soon that's over, and you're left with nothing but the past, when things were exciting. Even though you thought it only a job.

"But I could grow maudlin."

"You could, easily," said Dierdre. Then she looked at the plotboard. "I see Watchmost has abandoned his other mission. The search is starting." She turned the chrome reflector of her helmet toward her great-granduncle. "You're going to direct it from here?"

"I'm going to try."

"With all the search ships arriving so far apart? Are you up to it?"

"Yes. But I'll have to depend on you for help. Your mind is much quicker than mine has been in a long time. And you know Billy better than I do. Unusual, but you do."

"We get along okay," said Dierdre.

They were all three silent for a moment. The technician above them on his platform stretched his arms and legs.

"Jiminez," said Doctor Snorkel, "I want the three best plotters here, on duty."

"They're already on the way. We're going to work four-hour shifts."

Doctor Snorkel raised his eyebrows. "You should be checked for psi powers."

"Doc, you work at a job twelve years, you gotta know what's going on."

Max noticed the change in tone between the two. They did not stand on the formalities during a crisis.

Dierdre sat still, her head up.

"What are you thinking?" asked Maxwell.

She turned to him. "You've got regular beacons broadcasting toward where she disappeared?"

"Certainly." said Snorkel.

"Of course, we can barely see the messages..."

"What?"

"Morbid thoughts, Uncle Max. About what it would be like to be out there with no way of making contact, watching the messages come by and knowing there's nothing you can do but wait."

Maxwell Big-Eyes looked at his great-grandniece. "You're certainly not very much like your brother," he said.

It was like moving at high speed next to a great looming wall. There was a feeling of impending collision, of the end coming quickly at any time.

Billy swung the *Argus* to face the plasma cloud on a tangential course. All his concentration and vision were directed toward the opaque object; he still did not know what went on inside. There was confusion there, even in the X ray. It was the damnedest thing Billy Big-Eyes had ever seen. Even the *Argus'* instrumentation did little. He depended on the gravity sensors to tell him what was inside the plasma sheet.

All they told him was that something was inside. There were gravity wells of some sort. They seemed to be in constant motion and followed no set pattern.

He broadcast on the Scout Relay. He sent out diagrams which looked like wingtip vortices on old aerodynamic bodies. He waited for the data returns.

But he knew before the answer came that he needed to enter the plasma cloud to get any more information. Tension and anxiety rose in him. What he did could be very dangerous and very important. Or perhaps it could just be dangerous.

"I'm going in now," he broadcast, and set course to swing the *Argus* in, then out, of the cloud.

The crystal latticework gleamed dully in the various spectra, like an icicled geodesic dome. Billy looked out through the mirrors of the low-spectra reflectors to the dull-orbed stars around him, to the glowing curtains of dust in the soft night, the zip of interstellar garbage.

The cloud moved slowly to the side, then loomed ahead. He intended to skirt the edges of the central mass, dip in, skim out again. He would use himself and his ship to the utmost on the first penetration. It would be blinding in there in many of the frequencies. Unless he or his instruments were very sharp on the initial skim, he would have to repeat the maneuver several times until he found the answer or until it became too dangerous, too much a gamble with the Big Sleep.

In which case the cloud would have to be marked "unknown" and put on the charts.

That would be the first time those words would appear in any sector explored by Billy Big-Eyes. In the three years he had been a Scout, he had found more of lasting value than any other. He had never failed to determine exactly the nature of objects in his path. No subsequent black holes had been found, even after secondary colonization had begun.

Billy did not want this to be his first professional failure, either of his nerves or his limitations.

He sighed, and swung the lacework ship over like a shark.

Maxwell worked quickly with the readouts of the plotboard.

Snorkel and Dierdre were talking in a corner of the room. In deference to the Scouts, Snorkel and the other technicians were wearing bifocal infrared goggles. The room was now lighted totally on that wavelength.

Words drifted down to Maxwell. ". . . more surgery . . . upside down . . . way it used to be . . ." Then Dierdre's laughter started, joined by Snorkel's.

"Private joke?" asked Maxwell.

"No," said Dierdre, moving toward him, her shoulders still shaking with laughter. Max looked through her helmet to her smiling face with its eyes the size of large hen eggs. She could not as yet see in the X ray, like he, but he knew she could see his face in the infrared, where his eyes absorbed the light. "We were talking about Nelson Watchmost and Gini Oculli. High school romances. I didn't think you'd be very interested."

"I shouldn't be. But everything about the Sighted families interests me sooner or later. I might as well try to think of the future a while, as well as the past. Does it look as if the two of them will choose each other? Or be donor parents?"

Dierdre looked at Snorkel. "That's what we were talking about. No, I don't think so. They're just having fun. But the Ocullis are watching very closely. They're upset. They want Gini to mate with a Scoutmaker. Some of the Ocullis think it would be a gesture of goodwill toward the newest of the Scout Families."

"The Ocullis have their hearts in the right places," said Maxwell, "though some of them have their heads up their anii."

"That is the image they're fighting," said Dr. Snorkel.

"Yes," said Max. "But you and I know that's why, rather than out of the democratic goodness of their hearts. They want to fight the nouveau riche image they've acquired. The easiest way is to be nice to a family even more nouveau than they."

"Reverse snobbery." said Snorkel.

"Perhaps," said Dierdre, looking at Snorkel, "the Service would like it better if they could choose *who* mates with *whom*?"

"No," he said. "That's individual prerogative. All the families have the abilities we need, all the right genes, few recessive traits. It would only work if we knew exactly how each individual would turn out beforehand. Or work the genetic changes to bring about Sight. But we can't. All we can do is use amniocentisis, determine which traits are most pronounced, which ones we'll have to concentrate on later.

"And the Sighted Families know more about their own lines than they claim. Most heads of the families get the gene data on the offspring as soon as it's available.

"Max thinks we have a cabal about the chaos you go through in training. I think the Families have a session every generation or so in which they decide who will be with whom, so far as genetics go. It works both ways."

Dierdre moved her arms up to wrap them around her bare shoulders. "Then someone like Sally comes along," she said, "and doesn't go along with anybody's wishes, not even her own. Not Billy's, her family's, nobody's. I don't think she knew what she wanted, or how to get it."

"You're wrong, Dierdre," said Snorkel. "She knew too well what she wanted. That's why she's lost, right now."

"Whatever it was," said Dierdre, "it wasn't Billy."

The *Argus* entered the plasma wall. It had run beside it like a boat along the length of a long breakwater. There was no shock as it entered.

Billy Big-Eyes watched his instruments, saw them adjust to the plasma flow, the changed environment outside the ship. The gravity sensors did not define the stress within the cloud. The indicators moved and swayed but would not settle.

Billy was busy. He looked about him. The reflectors of the ship shone into his eyes, pushing all the spectra in, letting him see what was there. Half his attention was on his instruments, half on what his eyes told him.

In the X ray were huge swaying masses of gas, thick and opaque, like tarpaulins thrown over his vision. They swirled, they cleared, yet he still could not see through them.

They rotated like a cosmic maelstrom with no regular rhythm or order.

The ship hove closer, slowly, moving through plasma roils without effort. Too easily for Billy's liking, too effortlessly for him not to be nervous...

The instruments swung over, gave definite readings, settled in a regular gentle pulse.

His printouts showed two steadily rolling masses, tumbling around each other like millstones, gravity wells spinning away from them like swirls of mist. They twisted and pulled, broke away from the masses like smoke.

At the same time his vision penetrated the rolling swells of gas and plasma, and he saw into the heart of the great mystery he had been trailing across the skies like a wounded bear.

Shivers ran up Billy's spine as he realized what he had found. Then he laughed and turned his crystal ship out of the great pulsing cloud.

He broadcast his findings back to control.

He had found binary black holes. Two rotating masses locked in a double-system. The find would raise great questions about the physics involved. It was impossible that they had formed from a single stellar mass, even more unlikely that they formed from a binary system at the same instant. The possibility of the capture of a secondary black body by another was remote; even then something besides a stable binary should have been formed. Billy's find would question the theories behind the formation of rotating black holes.

In the end, they would be academic curiosities. For, as power sources, a binary system with its tides, fluctuating gravity wells and plasma field would be useless as teats on a boar shoat.

The questioning and theory would come later, by others less interested in exploration itself. As soon as Billy Big-Eyes brought the *Argus* out of the plasma cloud and was safely away, his granduncle Maxwell told him that Sally Lemur-Potti was missing and presumed lost.

"Of course I'm going," said Billy.

"I can order you not to."

"I'd rather you wouldn't."

"I know that. But it would be foolish for you to try. The search is under way. You're much too far from the sector. We'll find her by the time you get turned around."

"I'm already turning around."

There was a pause. "So I see. You leave me very little choice, Billy. I'm ordering you to proceed with your planned mission. *Before* you reach that slingshot point you've plotted. I'll have that backed by a directive in a few moments."

Silence.

"Billy, give me your answer."

The silence broke.

"Don't do this to me, Uncle Max. Don't send a directive I'll have to ignore."

Maxwell ran his hands through his hair. "I'm telling you not to do it, Billy. It'll be a big mistake. We can find her before you get there. We'll know what happened to the *Nightwatch* before you get out of your assigned sector."

"What if you don't? No, that's not what I want to ask. The real question is whether she's dead or not, isn't it?"

Maxwell's lips turned down as he paced back and forth across the center of the plotroom.

"All right, Billy, listen to this: I'm ordering you not to leave your assigned sector, or abort your present mission. That is that."

Dierdre, from her chair in the corner, said, "Orders never stopped you on the Wilson thing."

"Oh, be quiet, Dierdre!" Maxwell glared at his great-grandniece. "That's why I'm doing this, so he won't make the same mistake!"

"Then I'm going to refuse your orders," said Billy Big-Eyes, over the Scout Relay.

"I'm not going to let you do that!"

"Max!" said Snorkel, holding out his hand. "Calm yourself down."

"I have her last position and speed," Billy's voice came over the speaker. "I don't need anything else. What if I'm the only one who *can* find her, Max?"

"Wait," sighed Maxwell Big-Eyes. He slumped his shoulders, sat heavily in his chair. "Just wait." He rubbed the tip of his nose with fingers. "It's Systems' policy. You know you'll be wasting your mission, mismanaging the ship. You'll be late. You'll come into the sector ass-backwards. Chances are, you'll pass her position..."

"Max, I had the same training as you. Only I had all *your* experiences in the classes, and you didn't. I know all that. I know how to search frontwards, backwards, upside-down. I knew how *you* found Wilson and Termire, which is more than you did at the time. This argument is a waste. Are you going to help me, Uncle Max, or do I have to do it all myself?"

The only sound for a long time was that of the relays transferring information to the plotboard. Snorkel stood with one of his thumbs in his mouth, chewing at the nail. Dierdre scratched her arm.

"Okay. I'll help you, Billy," said Max. "I don't know how long we can keep the Council off you. But we'll try, we'll try."

Dierdre and Snorkel kept their eyes off Maxwell. They studied the intricate path trajectories on the plotboard.

"Thanks, Uncle Max."

"Dierdre's here, Billy. She's going to help."

"Fine."

"I'll get back to you. Take it easy for a while."

He signed off. He sat with the speaker held idly in his hand. His foot tapped some unknown rhythm on the floor.

Dierdre came to him and hugged him. "Thank you, Uncle Max. I'm proud of you."

"You shouldn't be," said the Chief of Scouts. "I'm doing a stupid thing. I'm letting him do worse. He'll repeat the mistake I made years ago." Maxwell brightened a little. "Well, Otto, let's go see the Director. While we're on our way there, we'll figure out some way *not* to tell her why we're letting Billy do this. For the moment, I can't think of a single reason."

"Let's eat, too," said Dierdre. "I'm hungry."

"Only if Otto promises to find us some place where the music won't hurt my eyes," said Max.

Sleep was not easy for Scouts at any time. Billy knew that he would have to get rest. He had not had a sleep shift in the nineteen hours he had been pursuing the plasma cloud. He could not afford to be without sleep in the ordeal ahead.

He traveled down the long tubeway from the focus room to his crew compartment. Both the tubeway and the room below were walled with reflectors which turned aside many of the wavelengths and frequencies coming through. The inner workings of the walls also gave off pleasing white noises on wavelengths designed to soothe the Scouts.

Billy undressed and climbed onto the couch. Gentle wafts of air blew through the room. He took off his large chrome helmet, leaving only his light protective harness. Opening this, he placed the sleep headgear over his face. This covering bathed his grapefruit-sized eyes in gentle solutions which washed, cleaned and massaged them. The Scouts had no eyelids, and the blinking reflex had been bred out of them.

Shielded speakers, which were not magnetic, played music to Billy, usually, but not always Pre-Systems "classical," the music of abandoned Earth. The walls poured out their white noise under this.

Billy reached out, while the bed began to massage him, while his eyes and ears were bathed in liquids and sounds, and moved his fingers and toes over the tactile surfaces at the edge of the couch. They turned now smooth or rough, soft or hard, in random patterns.

Massaged and lifted, hushed and cooed, he looked into the visible spectrum where all was dark and slept.

The great crystal ship *Argus* flew through the night, watching over Billy and its course, rounding the sector in a long, slow curve up into its Acceleration Mode which would take them toward the lost Sally Lemur-Potti. She would be an infinitely small dot on the large black night of the galaxy.

The only lights in the ship glowed in the soft infrared and ultraviolet. Like its namesake, the *Argus* watched and flew and waited dutifully for Billy to awake.

After they had napped and eaten and been to their homes, Max, Snorkel and Dierdre returned to the plotroom.

Nothing had happened. Only routine reports on the search had come in. The Watchmost Scout had begun pie-slicing his sector into usable cones. One of the Scoutmakers would take a portion of it in a few hours, as soon as she entered the coordinates. It looked to be a long and monotonous search unless something turned up unexpectedly. The chance of finding Sally Lemur-Potti diminished with each hour.

Billy was still asleep; he would be on sleep-shift a while. He was nowhere close to the search patterns of the other ships. He would enter the probability cone long after the others had gone through the most likely portions.

Dierdre was working with a pocket printout. Her fingers moved over the keys. She wrote figures on a memory pad, coding them with letters before they disappeared to be replaced by others. Occasionally, she would key one back and add it to the figures she worked on.

Maxwell watched with some amusement.

"You haven't memorized them yet?" he asked when she stopped.

"Everybody knows only you and Gilmore Oculli commit things like that to memory. No, I use the safe way, pad and stylus. If I do something wrong, I can find where I messed up. Hey!" She looked at her great-granduncle. "Why did you send Scoutmaker on that trajectory? By the book, that shouldn't start until they have a twenty-five-loop grid."

"I'm hoping we'll have a lot of luck. The two inmost ships can start sweeps and cover about as much as three. I'm hoping the *Nightwatch* will be in one of the most probable areas. But I'd really like to have five ships there already, instead of three..."

"You'll have, soon," said Dierdre, "but I'd advise using the standard pattern. Really, and you might have to get through it more than once, if something really bad's happened. There's an *awful* lot of territory out there. You were right, it'll be a miracle if she's found on the first sweep."

"It's always that way," said Maxwell Big-Eyes. "You haven't been out yet, haven't seen the Deeps. Where this place is nothing more than a coordinate, because there are so many better places to use as reference points."

"All we know is that something happened out there. Communication cut off in mid-sentence. She was chasing a probable. Her data looked perfectly normal, nothing dangerous. She was too far from the probable for any known forces to affect her ship. Unlikely, I know, but I'm working on the assumption of massive shipboard failure.

Dierdre looked at the pad held in one of her thin hands, held it up.

"If only it didn't come down to a bunch of numbers," she said.

"It always does, Dierdre. Much as we don't want it to."

"I mean," she said, "there's a person out there, so important to someone he's willing to stand up to you, the Council and everybody to get to her. But finding her comes down to a bunch of numbers that get bigger and bigger every hour."

Maxwell shook his wrists, ran thick fingers across his neck. "Numbers are tools, Dierdre. Men and women made them, based their sciences on them, their technology. When science fails, they have to fall back on the numbers."

He expected her to say more, be upset, to bring up the words "not fair." She didn't. She sat silently a moment, then went back to work.

Maxwell found himself nodding. There was nothing anyone could do right now that wasn't being done.

Sleep did Billy no good.

He had had only vague, disturbing dreams which he could not remember on waking. It would be the hours that he was conscious now that would hurt him, rather than those he spent sleeping.

He cleaned and relieved himself, ate and put his chrome helmet on. He climbed up the long tubeway to the focus and took his place at the controls. He punched in his course evaluations and changes, all the data he had on the lost ship, and the probable search patterns the other Scout ships would take.

He did not call Max yet. He wanted to think. He also wanted to get away from thinking for a while.

He sat back in his chair and watched the stars go by in exceptionally long waves at the very edge of the ship's capacity. These were the only frequencies in which he could see out when the *Argus* was in High Acceleration mode. Here the stars were black mats on a gray background. All he could see of his environment was the ship itself, ghostlike, and the pulse of the engines behind him. The rest was gray restlessness and lumpy stars where gravity itself bent around them in long waves.

Was it just a few hours ago he had chased down the binary black holes? Already it seemed half a lifetime away, something he had done in childhood, or which he had read about and remembered.

That had been his job, though; this was something else.

He did not know what he would find at the end of the search, or whether he wanted to be there when the end was known. It was something he had to do, out of a host of old allegiances and feelings, and the bitter remembrance of love.

He sat in the control room and did not know, once again, if he were still in love with Sally Lemur-Potti.

It had begun four years ago, when he was recovering from his fifth major operation. Sally, a year older than he, had already soloed. She had been in the hospital for a minor surgical correction. They had met there.

He remembered the first night they had walked under the stars, under the soft infrared glow from the star cluster, across the soft sands and mosses of Fremont, home world of the Scouts.

It had been warm and fragrant. Billy was outside at night for the first time since his operation. Night and day had little meaning for Scouts; in the daytime there was a rather large, harsh ultraviolet source point above the horizon. It moved from east to west. Billy's operation was the most major one, where recovery was longest, where the patient could do little but study and listen.

Both he and Sally wore their light protective head harnesses, form-fitting and much more comfortable than the chrome Scout helmets they would later take up.

To each other, they were soft-glowing red outlines, human shapes walking on a smooth background.

"Don't worry about it." said Sally Lemur-Potti.

Her face was turned toward his. It showed the two dark centers of her large eyes where they absorbed the infrared. He knew he looked the same to her.

The Sighted Families preferred infrared and ultraviolet for their usual vision. It had become habit; perhaps it had started with the desire, long ago, to stay as near human sight as possible. No one was sure.

"But I'm so sick of doing nothing," said Billy. "Of listening to tapes, studying. I don't feel like I'm doing anything. I'm standing still."

"I felt that way too," she said, "really I did, I'm not just saying that. I thought I'd never get into the Deeps, or fly, or anything. But I have."

"Snorkel keeps telling me that. He's seen them all come and go, but he can't know what it's like to be Sighted and then have to wait. He says we all go through the despondency just about now. We've been in the program too long without anything really happening, just alteration after alteration, study after study, nothing on top of nothing else."

They sat on a soft moss hillock under the glow of the Shitpot Nebula. Sally took his hand so naturally that he did not notice it.

"He's right." Sally turned her head toward the zenith. "See up there? What do you see, the nebula in IR and UV, the long flickers of the short radio waves? Right? Well, to me, in the X ray, the thing is a bunch of haloes, like water on a screen, with dots rising and falling all along it.

"And..."—she turned her head toward the southern horizon—"you know what? You squint your eyes, you get lucky, you know what you see? Sometimes, walking, you see little spots. You switch to X ray. It's hard on a planet, you can't see the horizon, you have to stand still.

"Anyway, you look at the dots. They come down all the time, secondary particles. But every once in a while you see a primary, bright like a drop of burning lead. And sometimes... sometimes they come up out of the ground. They really do. They've hit kilometers away, and get deflected; they come up out of the ground like a spent bullet, getting slower all the time. They break apart.

"There're fireworks everywhere, Billy. Little pieces of light, and particles always moving, zipping around. There's nothing like it."

He watched her. She was sitting up, moving her small hand-blobs around, taking in all the sky above them with motions of her softly glowing arms.

"And long radio! Wait till you see that! Big loops in the night, like giant moving fingerprints, with lines and whorls. You need the ship for that, with the reflectors, but wait till you see it. They're tremendous. And the ships themselves.

"They bring in everything out there so clear and sharp. You think you're ready for the first views, after the trials with the small reflectors, but you're not. You're sitting out there in the Deeps by yourself, with no planet under you, no horizon. The ship itself is the only thing that matters, and the seeing is good, there's something to look at everywhere you point the ship. You can live a lifetime out there in a few moments. Billy, you don't know how good it feels, how..."

Billy had become tense, tight with the sound of her words, so moved he wanted to reach out, touch her, hold her, make her be quiet while the wonder of her speech settled in him; he wanted to keep her quiet so the thrill inside him would stay.

He put his arms around her and she was still and very quiet.

"Nobody ever talked about the Deeps like that," he finally said. His despondence had passed. He felt some kind of new hope inside himself. Uncle Maxwell and the others only told him he would like it once he got out there. That had grown thin in the months he was in surgery and recovery, during the drug treatments and training. Now it didn't seem such a dead end. He was more anxious than ever to get out there. Now he *believed.*

Sally extended one of her soft-glowing hands on the end of her shining arm from her shimmering body and touched his face. "You'll see when you get out there," she said. "You'll see what it's like."

They stared up at the cluster overhead.

The ship warned him that it was coming out of Acceleration Mode. His reverie ended.

He called on the Scout Relay frequency. The overlag would keep his message suspended until the moment he dropped below light-speeds. The *Argus* would file its own stress reports automatically and put the information in its flight recorder. The recorder also monitored its position constantly and held as much data on a flight as the Scout programmed it to take. It served a function of which most Scouts were incapable; it remembered everything about a mission, stresses, where it had been, anything which affected it. The recorder, Billy knew, would have a huge load of information on the binary black holes he had found. So his mission had been important. He knew his Uncle Maxwell was against his search-and-rescue mission for good and valid reasons.

It still did not help his feelings. His emotions were compounded of many hurts. There was the possibility that he was still in love with Sally, after three years, after her indifferences and the pain she had caused him.

The front part of his mind told him he was feeling concern any Scout would feel when another was missing. He would expect the same from the others. The Sighted Families held together. That he would go out of his way was expected by Scouts, if not by the Control people. Uncle Max was in the unenviable position of being Chief of Scouts and still responsible to Control.

When Maxwell Big-Eyes had taken up the search for a mission colony ship, long after others had given up, he had been on more solid ground from the view of Control, but still irresponsible. The only thing that had saved him was success.

Billy assumed the *Argus* would bring him out where he wanted. His search would begin soon, and he set to work on patterns and the castings he would make when he dropped from High Acceleration.

It was quiet in the unknown gray space, with not much showing outside, and Billy worked for a long time on time on his calculations.

"He's out." said Jiminez.

Nine days after the search began, Billy came out of High Acceleration. In that time none of the other Scouts had picked up the slightest hint of what happened to the *Nightwatch*. There was no beacons, signals of any kind, no sporadic interference in those sectors the ship was most likely to appear.

Unlike the sea, sudden catastrophe leaves no signs in space. On water many things by their nature float; wood, plastics, heavy objects with air trapped inside, oil, wastes. In the Deeps, accidents happen, and the powers that propel the ships are so great that everything can be obliterated. Things not vaporized are broken to tiny pieces and flung to all directions. This debris moves out with the force of the initial blast and quickly disperses.

Or in the case of some quick and total power failure, the ship becomes a dead piece of metal and crystal, on whatever path it was following, with no sign except the residual radiations from its engines. Even a Scout would have to be very close to see or detect that, on the immensity of the Night.

Billy's ship came out exactly where he planned. Others in the search had begun much more toward the homeward direction, near the point of last contact. Two of the ships, the *Many-Orbed* and the *Lookmeover* had been as far in as Billy Big-Eyes, but in other directions.

Dierdre talked to her brother a few minutes after the ship slowed enough to allow communications.

"I've checked your figures."

"And?"

"I think you should move on closer courses. Intersect the probables as often as you can. You've got these open circles planned."

"Max?"

"Yes?"

"Max, is Dierdre right?"

"I don't know. It makes sense, by the book. But we've run this one by the book since the second day, and we've had no results. Yvonne Mustafa . . . er, Oculli, we've got her on a simulated power loss run. You'll pick her up in a day or two, she's got a beeper going so you won't mistake her. Ignore it if you can. Control wanted the solidstates to run the simulation, but I told them I haven't come up with anything so far. Not their fault.

"Billy, something bad must have happened to the ship out there. I hope you realize that?"

"Max . . ."

"I know, I know. Look, I'm beginning to think we're *not* going to find anything out there. Maybe some debris . . ."

"It's possible that it is only the ship which is in trouble," said Dierdre.

"That *was* possible," said Max. "I had great hopes, in the first week. Unless she's dead, she would have tried some way of signaling by now, anything. Radio, spark-gap transmitter, anything. Flares—even if you couldn't see them, you'd pick up the bursts, the ship would squawk.

"This is something I didn't want to say. Either everything—the ship, Sally—is gone, or it's still there and Sally's dead. And if so, the ship's somewhere we're not looking. We won't find them, either way."

"If she's there, I'll find her." said Billy.

"I know you believe that, so I won't say anything."

"I'll run the search like I planned, Max."

"Okay." Max paused. "Something else, Billy. Control's given us seventy-eight more hours. Then the search stops, except for passive beacons. You'll all be on Recall."

"Max, I just got here."

"You knew it would be like that when you started, Billy. I haven't told them you're there yet. Don't compromise this order. The Recall will include you. That's all."

"Max . . ."

"Billy, I'll be here in the search control, so will Dierdre. When the Recall goes out, I want to see you in an Acceleration Mode. Until then, anything you need from us, let us know."

"All right."

Billy contacted the nearest Scouts, watched his and their relay beams lock instantly, once again in the giant cactus designs peculiar to their frequency.

The Scouts could not see each other, except as directions in which their beams originated. Both the *Many-Orbed* and the *Lookmeover* were finishing large sweeps of search. Billy fed data to them, turned on his identifying beacon and entered his initial pattern. He would intersect those of the two ships and the probable path of the *Nightwatch* at many points, but also swing away in open arcs from the others. His search path was also separated in time; sometimes he would cross ahead of the other two ships, sometimes behind.

There was noise and movement on every frequency. No matter where he looked, Billy's attention was distracted by something.

He kept himself mostly in the infrared. This was a region of younger stars, where the soft, dull background was broken by brilliant splotches. He occasionally searched the X ray, looking into stars and their photospheres. It was possible her ship had been captured like a moon by one, its noise and stellar wind interfering with communication. Shielded in her rest compartment, Sally could live through the ordeal, though the *Nightwatch* would begin to crystallize and fall apart.

There were no foreign dots on the shells of the suns, no tiny traces of garbage like flour dropped from a leaking sack.

There were no softly glowing dots signaling the burned engines of a ship coasting through the night, no matter how long or hard he looked, no matter what wavelength.

His crystal-work ship picked up no unknown beacons, no sparks; his eyes saw no lights, flares or reflections he could not name.

Billy's responses were mechanical. He was paying attention to things around him; the view, his instruments, the chatter on the frequencies, the dip of his gauges as the long cycle of gravity waves passed through his ship each hour.

But there was nothing he was looking for, anywhere. He would know something amiss as soon as he saw or heard it. *Nothing wrong out there*, nothing he *wanted* to see.

Where was she, where was her ship, where?

Billy remembered things:

They had become lovers soon after the night under the stars. It surprised neither of them. At first they were happy for days, then weeks, then months. They talked, they studied, they worked, they slept, they made love, they wasted time together.

Billy fell in love with Sally Lemur-Potti.

She never said she was in love with him.

But she was happy with him, they had good times, and Billy did not push her about it, after the first. He thought whatever she felt for him would turn to love, and that with her it was a slow, growing process. He could wait.

He lost his despondency, threw himself into his studies and the adaptations he would have to make, he became *nice* again, after months of quiet anger. He got his confidence back.

It was the best time to be in love in the history of mankind. The worlds were rich in both people and resources. Each of the Talented families had its own homeworld, with a diverse gene pool, with many accommodations to the needs of the talents.

The government of the Systems was a benevolent one. It had

been compared with the Byzantine Empire on old Earth, but without the religions and the wars. It was a true commonwealth of worlds; its job was to portion out the resources, the manufactury, the exchange of culture and ideas among the planets of the settled stars.

There were more than a thousand worlds which were the abode of man. These stretched from the Secondary Worlds, within ten light-years of old Earth, to those scattered far away from them.

Among the homes of man, abandoned Earth was not numbered. It had been left to the dolphin, the whale and those pongoides who had chosen not to leave four thousand years before.

It was the best time in the history of man to be in love.

Five months after they had begun living together in his home, Sally received her first station assignment. She had recovered from the minor surgery which opened the longest of the radio waves to the Scouts. It was time for her to leave.

They lay in bed, two soft-glowing forms in the dim UV light from the shielded walls of the house. They were naked except for the lightest headpieces which supported their eyes. The night outside was quiet. Billy had not shut the shielded windows which kept out chance radiations, spectra garbage from engines, tools and lights that might disturb their sleep.

"I love you," said Billy Big-Eyes.

"Mmmmm. That's nice," said Sally Lemur-Potti.

"You won't say you love me?"

"It won't make any difference, will it?"

No. "I suppose not."

"Then why ask?"

"I don't know."

They lay quietly for a while. It would have been a beautiful night outside if they had been able to see it. The Shitpot would have been glowing quietly overhead, silently roaring. Streaks of cosmic ray would have danced in Sally's sight. Billy would be altered for X ray next month.

She put her head across his chest.

"Your heart beats very slowly," she said.

"It always has. I was born that way."

"I sometimes listen to it while you sleep."

"Do you?"

"Yes."
"You'll meet new people on Complex."
"I suppose so."
"Lovers, and everything."
"I suppose so."
"I love you, Sally."
"That's good."
They kissed.

He was in the transit tunnel above Fremont when she left. The place was lit with visible light which gave off scratchy X rays. Billy was there with Sally's family.

They all made small talk. She would be back in eleven months.

Her flight was ready.

"It'll be the last time somebody else does the piloting for a while," she said.

She embraced each member of her family. Billy grabbed her and hugged her.

"Hurry back," he said. "I'll miss you."

"I'll miss you, too," she said. He could see the dark pulses of her eyes under the helmet, but nothing of her expression, her features.

His chest hurt.

He held her close, as if no one had ever been parted from one they loved in the whole history of the Universe.

"I love you, Sally."

"That's good," she said. Then she laughed, to show it was the response he expected of her. Then she held him very tight while the last call was made for her flight.

She left.

Billy wished that the Sighted Families still had the physical ability to cry.

Their messages across the worlds were at first both frequent and full of emotion. Then her answers were shorter and took longer in coming.

He was in the hospital the first few months and looked forward to nothing more than the daily message deliveries.

She told of her life there, her adaptations, her first mission, purely routine, and the people, both Sighted and unsighted, whom she met there.

He was in emotional stasis, waiting for the effects of his new vision to sharpen. He knew she was far away, and could not relate to what it was like to be in training, in the surgical rooms.

Seven months after she left, she sent word that she had fallen in love, for the first time in her life, with Emory Quardon, the son of a Territorial Governor, and that he was in love with her.

Billy's last four months of training passed in a haze of dull, routine days and endless insomniac nights. They were broken by brief periods of happiness when he became the lover of one woman or another. But it was not the same.

Snorkel had come to see him one night. They talked.

"I *can't* hate her," he said.

"Sure you can. You've been hurt." said Snorkel.

"But I *can't* hate Sally. I loved her too much to ever be able to do that."

"Right now, you don't think you can be hurt anymore. Wait till she comes back, Billy. You think you're ready for it, but it's not true. You'll see her, and all of it will come back to you in a rush. It'll be like somebody stepped on your chest."

"Oh, fuck you, Snorkel!"

"Right now you mean that," said Snorkel, rising to leave. "Tomorrow morning you won't." He left.

He was right.

About what would happen when Sally came back, and about not meaning what he said to Snorkel.

The first sight of her made him know the meaning of pain all over again.

They spoke a few times. Then he did one of those things people always do. He went to her one night and tried to make her understand how much he loved her, how much she had hurt him. At the center of it was his love for her.

She would not listen, and gave him a speech she must have rehearsed for six months before her return: I never loved you. I never said I loved you.

Billy knew she meant it.

Three months later, Emory Quardon came to visit her.

Billy never saw them together because he did not want to see them together.

Quardon left one day soon after he arrived. Billy heard that Sally Lemur-Potti gave him a speech much like the one she had given Billy.

By then Billy had toughened enough to leave her alone. He found himself worrying about her sometimes, but he never saw her unless it was a social occasion in the company of others.

In the three years since, both Billy and Sally had distinguished themselves. For a while Sally threw herself totally into her work. She was a woman not quite sure of what she wanted, so she tried all the things she might possibly like. One by one she eliminated them, until she was left with her career, her few lovers, parties, some friends.

She was not vindictive in her whims, her attachments and disengagements. It was that she was slowly finding her way to what she wanted. Those things and people which did not change as she did were left behind like so many cicada shells.

She did not turn against old lovers, friends or co-workers so much as she outgrew them.

Billy did somewhat the same; he had fewer lovers, no real love. He still hurt. He wanted to find another who had been as good for him as Sally. It was impossible.

They had lived separate lives, and time had passed.

Time passed.

Billy came to himself in the focus room of the *Argus*, his mind catching up with his actions. He was watching, and ignoring a piece of natural debris far away.

Time passed.

So much debris, so much garbage. Even the unsighted would have a hard time imagining *this* space as empty. To the Sighted, it was a cluttered circus. Plasma, gas clouds, breeding grounds for comets, solar tides and winds, radio messages, radio noise, particles and monopoles zipped by. Everything had to be watched.

Everything.

The search was drawing to its last scheduled hours. Billy had not slept in a long time, but he would not leave the focus room for any reason.

Yvonne Oculli came on the main Scout frequency.

"I have a radiation source," she said.

The words fell like rocks onto Billy's ears. He punched in. The ship console showed him several curves and courses, enlarged until the plot followed the dot on the immense night that was the Oculli ship.

"I'm in pursuit," she said. Her ship broadcast data. The

Argus and two other Scout ships triangulated her. Their own plotboards glowed softly, getting a true fix on her position.

Billy found the Oculli ship was several times too far away for him to reach it by the end of the scheduled search time. They would extend it, of course, even though the Oculli ship would reach the object long before then.

"I'm having trouble keeping a fix on it," said Yvonne Oculli. "Anyone got it?"

The plotboards remained clear of all data except that her ship broadcast.

Billy looked back over his shoulder; there was nothing there but the great crystal reflectors of the *Argus*. He wished that even for a millionth of a second he could see through the light-year of lead, see the object the other Scout ships was chasing, know what it was.

If only he could see it.

"Tighten your patterns toward the search area," said Maxwell Big-Eyes, "but don't break them off until we know for sure what Yvonne's after."

On the plotroom wall ships broke off their predicted courses and moved like a pod of whales forming up slowly.

Dierdre and Max scanned the charts.

"A cone. In the middle. A ship *could* have gotten through undetected so far. It was Oculli's good luck to catch it. She under power?" he asked Jiminez. "Good."

"I've got a definite fix. I'm starting an intercept now," said Yvonne.

"Don't let your safeguards down," Max spoke. Yvonne was only on her third mission but had acted commendably so far. He did not want her to get overanxious.

"Let me handle the ship, Chief," she said.

"Sorry."

"I'm doing this by the book. It'll take a while. I'm not in *any* kind of visual range, I'm on instruments, and all they tell me is how far away, and how weak, the source is. I'll have it in an hour or so. A visual maybe before then. It's . . . it looks very small on the detectors. Don't get your hopes up."

"Jiminez," Max turned to him, "run a lost-probe check on the adjoining sectors, see if anything was heading that way, say . . ."

". . . two centuries ago," said Dierdre.

"...two hundred years..." Max's voice trailed off.

"Will do," Jiminez said, his hands running over buttons, displays.

Occasionally, Scouts ran across probes sent out centuries before light-speeds had been achieved. These had been launched when man first reached across space in rams and photon ships. Most probes had ceased functioning long ago. Many arrived at worlds to find men already waiting for them.

Sometimes their power sources were still active, only their systems broken down, crystallized or pitted away. Sometimes these probes fell as meteors on mankind's worlds, sometimes they were spotted by normal craft. Usually they passed silent, inert, of only archaeological interest.

Max wondered at the tenacity of his ancestors. With nothing but the bodies and simple talents evolution had given them, and desire, they made beachheads on the night with small, slow craft which had long outlived their purposes.

Perhaps Yvonne was chasing one of these, a probe forgotten by even the few ships which had encountered it across the years. Max hoped not. He hoped her estimates were wrong, and that she was following the ship *Nightwatch*. They would soon know.

Billy listened to the hour unravel like a garment; he hung on each word, watched the intricate play of paths on the location grids. But with his mind and eyes and senses he was watching around him for a sign, anything out of the ordinary. He would not rest; he was tired, the tension made him hurt through his shoulders and back.

Sally used to rub his back.

He slammed his fist on the control console.

Sally.

Did it come down, after all, to love? He had thought for three years now that he was beyond it, that the emotional scars had healed, not well, raggedly, but healed nonetheless.

He stared at the night, the Deeps he shared with the other Scouts, perhaps with Sally. It was not hostile, it was a giant indifference filled with electromagnetic phenomena. It was immense, and you got lost quickly if something went wrong. But it did not hurt people.

Only people hurt people.

His chest tightened, his head ached. He wanted to cry for the first time in three years, to relieve his frustration with sobs. But he couldn't. His job was to watch and wait and use his abilities as best he could. To find the lost Scout.

The least he could do was not cry about it.

"An engine. Torn off all raggedy. Maybe some port tubes attached. No sign of webwork, focus or crew compartment. Scans show nothing else. I'm checking it visually. All I get is inert equipment."

"Take your time," said Max.

"I'm sorry, Chief. I hoped there'd be more here than this."

"It's okay. Remember to beacon-mark it."

"By the book. Uh, Chief, you could run a backward..."

"We're already doing it."

The SSI's were busily plotting the backward trajectory of the engine remnants from the *Nightwatch*, its mass, its probable future path.

Dierdre watched while it ran through the program on screen. She turned to her uncle.

"That's what I was afraid of," he said. He broadcast the program onto the Scout frequency, let it run into each ship's console. "Here's what we get on a backward trajectory."

Billy Big-Eyes watched.

It was as good a simulation of an explosion in reverse as Billy had ever seen. In reverse, it would be an explosion, with only the engine remnant's path able to be followed out of all the infinite possible trajectories of debris.

The engine had been flung away from the ship by an explosion of some sort which ripped through the *Nightwatch*. The rest of the ship could be an ever-widening globule of debris moving somewhat along the initial path of the ship.

Sally could be anywhere, moving in any direction.

Or there could be no more Sally, no more *Nightwatch*.

"Make one more sweep of your sectors," said Max, "then get ready to bring them home. Put out the beacons and mark them."

That was all in the book, he didn't need to tell them. He felt old and useless and empty. "We'll still be here until we get a Recall check on all of you. Keep looking, but have your Acceleration programs ready."

He signed off.

"Christ!"

"Odd," said Dierdre. "I've never heard anybody but Chester say that."

"It comes easy," Max said. "It's about the last good curse we had. We've lost most of our gods, and all the good curses with them."

Doctor Snorkel came in, his mustache unkempt, his hair kinky. He carried food from the commissary for himself, Max and Jiminez, and a drink for Dierdre. Her helmet would open, but the harness she wore after the operation allowed only straws to enter the mouthpiece.

"I heard," he said, before he sat.

Dierdre opened the hinged front of the egg-shaped helmet. The room glowed redly in the IR. She looked around.

"How are the eyes?" asked Snorkel.

"Itchy."

"You need lots of rest."

Max spoke. "We all need rest, none of us more than those out there." He indicated the board. "They'll be glad to get rest, let the ships do all the work for a while."

Snorkel was looking at the plotboard along with Dierdre.

Max looked from one to the other.

"I don't think he's going to come on Recall, you know?" said Dierdre.

"I know."

"I didn't want to bring it up," Snorkel put in.

"Nothing has to be said until after the Recall. It's not official until then."

"You may as well get ready for it," said Dierdre.

Max sighed. His age and experience were leaning on him like an overturned bookshelf.

"She's dead," he said. "She's got to be."

"It's not us you have to convince."

"I'm trying to convince myself."

"It's like artificial respiration," said Dierdre. "You're not supposed to quit trying to revive someone until you're sure they're dead. And the only time you're sure they're dead is the minute you decide to quit trying. That's the only time."

"He loves her that much?"

"I don't know if it's love or the idea of love," said Snorkel.

"Billy was the closest thing to the classic case of someone trying to die of a broken heart, or acting like it, anyway. He was tough, though, and didn't. He kept at it, kept working, got better. Somewhere in there he realized what he was doing to himself. So he quit it, quit the posing. But he kept the real feeling inside."

"That's the longest I've ever heard you talk about one person, Otto," said Max.

"That's the longest I ever want to talk about one person."

"He won't come back until he's sure," said Dierdre.

"When will he be sure?"

"When he comes back." said Snorkel.

The Recall came. Billy watched the other ships go into Acceleration Modes and become probability lines on his plots.

So much to do, so much to cover out there. So much noise, so much light.

The great crystal ship *Argus* swung in closer toward the beacon marking the engine remnant, though it was still a day away at this speed.

"Billy, this is Dierdre."

"Hi, kid, how are you?"

"Terrible."

"Eyes hurt?"

"Skin, too. A rash."

"Oh, that. That'll go away."

"So Snorkel tells me. Billy..."

"How's Uncle Max?"

"He's right here. He's hurt."

"Oh, Dierdre..."

"Billy, come back please? For me, at least, if you can't for him?"

"Dierdre, I can't. I just can't, not yet."

"I know you don't think you can, Billy, but you can. Just do it. You can't have slept any, or anything. You couldn't see anything if you found it. I've just started alterations, and I can probably see better than you, right now..."

"No, you can't. You'll be able to one day, kid. You'll be better than me and Uncle Max and Uncle Chester put together. I'm okay though. I'm taking some stuff, and I can see pretty well, still."

"Oh, Billy, there's no way Sally—"

"William! This is Snorkel. What the hell are you taking?"

"...Uh, Myoptine. Just a few grains. Don't worry, Doc, I know my limits."

"That's great, William, just great! Not only are you going to keep at it till you drop, you're going to burn your eyes out doing it. *Do not* take any more, Billy, I mean that. You want to be blind? Really blind? Imagine it. I hope you can. I hope it makes you shake. Don't play around with that stuff. Put your ship in Acceleration and get to sleep and get back here. You've got me worried now."

"Okay, Doc, no more, no more. I'll leave it alone. Just something to keep me awake, just a little longer. I could figure out something but..."

"Two milligrams BNK every six hours for... twelve hours. That's it. No more. Then turn around and head it back home."

"Two BNK. Okay, Snorkel. Put Dierdre back on, will you?"

"Billy?"

"Yeah, kid. 'Come back.' I know."

"Come back."

"Another half-day, like the doctor says. That's all. I'm really getting tired. I know when I'm beat. Kid..."

"What, Billy?"

"I hope you never have to do anything like this. It tears your heart out. It really does."

Dierdre turned away from the speaker. Billy signed off.

"My god," said Snorkel, shaking his head. "Myoptine, my god. Letting his head turn off while his eyes keep watching. My god. Save us from love, save us from love."

Dierdre's shoulders were shaking. Maxwell went to her and held her, but the shaking did not stop for some time.

Billy Big-Eyes was alone now, as alone and more tired than he had ever been. He'd gone past the point of caring. His head was made of dough, his arms and legs lead. His face belonged to someone else. The drug had made his eyes burn. Snorkel had been right. It was just that the tiredness and the immensity and the activity around him had begun to get to him for the first time. He realized he was out in the Deeps and that it was bigger and more full of movement and noise than man could really imagine. On the surface of a planet it was impossible to believe, you were bounded by the stars above you, the ground at your feet, the hori—

Out of the corner of his eye he saw an instrument gauge *move*.

He looked at the console. He stared at it, trying to make something move again by force of will. The gauges remained steady.

Myoptine was not an hallucinogen. The BNK was supposed to cut down fatigue poisons, the ones which caused visions, at the expense of the body's insulin. He knew a gauge had moved.

He cleared the console and punched through the instruments one by one. He studied them. He moved sections, working one at a time until he memorized them all. Then he quick-patched a program to make *all* the gauges line up at their optimum readings. He watched. His hands gripped the chair arms.

"Move, damn you!"

Several of the beacon receivers pulsed regularly, normally. They distracted him. He moved uprange, but it was useless. The warning light spectra made them glow, and they impinged on his consciousness.

"Max! Max!" he called. "Who's there?" still watching the corner console.

"This is Max, Billy. What is it?"

"Max, kill the beacons, kill everything. One of my detectors moved."

"We can't kill the beacons, not this second. You know that."

"Damn it, Max, kill something!"

"Billy, this is Snorkel here too. What is it?"

"Get Max on, Snorkel, Goddamn it!"

"I'm still here, Billy. What did you see?"

"A detector. It moved once. I can't get a reading."

"Was it a beacon?"

"No, Max. No! Something else, some other frequency. Too much noise and garbage out here. The beacons are bothering me. Kill 'em. I'll damp the hydrogen and oxygen emissions. But kill the beacons, Max, for just a while."

A few moments later, they did.

It was quiet in the focus room, really quiet. There was no stellar noise, no flicker of solar winds, no crackle of ionized matter. Billy killed his engines, drifted on a curved path. He listened and looked and watched his detectors.

* * *

"Is he breaking up out there?"

"I don't know. The drug may have something to do with it, or fatigue. He could have taken something he didn't tell me about. I doubt that. If we had biotelemetering, like in the old days, I might know more. But he's so tense up there I couldn't get good readings anyway."

"Dierdre asleep?"

"Yes."

"Wake her. We may need her to talk to him." Max looked at his friend of thirty years. "I'm afraid right now for him, Otto."

"So am I."

The needle flickered *once* again.

There were many people in the plotroom a few hours later, including the Assistant Director. Her name was Smedd. She was pleasant but businesslike.

"The crew compartment?" she asked.

"Either that," said Snorkel, "or the low-pulse generator in one of the maneuvering engines. Nothing else aboard puts out waves on that frequency."

"The crew compartment wave is a shield against low-frequency which might disturb sleep," said Max. "They've been in ships as long as there have been Scouts. We're hoping she was able to get to that part of the ship after the explosion."

Smedd placed her knuckles together. "That still doesn't explain why Big-Eyes didn't answer the Recall."

"We're checking on that now." Max said. "It's possible he was near interference when Recall came, and he never got it."

"I know nothing can stop the Scout frequency, Maxwell." she said.

He looked to Snorkel for help. He started to speak.

"Don't implicate yourself in this ruse, Otto." she said. She turned to her assistant. "Big-Eyes, in the ship *Argus*, is chasing possible remains of the ship *Nightwatch*. Big-Eyes did not answer Recall and is therefore in violation of his directives." She looked up. "That's the official message." She looked at her assistant. "Now hold it, and wander around the building for a while so you can't be found. Be back here in an hour."

She turned to Max. "You shouldn't wear your small mask, Maxwell. It shows too much of your face. I want an explanation of all this, straight."

"Allow Dierdre to fill you in, Ms. Smedd. I'm very tired. I want to look at that board and listen to Billy and find out where in God's name the *Nightwatch* is."

Smedd walked to Dierdre. They began to talk.

"Billy?"

"Yes, Max?"

"We're running the beacons as fast as we can. We'll get you a fix on it. The pulses still regular?"

"Yes. Every six minutes."

"At least, whatever is making them is still in one piece. If it's the maneuver engine, that means it's a big hunk of metal. If it's the crew pulser, it may be the whole section or just the source, which is about as big as your hand. And it's not a frequency you'll be able to see head-on when you take the ship toward it. You'll have to move in on instruments so you don't overrun. Or hit it."

"I've been trying to think of all that, Uncle Max. It isn't too easy."

"I know. Hang with it a while, Billy." Max realized as soon as he said it how really bitter he could be with himself sometimes.

"We got it, maybe," said Jiminez, excitedly.

It was like doing the pencil thing in the mirror, trying to look at something held in front of you in reverse and drawing a line in a circle.

Billy had to triangulate from the beacons, alter his course, triangulate, try to determine the speed and angle, recheck to see if one or the other were changing. Always, maneuver, recheck, maneuver, check.

He was intent on the intercept and ignored the space around him as much as possible. It was only a backdrop to the thing he was doing. Occasionally he scanned it up and down the spectra, watched a star or a gas cloud and dust particles.

Somewhere ahead was what he *knew* was the crew compartment. He had been broadcasting since the moment he located it, his relays racing ahead of him. He watched them go, telling the *Nightwatch*: help is on the way hold tight please answer if you can help is on the way...

There had been no answer.

There had been no answer for the thirteen days of the search.

He kept imagining this as a maneuver, a challenge; he kept backing his ship down into parking orbit with it, talking to it, his beacons telling the object who he was and when he would get there and that it was all right.

There was no answer.

Billy was tired, he had to remember when he started to do things in the wrong sequence, or too quickly, or forgot to check steps.

By rote, by care, he moved his ship in.

It was more than the shielded crew compartment hanging twenty kilometers away from him. There was the focus room, the tubeway and three square kilometers of wrecked lacework reflectors.

He had known this from hundreds of kilometers back, when he determined and finally saw what was there.

He sat and watched the wreckage for a few seconds while his ship told him over and over that it was docked in orbit with the object.

Then he got up out of his seat and went down the tubeway to the work section.

Scouts were never meant to leave ships in the Deeps. That they could was a safeguard men like Chester Big-Eyes had had built into the ships, whether needed or not.

Billy came out the small access port in a shielded pressurized suit, its helmet transparent and huge to allow his chrome helmet room inside. He carried with him an empty suit, tools, a small propellant unit, communications gear.

He had never seen the outside of a ship in the Deeps. No living Scout ever had.

He moved to the area outside the focus room and kicked off, moving slowly across the great expanse of the reflector network. From the focus room, you never noticed how *big* it was. It was mostly behind you. Here, it was like sailing above the surface of an ocean, the surface of a moon built by spiders who worked with wire and ice.

He talked to the object hanging off the dully glowing horizon of his ship. It floated like an island, so close to the big metal archipelago of the *Argus*. It was unrecognizable as the *Nightwatch*. As any ship.

One section of the side glowed *very* deeply in the infrared. The metal must have been slagged there.

Sally he said Sally it's me.

There was no answer and had been none for thirteen days.

He looked at the ship in the infrared. He could not bring himself to look in the X ray.

His duty as a Scout was to get the other Scout safely back to Fremont.

He talked, amplified by his ship, to the wreckage, to Sally.

I've made it all this way, I'll get you back home.

Us Scouts have to stick together.

He reached the access door of the *Nightwatch*.

Now it was this wreckage which was the island, dwarfed by the continent of the *Argus* overhead, glowing bloodily in the IR, like wicker in a pool of magma.

The door opened easily when he pulled. What he really noticed was the crystallized scorch along the right side of the ship where the starboard engine must have exploded like a burst paper bag.

Millions of roengtens loosed in the night and the ship.

Sally he said up the dark tubeway as he cycled the lock and all kinds of waves shone around him from the focus room above, Sally I love you I love you I love you.

Sitting in her chair so small so beautiful so lovely where she was when the ship blew up, the woman he still loved with all his heart.

He crossed back through the boiling purple ultraviolet night around the *Argus*, across the immensity of the crystal lacework of his ship.

In one hand, he held the arm of the filled, but still unpressurized extra suit, guiding it gently.

In the other, he carried the flight recorder from the *Nightwatch*. The instrument was the second most important piece of equipment on a Scout ship.

Overhead, the music of the spheres hurt his eyes.

THE GODS OF REORTH

by Elizabeth A. Lynn

Once long ago writers were paid by the word for their stories. Legend has it that 2¢ rates were responsible for the greater part of Victorian literature. Genre publishing (largely a twentieth-century phenomenon) has never given over the practice, and unfortunately a great deal of the worst writing in the science fiction field attests to this. We all guard against it constantly but the compulsion is always there to churn away at the typewriter. Elizabeth A. Lynn has never been cowed by the inevitable pressure to produce flabby verbiage. She writes what she pleases, in the form that pleases her best, and her spare, fresh style is a joy. Lynn has produced in a very short time a body of work which is of the highest caliber. And it's pure good writing without any artificial ingredients. Read and enjoy.

This is the story of a goddess Who had once been a woman named Jael, and what She did.

She lived in a cave on an island. Around Her island of Mykneresta lay others: Kovos and Nysineria, Hechlos, Dechlas, and larger, longer, fish-shaped Rys, where the Fire God lived within his fuming, cone-shaped house. She was the Goddess. From Her cave sprang the vines and grains that women and men reaped from the fertile ground; from the springs of Her mountain welled the clear water that made the ground fertile, and gave life. Her mountain towered over the land. When She grew angry the lightning tore from the skies over Her cave, and the goats went mad on the mountainsides. *"Hard as frost, indolent as summer rain, spare us, spare us, O Lady of the Lightning,"* Her poets sang. Sometimes the music appeased Her, and then She smiled, and the skies smiled clear and purple-blue, as some said Her eyes must be. But they were not: they were dark and smoky-green, like the color in the heart of a sunlit pool, touched to movement by a summer shower.

They smoked now. Above Her cave lightning reached webbed fingers to the stars. "The Lady is angry," whispered the villagers. Inside the vast cavern that was Her home She stood staring at a pulsing screen. It burned and leaped with pinpoints of light. She read the message from the screen as easily as a scribe reads writing, and Her fingers sent a rapid reply out to the waiting stars.

WHY DO THE MEN OF RYS ARM FOR WAR?

MYKNERESTA IS A PEACEFUL AND FRUITFUL PLACE.

A moment passed, and the patterns answered, scrolling lines of amber fire on the dark, metallic screen.

PROBABILITIES PROJECT RYS AN EMPIRE.

THIS IS DESIRABLE. DO NOT IMPEDE.

Jael stared at the fading pattern, and swept a fierce hand across the board. The message vanished; above the cave's roof, fireballs rolled and then disappeared down the sides of the mountain.

This is desirable. In her mind, the silent screens retained a voice, a cool, sardonic, male voice. War! She scowled across the room. An ugly, evil thing she knew it was—though she had never seen a war. She did not desire war on Mykneresta. Yet it was "desirable" that Rys become an empire. Were the worshippers of the Fire God to rule, eventually, all of the planet Methys? She snorted. The Fire God had once been only a man, named Yron. Long ago, when they had been much younger, they had used the lumenings, the lightscreens, to talk with one another across the planet. But that had been an age ago, it seemed. She did not want to talk to Yron now.

Are you jealous, she asked herself, because his children will rule a world, and yours will not? She caught herself thinking it, and laughed. What nonsense to be feeling, that she, who had seen five worlds, and governed four, should care who or what ruled on a little planet round a little sun, whirling on an arm of a vast galaxy, a galaxy ruled by Reorth. Yet—Methys was important. Long-term assignments to undeveloped planets were not made unless they were important. Somewhere on a probability-line Methys was a key, a focus of power. Somewhere on Reorth, in the great block-like towers that held their machines, a technician had seen this world matched to a time within a nexus of possibilities, and had decided that, changed thus and so, moved in this or that direction, Methys could matter. *Do not impede.* Reorth wants a war.

Jael stepped away from the cavern which held the lumenings, the spyeyes, and all the other machines that made her Goddess. She walked along passageways, grown with fungus that glowed as she passed it, and ducked through a door cut into the rock. Now she was outside. Above her the night sky gleamed, thick with stars. Wind whipped round the granite crags with words hidden in its howls. She rubbed her arms with her hands, suddenly cold. It was autumn, drawing close to winter. I wonder how Yron likes living in his volcano, she thought, all smoke. That made her smile. With the bracelets on her slim wrists she drew a cloak of warmth around herself, and sent ahead of her, along the hard ground, a beam of yellow light. Slowly she walked down the mountainside, listening, smelling, tasting the life that roamed in the darkness. Once a cougar leaped to pace beside her, great head proud. She reached to stroke it. It sprang away, regarding her with widened eyes. She could compel it back—but even as she thought it, she rejected the thought. It was part of the night, with the wind and the starlight. Let it run free.

She came at last to the path which led to the villages—a worn and hidden path it was, and even she could not remember when it first was made. One bright star shone through the tree trunks. She stared at its flickering yellow light. It was not a star, but flame. Curious, she dimmed the light from her bracelets and walked toward it. Who would dare to come so far up the mountainside? It was almost a sacrilege. Perhaps it was a poet; they did strange things sometimes. Perhaps some traveler, lost and tired and unable to go on, had dared to build a small fire almost at Her door, praying Her to spare him in his hour of need.

But it was more substantial than that; it was a house, a rough-hewn cabin, and at the side of the house was a rain barrel, and there was a yellow curtain at the window. Marveling a little, Jael went up to the curtain and put her eye to the gap where it flapped.

She saw a small room, with a neat pallet on the floor, a table, a chair near the hearth, a candle on the table. From the low rafters, like bats, hung bunches and strings of herbs, roots, leaves, a witchwoman's stock. A woman sat on the chair, bending forward, poking at the fire with a long forked stick.

Jael understood. This was a woman who had chosen, as was her right, to live alone; to take no man and bear no children; to be, instead, wise-woman, healer, barren yet powerful in her choice, for did not the Goddess honor those who chose to be lonely in Her service? She watched. The woman rose. She went to a chest beside the bed, took out a sheepskin cape, and began to pick the burrs from it.

Suddenly she turned toward the window. Jael drew back instinctively, and then caught herself and used the bracelets to blur the air around her, so that she could stand still and not be seen. Gray eyes seemed to look right into hers; gray eyes like smoke, framed by the smoke of long dark hair.

Then the dark head bowed, and was covered by the cloak's hood. She walked to the door. Jael blurred herself wholly to human eyes and waited as the witchwoman opened the door and closed it behind her. She wondered (even She) where, on the Lady's mountain, even a witch would dare to go.

She walked along the path that followed the stream bed. Jael followed behind her, hidden and silent. As the pool by the waterfall, she knelt. Jael smiled. This was one of Her places; it was not so long ago that She had showed Herself, under the glare of a harvest moon, to an awed crowd. Now the stream bed was clogged with fallen leaves, but it was still a holy place. The waterfall was a small but steady drip over the lip of rock to the clear dark pool below.

The witchwoman knelt on the flat stones that ringed the pool's edge, staring into the fecund depth of water. Her face was grave and still. At last she rose, and made her way to the path. Her silent homage made Jael hesitate. But she decided not to follow the witchwoman to her cabin. Instead, she returned to her cave. Stalking to the lumenings, she lit them with a wave of her hand, and then, irresolute, stood thinking what to say.

She decided.

EXPLAIN NEED FOR EMPIRE AT THIS TIME.

The lights pulsed and went dim. She waited. No answer appeared. Oh well—they might answer another time. The question would surprise them. Jael remembered years of famine, of drought, of blight. Once She had sent a plague. It had hurt, watching the inexorable processes of disease and death sweep over Her people. She had not asked reasons for that.

War is different, she thought.

But how can I know that? I have never seen a war. Perhaps it is just like a plague. But plague is natural, she thought. War is made by men.

What's this? she asked herself. That plague was not "natural," *you* made it, with your training and your machines. What makes this different? Woman of Reorth, she said sternly, naming herself in her own mind, as she rarely did, how are *you* different than a war?

The next day brought no answer from the lumenings, nor did the one after that, nor the one after that.

Autumn began the steep slide into winter. Round the Lady's mountain it rained and rained, gullying the fields, now stripped of grain, and washing the last leaves from the thin trees. The waterfall sang strongly for a time.

Then one morning the ground was white and cold and hard, and ice spears tipped the trees and fences, and hung from the eaves. Village children drove their herds into barns, whooping and shouting, snapping willow switches from the dead branches of the willow trees. Men gathered wood; women counted over the apples and dried ears of corn that filled the storerooms, and prayed to the Goddess for a gentle winter. Mountain goats watched the stooping wood gatherers with disdainful eyes, their coats grown shaggy and long, for in winter the hunting stopped. In Rys and allied Hechlos the mining ceased. Only in the smithies the men worked, forging swords and knives and shields and spear and arrowheads. In the smithies it stayed warm.

Sometime during the winter procession of ice, snow, and thaw, Reorth answered. The lumenings lit, held a pattern for a few moments, and then went dark.

It was the outline of a machine, sketched in light. For weeks Jael could not think what it might mean. She had decided to dismiss it as a misdirected transmission, meant for someone, when one night she dreamed. It was a dream of Reorth, of home. She woke, weeping for a world she had not seen in three hundred years, and, in the darkness of her cave, heard herself say aloud the name of the machine.

It was a chronoscope, one of the great machines that scanned the timelines. She had not seen one in—in—she could not remember how long. Rage filled her. Was she a child, to be answered with pictures? The contemptuousness of the response brought her in haste to the screen, fingers crooked, ready to scorch the sky with lightning.

But she caught her hands back in mid-reach. The folk who had sent her here would not be impressed with her anger. The answer was plain, as they had meant it. The need is there, seen in the timelines. You know your job. Do as you are told.

Do not impede.

* * *

The year moved on. The waterfall over the pool froze into fantastic sculpted shapes, thawed, fell, froze again. The pool did not freeze. Only its color changed, deepening under stormy skies to black. The villagers did not visit it, but the witchwoman, Akys, did, coming to kneel on the icy, slippery stones once or twice each week.

The witchwoman's cabin by the streambed was as far up the Lady's mountain as the villagers would venture. They came reluctantly, drawn by need: a sick child, a sick cow, an ax wound. The women came first, and then the men. This was as it should be, for men had no place on Her mountain.

More rarely, the witchwoman went to the villagers, down the steep pathway from her home to the rutted village streets. How the knowledge came she was never sure, save that it did come, like a tugging within her head, a warning that something was amiss in wood or village. Once it was a girl who had slipped gathering kindling and wedged her legs between two rocks. Akys had gone down to the village to fetch the villagers and bring them to the child. Once a fire started in a storeroom; they never discovered how. Had Akys smelled the smoke? She could not tell, but with knowledge beating like the blood in her temples against her brain, she came scrambling down the path to call the villagers out from sleep, and helped them beat the flames out in the icy, knife-edged wind.

In the thick of the winter, trying to gather twigs on the stony slope, the witchwoman would find firewood outside her door, or apples, cider, even small jugs of wine, to warm her when the ashes gave no warmth, and the wind thrust its many-fingered hands through her cabin's myriad chinks. After the fire they left her a haunch of venison. She was grateful for it, for the hares and sparrows grew trapwise, and her snares often sat empty.

To pass the shut-in days in the lonely hut, the witchwoman cut a flute from a tree near the Lady's pool, and made music. It floated down the hillside, and the village children stopped their foraging to listen to the running melodies.

Jael heard them, too. They drew her. The quavering pure tones seemed to her to be the voice of winter, singing in the ice storms. Sometimes, on dark nights, she would throw on her cloak of green cloth—a cloak made on Reorth—and go past the pool, up to the shuttered window of the witch's house, to listen.

The music made her lonely.

On impulse one night, she shifted the lumenings to local and called across the islands to Yron. She called and called. Then she called Reorth.

YRON DOES NOT ACKNOWLEDGE TRANSMISSION

The reply came at once.

YRON RECALLED 20 YEARS AGO, LOCAL TIME.
NEW ASSIGNMENT ACCEPTED. COORDINATES
FOLLOW.

There was a pause. Then a set of planetary coordinates flashed across the screen.

Jael shrugged. The transmission continued.

YOUR RECALL UNDER CONSIDERATION.

WOULD YOU ACCEPT REASSIGNMENT?

TAKE YOUR TIME.

* * *

Akys did not know when she first began to sense the presence of a stranger near her home. It came out of nowhere, like the gift of warning in her head. Especially it came at night, when clouds hid the moon and stars. At first she thought it was the wild things of the mountain, drawn by her music. But beasts leave signs that eyes can read. This presence left no sign—save, once, what might have been the print of a booted foot in snow.

On a day when the sun at noon was a copper coin seen through cloud, she heard a knock at her door. She thought, Someone in trouble? Her gift had given her no warning. She stood, laying the flute aside, moving slowly with weariness and hunger, for her snares had shown empty for three days. She went to the door and opened it.

A woman stood under the icicled eaves. She wore a long green cloak, trimmed with rich dark fur. From her fingers dangled two partridges.

"Favor and grace to you," she said. Her voice was low and gentle. "My name is Jael. We are neighbors on the mountain. I have heard your music in the evenings; it gives me much delight. I wished to bring you a gift." She held out the birds. Her hair, escaping from its hood, was the bright auburn of a harvest moon.

Akys stepped back. "Will you come inside? It's cold on the doorstep."

"Gladly," said the stranger. She dropped her hood back, and stepped into the small, smoky house.

Taking the birds from the slim hands, Akys said, "I didn't know I had any neighbors."

Her quick eyes caught the tint of gold as the cape shifted. Who was this woman, dressed so richly and strangely, who called her "neighbor" and brought her food?

"My name is Jael," said Jael again. "I am new come to this place. I lived before in . . ."—she seemed to hesitate—"Cythera, west of here. Now I live near the Lady's well."

"I do not know that place, Cythera," said the witchwoman. She began to strip the feathers from the birds. "Are you alone?" she murmured.

Jael nodded. "I have no man," she said.

"Then will you eat with me tonight?" said Akys. "It is hard to come to a new home alone, especially in winter. And they are your birds, after all."

Jael came to the hearth, where Akys sat cleaning the birds. Kneeling, she stretched out her hands to the warmth. Her fingers were slender, unscarred by work. On her wrists wire bracelets shone gold in the firelight. The flame seemed to leap toward them.

She glanced up, into Akys' gray eyes. "Forgive my silence," she said. "I may not speak of my past. But I mean you no harm."

"I can see that," said Akys. "I accept your gift and your silence." She has a vow, she thought. Perhaps she has left wealth and family behind, to serve the Lady. That is noble in one so beautiful and young.

She picked up the bellows and blew the fire up, and dropped the cleaned partridge in the pot. "I am alone, too," she said matter-of-factly.

"So I see," said Jael, looking around at the one room with its narrow pallet, and single chair. "You've not much space."

Akys shrugged. "It's all I need. Though I never thought to have visitors. I might get another chair."

Jael tucked her feet beneath her and settled beside the fire. "Another chair," she agreed quietly, "for visitors—or a friend."

Through the rest of the short, severe winter the two women shared food: birds, coneys, dried fruits, nuts, and clear water. In the thaws, when the snow melted and the streams swelled, they make hooks and lines to catch fish. They hunted the squirrels' stores from the ground, and gathered wood for the hearth. Jael's hands and cheeks grew brown, chapped by wind and water.

"Akys!" she would call from the house, flinging wide the door.

And Akys, kneeling by the stream, water bucket in hand, felt her heart lift at that clear, lovely call. "Yes!"

"Can I stuff quail with nuts?"

"Have we enough?"

"I think so."

"Slice them thin." She brought the bucket to the house. Jael was chopping chestnuts into bits. She watched warily over Jael's shoulder, wondering as she watched how the younger woman had managed, alone. She did not know the simplest things. "Be careful with that knife."

"If I dull it," Jael said, "you'll have to get the smith to sharpen it for you again."

"I don't want you to cut yourself," said Akys.

Jael smiled. "I never do," she said, "do I?"

"No."

Jael set the knife down and pushed the sliced nuts into the cavity. She trussed the bird with cord, held it, hefted it. "It's a big one. I'm glad you got that new pot from the village."

"I hate asking for things," said Akys.

Jael said, "I know. But you can't build an iron pot the way you can a chair." Crossing the room, she dumped the bird into the cauldron. "And tomorrow I want to fish. I'll bring some metal hooks with me when I return in the morning."

Akys said, quietly, "Why don't you stay the night?"

Jael shook her head.

During the days she became a human woman. She learned, or relearned, for surely she had known these skills before, to chop wood, to skin, clean, and cook animals, to fish, with coarse strings of hemp she had twisted herself, and a willow pole. She got cold and wet, went hungry when Akys did, and climbed to her cave tired and footsore. But she always went back at night. Fidelity had made her set the lumenings to Record, and she turned them on each evening, awaiting—what? Sometimes she told herself she was waiting for her recall. Touching her machines, she was once more the Goddess. But in the morning, when she went back down the slope to Akys, the reality of Reorth receded in her mind, and all its designs became bits of a dream, known only at night, and she did not think of recall.

Akys never asked questions. The brief tale told at their first meeting remained unembroidered, and Jael had half-forgotten it. She felt no need to have a past. Sometimes Akys looked at her with a stir of inquiry in her gray eyes. But if questions roiled her mind, they never reached her tongue.

Spring broke through winter like water breaking through a dam. They measured time by the rise and fall of the river. In spring the fish came leaping upstream, and if you held out a net—ah, if you just held out your hands—they would leap to the trap, bellies iridescent in the sunshine. In the white rapids they looked like pieces cut from rainbow.

"I want to bathe in the river!" cried Jael.

"It's too cold now," said practical Akys. "You'll freeze."

"Then I want summer to come." Jael pouted. "Why does the year move so slowly?" she demanded, flinging her arms wide.

Yet in the cavern at night, she saw the year moving swiftly, and wished that her power extended to the movement of the planet in its course around its sun.

The spyeyes set to Rys told her that armies and ships were gathering. They will be coming in the fall, she thought. They will be ready then. Spykos, king of Rys, was drawing men from all his cities and from the cities of nearby Dechlas. He cemented his alliance with Hechlos by marrying his daughter to Hechlos' king's son, and the goddess within Jael-the-woman raged, that these men could see women as so many cattle, bought and bred to found a dynasty. Spykos raided the harbor towns of Nysineria and Kovos—in winter!—distracting them, frightening them, keeping them busy and off guard. Jael watched the raids with a drawn face. It hurt, to see the villages burn.

What will you do?

This was the question she did not allow herself to hear. If she heard it, she would have to answer it. It kept her wakeful at night, walking through her caverns, staring at the dark, unspeaking lumenings.

Akys scolded her. "What's wrong with you? Your eyes have pits under them. Are you sleeping?"

"Not very well."

"I can give you a drink to help you sleep."

"No."

"Won't you stay here? It tires you, going home at night."

Jael shook her head.

Summer came to the mountain with a rush of heat. The children herded the beasts up to the high pastures again. The crags echoed to their whistles and calls and to the barking of the dogs. The heavy scents of summer filled meadows and forests: honeysuckle, clover, roses, wet grass steamy after a rainstorm.

Akys said, "You could bathe in the river now."

They went to the river, now strong and swift in its bed. Jael flung off her clothes. Her body was slim, hard and flat, golden-white except where weather had turned it brown. She dipped a toe in the rushing stream. "Ah, it's cold!" She grinned at Akys. "I'm going to dive right off this rock!"

Akys sat on the bank, watching her, as she ducked beneath the flowing, foamy water, playing, pretending to be a duck, a salmon, an otter, a beaver, an eel. Finally the cold turned her blue. She jumped out. Akys flung a quilt around her. She wrapped up in it, and rolled to dry. The long grass, sweet with the fragrance of summer, tickled her neck. She sat up.

"Hold still," said Akys. "You've got grass all over your hair." She picked it out with light, steady fingers.

Jael butted her gently. "Why don't you go in?"

"Too cold for me," said Akys. "Besides, I'd scare the fish." She looked at Jael. "I'm clumsy."

Jael said, "That's not true. You move like a mountain goat; I've watched you climbing on the rocks. And you're never clumsy with your hands. You didn't pull my hair, once."

Akys said, "Yes, but—you look like a merwoman in the water. I'd look like an old brown log."

Jael said, "I'm younger than you. I haven't had to work as hard."

"How old are you?" Akys asked.

Jael struggled to see her face through timebound eyes. "Twenty," she lied.

"I'm thirty-two," said Akys. "If I had had children, my body would be old by now, and I would be worrying about their future, and not my own."

Jael let the onimous remark pass. "Are you sorry that you have no children?" she said.

"No. A promise is a promise. For the beauty I lack—a little."

"Don't be silly." Jael bent forward and caught Akys' hands between her own. The quilt slid from her shoulders. "You *are* beautiful. You cannot see yourself, but I can see you, and I know. Do you think you need a man's eyes to find your beauty? Never say such nonsense to me again! You are strong, graceful, and wise."

She felt Akys' fingers tighten on her own. "I—I thank you."

"I don't want your thanks," said Jael.

That night, Jael lay in Akys' arms on the narrow, hard, straw-stuffed pallet, listening to rain against the roof slats, pat, pit-pat. The hiss of fire on wet wood made a little song in the cabin.

"Why are you awake still," murmured Akys into her hair. "Go to sleep."

Jael let her body relax. After a while Akys' breathing slowed and deepened. But Jael lay wakeful, staring at the dark roof, watching the patterns thrust against the ceiling by the guttering flames.

Autumn followed summer like a devouring fire. The leaves and grasses turned gold, red, brown, and withered; the leaves fell. Days shortened. The harvest moon burned over a blue-black sky. The villagers held Harvest Festival. Like great copper-colored snakes the lines wth torches danced through the stripped fields, women and children first, and then the men.

Smoke from the flaring torches floated up the mountainside to the cabin. Akys played her flute. It made Jael lonely again to hear it. It seemed to mock the laughter and singing of the dancers, and, as if the chill of winter had come too soon, she shivered.

Akys pulled the winter furs from her chest, and hung them up to air out the musty smell. She set a second quilt at the foot of the pallet.

"We don't need that yet," said Jael.

"You were shivering," said the witchwoman. "Besides, we will."

One night they took the quilt out and lay in the warm dry grass to watch the stars blossom, silver, amber, red, and blue. A trail of light shot across the sky. "A falling star!" cried Akys. "Wish."

Jael smiled grimly, watching the meteor plunge through the atmosphere. She imagined that it hit the sea, hissing and boiling, humping up a huge wave, a wall of water thundering through the harbors, tossing the Rysian ships like wood chips on the surface of a puddle, smashing them to splinters against the rocks. I wish I could wish for that, she thought.

"What are you thinking . . . ?" said Akys.

"About Rys."

"The rumors . . ."

"Suppose," said Jael carefully, "suppose they're true."

Akys lifted on an elbow. "Do you think they are?"

"I don't know. They frighten me."

"We're inland, a little ways anyways, and this village is so close to Her mountain. They wouldn't dare come here."

Jael shivered.

"You dream about it, don't you?" said Akys. "Sometimes you cry out, in your sleep."

Later she said, "Jael, could you go back home?"

"What?"

"To that place you came from, in the west, I forget its name."

"Cythera."

"Yes. Could you go back there? You'd be safer there, if the men of Rys do come."

"No," said Jael, "I can't go back. Besides, I know you won't leave this place, and I won't leave you."

"That makes me happy and sad at the same time," said Akys.

"I don't want to make you sad."

"Come close, then, and make me happy."

They made love, and then slept, and woke when the stars were paling. The quilt was wet beneath them. They ran through the dewy grass to the cabin, and pulled the dry quilt around them.

Jael went back to the cave the next night.

This is madness, she told herself on the way. You cannot be two people like this; you cannot be both the Goddess and Akys' lover. But around her the dark forest gave no answer back, except the swoop of owls and the cry of mice, and the hunting howl of a mountain cat.

She went first to the lumenings, but they were dark. In all the months she had stayed away, no messages had come. Next she checked the spyeyes. Ships spread their sails across the water like wings, catching the wind, hurrying, hurrying, their sails dark against the moonlit sea. She calculated their speed. They would reach the coast of Mykneresta in, perhaps, four days. She contemplated sending a great fog over the ocean. Let them go blundering about on reefs and rocks. If not a fog, then a gale, a western wind to blow them back to Rys, an eastern wind to rip their sails and snap their masts, a northern wind to ice their decks... She clenched her teeth against her deadly dreaming.

She waited out a day and a night in the cave, and then went back to Akys.

The witchwoman was sitting at her table with a whetstone, sharpening her knives.

"You have some news," said Jael. "What have you heard?"

Akys tried to smile. Her lips trembled. "The runner came yesterday, while you were gone. They have sighted ships, a fleet. The villages are arming." Her face had aged overnight, but her hands were steady. "I walked down to the forge and asked the smith for a sharpening-stone. I have never killed a man, but I know it helps to have your knife sharp."

"Maybe they will not come here," said Jael.

"Maybe." Akys laid down one knife, and picked up another. "I went to the Lady's pool yesterday, after I heard the news."

"And?"

"There was nothing, no sign. The Lady does not often speak, but this time I thought She might. . . . I was wrong."

"Maybe She is busy with the fleet."

Akys said, "We cannot live on maybes."

"Have you had anything to eat today?" said Jael.

Akys stayed her work. "I can't remember."

"Idiot. I'll check the snares. You make a fire under the pot."

"I don't think I set the snares."

Jael kissed her. "You were thinking of other things. Don't worry, there'll be something. Get up now." She waited until Akys rose before leaving the little hut.

She checked the snares; they had not been set. I should never have stayed away, she thought. She stood beside a thicket, listening for bird sounds, keening her senses. When she heard the flutter of a grouse through grass she called it to her. Trusting, it came into her outstretched hands, and with a quick twist she wrung its neck.

She brought the bird to the table and rolled up her sleeves. Akys was poking up the fire. "I chased a fox from a grouse," Jael said. "Throw some herbs into the water."

In bed, under two quilts, they talked. "Why do men go to war?" said Akys.

"For wealth, or power, or lands," said Jael.

"Why should anyone want those things?"

"Why are you thinking about it? Try to sleep."

"Do you think She is angry with us, Jael, for something we have done, or not done?"

"I do not know," Jael answered. She was glad of the darkness, glad that Akys could not see her face.

"They have a god who lives in fire, these men of Rys."

"How do you know?"

"The smith told me. He must like blood, their god."

"Hush," said Jael.

Finally Akys wept herself into an exhausted sleep. Jael held her tightly, fiercely, keeping the nightmares away. So Akys had held her, through earlier nights.

In the morning they heard the children shrilling and calling to the herds. "What are they doing?" wondered Akys.

"Taking the cattle to the summer pasture."

"But why, when it is so late—ah. They'll be safer higher up. Will the children stay with them?"

Jael didn't know.

That night, when she wrapped her cloak around her, Akys stood up as if to bar the door. "No, Jael, you can't go back tonight. What if they come, and find you alone?"

Jael said, "They won't find me."

"You are young, and beautiful. I am old, and a witch, and under Her protection. Stay with me."

Under her cloak Jael's hands clenched together. "I must go," she said. "I'll come back in the morning. They won't come at night, Akys, when they can't see, not in strange country. They'll come in daylight, if they come at all. I'll come back in the morning."

"Take one of the knives."

"I don't dare. I'd probably cut myself in the dark."

"Don't go," pleaded Akys.

"I must."

At last she got away.

At the cave, she would not look at the spyeyes. She had told Akys the truth, they would not come at night, she was sure of that. But in the morning . . . She twisted her hands together until her fingers hurt. What have you chosen, woman of Reorth?

She couldn't sleep. She sat in the cavern with her machines, banks of them. With them she could touch anyplace on Methys, she could change the climate, trouble the seas, kill. . . . The bracelets on her wrists shimmered with power. She dulled them. If only she could sleep. She rose. Slowly, she began to walk, pacing back and forth, back and forth, from one side of the cave to the other, chaining herself to it with her will.

You may not go out, she commanded herself. Walk. You may *not* go out. It became a kind of delirium. Walk to that wall. Now turn. Walk to *that* wall. Turn. Do not impede. Walk. This is desirable. Walk. Turn. You may not go out.

In the morning, when the machines told her the sun was up and high, she left the cave.

She went down the path toward the hut. The smell of smoke tormented her nostrils. She passed the pool, went through the trees that ringed it, and came out near the river. The cabin seemed intact. She walked toward it, and saw what she had not seen at first: the door, torn from its hinges, lying flat on the tramped-down, muddied grass.

She went into the cabin. Akys lay on the bed, on her side. There was blood all around her, all over the bed and floor. She was naked, but someone had tossed her sheepskin cloak across her waist and legs. Jael walked to her. Her eyes were open, her expression twisted with determination and pain. Her stiff right arm had blood on it to the elbow. Jael's foot struck something. She bent to see what it was. It was a bloody knife on the stained floor.

Jael looked once around the cabin. The raiders had broken down the door, to find a dead or dying woman, and had left. It was kind of them not to burn or loot the tiny place, she thought.

She walked from the hut. Smoke eddied still from the village below. She went down the path. She smelled charred meat. The storehouses were gone. They had come burning and hacking in the dawnlight. She wondered if they had killed everyone. There was a body in the street. She went to look at it; it was a ewe-goat with its throat slit. A man came out of a house, cursing and crying. Jael blurred Herself to human eyes. She went in through the broken door. There were dead women in here, too: one an old lady, her body a huddled, smashed thing against the wall, like a dead moth, the other a young woman, who might have once been beautiful. One could not tell from the things they had done.

Had they killed only women, then? She left the house. No, there was a man. He lay against a wall, both hands holding his belly, from which his entrails spilled. Flies buzzed around his hands.

Around Her the sounds of weeping rose and fell.

She walked the length of the street, and then turned, and walked back again, past the dead man, the dead ewe, the granaries smoking in the sunlight. They had left enough people alive in the village to starve through the winter. She followed the river past the cabin, past the pool. Just below the cabin She hesitated, drawn by a change in the mutter of the stream. The raiders had tossed a dead body into the clear water, and wedged it between two big rocks, defiling it.

She returned to the cave.

She lit it with a wave of Her hand. The light flamed and stayed, as if the stone walls had incandesced. Surrounded by bright, bare, burning stone, Jael walked to Her machines. She flung a gesture at the lumenings: the points of light whirled crazily, crackled, and died. The screen went blank. She passed Her hand over it; it stayed blank, broken, dead.

She smiled.

She turned to a machine, setting the controlling pattern with deft fingertips. She had not used this instrument since the plague time, when She had had to mutate a strain of bacteria. Meticulously She checked the pattern, and then tuned it finer still. When She was wholly satisfied, She turned the machinery on.

It hummed softly. A beam went out, radiation, cued to a genetic pattern. It touched Spykos of Rys, where he lay in his war tent outside the walls of Mykenestra's capitol, the city of Ain, with a twelve-year-old captive daughter of that city whose home and street his soldiers were busy burning to ash. It touched the guard outside his door. It touched the soldiers pillaging the city. It touched the little bands of raiders raping and killing in the countryside.

It touched the nobles of Rys. It touched Araf, Hechlos' king, where he lay with his third wife, and Asch, his son, where *he* lay with a slave girl whose looks he'd admired, that morning. His new wife slept alone. It touched the nobles of Hechlos, the high families of Dechlas.

It touched every male human being over fourteen on the six islands. It did not kill, but when it encountered the particular genetic pattern to which it had been cued, it sterilized. The men of Kovos, Nysineria, and Mykenestra it ignored. But on Rys, Hechlos, and Dechlas, and wherever it found men of that breed, it lingered. No seed, no children; no children, no dynasty; no dynasty, no empire; no empire, no war.

At last She shut it off. Around Her the stones still burned with light. She looked once around the cave that had been Her home for three hundred years. Then, using the bracelets, She set a protective shield around Herself, and summoned the patient lightning from the walls.

To the remaining villagers who saw it, it seemed as if the

whole of the Lady's mountain exploded into flame. Balls of fire hurtled down the mountainside; fire-wisps danced on the crags like demented demons. Stones flaked and crumbled. "It is the Fire God of Rys," the villagers whispered. "He has come to vanquish the Lady." All through the night they watched the fires burn. By morning the flames seemed gone. That day some brave women crept up the path. Where the Lady's pool had been was a rushing stream, scored by the tips of jagged rocks like teeth. Above it the mountaintop was scoured into bare, blue ash. The Lady had fled. The grieving women stumbled home, weeping.

No seed, no children.

With the coming of the first snow, word came to Mykenestra, carried by travelers. "The women of Rys are barren," they said. "They bear no children." And in the villages they wondered at this news.

But in the spring, the singers one by one came from their winter homes, to take their accustomed ways along the roads. They told the news a different way. "The Fire God's seed is ash," they cried, "He burns but cannot beget," and they made up songs to mock Him, and sang them throughout the marveling countryside. No children, no dynasty. They sang them under the walls of the brand new palace that Spykos of Rys had built in Ain. But no soldiers emerged to punish them for this temerity, for the brand new palace was empty, save for the rats. No dynasty, no empire. There was war in Rys over the succession, and Spykos had gone home.

It was the women who brought the truth. They came from Rys, from Hechlos, from Dechlas. Leaving lands, wealth, and kin, they came to the islands their men had tried to conquer. They came in boats, wives of fishermen, and in ships, wives of nobles. Wives of soldiers and merchants, kings and carpenters, they came. "Our men give us no children," they said. "We bear no sons for our fields, no daughters for our hearths. We come for children. Have pity on us, fold of Mykneresta; give us children, and our daughters will be your daughters, and our sons, your sons." No empire, no war.

Then the whole world knew. The poets sang it aloud: "The Lady is with us still, and She has taken vengeance for us." In Ain they rebuilt Her altar, and set Her statue on it, and they made Her hair as red as fire, and set hissing, coiling snakes about Her wrists, so real that one could almost see them move. Even on Rys the poets sang, and under the Harvest Moon the people danced for Her, keeping one eye on the Fire God's mountain. But it stayed silent and smokeless.

On Mykenestra the trees and bushes grew back on the Lady's mountain. One day in late summer, when the streams were dry, some rocks slid and fell. After the rain a pool formed, and it stayed. The old women went up the path to look. "She had returned," they said.

In spring the next year a woman came to the village. Her face was worn and weathered, but her back was straight, and though her red hair was streaked with gray, she walked as lightly as a young girl. "I am vowed to the Lady," she told the villagers, and she showed them the bracelets, like coiled snakes, on her slim brown wrists. "I am a healer. I have been in many lands, I have even been to Rys, but now I must come home. Help me build a house."

So the villagers built her a cabin by the curve of the stream, below the Lady's pool. They brought her meat and fruit and wine, when they had it, and she tended their sickness and healed their wounds. They asked her name, and she said, "My name is Jael."

"Have you really been to Rys?" they asked her.

"I have," she said. And she told them stories, about cities of stone, and tall men with golden hair, and ships with prows like the beaks of eagles, and streets with no children.

The children of the village asked, "Is it true they killed their king, because they thought he brought the Lady's Curse?"

"It's true," she said. "Camilla of Ain rules in Rys, and she is a better ruler than Spykos ever was or ever could be."

"Will they ever come again?"

"No, they never will."

A girl with brown braids and a small, serious face, asked, "Why did they come before?"

"Who knows? Now, be off with you, before night comes."

The children ran, save for the brown-haired girl. She lingered by the door. "Jael, aren't you ever afraid, so close to Her holy place?"

"How could I be?" said the healer. "This is my home, and She is good. Go on now, run, before the light goes."

"May I come back tomorrow?" said the girl.

"Why?" said Jael.

"I—I want to learn. About herbs, and healing, and the Lady."

"Come, then," said Jael.

The girl smiled, like a coal quickening in the darkness, and waved, and ran like a deer down the path beside the stream. Jael watched her go. Above her the clouds spun a net to catch the moon. She stood in the cabin doorway for a long time. At last the cold wind blew. Turning from the night, she pulled her green cloak close about her throat, and closed the cabin door against the stars.

SERGEANT PEPPER

by Karl Hansen

Biology has been rather the neglected science in science fiction writing, the traditional emphasis being on physics and all its ramifications. But as work in the biological sciences gallops along, and as science fiction strives to look as much inward as outward, we will (one hopes) see more stories that play with biological extrapolations. To wit, "Sergeant Pepper," a striking vision of some future applications of neurobiological insights...

A black queen stared at me: the Bitch of Spades.

Night came quickly on Titan. Outside, thick hydrocarbon fog rolled over steep mountain slopes covered with crystal forest. Before long, we would hear the banshee howls of elves as they swooped from tree to tree, before eventually settling into the trees ringing the base's perimeter, there to taunt us with their shrieks throughout the night. Maybe they mourned their dead—the ones we'd killed that day. Maybe that's why they wailed so. It didn't matter.

I was only interested in gambling, and in playing the game.

No matter how much psionic influence I tried to exert on my poker crystal, I couldn't transmute the queen to the jack of diamonds. She continued to smirk at me from her facet in the pentagonal crystal. I never had been worth a dog at telekinesis.

"Never draw to an inside straight," was the only advice my old man ever gave me before he died. Sometimes I wished I'd listened. He'd never had a chance to lay much more on me; I hit the road when I was twelve, and had been running away from home ever since. I had killed my first man in a fair fight before I made it to thirteen. I'd lost count of how many I'd killed by the time I was sixteen and old enough to join the Corps. And there was certainly no point in keeping track after that. Fortunately, the Corps didn't ask too many questions about their recruits' previous lives and activities. They didn't look for skeletons in closets. What did they care? They assumed there was something prompting a recruit to want to join the Corps and undergo hybridization to a combrid. They knew you were running away from something: poverty or wealth, no difference. When you emerged from the transformation tank it was to a clean slate. You had a new life to live. Past mistakes were forgotten. Lucky us.

I quickly calculated how deep I was into the pot. Pretty deep, all right. Almost a grand. I had no choice. I was going to have to bluff my way out of this mess.

Because I'd stayed a sucker for an inside straight. So when diamond face-cards started rolling up in my crystal, they lured me into jazzing up the pot. Besides, it wasn't that bad a draw—I held four to a flush, or four to an inside straight. The jack of diamonds would have given me a royal flush. Not a bad draw at all.

Then the bitch queen rolled up.

Busted.

A crummy pair of queens. (I was holding the diamond queen as my hole card.)

But maybe I could make them think I was holding a jack

instead. A royal straight wasn't a bad hand in stud poker. If you had one. I didn't.

So I waited for Vichsn to bet. She was high with a pair of tens showing. She threw in a C chip.

I bumped her a grand.

No point being timid now. Go for broke. And I would be broke if she didn't bluff. Not only were all my winnings tied up in this one pot, but so was the week's pay I'd started with. There was not much to do at base anyway, but with no money it was even worse. It could be a very boring week until next payday.

I made sure my face was held in a mask of careful nonchalance. It wasn't that hard. I'd risked my life too many times for less money than was in the pot. Gambling sometimes seemed silly and futile compared with the big risk. But it was better than nothing.

The other crystals went blank one by one as players folded. My bluff was working.

The bet passed to Vichsn again. Light gleamed from her oiled scalp, which was convoluted into ridges by buried vitalium wires. Her occular membranes snapped shut for a moment, then dilated. She looked into my eyes, running the tip of her tongue along the edge of fine, white teeth. She'd been trying to distract me all night by letting her tunic fall open as she threw chips into the pot, revealing glimpses of her breasts. Not that I minded. I enjoyed the show. It took more than a few flashes of taut, young nipples to distract me away from gambling. Well, maybe not all that much more.

A bare foot touched my leg under the table, then stroked my shin.

Vichsn smiled. "I think you're trying to buy the pot," she said.

"It'll only cost you a grand to find out." I knew my voice carried just the right amount of flippancy. I really could care less.

Vichsn toyed with the chips in front of her. Her toes continued to play footsy with my leg. She must be holding the third ten. Three of a kind wasn't a bad hand in stud. But she was thinking I had filled my straight. A straight beats three of a kind on every moon in the system. Her other two cards showing were a six of hearts and a jack of clubs. No help there. She had to be holding a ten.

"I don't think you've got that jack," she said. "I think you're trying to bluff your way out." She smiled. Her skin gleamed like obsidian. She wasn't going to bluff. Dogs.

Vichsn counted out her chips carefully, stacking them into a neat pile. She looked at my face. Her eyes shone blue with retinal reflections. She pushed her stack of chips into the center of the table, then delicately tipped them over so they spilled and mingled with the others. They skittered over the green felt of the table.

"Call," she said.

"Dogs," I said, and illuminated the side of my crystal facing her. The queen's image formed. "Two ladies. What's your hole card?"

"Two pair," she said. A jack of diamonds showed on her crystal. No wonder she didn't bluff out. She was holding the fourth jack. My jack. She knew all along I didn't have my straight. Sneaky little tart.

As Vichsn gathered in the chips, I got up to leave. I was broke and I didn't want to have to play with her marker. I knew how she'd want it redeemed. Be more fun to listen to the elves' taunts. Well, almost.

As I turned, I saw the Captain standing in the doorway. He was smiling like a sand-cat. "Had enough poker lessons for tonight, Detrs? Looks like you're into Vichsn pretty deep already. Ready to call it quits for the day?" He leered at Vichsn. "While you're still capable of redeeming your marker?"

"I suppose. Frogging run of bad luck." I stood up from the table.

Vichsn winked at me. "Later," she said.

"What's up?" I asked the Captain as I walked outside with him. He was short and stocky, but had the forearms of a home-run hitter. I'd seen him decapitate an elf with one chop of a combat glove. The Captain didn't smile very much. I'd never asked him why. You didn't ask those kinds of questions. But he was smiling now.

"We're finally getting another medic," he said when we got outside. "And about damn time. It's been almost two months since Doc bought his."

"Wasn't there some hangup luna-side?" Earth's moon was where the Corps had most of its hybridization tanks and training facilities.

"Yeah, they're bringing out a new series of corpsman and ran into a few production delays. Something about needing a certain personality profile. But the tanks are on line now. They're putting out ten a week. The new medics are supposed to be the hottest thing since the autopulser. Completely self-contained. Entirely autosynthesizing. And we've got one waiting. So I want you to grab a skimmer and move ass over to the port and pick her up."

"But it's almost dark." I put just a touch of a whine in my voice. "And it's a hundred clicks to the space port." Then I realized what he'd said. "Her?" I asked, suddenly interested.

"That's what I said. Don't you listen to the scuttlebutt? All the new medics are female genotype. Something about needing an X chromosome for the hybridization to be successful. Why do you think their mark designation is X-M-R?"

"I hadn't thought about it much." *Chi-M-Rho*. Chimera. "Chimera," I said out-loud. "So that's where the name comes from."

"Sure," he said. "Now move. It's almost dark."

We both knew what dangers night would bring.

Harsh sodium light glared from each of four guard towers, brightly illuminating the supply pad. I saw the chimera standing on the pad next to a gravship. The ship's hatches were open and stevedores were busily unloading it. I had no trouble recognizing her. She wore a cape with spec-five stripes on the shoulders above a medic's coiled serpent insignia. A duffel bag lay beside her. She stood nearly two meters tall, average height for a combrid, but weighed maybe eighty kilos—definitely on the skinny side. Her arms and legs were long and lithe. Her skin was black with anti-radiation pigment granules and gleamed with protective monomer sweat. Pretty standard adaptations. Just like any other combat hybrid. But if the rumors were true, her significant modifications would be internal. Chimera were supposed to represent a new generation of combrids.

I touched her shoulder.

She turned. Occular membranes contracted quickly, then dilated again. Jade eyes examined me dispassionately. Men used to fight wars over a face like hers. I thought I was in love. But I knew better. I could recognize the beginning of a testosterone shower.

"Lance Corporal Detrs," I said. "The Captain sent me to fetch you to the base." There was something wrong with my voice.

"Peppardine," she said. "Firiel Peppardine. I mean, Specialist V Peppardine." She laughed, then paused. Her face became lax.

Frogs, she probably expected me to salute or something. Noncoms fresh from the hypnotanks always did. So I didn't salute. The sooner she learned the realities of a combat situation, the better it would be for everyone. I slouched a little more than I already was, and gazed about laconically.

She must have gotten the message, because she shrugged and shouldered her duffel bag. I led the way to the skimmer.

Night had deepened. Fog rolled across the road like surf on a beach. A safe-zone had been cleared a hundred meters on both sides of the roadway. Yellow light glared from pulverized crystals. A force-field crackled in green fire at the edges of the safe-zone. Beyond that was virgin forest glittering in the diffuse glow of saturn-light. And laughing elves glided among trees of glass.

More than once, the force-field had been penetrated somewhere along the hundred kilometers of road between the base and the space-port. It had always happened at night. Elves were more devious in darkness.

So I was just a little nervous as I drove the skimmer back to base. I gripped the steering handle tightly. Sometimes they managed to slip airbears through the barrier and let them wander about the road. Skimmers weren't armored. They didn't provide much protection from the explosion that resulted from a collision with an airbear. I kept glancing from one side of the road to the other. But I wasn't so nervous that I didn't look at the chimera every chance I got. She was worth looking at. I hoped she'd let her cape fall open a little now we were in the skimmer, but she kept herself demurely covered. My gaze seemed to linger unconsciously on her hands. I couldn't help but look at them. I'd heard rumors. She had long, supple fingers. Their pads were formed into tree-frog suction cups, like those of sailors, to better cling to polished surfaces. She didn't have fingernails. Instead, each finger had the retractable claw of a cat. I couldn't help but wonder if the stories told about those claws could be true.

She must have sensed my interest, for she bared her claws

quickly, then retracted them again. But before they disappeared, I saw a wet, blue gleam. Nights could be dull at base. Those claws could make them interesting. She smiled, showing her teeth. They shone like cut sapphires. Then she laughed. Viper heat-organs glowed from ridges above her eyebrows.

"Where are you from?" I asked, hoping idle conversation would distract my thoughts. From dark forest. And her hands.

She smiled. "A place called Nyssa. Have you been there?"

"Once," I answered. "A long time ago." I'd been most everywhere on Earth once. Especially places the beautiful and rich considered chic. Nyssa was very chic. I wondered what a resident of there was doing here. But you didn't ask that kind of question in the Corps. Because you wouldn't want to answer it. Everyone had their reasons. Some were more sordid than others, but all were valid. "An interesting place, Nyssa," I said.

"Do you think so? I suppose. I was a Lady there. Married to a Lord of Nyssa." She stopped speaking.

Ahead, shadows moved. I stomped on the accelerator and banked into a hard right turn. Ten G's pushed against me, pinning my flesh against wombskin cushions. I heard Peppardine gasp in surprise, as her breath was squeezed from her lungs.

"Toad!" I said with my own exhalation.

A pulse of red light flashed through a momentary gap in the road's force field. Pavement bubbled into vapor where the skimmer would have been.

I thumbed the firing stud of the quad-fifty mounted on the roof of the skimmer. A computer-sight was already aiming it. Before the breech in the field closed again, four fifty-millimeter pulser beams of a nanosec duration fanned through it. Spent photonuclear cases streamed into the air behind the skimmer. In the forest, crystal trees exploded into millions of sharp fragments. I knew the unseen elves were dead, impaled by tiny slivers of glass. They didn't wear combat armor. They couldn't fly with the extra weight. Their mistake.

I eased off the accelerator and let the skimmer coast to a more maneuverable speed. The lights of base glowed on the horizon. We were almost home.

I looked at the chimera. Ten claws gripped the arms of her seat. But she was smiling.

"You saw?" I asked.

"Of course. More than you imagine." She licked her lips with blue saliva. "Did you have to kill them that way?"

"No."

Her eyebrows arched. "Then why?"

"Because I wanted to. I like killing elves. And there's no way they can claim to be civilians if they're dead."

"I see." She touched my leg. Her fingers puckered my skin. Her cape had opened along its slits. I glimpsed smooth pectus muscles, adolescent breasts, pubic hair fine as spun carbon.

Excitement swirled inside. It had been a long time since we'd had a new player in the outfit. Or at least it seemed like a long time. Everyone had bedded everyone else. But there'd never been anyone like this chimera. I thought of the blue fire carried in her claws. Peptide could warm up the night. Scenarios flashed in my mind. I smiled to myself.

I put my hand on her leg. Her skin was soft to the touch, but with a firmness underneath due to intradermal polymer-mesh reinforcement. She moved my hand along her thigh. Sharp claws scratched the back of my hand. I saw promise hidden in her eyes.

Then we were gliding into base. I was being tossed about by a testosterone storm. You know, hot to trot. I stopped the skimmer and dilated its doors. I carried Peppardine's duffel this time, leading the way to her hut. But at the door, she turned. Nictitating membranes had closed.

She was different; something had changed.

"Let me show you your quarters," I said, intimation in my voice.

"That won't be necessary." Her voice had become flat. Something was wrong.

"Okay." I was desperate. "But after you've unpacked your gear, come over to the noncom club. I'll buy you a mnemone stick."

"I think I need to be by myself."

"Maybe I can help?"

"I don't think so." She looked at me in a way I remembered.

But I was too tight with sex steroid to care about my pride. "You'll come later?" I knew she wouldn't. I knew that look. I knew that game. But why?

She turned and entered her room. She paused inside the door and looked back. "I was once a Lady of Nyssa," she said, and her voice told me she'd lost more than I would ever have. Because my nobility had not been taken away from me. I had run away from mine. I was an orphan by choice.

The door hissed shut.

I waited by myself at a corner table in the club. A mnemone stick fumed from a bong sitting in front of me. I'd only taken one hit. My thoughts were disturbed enough already. I kept thinking about the sudden change that had come over Peppardine—one minute she was teasing me like a Venusian in heat, and the next she was as frigid as an Anti-Recombinant fanatic. And I kept feeling sorry for myself. Because it wouldn't have mattered except she'd thrown me into a testosterone crisis. All that sex steroid had to be dissipated some way. I knew Peppardine was not going to show up. But I wanted her in the worst way.

Someone sat down at my table. Mnemone fumes blurred my vision. For an instant, hope flared. Then nictitating membranes blinked away the film. I saw Vichsn sitting across from me. She picked up the bong and sucked mnemone deep into her lungs.

She exhaled slowly. Blue eyes appraised me.

"What's she like?" Vichsn asked. "Though it appears you've struck out."

"Who?"

"Who? Who do you think? The new medic. The X-M-R. Didn't you pick her up at the space port?"

"Sure."

"Is what they say about them true?" Her smile was a leer.

"What do they say about them?" I thought of her wonderful claws.

"You've heard the stories. They say they have the kiss of death now. Each finger can inject a different neuropeptide hormone. They hold a hundred electric eels between their hands. They can kill in a dozen ways now. But they're supposed to have been killers before. What's she like?" A bare foot stroked my leg under the table.

"She seems okay." But I thought of her fingers, each with a long, curved claw, hollow, connected to a modified venom sac in its finger's pad. And a blue gleam. Her peptides could bring unimaginable euphoria—the ultimate natural high. I glimpsed again her body, with smooth muscles rippling. I'd thought I was going to get to receive her blue joy. Again testosterone fire flared. Corpus cavernosum engorged with blood. I hoped

Vichsn wouldn't notice the bulge in front of my pants. "She says she was a Lady of Nyssa," I added as an afterthought.

"You know what else they say?"

"What?"

"The ones who become chimerae all have something in common." She smiled in a sly, sinister way. "They were given a choice—chimerae or the cyborg factories."

"And why was that?" But a scenario flashed in my mind: a glimpse of something nasty, something that would even shock the jaded sensibilities of the wealthy Lords and Ladies of Nyssa; craziness, raging passion, fury in the dark of night.

"They say they killed their lovers. They each committed a crime of passion. Something about a particular personality profile being necessary to engram the X-M-R patterns. But then genosurgeons always double-talk. What do you think about her?"

"What about her?" Why was I on the defensive?

"Did she do it? Did she tell you about it? Did she kill her lover?"

"I wouldn't know. I didn't ask." But I saw a mutilated body sprawled amid sonic sculpture and mutable holograms. Singing jewelry adorned his nose, ears, fingers, and toes. A spidersilk cape was tattered and bloody. Every fax in the system had carried the holo. Even on Titan. Scandal was news. A dead Lord was scandal.

Vichsn leaned over to kiss me. Her tongue probed my mouth. I felt taut nipples pressing against my chest.

I let her lead me out of the club, through swirling clouds of yellow hydrocarbon fog, across the commons past parked hoverbuses, into her hut with its waiting bunk of pulsating wombskin. She pulled privacy curtains around us, telling her roommates they were not welcome to join us tonight.

Later, when my androgen rush had subsided, we lay together in the quiet. I stroked the hollow of her back. I let childhood memories surface.

"You're thinking of that chimera," Vichsn said accusingly.

She was right. "Are you hurt?" I asked.

She thought for a moment. "No," she laughed. "Think about her all you want. And think about her lover." She laughed again.

There was something unpleasant about the way she did.

* * *

I woke to the clang of the battle gong calling general quarters.

Cursing under my breath, I leaped out of bed and pulled on my combat armor and boots. I shouldered my battle pack, grabbed my assault rifle and a bandellero of ammo, and trotted out of the barracks.

Vichsn fell into step beside me.

She looked splendid in her battle gear: body armor fit her as tight as exoskeleton, gravboots barely touched the ground, ammobelts crisscrossed her chest. Her face was hidden behind a mirrored helmet visor. Yet I knew it was her. I knew her moves. She flipped up her visor. I saw the mouth that had kissed me the night before. Her lips were smiling.

We joined the stream of other combrids running across the commons.

A hoverbus waited, hatches open.

We climbed in and strapped ourselves into our seats. Other combrids filed past. Except for the whine of turbines warming, it was quiet. Combat armor was flexible and made no noise as it moved; a polymer coating deadened any sound produced on its surface. Elves' ears were very good. Even a little noise could be fatal. No one spoke. There was nothing to say. Later, when speech was necessary, it wouldn't be verbal—there was a network of vitalium wires buried beneath our scalps. Their proximal ends terminated within cerebral cortex. Neuropotentials generated within our speech centers would be picked up by transducers in our helmets and transmitted on microwaves. The elves had not yet devised a way to jam the frequencies we used. Other cerebral centers controlled the servos in our armor, boots, and power packs.

The hatch closed and the hoverbus lifted into the air. Overhead, the force field winked as we flashed through a breech produced by phase generators in the hoverbus. Then we settled into smooth flight, skimming the tree-tops.

I stared out the window. Jagged mountains covered with dense forests of crystalline trees passed below. A century before, Titan had been lifeless. Terran ecoengineers had devised an ecology using genetically engineered plants and animals, specifically adapted to the moon's environment. Fifty years later the first colonists had landed. They were of human stock, but had also been adapted to the native conditions of Titan. They called themselves men. We called them elves. They were tall with hollow, pneumaticized long bones. A flap of skin stretched between their arms and legs. They could glide for great distances in weak gravity and heavy hydrocarbon atmosphere by extending their limbs to make a taut airfoil out of their pseudowings. They had large, pointed ears to collect ultrasonic pulses emitted by bat voice-boxes, allowing them to maneuver through dense forest in complete darkness. Lemur eyes easily pierced the murk of hydrocarbon mist. Dense gray fur and brown adipose under their skin insulated them from the cold. They were completely at home in the forests of glass we passed over. A battalion of eleven guerrillas could be concealed there—or only a ragged band.

That was the trouble with counter-insurgency. Guerrilla forces fought on their terms, revealing themselves only when it was to their advantage. Intelligence estimates of their numbers usually had an uncertainty factor to a power of three. And there was a similar situation on every habitable moon and planet of the outer system. The Corps was spread dangerously thin trying to contain a dozen simultaneous rebellions. Self-determination had become a universal rallying cry. The Hybrid Wars had been fought for over a century. The end was not in sight. Earth could not afford to lose her colonies. The terran economy depended on them as consumers of high-technology goods and providers of raw materials. Imperialists distrusted changes in the *status quo*. So the Corps was charged with maintaining the old order. And we were hard pressed to manage it.

Part of the problem was that the colonists had been adapted to the peculiar environment of their planet/moon. They had been bioengineered using the techniques of recombinant DNA to fit a particular niche. They could never be human again, having become true-breeding hybrids. Their progeny didn't consider themselves human, nor were they. And their specialization gave them an advantage over the combrids of the Corps. We also had been hybridized, but our adaptations were generalized ones, so we could remain mobile and fight anywhere in the system. But universality created certain inherent disadvantages: we had to breathe oxygen, drink water, eat terran food concentrates. Which meant we had to maintain supply lines to Earth. We couldn't live off the land.

Nor were we true-breeding. Our germ cells were unaltered. Our progeny (should we live long enough to leave the Corps to have any) would be unaltered humans. The Lords of Earth didn't want a warrior caste to develop. Besides, it was more economical to bioform combrids from adult humans than breed them; that way you didn't have to worry about feeding them as infants and children.

I guess because I too was a hybrid I could understand the elves' feelings. It was difficult for them to have any loyalty to the Lords of Earth—who had become an alien species living on an inhospitable planet. But that didn't make me like them any better. I'd lost a lot of buddies to their traps. Terrorist tactics frogged me off. There was nothing I liked better than seeing an elf in my gun-sight. That was the only time they could be trusted. Devious little toaders, they were.

Chances were, I'd lose another buddy before the day was over. One less bed partner would be in the pool.

We were going on a search-and-destroy mission. That's what High Command called it, anyway. Us grunts had another name for it—target practice. Only we were the targets. Intelligence had located what they thought was a rebel camp. Our job was to confirm that intelligence and destroy it if it existed. Of course it was just as likely to be a dummy camp baiting a trap for us to walk into. Paid informants worked both sides of the street. Spy satellites were fallible. But we had to investigate to know one way or the other. Like I said, target practice.

But the military options of the Terran government were limited. The use of excessive force carried the certain risk of swaying public opinion to the rebel cause, as well as possibly interrupting the flow of resources the government was trying to protect. As had been demonstrated countless times before, military force was useful only if it could be used to implement policy. Heavy cruisers with catalytic torpedoes, though capable of destroying a planet, were impotent weapons if one's adversaries knew you didn't have the balls to use them, or if they had enough balls or fanaticism not to care if you did blow them into the next orbital plane. So our military intervention became more of a police action. And that was frustrating. Actual confrontation was rare. Sneak attacks and ambushes were common. By elves. We weren't allowed to use such tactics.

Even if this was an actual rebel camp, it would most likely be abandoned by the time we arrived. The elven observers that constantly watched our base would have reported our departure and the direction of our subsequent flight would be monitored.

They would have plenty of warning and lots of time to set their traps.

Titan was their world. The elves were adapted to it, not us. They could live off the land and fight with just the equipment they could carry on their backs. We were forced to look for them. So they could snipe at us from concealment and leave nasty booby traps behind for us. They could poison our food and contaminate our water. They tried to taint our oxygen converters. They mutated strains of venereal disease, then tempted us to bed pelts infected with it. They fed their babies liquid *plastique* and abandoned them for us to find, detonating the explosive by remote control. There was no safe place to step. Not one minute of the day was secure. The life of a combrid on an off-world garrison was one of constant anxiety.

No wonder we eventually went bonkers and had to be shipped earth-side snowed with endolepsin. Unless we were killed in the attempt to subdue us. Or unless we were bonkers to begin with and liked the threat of death.

Let's just say I was in a grim and introspective mood as the hoverbus streaked through the methane fog of Titan.

I noticed Peppardine sitting alone toward the front. That seemed strange. Combrids were a randy breed. Normally all we thought about was fighting and sex. Or sex and fighting. Or just sex. It seemed unusual that someone wasn't putting the moves on her. She looked just as good to me now as she had last night. Still gave my dingle a tingle, so to speak. But Vichsn had me trapped in an inside seat. I knew she wouldn't let me change seats so I could reacquaint myself with the chimera. No big deal. There'd be plenty of time to try to get inside her tunic, I reasoned. No hurry. She wasn't going anywhere now. So what if she'd been a Lady of Nyssa. She wasn't now. She'd soon realize I was as good as anyone in the outfit, and better than most. Maybe I would tell her of my own nobility. I wasn't afraid of it now. Strange that no one was trying to beat me to her, though. Maybe we should have a few sex steroid levels checked.

Then the hoverbus descended.

It was a typical landing. The fishbait pilots figured the less time they spent motionless close to the ground, the less chance they had of being shot down. They had it figured right, of course. So they flew directly over the drop zone, fell a couple of thousand meters straight down, pulled ten G's decelerating, then hovered a few meters over the ground. Our pilot was no exception. And all the time she was screaming over the intercom for us to get ready to jump. The jump gong beat like a drum. She'd blown the rear hatch while we were still a thousand meters up. Now she squawked like a buggered hen for us to get our tails out.

By this time, we had all crowded into the aisle and were shuffling toward the rear. The hoverbus was already moving forward. As each two combrids jumped out, the two behind followed close behind, knowing they would land a few meters away on the ground.

Vichsn and I crowded toward the rear hatch, pushed from behind. Everyone knew the pilot's nerve would soon fail. They were supposed to give you a full minute to evacuate the hoverbus. But the pilots usually cheated by thirty seconds. You risked a broken leg if you were among the last to jump. So you didn't let the ones in front of you dawdle too long.

The open hatch came closer.

We were standing on the edge. Vichsn and I jumped together. I bent my knees, but there was little shock as I hit the ground after drifting ten meters through the weak Titanian gravity.

Overhead, the hoverbus whined.

The pilot's nerve had broken. Already it accelerated upward. Combrids continued to dribble from the hatch, even as the hoverbus climbed.

Catsucking pilots anyway.

The chimera was the last to jump. When she did, the hoverbus was at least a hundred meters up. She leaped into the air, extending arms and legs to create as much resistance as possible against the thick hydrocarbon atmosphere, thusly slowing her fall. As she neared the ground, she doubled up and rolled as she struck. After two somersaults, she came up on her feet smiling. A nifty maneuver. She'd had a good take on the hypnotraining. She'd be all right.

The Captain spoke softly in my mind. I checked off, then listened as the others did the same one by one. The last to report was Peppardine. All were present. There were no drop injuries. No thanks to our sheepdip pilot.

"Detrs," the captain said, "you take the point. Bearing oh six oh."

Dogbreath! I thought. The point was the worst place to be.

Well, usually the worst. You were the bait, to try to get the enemy to reveal themselves. You were the target for target practice. Only sometimes they let you pass, so they could blow away your buddies who followed. Either way, it was not a fun place to be. In a cross-fire, it didn't matter whether friend or foe pressed the firing stud of the pulser that fried you. You would be just as dead from one as the other.

We fanned out from the drop zone, walking in a half-crouch on the balls of our feet, weapons held at ready. I was ahead of the rest. Vichsn was behind to my right. I glanced to the left. Trinks was there. He was a good man to have close any time, but particularly when the shooting started. He'd saved my skin before. I owed him a few already.

The drop zone was a natural clearing in the forest a few clicks away from the suspected elf camp. That could mean trouble. Elves had a nasty habit of booby-trapping the open areas around their real camps, knowing we'd have to land in them. So I walked slowly and cautiously, careful of where I stepped, and watched the monitors along the top of my visor. Any metal would be detected by the varience it produced in the sensing electromagnetic field put out by the antennae of my helmet. Which was why elves seldom used metal mines anymore. Plastic explosive with sonic detonators was more difficult to detect. As were bug bombs and gas pots. But *plastique*, virulent bacteria, and enzyme poisons could be smelled. Olfactimeters sniffed thick hydrocarbon air for any telltale odor. Sonic triggers resonated to the sonar I put out, and hopefully would detonate to its pings before the sound of my footsteps tripped the mine.

That's why you took it real slow when you could. You wanted to give your sensors lots of time to probe the area in front of you. You didn't want to blunder into any little surprises.

We crossed the clearing in a zigzag fashion, avoiding buried mines, gas pots, and bug bombs. Yes, they were there. Fortunately, none detonated. The surrounding lethality suggested there might be a real elven camp nearby. There would be fewer booby traps among the trees. You were pretty safe from them there if you resisted the temptation to walk on a trail. But there were other dangers in the forest.

I entered the trees a few meters ahead of the rest. I knew they would be scanning the forest, hoping my entrance would stir up something. But it was quiet. I walked slowly and carefully. The trees were about a meter in diameter and stood several hundred meters high. They were composed of aggregates of oxide crystals and polymeric hydrocarbons: emerald, tourmaline, sapphire, amethyst, aquamarine, and chrysoberl matrix completed with polyethylene, polyvinyl chloride, polybutadiene, polyisoprene, and a dozen other natural polymers. They "grew" by continually adding complexes to their substance. The complexes naturally tended to form tubular structures, so growth occurred in a linear fashion, at the ends of the tubes. They would have collapsed in a one-G field, but could be free-standing in the lesser gravity of Titan. They were "alive" by the standard criteria: individual complexes were organized into a greater whole and kept in organization by the expenditure of energy of crystallization, thereby conserving entropy. They reproduced by direct "budding" at the distal ends of their tubules, casting "seed" complexes to the wind.

If not for the elves, the crystalline forests of Titan could have been quite a tourist attraction. Swirling hydrocarbon mist condensed on the facets of leaves—liquid pentane and butane dripped from their undersides. On the rare occasions the mist lifted, Saturn-light blazed from billions of gemstones embedded in transparent plastic in a myriad of dazzling color.

But there were elves.

No tourist in his right mind would visit Titan for pleasure.

And I should have been more concerned about what lurked in concealment within the forest, than admiring its unique beauty.

I heard Vichsn's warning whisper in my mind too late. Already I felt strong legs cradling me. Long carbide claws clicked against my armor. A furry body embraced itself around my head.

I did manage to call myself a flyblown dumb son-of-an-elf before I froze, holding every muscle as still as I could. I tried not to move at all. If I did, I'd be dead in a few millisecs.

The most dangerous of elven traps were airbears. One had just fallen on me, clinging around my head. They were creatures bioformed from Terran koalas. But their modifications were more than those required to adapt them to the environment of Titan. Sure, they had respiratory and digestive functions switched like all Titanians: they breathed their food and ate their oxygen. Titanian lungs extracted hydrocarbons to be used as substrate for oxidation. Titanians derived elemental oxygen from the enzymatic degradation of crystal complexes in their alimentary tracts. They had plasmids in their cells with the coding for enzymes to convert methane and heavier hydrocarbons into carbohydrate. Otherwise their biochemistry was not much different than standard Terran; they just got the raw materials in a different fashion.

But elven genosurgeons possessed a sense of the macabre. For instead of storing free oxygen bound in brown adipose tissue, as did other Titanian creatures, airbears secreted it in distensible bladders that trailed from their backs. And they had eel bioelectricity organs in the membranes of their oxygen bladders.

They were, in effect, living bombs.

Pure oxygen exploded just as violently in the hydrogen/methane air of Titan, as flammable gas would in the oxygen-rich air of Earth.

Airbears' heavy bodies were almost counter-balanced by their oxygen-filled bladders. They floated among the upper branches of the crystal forest, browsing on buds and leaves of crystalline oxides. Carbide teeth ground the gems to powder. Plastic matrix passed through their gut and became feces, binding the silicon, aluminum, beryllium, iron, chromium, calcium, magnesium, and boron residues left after oxygen was extracted. They were perfectly harmless as long as they stayed up in the trees. But if a combrid, or anything else with an unaltered Terran metabolism, should pass below them, they immediately let go of the branch they were clinging to and dropped to the ground. It seems they were attracted to free oxygen. Our higher body temperatures caused us to lose minute traces of pure oxygen, which boiled through both protective monomer and armor. Airbears thought we were walking dessert. They clung to whomever happened to be below them.

As it happened, that was me.

Airbears actually were gentle creatures. They didn't normally hurt anything. But they were easily startled. The elven genosurgeons made them that way.

You were okay if you could slowly extricate yourself from their grasp. But if you scared them, they involuntarily discharged their electricity organs. This both disrupted oxygen bladders and provided a spark to ignite the contents of the bladders. The air exploded as hydrocarbon atmosphere burned with pure oxygen. The resulting concussion was relatively minor—unless you happened to be the one standing at ground zero. Then it was enough to flatten your combat armor like a crushed beer can. The flesh inside tended to take on a look of undifferentiated protoplasmic jelly.

I saw furry lips pressed against my visor, then a rough tongue scratched across the surface, as the airbear tasted lingering traces of elemental oxygen. I didn't dare move. Let the creature get settled, I said to myself. To the others: "Don't come any closer, meat. And no sudden moves, please. I don't want to be smeared into pulp." Not that I had to worry about the others getting too close. They knew there probably were more airbears overhead. No one would be anxious to be in my predicament. And if they were too close when my airbear detonated, they'd suffer the same fate as me.

I was desperately trying to devise a plan that would gently extricate myself from the bear's hug, when I saw movement at the edge of vision. Someone was coming toward me.

"Stay clear, frog it!" I said as emphatically as I dared. They said even voice vibrations could spook an airbear. But I took the chance and vocalized anyway; it wasn't any fun to curse silently.

"Hold still," came a voice in my mind. "I know what I'm doing." I recognized that voice right away. I'd been remembering snatches of conversations all day.

Peppardine approached slowly, walking with barely perceptible steps. Despite my situation, I almost had another testosterone storm. Combat armor fit skin-tight. Hers did her body credit—smooth musculature, firm belly, taut breasts, long, supple legs. She moved with lithe grace—they must have used considerable feline DNA in her xenogene complement. After what seemed like a long, hot summer on the bright-side of Mercury, the chimera stood beside me.

I realized I was holding my breath. I let it out slowly. Water misted on the oxygen bubble surrounding my nose and mouth. I saw my face reflected from the inside of my visor; sweat beaded from my forehead.

The airbear began to suckle on my visor.

I sure as Akron hoped the chimera knew what she was doing.

She did.

Peppardine stood behind me, moving in close enough for our

bodies to touch. Even through two layers of combat armor, I felt her nipples brush against my back and her pelvis press into my buttocks. She reached around carefully with both arms. I saw a curved claw slide out of a finger. A blue drop of liquid clung to its tip.

I knew her helmet visor was thrown back. She had little need for artificial sensors. The viper pit-organs in her eyebrows scanned the bear, outlining the warmer tracks where blood flowed in vessels beneath its skin. Her claw neared the bear's arm, smoothly passed through its fur, and slipped beneath skin to pierce a vein. So sharp were her claws, the bear never felt the prick in its skin. Neuropeptide coursed like blue fire into its bloodstream. I watched with fascination; the peptides carried by Peppardine's claws had been the subject of several hours speculative fantasy by me. I wondered if the airbear felt the same euphoria I would have. I decided it would; its neurophysiology had not been significantly modified. The overdose of endorphine quickly went to the airbear's brain; its grip weakened, then relaxed. It floated face up in the air beside me. The chimera came around and held it gently between her hands. Her claws had retracted.

"Though unconscious from endorphine," she said, "it could still reflexively discharge its spark." She pulled the lax body lower, gently, bringing its face close to hers. Its eyes stared wide open. The chimera pursed her lips. She nodded her head. A glob of blue spit formed on her lips, hung for a moment, then dropped like a sapphire tear. The droplet seemed to hesitate as it hit her oxygen bubble's surface-effect membrane, but only flattened a little, then passed through. It splattered into the bear's eye, spreading into a blue film to cover the conjunctiva. The bear's fur shook with fasciculations briefly, then was still. Legs hung limp from the body. Oxygen bladders hung suspended over the body.

"Endolepsin laces my saliva," Peppardine said. "A drop in the eye is enough to paralyze every nerve. Its bioelectricity cells can never fire now." She turned to me and smiled. "You owe me a favor now. When can I collect?" Again the intimation. Would she deliver this time? I wondered. Then a shiver ran up my spine. I looked at the airbear, paralyzed with euphoria, soon to die of pleasure. Playing with her claws would be a dangerous game. She could either please or punish. Her kiss could either soothe or kill. I remembered stories of depraved frenzy hidden behind the walls of paralyzed force of one of Nyssa's floating towers—golden chains, spidersilk ropes, shining knives with jeweled blades, braided whips, rituals of torment in the night—and a sudden burst of violence ending it all. Yes, a very dangerous game. A game I should enjoy.

"Come on, Detrs," Vichsn said from behind. "Get moving. We don't have all day."

I turned to look at her, but her face was hidden behind the mirror-surface of her helmet visor. I'd thought I'd heard something in her voice. Something that pleased me. Maybe she was worried about Peppardine and me. Fine. Let her worry. If I had my way, she'd soon have something to worry about.

"Let's go, Detrs," the Captain said. "And be a little more careful this time.

I was more careful, but we didn't encounter any more airbears.

We moved slowly through the crystal forest. Broken shards of shed leaves lay scattered on the ground. Sometimes a crunching sound was heard when someone accidentally stepped on one. When that happened, we all froze, expecting to see flashes of pulser fire from concealed snipers. But none came until we approached the elves' abandoned camp.

All that remained of it were the skeletons of crisscrossed saplings that had been their lean-to shelters, with smoldering cinders of oxide crystals in front, where their campfires had been.

The Captain has us disperse around the periphery. Combrids scattered from tree to tree, using the trunks for cover, before finally taking positions at various vantage points. We watched the deserted camp for a long time. Sometimes elves left nasty surprises. Especially if they had sufficient warning before they left.

I cursed the spooks at Corps Intelligence as I waited. They were safe in their spook houses in orbit around Titan. When one of their sensors buzzed, we were the ones sent into the forest for target practice. Then I cursed the Lord Generals of High Command for good measure.

Everything stayed quiet. There was no detectable movement in the camp. Helmet sensors showed only an ebbing infrared glow where campfires cooled.

Finally, the Captain had six of us advance, keeping the rest of the platoon in concealment. As before, I was on the point; Vichsn and Trinks flanked me, but were a little behind. Three other combrids followed.

As I entered the camp, I scanned the surrounding forest carefully. Everything remained quiet. Sensing fields were not disturbed. Bur drops of sweat had formed along my back. Something was wrong. I'd learned a long time ago to trust my intuition. I knew we were walking into a trap, but there wasn't a mousey thing I could do to avoid it. We were bait, to force any elven snipers into revealing themselves. Target practice.

I was almost to the center of the camp when the trap was sprung. My intuition saved me. All six of us were well within the clearing. The elves probably figured six were all they were going to get. Did I say elves? Make that elf, as it turned out. Anyway, the hairs on the back on my neck rose. I hit the ground, yelling a warning to the others at the same time. But my warning came too late. As I was going down, I sensed a quick flurry of movement behind crystalline foliage, followed by a burst of automatic pulser fire fanning out across the clearing. A bright pulse passed over me, where I had been millisecs before. But Trinks wasn't quick enough. I saw him crumple as a pulser quantum glanced off his body, partially deflected by his armor. His groans of pain sounded within my skull. But there wasn't much I could do for him. I was more worried about keeping myself alive.

The elf's fire had me pinned down; there was no cover to hide behind, nor did I dare try to move. I fired my own weapon into the forest in the general area where I'd seen the movement. Spent photonuclear cases bounded off my back. But I knew the elf had already swooped to another tree. He was more mobile than me.

I heard the Captain calmly telling the rest of the platoon to hold their fire and wait for the elf to show himself again. As soon as his pulser flashed, they were to sweep the section of forest with their beams. That the elf knew our tactics was the only thing saving me and the others caught in the open. The elf knew that as soon as he fired, a score of pulser bursts would stab into his general area. So he had to shoot on the move, as he was gliding from tree to tree. That made aiming his weapon a little difficult. But not difficult enough to suit me; clouds of rock vapor puffed around me where his shots hit too close for comfort.

The stand-off began to get a little tedious.

Each time the elf shot from concealment, a salvo of return fire burst into the forest, shattering oxide wood into tiny slivers that drifted through a polymer mist like floating glitter. But the elf was quick enough to avoid getting hit by either the beams or exploding fragments and fired again from another position. One elf was tying up an entire platoon of Corps combrids, while his comrades made good their escape.

But that was their plan, of course.

Trinks continued to moan in agony, clutching his belly. A combrid left the safety of the forest and darted across the clearing toward us. Pulser fire traced a smoking path behind the weaving and bobbing course taken by the combrid. Amazingly, he wasn't hit. Then I saw who *she* was. The combrid was the chimera. She dove beside Trinks and lay on the ground beside him. Her hands busied themselves. Fingers probed cleverly designed chinks in his combat armor. Hypodermic claws sought the veins underneath polymer-toughened skin and injected neuropeptides into sluggish blood. Endotalis flogged his failing heart, while endopamine toned blood vessels and raised blood pressure. Endosmin sealed leaking capillaries and endosteroid stabilized cell membranes. Endorphine obliterated pain.

When Trinks' physiologic functions became stable, the chimera used two other claws. Endophetamine sent synthetic courage to his basal ganglia. Endocholine speeded nervous transmission to thrice normal and strengthened muscle contractions by augmenting depolarization potentials.

All of which meant only one thing to a simple grunt combrid: Trinks stood up with blue fire in his eyes. The same fire coursed in his veins. He was now three times as strong and fast as he had been. And many times braver. He feared nothing. He felt no pain. He could do anything. He was berserk—overwhelmed with fighting rage, like a vengeful Norse warrior.

Trinks charged across the clearing, running toward the trees from which the elf sniper shot. It didn't seem possible a man could run that fast—his legs blurred with motion. A salvo of autopulser fire streamed from the forest, but the puffs they made in the ground were behind Trinks. The elf didn't believe a man could move that fast either, and didn't lead enough. In an instant. Trinks was across the clearing and among the tress. A moment later, I saw his pulser flash. Light flared upward, silhouetted against a sky of mist. An elven scream sounded, then the elf appeared in the air over the clearing, gliding on taut pseudowings. Singed fur marked the sites of pulser wounds. Pulser beams stabbed from the surrounding forest. Only charred remnants of the elf made it to the ground. Most of him became smoke that mingled with the mists of Titan.

I found Trinks propped against the side of a tree trunk. He had his visor flipped up. He looked at me through half-open eyes, blurred by nictitating membranes.

"Did I get the fairy?" he asked.

I nodded.

"Good. You want to make sure to do whatever you need to do before the rush goes away." He coughed blood and spat through his oxygen bubble on the ground beside him. There was a puddle of clot there already, like red pudding. "Horses, it's good before it goes. I think I could have taken a whole company of the devils by myself. But the fire burns out too quickly. And when it goes, there's nothing left."

"You'll be okay."

"Sure. Keep saying it. I believe you. Sure I do."

"Corpsman!" I yelled. Where was that catfaced chimera?

"Pepper," Trinks said, "that's what she shoots into you. Hot pepper." He looked beyond me. "Here she comes now. Sergeant Pepper." He tried to laugh, but coughed more blood instead.

The chimera knelt beside him. Her fingers busied themselves again. Trinks closed his eyes.

I went back to the camp and helped the others "sanitize" the camp. After a quick search and photo session for the spooks at Corps int., we set our own booby traps, leaving behind hundreds of needle mines, that would detonate should even an elf glide over one in the air. A shaped charge of plastic explosive threw needles of isotope into a 180-degree hemisphere. Each needle was a miniature nuclear device consisting of an isotope sandwiched with a fission catalyst. When the needle struck something solid, isotope and catalyst collapsed together, reaching a microcritical mass, which fissioned and exploded. The tiny nuclear explosions produced remarkable results, particularly if they occurred within a previously living body. Needle mines were almost as devious as elf-tricks. Almost. We had to post signs around the area, warning it was mined. Didn't want innocent civilians getting hurt. Frogging waste of time, all of it.

In the hoverbus, on the way back to base, the chimera held Trinks in her arms. The rest of us were quiet, each thinking our time would be coming. When turbulence buffeted the hoverbus and we were jostled, Trinks moaned with pain. His lips moved silently: Sergeant Pepper. Then the chimera would kiss his head, soothing away the moans. She murmured in his ear. Her whispers could not be heard by the rest of us. We didn't know what lies she told him. I should have noticed the strangeness that had come to hide in her eyes. But I was preoccupied.

When we docked at base, everybody got up and filed down the aisle. I paused as I passed the chimera and Trinks. His eyes were closed. I touched her shoulder.

"How is he?" I asked, remembering things I should have left forgotten.

"Dead," she answered simply, in a flat voice. Wrongness faded from her eyes.

"What happened? Why didn't you do something?"

"I did everything I could. There was nothing more to do. He didn't cry, nor hurt too much. He didn't cry," she said again.

I thought I saw a wet gleam behind her nictitating membranes, before I was crowded ahead by the other combrids.

Later, I found the chimera standing alone at the base perimeter. Beyond the green-crackling force field, bright forest gleamed in Saturn-light, hydrocarbon fog glowed like a will-o'-the-wisp. Dark flutterings marked the passage of elves among the trees. Occasionally, when the elves revealed too much of themselves, pulser beams stabbed into the murk as automatic sensors reacted to the disturbance.

I stood beside Peppardine.

"Sergeant Pepper," I whispered.

"What?" she asked, turning to face me.

"Nothing. Only a name Trinks called you before he died. Sergeant Pepper. Short for Peppardine."

"Or peptide?"

"I suppose." I shrugged. It didn't matter now. "You did what you could," I said. "And Trinks did get the sniper. I know that was important to him. You don't like the elf that kills you to get away."

"I'm glad then." She turned away, bringing her hands to her face. She was crying. But I mostly stared at her hands, thinking of the claws held within them. It was time for night-games to begin. I was ready this time. I'd learned a little since I'd run away from home, fleeing the endless rituals of decadence staged by my parents. But I found you couldn't run away from it. I'd tried to lose myself among street-people and tried to learn their games. I had never told anyone I was the scion of old Earth nobility, son of Lady and Lord. I'd never mentioned the vast estates, fast skimmers, blue-water yachts, and polo ponies that had been my heritage. Because for a long time, I'd been afraid of the raw emotion brought out by the games the nobility played to overcome the ennui of idleness. I had once been a victim of those games. Until my parents died. I was afraid of my secret, so I ran. But now I couldn't be discovered. I'd come too close to dying and had killed too many men to be afraid of feelings. It was almost time I claimed my legacy. So when the chimera who had been a Lady of Nyssa surfaced in my life like a specter from the past, I was ready. She would be my test. I could play her games. And I would win.

I touched her shoulder. I saw something at the edge of the forest I wanted her to see.

She took her hands away from her face and looked up.

I pointed to the trees beyond the force field. A small shape was hurled into the air in our direction. Almost immediately, autopulser beams stabbed out. One of them hit the shape. It fell to the ground smoking.

"What was that?" she asked.

"An elf baby."

"What do you mean? A baby . . ." Her eyes widened in mock surprise.

"When one of their babies dies, they throw the corpse out like that, knowing the computers controlling our autopulsers can't distinguish between the living and the dead. Then they claim we're shooting innocent babies, and have the charred bodies to back the claims. Elves have no scruples. They use whatever they have. What else is a dead baby good for?"

Suddenly she was holding me tight. Her sobs were muffled against my chest. I stroked her back, trying to smooth away the hurt. She almost had me fooled.

"How can they do that?" she asked.

"They're not like you and me," I lied. Because they were the same. "But you'll get used to it."

"Will I? Is that what happens? Do you become cold with no

feelings? Is that how you protect yourself? By not caring."

"You guessed it." What else could I say? She was right. But she'd known that all along. She hadn't fooled me.

I walked her back to her quarters. Fog deepened. Mist swirled, mixed with hydrocarbon snow. In the forest, elves wailed in mock mourning of their dead baby.

At her door, she paused. This time I saw it in her eyes.

She invited me inside.

Waking, the chimera stirred against me. Her eyes were dilated wide in darkness. She saw that I too was awake.

"A dream?" I asked.

She nodded. "I've been having a few lately."

"What do you dream?"

"Tonight about babies." Her voice softened. "About my baby."

"Your baby?"

She looked at me. "Didn't you know? My *dead* baby. I was once a Lady of Nyssa. Lords must have heirs. It's expected of them. But babies die, don't they? They die all the time."

"Just as Lords do?" She hadn't touched me with her claws. I'd wanted her to earlier, but she wouldn't. I thought I knew a way. Vichsn had given me the idea. *They killed their lovers*, she had said. "How do Lords die?" I asked, smiling. *How do children become orphans?*

She looked at me closely. "The usual ways," she said. "Don't you read the scandal sheets. With overdoses. Or smashed in the wreckage of racers. Or trampled beneath the hooves of ponies. They drown sometimes. The usual ways."

"And sometimes they kill each other. Duels? Arguments?"

"Sometimes."

"Jealous fits of rage?"

"Sometimes."

"It's simpler out here." I took her hand. "The elves kill us. Or we kill them. That's all." I pressed the tip of her index finger. A claw slid out of its sheath. "Let me see how it feels?" I asked.

A blue drop of peptide formed on the tip of her claw.

"Not yet," she said.

"When?"

"Later. There'll be time for that. I don't want it to be like that now."

"How do you want it, then?"

"I'm not sure." She took her hand out of my grasp. Five claws gleamed. "But not that way now." She kissed me, slipping her tongue into my mouth. I tasted bitter endolepsin. But it could not affect me that way. Digestive enzymes destroyed it. She had to kiss the CNS stud on my head. In that way, the neuropeptide could gain ingress to my brain. She bit my nose, then laughed.

"What's so funny?" I asked.

"I just had a silly urge. Quite tempting, really." She laughed again.

I waited for her to continue.

"Do you ever have any *animal* thoughts?" She smiled at the profanity.

"Don't be vulgar. They don't use that much xeno-DNA in our hybridization. Do they in yours?"

"Apparently. Sometimes the urges are overwhelming. Mostly feline. Cat-thoughts are so delicious." She put her arms around me. I felt claws scratch my back. "I pounce on little mice," she said. "I bat them with my paws. Sometimes I let them think they can get away, but as they dart across the floor, I reach out and hook them with my claws."

"And when you're through playing with them?" The game had begun.

"Cat-thoughts are so delicious." She smiled in the dark. "I bite off their little heads." She laughed. I'd heard that kind of laugh before. "They can't cry without their heads."

Later we slept again.

A battle gong beat its persistent song.

Combrids ran across the commons to their waiting hoverbuses. Wisps of mist wafted against the force field, dissipating when they touched it. Dawn glowed weakly on the horizon.

I shouldered my battle pack and joined the ragged lines of running combrids. I felt a hand touch mine. Vichsn ran beside me. She said something, but as we did not have our helmets on yet, her words were lost in the commotion.

We boarded our hoverbus and she sat beside me. Peppardine was already sitting in the medic's seat at the front of the bus. Soon forests of glass passed silently before us.

Vichsn brought her mouth close to my ear. "Did she tell you

about it?" she asked, speaking through barely parted lips.

"About what?"

"Did she tell you about how she killed her lover. You need to do that to qualify for X-M-R." She giggled. "And then you don't have a choice. That or the cyborg factories."

"You're jealous."

"I am not." She pretended to pout. She soon tired of that game though, and tried another. She put her hand on my leg and stroked it through combat armor. Tactile sensations were conducted quite well through the polymer fabric. She knew that. She let her hand roam higher. I looked up to see if Peppardine was watching; her eyes were hidden behind a lowered helmet visor. Vichsn whispered in my ear again. "What are they like?"

"What?"

"The chimera's peptides."

"Would you like to try them?"

"Does she swing both ways?" Her eyes opened wide in mock surprise. "Seems a little straight to me. If you know what I mean? A Lady and all. Can I join you tonight?"

"Oh, before then." I smiled slyly.

"What do you mean?"

"Get yourself wounded." I laughed at my little joke.

Vichsn pretended to pout again.

We were going on another routine mission. The spooks thought they'd located an elf munitions plant. They were wrong.

We spent all morning combing a thousand hectares of forest. We didn't find any sign of a factory. And we hadn't blundered into an elf trap either, for a change.

Vichsn and I rested, sitting together beneath a tree.

"You are jealous of Peppardine," I said.

"You mean, Sergeant Pepper."

"Where did you hear that name?"

"Everyone knows it. Why?"

"Nothing." I looked away.

"Does it bother you that I know her name?" She nudged my foot with hers.

"Of course not. Don't be silly."

"What kind of stories did she tell you to get you into the sack?"

"The usual." I smiled.

"I guess I'm not good enough for you now." She looked away. "I mean, a Lady and all. How can a simple, plain thing like me have a chance against the charms of a Lady. I was just temporary, wasn't I. Good enough until something better came along."

"It's not like that."

"Just a whore to play with. Is that all I mean to you?"

I turned her head so she faced me. "What's bothering you, Vichsn? This isn't the first time I've slept in another's bed. And you've slept with others too."

"No, only with you. Hadn't you noticed?"

I really had not paid that much attention to her sleep partners. But something in her voice told me she was telling the truth. A suspicion slowly grew. And with it, a sinking feeling. She really was a simple thing. She'd believed my lies. "Look," I said, "you know as well as I that either one of us could get killed at any time. This is no place to be foolish. If we live, we'll be rotated earthside eventually. If we don't live, it won't matter." I tried to remember what I'd told her. But it was hard to keep the stories straight. I'd been living lies for years. The hardest part was remembering to be consistent.

"But there has to be some kind of hope, doesn't there? Otherwise, what's the point of going on. What's the use of having all that money accumulating in the Bank of Earth, if you can't make plans to spend it? Didn't you mean anything you said?"

"Sure I did." I frantically tried to remember just what it was I'd promised her.

"You said we could go back to Earth and live together. Be the toast of the town, you said. War heroes returning victoriously to parades and speeches. With a nice little nest egg all saved up. Enough to last us the rest of our lives. Live happy ever after."

"It *could* be like that," I lied.

"And now *she* has to come. Rather be with your own kind, wouldn't you?"

"What are you talking about?" I knew I hadn't told her *that*.

"The Honorable Markus Detrs. Son of Lord and Lady. Orphan of nobility. Too good for a simple commoner."

"How did you find out about that?"

"The Corps compares retinal holographs with those stored in Buenos Aires. They want to know who their soldiers are. I know someone who works in Records. I found out who you are. But I kept telling myself it wouldn't matter. I almost started believing it. But *she* opened my eyes. Can't stay away from her, can you? Old Vichsn is easy to forget." She flipped down her visor, hiding her face behind its mirrored surface. "You were never planning to go back with me, were you?"

"I don't know. I don't know what I plan to do. Can't you understand that? It's all a game. Everything we do or say is just part of a game. Read the rules, play the game. Only sometimes the rules change."

"You're right," she said. "I'm just being silly."

We heard the hoverbus siren. It was time to go. The spooks had tired of hide-and-seek.

I followed Vichsn through the forest toward the clearing where the hoverbus had landed to pick us up. Her thoughts must have been preoccupied. Or maybe she thought we had to hurry to keep from being left behind by a nervous pilot. For whatever reason, she was moving too fast.

"Slow down," I said. "Be careful."

She didn't turn and continued to walk down a trail.

The olfactimeter in my helmet began screaming in my ear. A red star glowed on my sonar scope.

I yelled at Vichsn.

Too late.

An explosion shook the forest. Concussion waves bounced from tree trunks, setting them humming with resonation. A burst of light flashed through the forest, turning crystalline leaves too dazzling to watch.

I ran ahead. My own sonic field must have triggered the mine. Vichsn must not have even had hers on. Still, she'd just been caught in the edges of detonation. But she was pretty banged up, despite the protection of combat armor. I kneeled beside her and flipped up her visor. She opened her eyes and tried to smile. Her lips moved in silent whispers.

Shards of broken leaves drifted around us, still glowing with trapped light.

"Corpsman!" I yelled.

Then waited.

The chimera's fingers had done their magic.

Vichsn rested quietly on a stretcher in the back of the

hoverbus. She was still in her armor; it acted as external splints for broken bones. Apparently she had a few of those.

She had tried to speak to me once more before Peppardine had come, but I couldn't understand the words. All that came over the encephalowave was pain. But there was something in her eyes I wished I hadn't seen.

I stood beside her and held her hand. Her eyes stayed closed. If she moaned with pain, the chimera's touched a finger to her arm; a claw found a vein and endorphine soothed the hurting.

We were almost back to base when it happened.

I noticed something was different. For a moment, I couldn't figure out what it was. Then it came to me. Vichsn had been making raspy breathing noises. Now she was silent.

"Peppardine!" I yelled. "She's dying."

The chimera quickly came over and felt Vichsn's neck for pulsations. She must have found none, because she then detached Vichsn's carapace, exposing her bare chest. Peppardine placed one hand between Vichsn's breasts and put the other below the left breast.

"Clear!" she said firmly.

I made sure I wasn't touching the cot.

Blue electricity arced from between the chimera's fingers. Vichsn writhed in a quick convulsion.

There was no need to feel her neck this time. The chimera's hands were sensitive enough to feel the beating of a heart. Or the worm wriggles of fibrillation. Or the quiet of cardiac standstill.

A claw extended from Peppardine's left index finger, curving at least six centimeters long. She thrust the claw like a sword beneath Vichsn's breastbone, angling toward her left shoulder. I saw bright red blood fill the hollow claw as it penetrated the chambers of Vichsn's heart. Then the red was pushed back into the heart by the blue of neuropeptide. The claw was withdrawn.

The chimera again placed her hands where palm-prints had already been blistered into skin. Again electric fire flared. Again Vichsn convulsed. Again no heartbeat was produced.

"Do something else!" I shouted. Hysteria cracked from my voice.

"There's no more that can be done," Peppardine said. "Sergeant Pepper can do no more." She reached out to close Vichsn's eyes. "Her pain is gone. She didn't have to cry. No tears come from her eyes. Sergeant Pepper can do no more."

And she was right. But I didn't know that then. As Vichsn's hand cooled in mine, I didn't know a chimera was incapable of reversing an overdose of her own endorphine.

I sat alone at a table in back of the club. The room was as dark as my thoughts. Near the far wall, a bright cone of light illuminated the green felt of a gaming table. Players sat around the table: only their hands were visible, toying with stacks of chips or fingering their poker crystals; their faces were hidden in shadow. I heard snatches of friendly banter coming from the table. The game had not become serious yet.

Normally, I would have been playing also. But tonight, I didn't feel the urge to join the play. I'd not insulated myself from Vichsn as well as I'd thought I had. Her death bothered me more than I wanted to admit. Only once before had death bothered me so much. Then I had to run.

I told her it had all been a game. But I knew now that even that confession had been part of the game. I'd allowed myself to get too close and was trying to pull away. But it had been too late. I had meant what I'd said to her; I was only trying to fool myself into thinking I was lying. But players had to play the game. They only loved when they were playing. It was too late to go back. The game continued.

So I contented myself with the acrid company of mnemone fumes.

Then someone stood beside my table. Her eyebrows glowed in darkness like inverted smiles. I nodded for her to join me. I knew she could see clearly through the shadows. We knew who we were.

I offered her a mnemone stick. She refused. So I sucked its vapors deep into my lungs. There was a hurting somewhere that wouldn't go away. Mnemone pushed it deeper.

Peppardine sat across from me, saying nothing. Her eyes were flawed emeralds beneath smoldering eyebrows. Teeth shone with blue saliva. She appositioned her fingertips. Sharp claws peeked out.

I snapped open another mnemone stick.

In the dark, she moved against me. Her skin was slick with monomer sweat. She reached out and pulled me closer; her nipples pressed into my chest, her legs locked around mine. Lips nuzzled along my neck, then teeth nipped skin.

I whispered in her ear, hoping her sleeping mind would be open to suggestion. "I hurt deep inside. Only you can make it stop hurting. Chase away my ice with your fire."

She muttered in her sleep. "Don't cry, little man. Please don't cry."

Claws pricked, leaving tracks of blood across my back.

She leaped out of bed, waking me. She stood near the window, silhouetted by dawn light. Fog swirled outside. She seemed confused, disoriented. She looked about wildly. But after a few minutes the craziness left her eyes. She came back to bed and lay on the wombskin beside me and stared at the ceiling.

"Another dream?" I asked.

"I thought I heard him crying," she said. "I had to go to him, to make him be quiet. My man used to get mad if the baby cried." She looked at me. "But that was a long time ago. Why do I still hear him cry?"

"What happened?"

"To the baby?" She purposely misunderstood my question. "He died. That's all. Nothing more. He just died one day." She shivered. "Babies die all the time. But why do I still hear him cry? I tried to keep him quiet."

"And your man? What happened to him?"

"You wouldn't understand."

"I might. You see, I'm an orphan, myself."

"What do you know of the rages of nobility? We're not like common folk. We feel different passions." She paused. "But I'm not a Lady any more. They told me to forget all that. And I tried. Why won't my dreams let me forget?"

Sunlight waxed stronger, but was still pale compared to the sunlight of Earth. And darkness was deeper there. I saw a jeweled knife hilt protruding from his chest. But he'd been cut many times before the final thrust. You could see that even in the holos. I wondered what final act of cruelty had driven her to such frenzy. Yes, I understood the rages of nobility. One game ended. Another began.

The mists of morning rose.

We didn't go on any routine missions that morning. No hoverbuses left the base. The only daily order was that we were to keep combat armor and packs ready and be prepared for immediate mobilization.

That made us a little nervous.

High Command always planned some kind of routine missions; they tried to keep us too busy to think too much. So maybe something big was about to happen, and they were holding us back in anticipation of needing us later. There was only one thing worse than routine missions—real ones.

Combrids loitered about, talking together in small groups. Rumors circulated like oxide fire jumping among treetops.

In the noncom club, a poker game formed. I watched the game for a bit, not really interested in playing. But with nothing better to do, and tired of listening to idle rumors, I decided to play. I had trouble getting into the flow of play though; it didn't seem to matter very much. I played cautiously, not bluffing, folding if I didn't have the cards. And I didn't have the cards very often.

Once, when I looked up, I saw Peppardine come into the club. She sat alone next to the wall and watched us play.

Morning drifted into afternoon. Rumors intensified; there were mutters that a big elven offensive was being launched. Combrids fidgeted on their seats. Mnemone fumes wafted lazily in the air.

I was becoming bored. I grew tired of killing time with listless gambling. So I decided to up the stakes. On the next hand, I began betting big, raising the bet each round at least a hundred. I didn't care what kind of hand I had; I didn't even know what my hole card was. What difference was a couple of grand, one way or the other?

Besides, it was kind of fun watching the other combrids' faces as they tried to figure out what I had I was so proud of, what kind of game I was playing. But not as much fun as when Vichsn had been one of the players.

My first card up was a diamond queen. Eyebrows were raised when I led with a C chip, but nobody folded on me. I knew they would play along for a while. They paused to think, though, when I bet a hundred and raised another hundred on a four of hearts. There was even more thinking when I bet heavily on a ten of clubs. But everyone played along. They decided I was bluffing and trying to buy the pot. Which I was.

I was enjoying myself thoroughly. I almost forgot about

Vichsn not being there. Almost.

When another queen rolled up as my last card, I nearly laughed out loud. It was all I could do to keep from grinning like a sand-cat. Now I could really bluff. Two queens showing. Everyone would think my hole card was a queen. Three ladies. Not bad. So I threw a grand into the pot.

That really caused the other players to sweat.

I probably could have bought the pot.

But then the battle gong began clanging.

Everyone in the club jumped up and began putting on combat armor. Outside, combrids were already running across the commons. Hoverbuses began to warm their engines; the whine of grav-turbines filled the air.

I cursed under my breath. They would sound general quarters just as I was beginning to have fun. I pulled on my armor and picked up my pack. Then I noticed Peppardine was still in the room, standing across the table from me. I turned to leave, then paused. I illuminated the dark hole facet on my poker crystal for the first time.

I stared at it for a moment.

Then I had to laugh.

For the Queen of Spades stared back at me.

We were briefed while airborne in the hoverbus.

The Captain spoke in his usual clipped speech. He was so dry and laconic you had the urge to suck on your helmet nipple. It seemed the elves had launched a major attack on our space port, apparently in an effort to cut our lines of supply. Other than being a predictable move, it was a good idea. But the Lords of High Command knew what a tempting target the port would be, so it was heavily defended with triple force fields and double batteries of autopulsers. The elves had no real chance to break through its computer-directed defenses. In the past, they'd shown no inclination toward suicide attacks. So they must have some ulterior motive behind the attack. So High Command held back on sending combrid units to the port, waiting to see what would develop later in the day. They trusted the port's defense to the cold precision of battle computers firing autopulsers.

The elven attack continued unrelenting, but consisted of long-range bombardment with heavy pulsers. Their big guns parried with ours. They didn't mount a direct attack and risk exposing themselves to counter-attack. High Command became even more suspicious. The elves looked too vulnerable. A couple of our divisions were mobilized and feigned an attack. As expected, the elves put up only token resistance as they retreated deeper into the forest. They fought only enough to try to lure us into chasing them.

Then their real attack began.

Our depot at Cronus reported coming under heavy bombardment. Most of the Corps munitions and fuel were stored there. The elves hoped we would be too busy chasing their diversionary forces to defend the depot. Of course, it was just as heavily defended with force fields and autopulsers as the port. So they would need ground forces to try to knock out our computer guns. They knew that and so did we.

That's when our unit was mobilized.

Our hoverbus hung in the air over a clearing in the forest. We were supposed to be at the rear of the elven ground forces. They were going to be trapped between us and the autopulsers defending Cronus. A pincer maneuver. A glorious victory for Mother Earth. At least that was the plan. I remembered something about mice and men and plans. I wondered if elves were included in there somewhere.

We quickly filed out of the bus and jumped to the ground. I scrambled toward the trees and made it to their cover without incident. The hoverbus was already accelerating away. The whine of grav-turbines ebbed.

The Captain had us form a vee and we began advancing through the trees. Far away was the sound of heavy artillery, as faint as distant thunder. I had my sensors turned to max gain and had twelve diopters of magnification warping my visor. But the woods were quiet; nothing moved save us. My sensors detected no hidden surprises.

The forest held an eerie silence. Night approached. Fog thickened. Already hydrocarbon snow was falling, heavy and sticky with pentane and hexane rain mixed in. It was cold, at least eighty or ninety below. But combat armor kept me warm. Only my thoughts were chilled.

Ebbing light glittered from aggregates of emerald, sapphire, amethyst, and tourmaline. Serrated leaves sparkled like broken teeth. Underbrush broke into shards as we passed; fallen leaves screaked under combat boots. The trees were like giant fiber optic bundles; a translucent sheath enclosed tiny tubes that transported both hydrocarbon monomer and crystal composite upward, where the tubules fanned out at the tree's top and budded into leaves. Photopolymerization occurred in the leaves, and a matrix of complex crystals and polymer formed into geometric shapes. A forest of ripe glass dandelion heads. Silent for two or three kilometers.

Then the quiet was broken.

"Here they come!" shouted the Captain.

I saw elves swooping from tree to tree, firing their pulsers in midair. Tree trunks picked up the flash of the weapons firing. The light was conducted distally to set their leaves glowing. Foliage quivered to the shriek of hydrocarbon gas parting for the pulser beam, then shook with a sudden clap of thunder when sudden vacuum filled.

I fired my assault rifle at the swift-gliding elves in short bursts. Spent photonuclear cases arched into the air and clattered against the trunks of glass trees. I backed up slowly. The Captain was having us form a ring, with our backs to our fellow combrids. I took cover behind a fallen tree and fanned pulser beams at any elf that showed too much of himself.

We were just supposed to delay the elves, to make sure they couldn't escape. Reinforcements were coming to administer the coup de grace. The two divisions used earlier to fake an attack were already on their way to help. So there was no point being a hero. Just stay alive until help came. And worry the elves a little. Slow them up a little.

Which was exactly what I intended to do. I squirmed deeper into the ground beside my tree trunk, using the trunk as a rest for my weapon. I certainly didn't intend to be a hero. I planned to go back to Earth. A substantial trust had matured there while I was off to the colonies fighting with the Corps. I was ready to go back now. I wasn't afraid any more. My secret was safe. Nothing the Lords and Ladies could do would shock or worry me. I'd seen too much and done too much. I wouldn't reveal myself. There were atrocities they'd not dreamed. I would show them. I knew I was ready; I'd passed the test. I'd played the game with a Lady. If I could play with her, I could play with anybody. All I had to do now was make sure I lived to collect.

I upped the gain on the laser scope of my assault rifle and slowly scanned the forest. I saw an elf swoop to a tree and cling to it briefly, as he decided which way to launch himself. I centered the pale disk of the point-of-impact of the laser sight on him and touched the firing stud, squeezing off three quanta before he could move. Gray fur exploded. The elf crumpled and fell to the ground.

No problem. We could hold them here for hours, until our trap was sprung.

Me and my big mouth.

A moment later a concussion almost knocked me over. A patch of forest was missing in front of me.

"They've turned their big guns around," the Captain whispered in my head. "They'll have the range with the next salvo. We've got to move. Everyone retreat."

I agreed wholeheartedly. No hero me. I cautiously stood up. Pulser beams stabbed out of the forest through which we'd come. Glass exploded over my head. Sharp fragments of crystal pinged against my armor. If I'd been an elf, I would have been skewered. Lucky me.

We were trapped between two columns of elves.

"I can't move, Captain," I bawled into my cortical mike. "They've got me pinned down with snipers." It was the same for every combrid. We were caught. That had been their plan all along. They knew they couldn't breech the walls of the depot. They'd pulled a double feint, luring us into attacking with ground forces, then trapping us in the forest with their own ground forces, where our hoverbuses couldn't evacuate us, and their artillery could blow us into orbit. Devious devils. If I hadn't been the one about to be blown to bits, I would've admired their trickery.

But I was the one.

I waited nervously for the Captain to think of something. That's what they paid him for: to think for the rest of us. I hoped he'd come up with something real quick.

Then I felt myself being lifted into the air by a giant hand. Only there wasn't any hand. Just a concussion wave. With the clarity of expanded perception, where an instant becomes stretched forever, I saw the tree trunk I'd been hiding behind turn into vapor as a blast crater formed. I seemed to float high in the air for an eternity. I knew the initial blast had broken some bones; my right thigh and left forearm felt like hot coals had been placed under the skin and it hurt all over my chest when I tried to breathe. It felt like a knife was sticking into my left side—a ruptured spleen or perforated viscus, I thought. And they were right; your whole life does flash before you. I saw again the endless scenes of petty cruelty as my parents slowly destroyed each other. With me in the middle, about to be destroyed myself. I'd had no choice—it was them or me. And I'd planned it carefully to look like a double suicide. Slipped them both sleepy sticks. When they were unconscious, I'd hauled them into the bath, floated their bodies in the water. Veins opened easily. Water steamed crimson. But then I realized I'd never be able to live the lie. Lords and Ladies would guess the truth. So I ran. I'd been running ever since. Until now. Now I could go back. Now I could play the game. Except I was going to die.

The same hand that lifted me now flung me back to the ground, as the inner core of the photon-bomb imploded. Explosion/Implosion shells were quite popular with elves. Particularly nasty, they said. Frogs, do the dead lose their cynicism? I hoped so. Blackness closed around me.

I woke with fire burning inside.

Fingers sought secret places; claws sought blood.

Cat-eyes peered into mine.

I recognized Peppardine's face. The chimera smiled.

I wasn't dead!

I was strong. Pain evaporated like morning mists and was forgotten. I wasn't scared. I could do anything. And I was strong. Dogs, how strong!

"You are well, Soldier," she said. "You live to fight again. Be my hero." She lifted my visor. Our oxygen bubbles touched, then fused. She kissed my lips. I saw the wrongness in her eyes again. "You know what to do, Berserker." The lips smiled. Teeth shone with blue promises.

I did know what to do.

My weapon lay beside me. I picked it up and worked the action. A photonuclear case slipped easily into the chamber. It wasn't damaged. But I was, I knew that. But it didn't matter. Endosmin sealed torn blood vessels and stopped their bleeding. Endotalis flogged my heart. Endocholine speeded nervous transmission and strengthened muscles. Combat armor splinted broken bones; endosmin would keep their jagged ends from bleeding as they ground together when I ran. Pain was obliterated by endorphine.

I was strong. I was fast. I was brave . . . so brave.

I laughed.

Then ran.

I cut through the forest, weaving back and forth among the trees, bobbing up and down. Pulser beams followed me, hitting the ground where I had been. I was too quick for them. Craters from E/I shells formed around me, but the concussion waves couldn't topple me. Then I was beyond their zone of fire and among the elves. Everything was in slow-motion. Elves hung from trees. They were incredibly slow. Before they could point their pulsers toward me, I'd shot them out of their trees. I ran faster than the wind. I darted in and out as quick as a frightened coyote. Only I wasn't frightened. Just brave.

I came to an elven battery, bursting into the clearing where they had their gun set up before they even knew I was approaching. I emptied a clip into it, spraying the pulser beams into the gunners. They all lay dead, fur smoking. I jammed another clip into place. But all was quiet.

I examined the artillery piece. The controls looked easy enough. Just like the spooks had outlined once at an orientation.

I hauled the dead elf gunner out of his chair and sat in it myself. I pushed control buttons; the detonation tube swung smoothly on gimbals. Light flashed from other batteries along the same ridge this one was placed. I didn't need to do anything fancy. Just point the tube in the direction of the flashes and center the computer-sight on the battery. Then pull the trigger. And a click away there'd be another flash of light. Brighter. And louder. Then move the cross-hairs down the ridge. The gun loaded itself. Soon the only flashes were from the shells I fired.

There was but one more duty to be discharged. (I could still smile at my pun.)

I centered the cross-hairs of the gun on its own stacked crates of photonuclear cases and locked the controls in place. I dialed in a ten-second delay and pulled the trigger.

Then ran again.

I was well across the clearing before the ammo detonated. Random light flared as bright as novae. Another giant's hand knocked me down. I couldn't get back up. No matter. The game was almost over. Next move, please.

* * *

Hoverbus turbines whined.

A black queen haunted my dreams. I opened my eyes. A face watched mine. Prismatic card-eyes became green cat-eyes, following mine.

I hurt all over.

I didn't think that much pain was possible.

I lay on a stretcher in the front of the hoverbus. I could hear combrids talking. They said I was a hero, sure to get a medal, maybe the Legion of Merit. That I saved a whole division by taking the elven batteries. Reinforcements had arrived. We'd won.

It didn't much matter to me.

I hurt all over.

A moan pushed through my lips. I felt a claw pierce my skin. Warmth flowed up my arm. Then the pain was gone, chased away by the blue glow of endorphine.

"There, there," the chimera said. "Does my baby hurt? I'll make it better. Don't cry. You know he doesn't like to hear you cry." There was something wrong with her eyes. The same wrongness I'd seen in my mother's. "Remember when I had to hold the pillow over your face," she crooned, "to keep you quiet? Don't make Mama do that again." Suddenly I understood the madness behind the words. Somehow the holos hadn't found out about her dead baby. I saw two mind images superimposed: the faces of Trinks and Vichsn. The chimera had comforted both. Both should have made it back to base alive. Neither had. Now I knew why. I remembered feeling the same madness once.

The chimera stroked my head. Sharp claws left scratches in my skin. I tried not to wince. I found I couldn't move my arms and legs; they were held by straps.

Pain began to gnaw deep inside again.

The chimera kissed my cheek. "Is my baby warm enough? What can Mama do for baby? Only please don't cry. Don't make me get the pillow out." I knew what game she played in her twisted mind. I'd been foolish to think I could escape the lies. And I'd only been lying to myself when I thought I could go back to Earth. There was no escape. Only endless games.

Pain washed over me in waves. I bit my lip hard to keep from crying out. I tasted the salty taste of blood. I had to keep from crying. Base couldn't be much farther. I could make it. Only one more game. I could bluff my way out of this mess.

Tears formed in the corners of my eyes. I blinked, squeezing them down my cheeks. I screamed inside, but none escaped my lips.

"There, there," the chimera crooned, her mind lost to warped fantasy. "Let Mama kiss the hurt away."

THE PRINCESS AND THE BEAR

by Orson Scott Card

Orson Scott Card says he wrote this story for fun, and because he loved it. So did we. It is an unabashed fairy tale, missing only the "once upon a time." But it's full of beauty and magic, romance and betrayal, pain and joy. It's a timeless sort of tale, one which we'll read to the children in our lives, only to find that it soothes the constant child we carry forever in ourselves...

I know you've seen the lions. All over the place: beside the doors, flanking the throne, roaring out of the plates in the pantry, spouting water from under the eaves.

Haven't you ever wondered why the statue atop the city gates is a bear?

Many years ago in this very city, in the very palace that you can see rising granite and gray behind the old crumbly walls of the king's garden, there lived a princess. It was so long ago that who can ever remember her name? She was just the princess. These days it isn't in fashion to think that princesses are beautiful, and in fact they tend to be a bit horse-faced and gangling. But in those days it was an absolute requirement that a princess look fetching, at least when wearing the most expensive clothes available.

This princess, however, would have been beautiful dressed like a slum child or a shepherd girl. She was beautiful the moment she was born. She only got more beautiful as she grew up.

And there was also a prince. He was not her brother, though. He was the son of a king in a far-off land, and his father was the thirteenth cousin twice removed of the princess' father. The boy had been sent here to our land to get an education—because the princess' father, King Ethelred, was known far and wide as a wise man and a good king.

And if the princess was marvelously beautiful, so was the prince. He was the kind of boy that every mother wants to hug, the kind of boy who gets his hair tousled by every man that meets him.

He and the princess grew up together. They took lessons together from the teachers in the palace, and when the princess was slow, the prince would help her, and when the prince was slow, the princess would help him. They had no secrets from each other, but they had a million secrets that they two kept from the rest of the world. Secrets like where the bluebirds' nest was this year, and what color underwear the cook wore, and that if you duck under the stairway to the armory there's a little underground path that comes up in the wine cellar. They speculated endlessly about which of the princess' ancestors had used that path for surreptitious imbibing.

After not too many years the princess stopped being just a little girl and the prince stopped being just a little boy, and then they fell in love. All at once all their million secrets became just one secret, and they told that secret every time they looked at each other, and everyone who saw them said, "Ah, if I were only young again." That is because so many people think that love belongs to the young: sometime during their lives they stopped loving people, and they think it was just because they got old.

The prince and the princess decided one day to get married.

But the very next morning, the prince got a letter from the

far-off country where his father lived. The letter told him that his father no longer lived at all, and that the boy was now a man; and not just a man, but a king.

So the prince got up the next morning, and the servants put his favorite books in a parcel, and his favorite clothes were packed in a trunk, and the trunk, and the parcel, and the prince were all put on a coach with bright red wheels and gold tassels at the corner and the prince was taken away.

The princess did not cry until after he was out of sight. Then she went into her room and cried for a long time, and only her nurse could come in with food and chatter and cheerfulness. At last the chatter brought smiles to the princess, and she went into her father's study where he sat by the fire at night and said, "He promised he would write, every day, and I must write every day as well."

She did, and the prince did, and once a month a parcel of thirty letters would arrive for her, and the postrider would take away a parcel of thirty letters (heavily perfumed) from her.

And one day the Bear came to the palace. Now he wasn't a bear, of course, he was *the* Bear, with a capital B. He was probably only thirty-five or so, because his hair was still golden brown and his face was only lined around the eyes. But he was massive and grizzly, with great thick arms that looked like he could lift a horse, and great thick legs that looked like he could carry that horse a hundred miles. His eyes were deep, and they looked brightly out from under his bushy eyebrows, and the first time the nurse saw him she squealed and said, "Oh, my, he looks like a *bear*."

He came to the door of the palace and the doorman refused to let him in, because he didn't have an appointment. But he scribbled a note on a piece of paper that looked like it had held a sandwich for a few days, and the doorman—with grave misgivings—carried the paper to the king.

The paper said, "If Boris and 5,000 stood on the highway from Rimperdell, would you like to know which way they were going?"

King Ethelred wanted to know.

The doorman let the stranger into the palace, and the king brought him into his study and they talked for many hours.

In the morning the king arose early and went to his captains of cavalry and captains of infantry, and he sent a lord to the knights and their squires, and by dawn all of Ethelred's little army was gathered on the highway, the one that leads to Rimperdell. They marched for three hours that morning, and then they came to a place and the stranger with golden brown hair spoke to the king and King Ethelred commanded the army to stop. They stopped, and the infantry was sent into the forest on one side of the road, and the cavalry was sent into the tall cornfields on the other side of the road, where they dismounted. Then the king, and the stranger, and the knights waited in the road.

Soon they saw a dust cloud in the distance, and then the dust cloud grew near, and they saw that it was an army coming down the road. And at the head of the army was King Boris of Rimperdell. And behind him the army seemed to be five thousand men.

"Hail," King Ethelred said, looking more than a little irritated, since King Boris' army was well inside our country's boundaries.

"Hail," King Boris said, looking more than a little irritated, since no one was supposed to know that he was coming.

"What do you think you're doing?" asked King Ethelred.

"You're blocking the road," said King Boris.

"It's my road," said King Ethelred.

"Not any more," said King Boris.

"I and my knights say that this road belongs to me," said King Ethelred.

King Boris looked at Ethelred's fifty knights, and then he looked back at his own five thousand men, and he said, "I say you and your knights are dead men unless you move aside."

"Then you want to be at war with me?" asked King Ethelred.

"War?" said King Boris. "Can we really call it a war? It will be like stepping on a nasty cockroach."

"I wouldn't know," said King Ethelred, "because we haven't ever had cockroaches in our kingdom."

Then he added, "Until now, of course."

Then King Ethelred lifted his arm, and the infantry shot arrows and threw lances from the wood, and many of Boris' men were slain. And the moment all of his troops were ready to fight the army in the forest, the cavalry came from the field and attacked from the rear, and soon Boris' army, what was left of it, surrendered, and Boris himself lay mortally wounded in the road.

"If you had won this battle," King Ethelred said, "what would you have done to me?"

King Boris gasped for breath and said, "I would have had you beheaded."

"Ah," said King Ethelred. "We are very different men. For I will let you live."

But the stranger stood beside King Ethelred, and he said, "No, King Ethelred, that is not in your power, for Boris is about to die. And if he were not, I would have killed him myself, for as long as a man like him is alive, no one is safe in all the world."

Then Boris died, and he was buried in the road with no marker, and his men were sent home without their swords.

And King Ethelred came back home to crowds of people cheering the great victory, and shouting, "Long live King Ethelred the conqueror."

King Ethelred only smiled at them. Then he took the stranger into the palace, and gave him a room where he could sleep, and made him the chief counselor to the king, because the stranger had proved that he was wise, and that he was loyal, and that he loved the king better than the king loved himself, for the king would have let Boris live.

No one knew what to call the man, because when a few brave souls asked him his name, he only frowned and said, "I will wear the name you pick for me."

Many names were tried, like George, and Fred, and even Rocky and Todd. But none of the names seemed right. For a long time, everyone called him Sir, because when somebody is that big and that strong and that wise and that quiet, you feel like calling him sir and offering him your chair when he comes in the room.

And then after a while everyone called him the name the nurse had chosen for him just by accident: they called him the Bear. At first they only called him that behind his back, but eventually someone slipped and called him that at the dinner table, and he smiled, and answered to the name, and so everyone called him that.

Except the princess. She didn't call him anything, because she didn't speak to him if she could help it, and when she talked about him, she stuck out her lower lip and called him That Man.

This is because the princess hated the Bear.

She didn't hate him because he had done anything bad to her. In fact, she was pretty sure that he didn't even notice she was living in the palace. He never turned and stared when she walked into the room, like all the other men did. But that isn't why she hated him, either.

She hated him because she thought he was making her father weak.

King Ethelred was a great king, and his people loved him. He always stood very tall at ceremonies, and he sat for hours making judgments with great wisdom. He always spoke softly when softness was needed, and shouted at the times when only shouting would be heard.

In all he was a stately man, and so the princess was shocked with the way he was around the Bear.

King Ethelred and the Bear would sit for hours in the king's study, every night when there wasn't a great banquet or an ambassador. They would both drink from huge mugs of ale—but instead of having a servant refill the mugs, the princess was shocked that her own father stood up and poured from the pitcher! A king, doing the work of a servant, and then giving the mug to a commoner, a man whose name no one knew!

The princess saw this because she sat in the king's study with them, listening and watching without saying a word as they talked. Sometimes she would spend the whole time combing her father's long white hair. Sometimes she would knit long woolen stockings for her father for the winter. Sometimes she would read—for her father believed that even women should learn to read. But all the time she listened, and became angry, and hated the Bear more and more.

King Ethelred and the Bear didn't talk much about affairs of state. They talked about hunting rabbits in the forest. They told jokes about lords and ladies in the kingdom—and some of the jokes weren't even nice, the princess told herself bitterly. They talked about what they should do about the ugly carpet in the courtroom—as if the Bear had a perfect right to have an opinion about what the new carpet should be.

And when they did talk about affairs of state, the Bear treated King Ethelred like an *equal.* When he disagreed with the king, he would leap to his feet saying, "No, no, no, no, you just don't see at all." When he thought the king had said something right, he clapped him on the shoulder and said, "You'll make a great king yet, Ethelred."

And sometimes King Ethelred would sigh and stare into the fire, and whisper a few words, and a dark and tired look would steal across his face. Then the Bear would put his arm around the king's shoulder, and stare into the fire with him, until finally the king would sigh again, and then lift himself, groaning, out of his chair, and say, "It's time that this old man put his corpse between the sheets."

The next day the princess would talk furiously to her nurse, who never told a soul what the princess said. The princess would say, "That Man is out to make my father a weakling! He's out to make my father look stupid. That Man is making my father forget that he is a king." Then she would wrinkle her forehead and say, "That Man is a traitor."

She never said a word about this to her father, however. If she had, he would have patted her head and said, "Oh, yes, he does indeed make me forget that I am a king." But he would also have said, "He makes me remember what a king should be." And Ethelred would not have called him a traitor. He would have called the Bear his friend.

As if it wasn't bad enough that her father was forgetting himself around a commoner, that was the very time that things started going bad with the prince. She suddenly noticed that the last several packets of mail had not held thirty letters each—they only held twenty, and then fifteen, and then ten. And the letters weren't five pages long any more. They were only three, and then two, and then one.

He's just busy, she thought.

Then she noticed that he no longer began her letters with, "My dearest darling sweetheart pickle-eating princess." (The pickle-eating part was an old joke from something that happened when they were both nine.) Now he started them, "My dear lady," or "Dear princess." Once she said to her nurse, "He might as well address them to Occupant."

He's just tired, she thought.

And then she realized that he never told her he loved her any more, and she went out on the balcony and cried where only the garden could hear, and where only the birds in the trees could see.

She began to keep to her rooms, because the world didn't

seem like a very nice place any more. Why should she have anything to do with the world, when it was a nasty place where fathers turned into mere men, and lovers forgot they were in love?

And she cried herself to sleep every night that she slept. And some nights she didn't sleep at all, just stared at the ceiling trying to forget the prince. And you know that if you want to remember something, the best way is to try very, very hard to forget it.

Then one day, as she went to the door of her room, she found a basket of autumn leaves just inside her door. There was no note on them, but they were very brightly colored, and they rustled loudly when she touched the basket, and she said to herself, "It must be autumn."

She went to the window and looked, and it was autumn, and it was beautiful. She had already seen the leaves a hundred times a day, but she hadn't remembered to notice.

And then a few weeks later she woke up and it was cold in her room. Shivering, she went to her door to call for a servant to build her fire up higher—and just inside the door was a large pan, and on the pan there stood a little snowman, which was grinning a grin made of little chunks of coal, and his eyes were big pieces of coal, and all in all it was so comical the princess had to laugh. That day she forgot her misery for a while and went outside and threw snowballs at the knights, who of course let her hit them and who never managed to hit her, but of course that's all part of being a princess—no one would ever put snow down your back or dump you in the canal or anything.

She asked her nurse who brought these things, but the nurse just shook her head and smiled. "It wasn't me," she said. "Of course it was," the princess answered, and gave her a hug, and thanked her. The Nurse smiled and said, "Thanks for your thanks, but it wasn't me." But the princess knew better, and loved her nurse all the more.

Then the letters stopped coming altogether. And the princess stopped writing letters. And she began taking walks in the woods.

At first she only took walks in the garden, which is where princesses are supposed to take walks. But in a few days of walking and walking and walking she knew every brick of the garden path by heart, and she kept coming to the garden wall and wishing she were outside it.

So one day she walked to the gate and went out of the garden and wandered into the forest. The forest was not at all like the garden. Where the garden was neatly tended and didn't have a weed in it, the forest was all weeds, all untrimmed and loose, with animals that ran from her, and birds that scurried to lead her away from their young, and best of all, only grass or soft brown earth under her feet. Out in the forest she could forget the garden where every tree reminded her of talks she had had with the prince while sitting in the branches. Out in the forest she could forget the palace where every room had held its own joke or its own secret or its own promise that had been broken.

That was why she was in the forest the day the wolf came out of the hills.

She was already heading back to the palace, because it was getting on toward dark, when she caught a glimpse of something moving. She looked, and realized that it was a huge gray wolf, walking along beside her not fifteen yards off. When she stopped, the wolf stopped. When she moved, the wolf moved. And the farther she walked, the closer the wolf came.

She turned and walked away from the wolf.

After a few moments she looked behind her, and saw the wolf only a dozen feet away, its mouth open, its tongue hanging out, its teeth shining white in the gloom of the late afternoon forest

She began to run. But not even a princess can hope to outrun a wolf. She ran and ran until she could hardly breathe, and the wolf was still right behind her, panting a little but hardly tired. She ran and ran some more until her legs refused to obey her and she fell to the ground. She looked back, and realized that this was what the wolf had been waiting for—for her to be tired enough to fall, for her to be easy prey, for her to be a dinner he didn't have to work for.

And so the wolf got a gleam in its eye, and sprang forward.

Just as the wolf leaped, a huge brown shape lumbered out of the forest and stepped over the princess. She screamed. It was a huge brown bear, with heavy fur and vicious teeth. The bear swung its great hairy arm at the wolf, and struck it in the head. The wolf flew back a dozen yards, and from the way its head bobbed about as it flew, the princess realized its neck had been broken.

And then the huge bear turned toward her, and she saw with despair that she had only traded one monstrous animal for another.

And she fainted. Which is about all that a person can do

when a bear that is standing five feet away looks at you. And looks hungry.

She woke up in bed at the palace and figured it had all been a dream. But then she felt a terrible pain in her legs, and felt her face stinging with scratches from the branches. It had not been a dream—she really had run through the forest.

"What happened?" she asked feebly. "Am I dead?" Which wasn't all that silly a question, because she really had expected to be.

"No," said her father, who was sitting by the bed.

"No," said the nurse. "And why in the world, why should you be dead?"

"I was in the forest," said the princess, "and there was a wolf, and I ran and ran but he was still there. And then a bear came and killed the wolf, and it came toward me like it was going to eat me, and I guess I fainted."

"Ah," said the nurse, as if that explained everything.

"Ah," said her father, King Ethelred. "Now I understand. We were taking turns watching you after we found you unconscious and scratched up by the garden gate. You kept crying out in your sleep, 'Make the bear go away! Make the bear leave me alone!' Of course, we thought you meant *the* Bear, our Bear, and we had to ask the poor man not to take his turn any more, as we thought it might make you upset. We all thought you hated him, for a while there." And King Ethelred chuckled. "I'll have to tell him it was all a mistake."

Then the king left. Great, thought the princess, he's going to tell the Bear it was all a mistake, and I really do hate him to pieces.

The nurse walked over to the bed and knelt beside it. "There's another part to the story. They made me promise not to tell you," the nurse said, "but you know and I know that I'll always tell you everything. It seems that it was two guards that found you, and they both said that they saw something running away. Or not running, exactly, galloping. Or something. They said it looked like a bear, running on all fours."

"Oh no," said the princess. "How horrible!"

"No," said the nurse. "It was their opinion, and Robbo Knockle swears it's true, that the bear they saw had brought you to the gate and set you down gentle as you please. Whoever brought you there smoothed your skirt, you know, and put a pile of leaves under your head like a pillow, and you were surely in no state to do all that yourself."

"Don't be silly," said the princess. "How could a bear do all that?"

"I know," said the nurse, "so it must not have been an ordinary bear. It must have been a magic bear." She said this last in a whisper, because the nurse believed that magic should be talked about quietly, lest something awful should hear and come calling.

"Nonsense," said the princess. "I've had an education, and I don't believe in magic bears or magic brews or any kind of magic at all. It's just old-lady foolishness."

The nurse stood up and her mouth wrinkled all up. "Well, then, this foolish old lady will take her foolish stories to somebody foolish, who wants to listen."

"Oh, there, there," the princess said, for she didn't like to hurt anyone's feelings, especially not Nurse's. And they were friends again. But the princess still didn't believe about the bear. However, she hadn't been eaten, after all, so the bear must not have been hungry.

It was only two days later, when the princess was up and around again—though there were nasty scabs all over her face from the scratches, that the prince came back to the palace.

He came riding up on a lathered horse that dropped to the ground and died right in front of the palace door. He looked exhausted, and there were great purple circles under his eyes. He had no baggage. He had no cloak. Just the clothes on his back and a dead horse.

"I've come home," he said to the doorman, and fainted into his arms. (By the way, it's perfectly all right for a man to faint, as long as he has ridden on horseback for five days, without a bite to eat, and with hundreds of soldiers chasing him.)

"It's treason," he said when he woke up and ate and bathed and dressed. "My allies turned against me, even my own subjects. They drove me out of my kingdom. I'm lucky to be alive."

"Why?" asked King Ethelred.

"Because they would have killed me. If they had caught me."

"No, no, no, no, don't be stupid," said the Bear, who was listening from a chair a few feet away. "Why did they turn against you?"

The prince turned toward the Bear and sneered. It was an ugly sneer, and it twisted up the prince's face in a way it had never twisted when he lived with King Ethelred and was in love with the princess.

"I wasn't aware that I was being stupid," he said archly. "And I certainly wasn't aware that *you* had been invited into the conversation."

The Bear didn't say anything after that, just nodded an unspoken apology and watched.

And the prince never did explain why the people had turned against him. Just something vague about power-hungry demagogues and mob rule.

The princess came to see the prince that very morning.

"You look exhausted," she said.

"You look beautiful," he said.

"I have scabs all over my face and I haven't done my hair in days," she said.

"I love you," he said.

"You stopped writing," she said.

"I guess I lost my pen," he said. "No, I remember now. I lost my mind. I forgot how beautiful you are. A man would have to be mad to forget."

Then he kissed her, and she kissed him back, and she forgave him for all the sorrow he had caused her and it was like he had never been away.

For about three days.

Because in three days she began to realize that he was different somehow.

She would open her eyes after kissing him (princesses always close their eyes when they kiss someone) and she would notice that he was looking off somewhere with a distant expression on his face. As if he barely noticed that he was kissing her. That does not make any woman, even a princess, feel very good.

She noticed that sometimes he seemed to forget she was even there. She passed him in a corridor and he wouldn't speak, and unless she touched his arm and said good morning he might have walked on by without a word.

And then sometimes, for no reason, he would feel slighted or offended, or a servant would make a noise or spill something and he would fly into a rage and throw things against the wall. He had never even raised his voice in anger when he was a boy.

He often said cruel things to the princess, and she wondered why she loved him, and what was wrong, but then he would come to her and apologize, and she would forgive him because after all he had lost a kingdom because of traitors, and he couldn't be expected to always feel sweet and nice. She decided, though, that if it was up to her, and it was, he would never feel unsweet and unnice again.

Then one night the Bear and her father went into the study and locked the door behind them. The princess had never been locked out of her father's study before, and she became angry at the bear because he was taking her father away from her, and so she listened at the door. She figured that if the Bear wanted to keep her out, she would see to it that she heard everything anyway.

This is what she heard.

"I have the information," the Bear said.

"It must be bad, or you wouldn't have asked to speak to me alone," said King Ethelred. Aha, thought the princess, the Bear *did* plot to keep me out.

The Bear stood by the fire, leaning on the mantel, while King Ethelred sat down.

"Well?" asked King Ethelred.

"I know how much the boy means to you. And to the princess. I'm sorry to bring such a tale."

The boy! thought the princess. They couldn't possibly be calling her prince a boy, could they? Why, he had been a king, except for treason, and here a commoner was calling him a boy.

"He means much to us," said King Ethelred, "which is all the more reason for me to know the truth, be it good or bad."

"Well, then," said the Bear, "I must tell you that he was a very bad king."

The princess went white with rage.

"I think he was just too young. Or something," said the Bear. "Perhaps there was a side to him that you never saw, because the moment he had power it went to his head. He thought his kingdom was too small, because he began to make war with little neighboring counties and duchies and took their lands and made them part of his kingdom. He plotted against other kings who had been good and true friends of his father. And he kept raising taxes on his people to support huge armies. He kept starting wars and mothers kept weeping because their sons had fallen in battle.

"And finally," said the Bear, "the people had had enough, and so had the other kings, and there was a revolution and a war all at the same time. The only part of the boy's tale that is true is that he was lucky to escape with his life, because every person that I talked to spoke of him with hatred, as if he were the most evil person they had ever seen."

King Ethelred shook his head. "Could you be wrong? I can't believe this of a boy I practically raised myself."

"I wish it were not true," said the Bear, "for I know that the princess loves him dearly. But it seems obvious to me that the boy doesn't love her—he is here because he knew he would be safe here, and because he knows that if he married her, he would be able to rule when you are dead."

"Well," said King Ethelred, "that will never happen. My daughter will never marry a man who would destroy the kingdom."

"Not even if she loves him very much?" asked the Bear.

"It is the price of being a princess," said the king. "She must think first of the kingdom, or she will never be fit to be queen."

At that moment, however, being queen was the last thing the princess cared about. All she knew was that she hated the Bear for taking away her father, and now the same man has persuaded her father to keep her from marrying the man she loved.

She beat on the door, crying out, "Liar! Liar!" King Ethelred and the Bear both leaped for the door. King Ethelred opened it, and the princess burst into the room and started hitting the Bear as hard as she could. Of course the blows fell very lightly, because she was not all that strong, and he was very large and sturdy and the blows could have caused him no pain. But as she struck at him his face looked as if he were being stabbed through the heart at every blow.

"Daughter, daughter," said King Ethelred. "What is this? Why did you listen at the door?"

But she didn't answer; she only beat at the Bear until she was crying too hard to hit him anymore. And then, between sobs, she began to yell at him. And because she didn't usually yell her voice became harsh and hoarse and she whispered. But yelling or whispering, her words were clear, and every word said hatred.

She accused the Bear of making her father little, nothing, worse than nothing, a weakling king who had to turn to a filthy commoner to make any decision at all. She accused the Bear of hating her and trying to ruin her life by keeping her from marrying the only man she could ever love. She accused the Bear of being a traitor, who was plotting to be king himself and rule the kingdom. She accused the Bear of making up vile lies about the prince because she knew that he would be a better king than her weakling father, and that if she married the prince all the Bear's plans for ruling the kingdom would come to nothing.

And finally she accused the Bear of having such a filthy mind that he imagined that he could eventually marry her himself, and so become king.

But that would never happen, she whispered bitterly, at the end. "That will never happen," she said, "never, never, never, because I hate you and I loathe you and if you don't get out of this kingdom and never come back I'll kill myself, I swear it."

And then she grabbed a sword from the mantel and tried to slash her wrists, and the Bear reached out and stoppped her by holding her arms in his huge hands that gripped like iron. Then she spit at him and tried to bite his fingers and beat her head against his chest until King Ethelred took her hands and the Bear let go and backed away.

"I'm sorry," King Ethelred kept saying, though he himself wasn't certain who he was apologizing to or what he was apologizing for. "I'm sorry." And then he realized that he was apologizing for himself, because somehow he knew that his kingdom was ruined right then.

If he listened to the Bear and sent the prince away, the princess would never forgive him, would hate him, in fact, and he couldn't bear that. But if he didn't listen to the Bear, then the princess would surely marry the prince, and the prince would surely ruin his kingdom. And he couldn't endure that.

But worst of all, he couldn't stand the terrible look on the Bear's face.

The princess stood sobbing in her father's arms.

The king stood wishing there were something he could do or undo.

And the Bear simply stood.

And then the Bear nodded, and said, "I understand. Good-bye."

And then the Bear walked out of the room, and out of the palace, and out of the garden walls, and out of the city, and out of any land that the king had heard of.

He took nothing with him—no food, no horse, no extra clothing. He just wore his clothing and carried his sword. He left as he came.

And the princess cried with relief. The Bear was gone. Life could go on, just like it was before ever the prince left and before ever the Bear came.

So she thought.

She didn't really realize how her father felt until he died only four months later, suddenly very old and very tired and very lonely and despairing for his kingdom.

She didn't realize that the prince was not the same man she loved before until she married him three months after her father died.

On the day of their wedding she proudly crowned him king herself, and led him to the throne, where he sat.

"I love you," she said proudly, "and you look like a king."

"I am a king," he said. "I am King Edward the first."

"Edward?" she said. "Why Edward? That's not your name."

"That's a king's name," he said, "and I am a king. Do I not have power to change my name?"

"Of course," she said. "But I liked your own name better."

"But you will call me Edward," he said, and she did.

When she saw him. For he didn't come to her very often. As soon as he wore the crown he began to keep her out of the court, and conducted the business of the kingdom where she couldn't hear. She didn't understand this, because her father had always let her attend everything and hear everything in the government, so she could be a good queen.

"A good queen," said King Edward, her husband, "is a quiet woman who has babies, one of whom will be king."

And so the princess, who was now the queen, had babies, and one of them was a boy, and she tried to help him grow up to be a king.

But as the years passed by she realized that King Edward was not the lovely boy she had loved in the garden. He was a cruel and greedy man. And she didn't like him very much.

He raised the taxes, and the people became poor.

He built up the army, so it became very strong.

He used the army to take over the land of Count Edred, who had been her godfather.

He also took over the land of Duke Adlow, who had once let her pet one of his tame swans.

He also took over the land of Earl Thlaffway, who had wept openly at her father's funeral, and said that her father was the only man he had ever worshipped, because he was such a good king.

And Edred and Adlow and Thlaffway all disappeared, and were never heard of again.

"He's even against the common people," the nurse grumbled one day as she did up the queen's hair. "Some shepherds came to court yesterday to tell him a marvel, which is their duty, isn't it, to tell the king of anything strange that happens in the land?"

"Yes," said the queen, remembering how as a child she and the prince had run to their father often to tell him a marvel—how grass springs up all at once in the spring, how water just disappeared on a hot day, how a butterfly comes all awkward from the cocoon.

"Well," said the nurse, "they told him that there was a bear along the edge of the forest, a bear that doesn't eat meat, but only berries and roots. And this bear, they said, killed wolves. Every year they lose dozens of sheep to the wolves, but this year they had lost not one lamb, because the bear killed the wolves. Now that's a marvel, I'd say," said the nurse.

"Oh yes," said the princess who was now a queen.

"But what did the king do," said the nurse, "but order his knights to hunt down that bear and kill it. Kill it!"

"Why?" asked the queen.

"Why, why, why?" asked the nurse. "The best question in the world. The shepherds asked it, and the king said, 'can't have a bear loose around here. He might kill children.'

"'Oh no,' says the shepherds, 'the bear don't eat meat.'

"'Then, it'll wind up stealing grain,' the king says in reply, and there it is, my lady—the hunters are out after a perfectly harmless bear! You can bet the shepherds don't like it. A perfectly harmless bear!"

The queen nodded. "A magic bear."

"Why, yes," said the nurse. "Now you mention it, it does seem like the bear that saved you that day—"

"Nurse," said the queen, "there was no bear that day. I was dreaming I was mad with despair. There wasn't a wolf chasing me. And there was definitely no magic bear."

The nurse bit her lip. Of course there had been a bear, she thought. And a wolf. But the queen, her princess, was determined not to believe in any kind thing.

"Sure there was a bear," said the nurse.

"No, there was no bear," said the queen, "and now I know who put the idea of a magic bear into the children's head."

"They've heard of him?"

"They came to me with a silly tale of a bear that climbs over the wall into the garden when no one else is around, and who plays with them and lets him ride on his back. Obviously you told them your silly tale about the magic bear who supposedly saved me. So I told them that magic bears were a full tall-tale and that even grownups liked to tell them, but that they must be careful to remember the difference between truth and falsehood, and they should wink if they're fibbing."

"What did they say?" the nurse said.

"I made them all wink about the bear," said the queen, "of course. But I would appreciate it if you wouldn't fill their heads with silly stories. You did tell them your stupid story, didn't you?"

"Yes," said the nurse sadly.

"What a trouble your wagging tongue can cause," said the queen, and the nurse burst into tears and left the room.

They made it up later but there was no talk of bears. The nurse understood well enough, though. The thought of bears reminded the queen of *the* Bear, and everyone knew that she was the one who drove that wise counselor away. If only the Bear were still here, thought the nurse—and hundreds of other people in the kingdom—if he were still here we wouldn't have these troubles in the kingdom.

And there were troubles. The soldiers patrolled the streets of the cities and locked people up for saying things about King Edward. And when a servant in the palace did anything wrong he would bellow and storm, and even throw things and beat them with a rod.

One day when King Edward didn't like the soup he threw the whole tureen at the cook. The cook promptly took his leave, saying for anyone to hear, "I've served kings and queens, lords and ladies, soldiers, and servants, and in all that time this is the first time I've ever been called upon to serve a pig."

The day after he left he was back, at swordpoint—not cooking in the kitchen, of course, since cooks are too close to the king's food. No, the cook was sweeping the stables. And the servants were told in no uncertain terms that none of them was free to leave. If they didn't like their jobs, they could be given another one to do. And they all looked at the work the cook was doing, and kept their tongues.

Except the nurse, who talked to the queen about everything.

"We might as well be slaves," said the nurse. "Right down to the wages. He's cut us all in half, some even more, and we've got barely enough to feed ourselves. I'm all right, mind you, my lady, for I have no one but me to feed, but there's some who's hard put to get a stick of wood for the fire and a morsel of bread for a hungry mouth or six."

The queen thought of pleading with her husband, but then she realized that King Edward would only punish the servants for complaining. So she began giving her nurse jewels to sell. Then the nurse quietly gave the money to the servants who had the least, or who had the largest families, and whispered to them, even though the queen had told her not to give a hint, "This money's from the queen, you know. *She* remembers us servants, even if her husband's a lout and a pimple." And the servants remembered that the queen was kind.

The people didn't hate King Edward quite as much as the servants did, of course, because even though taxes were high, there are always silly people who are proud fit to bust when their army has a victory. And of course King Edward had quite a few victories at first. He would pick a fight with a neighboring king or lord and then march in and take over. People had thought old King Boris' army of five thousand was bad, back in the old days. But because of his high taxes, King Edward was able to hire an army of fifty thousand men, and war was a different thing then. They lived off the land in enemy country, and killed and plundered where they liked. Most of the soldiers weren't local men, anyway—they were the riffraff of the highways, men who begged or stole, and now were being paid for stealing.

But King Edward tripled the size of the kingdom, and there were a good many citizens who followed the war news and cheered whenever King Edward rode through the streets.

They cheered the queen, too, of course, but they didn't see her very much, about once a year or so. She was still beautiful, of course, more beautiful than ever before. No one particularly noticed that her eyes were sad these days, or else those who noticed said nothing and soon forgot it.

But King Edward's victories had been won against weak, and peaceful, and unprepared men. And at last the neighboring kings got together, and the rebels from conquered lands got together, and they planned King Edward's doom.

When next King Edward went a-conquering, they were ready, and on the very battlefield where King Ethelred had defeated Boris they ambushed King Edward's army. Edward's fifty thousand hired men faced a hundred thousand where before they had never faced more than half their number. Their bought courage melted away, and those who lived through the first of the battle ran for their lives.

King Edward was captured and brought back to the city in a cage, which was hung above the city gate, right where the statue of the bear is today.

The queen came out to the leaders of the army that had defeated King Edward and knelt before them in the dust and wept, pleading for her husband. And because she was beautiful, and good, and because they themselves were only good men trying to protect their own lives and property, they granted him his life. For her sake they even let him remain king, but they imposed a huge tribute on him. To save his own life, he agreed.

So taxes were raised even higher, in order to pay the tribute, and King Edward could only keep enough soldiers to police his kingdom, and the tribute went to paying for soldiers of the victorious kings to stay on the borders to keep watch on our land. For they figured, and rightly so, that if they let up their vigilance for a minute, King Edward would raise an army and stab them in the back.

But they didn't let up their vigilance, you see. And King Edward was trapped.

A dark evil fell upon him then, for a greedy man craves all the more the thing he can't have. And King Edward craved power. Because he couldn't have power over other kings, he began to use more power over his own kingdom, and his own household, and his own family.

He began to have prisoners tortured until they confessed to conspiracies that didn't exist, and until they denounced people who were innocent. And people in this kingdom began to lock their doors at night, and hide when someone knocked. There was fear in the kingdom, and people began to move away, until King Edward took to hunting down and beheading anyone who tried to leave the kingdom.

And it was bad in the palace, too. For the servants were beaten savagely for the slightest things, and King Edward even yelled at his own son and daughters whenever he saw them, so that the queen kept them hidden away with her most of the time.

Everyone was afraid of King Edward. And people almost always hate anyone they fear.

Except the queen. For though she feared him she remembered his youth, and she said to himself, or sometimes to the nurse, "Somewhere in that sad and ugly man there is the beautiful boy I love. Somehow I must help him find that beautiful boy and bring him out again."

But neither the nurse nor the queen could think how such a thing could possibly happen.

Until the queen discovered that she was going to have a baby. Of course, she thought. With a new baby he will remember his family and remember to love us.

So she told him. And he railed at her about how stupid she was to bring another child to see their humiliation, a royal family with enemy troops perched on the border, with no real power in the world.

And then he took her roughly by the arm into the court, where the lords and ladies were gathered, and there he told them that his wife was going to have a baby to mock him, for she still had the power of a woman, even if he didn't have the power of a man. She cried out that it wasn't true. He hit her, and she fell to the ground.

And the problem was solved, for she lost the baby before it was born and lay on her bed for days, delirious and fevered and at the point of death. No one knew that King Edward hated himself for what he had done, that he tore at his face and his hair at the thought that the queen might die because of his fury. They only saw that he was drunk all through the queen's illness, and that he never came to her bedside.

While the queen was delirious, she dreamed many times and

many things. But one dream that kept coming back to her was of a wolf following her in the forest, and she ran and ran until she fell, but just as the wolf was about to eat her, a huge brown Bear came and killed the wolf and flung him away, and then picked her up gently and laid her down at her father's door, carefully arranging her dress and putting leaves under her head as a pillow.

When she finally woke up, though, she only remembered that there was no magic bear that would come out of the forest to save her. Magic was for the common people—brews to cure gout and plague and to make a lady love you, spells said in the night to keep dark things from the door. Foolishness, the queen told herself. For she had an education, and knew better. There is nothing to keep the dark things from the door, there is no cure for gout and plague, and there is no brew that will make your husband love you. She told this to herself and despaired.

King Edward soon forgot his grief at the thought his wife might die. As soon as she was up and about he was as surly as ever, and he didn't stop drinking, either, even when the reason for it was gone. He just remembered that he had hurt her badly and he felt guilty, and so whenever he saw her he felt bad, and because he felt bad he treated her badly, as if it were her fault.

Things were about as bad as they could get. There were rebellions here and there all over the kingdom, and rebels were being beheaded every week. Some soldiers had even mutinied and got away over the border with the people they were supposed to stop. And so one morning King Edward was in the foulest, blackest mood he had ever been in.

The queen walked into the dining room for breakfast looking as beautiful as ever, for grief had only deepened her beauty, and made you want to cry for the pain of her exquisite face and for the suffering in her proud, straight bearing. King Edward saw that pain and suffering but even more he saw that beauty, and for a moment he remembered the girl who had grown up without a care or a sorrow or an evil thought. And he knew that he had caused every bit of the pain she bore.

So he began to find fault with her, and before he knew it he was ordereing her into the kitchen to cook.

"I can't," she said.

"If a servant can, you can," he snarled in reply.

She began to cry. "I've never cooked. I've never started a fire. I'm a queen."

"You're not a queen," the king said savagely, hating himself as he said it. "You're not a queen and I'm not a king, because we're a bunch of powerless lackeys taking orders from those scum across the border! Well, if I've got to live like a servant in my own palace, so have you!"

And so he took her roughly into the kitchen and ordered her to come back in with a breakfast she had cooked herself.

The queen was shattered, but not so shattered that she could forget her pride. She spoke to the cooks cowering in the corner. "You heard the king. I must cook him breakfast with my own hands. But I don't know how. You must tell me what to do."

So they told her, and she tried her best to do what they said, but her untrained hands made a botch of everything. She burned herself at the fire and scalded herself with the porridge. She put too much salt on the bacon and there were shells left in the eggs. She also burned the muffins. And then she carried it all in to her husband and he began to eat.

And of course it was awful.

And at that moment he realized finally that the queen was a queen and could be nothing else, just as a cook had no hope of being a queen. Just so he looked at himself and realized that he could never be anything but a king. The queen, however, was a good queen—while he was a terrible king. He would always be a king but he would never be good at it. And as he chewed up the eggshells he reached the lowest despair.

Another man, hating himself as King Edward did, might have taken his own life. But that was not King Edward's way. Instead he picked up his rod and began to beat the queen. He struck her again and again, and her back bled, and she fell to the ground, screaming.

The servants came in and so did the guards, and the servants, seeing the queen treated so, tried to stop the king. But the king ordered the guards to kill anyone who tried to interfere. Even so, the chief steward, a cook, and the butler were dead before the others stopped trying.

And the king kept beating and beating the queen until everyone was sure he would beat her to death.

And in her heart as she lay on the stone floor, numb to the

pain of her body because of the pain of her heart, she wished that the bear would come again, stepping over her to kill the wolf that was running forward to devour her.

At that moment the door broke in pieces and a terrible roar filled the dining hall. The king stopped beating the queen, and the guards and the servants looked at the door, for there stood a huge brown bear on its hind legs, towering over them all, and roaring in fury.

The servants ran from the room.

"Kill him," the king bellowed at the guards.

The guards drew their swords and advanced on the bear.

The bear disarmed them all, though there were so many that some drew blood before their swords were slapped out of their hands. Some of them might even have tried to fight the bear without weapons, because they were brave men, but the bear struck them on the head, and the rest fled away.

Yet the queen, dazed though she was, thought that for some reason the Bear had not struck yet with all his force, that the huge animal was saving his strength for another battle.

And that battle was with King Edward, who stood with his sharp sword in his hand, eager for battle, hoping to die, with the desperation and self-hatred in him that would make him a terrible opponent, even for a bear.

A bear, thought the queen. I wished for a bear and he is here.

Then she lay, weak and helpless and bleeding on the stone floor as her husband, her prince, fought the bear. She did not know who she hoped would win. For even now, she did not hate her husband. And yet she knew that her life and the lives of her subjects would be unendurable as long as he lived.

They circled around the room, the bear moving clumsily yet quickly, King Edward moving faster still, his blade whipping steel circles through the air. Three times the blade landed hard and deep on the bear, before the animal seized the blade between his paws. King Edward tried to draw back the sword, and as he did it bit deeply into the animal's paws. But it was a battle of strength, and the bear was sure to win it in the end. He pulled the sword out of Edward's hand, and then grasped the king in a mighty embrace and carried him screaming from the room.

And at that last moment, as Edward tugged hopelessly at his sword and blood poured from the bear's paws, the queen found herself hoping that the bear would hold on, would take away the sword, that the bear would win out and free the kingdom—her kingdom—and her family and even herself, from the man who had been devouring them all.

Yet when King Edward screamed in the bear's grip, she heard only the voice of the boy in the garden in the eternal and too-quick summer of her childhood. She fainted with a dim memory of his smile dancing crazily before her eyes.

She awoke as she had awakened once before, thinking that it had been a dream, and then remembering the truth of it when the pain where her husband had beaten her nearly made her fall unconscious again. But she fought the faintness and stayed awake, and asked for water.

The nurse brought water, and then several lords of high rank and the captain of the army and the chief servants came in and asked her what they should do.

"Why do you ask me?" she said.

"Because," the nurse answered her, "the king is dead."

The queen waited.

"The Bear left him at the gate," the captain of the army said.

"His neck was broken," the chief said.

"And now," one of the lords said, "now we must know what to do. We haven't even told the people, and no one has been allowed inside or outside the palace."

The queen thought, and closed her eyes as she did so. But what she saw when she closed her eyes was the body of her beautiful prince with his head loose as the wolf's had been that day in the forest. She did not want to see that, so she opened her eyes.

"You must proclaim that the king is dead throughout the land," she said.

To the captain of the army she said, "There will be no more beheading for treason. Anyone who is in prison for treason is to be set free, now. And any other prisoners whose terms are soon to expire should be set free at once."

The captain of the army bowed and left. He did not smile until he was out the door, but then he smiled until tears ran down his cheeks.

To the chief cook she said, "All the servants in the palace are free to leave now, if they want. But please ask them, in my name, to stay. I will restore them as they were, if they'll stay."

The cook started a heartfelt speech of thanks, but then

thought better of it and left the room to tell the others.

To the lords she said, "Go to the kings whose armies guard our borders, and tell them that King Edward is dead and they can go home now. Tell them that if I need their help I will call on them, but that until I do I will govern my kingdom alone."

And the lords came and kissed her hands tenderly, and left the room.

And she was alone with the nurse.

"I'm so sorry," said the nurse, when enough silence had passed.

"For what?" asked the queen.

"For the death of your husband."

"Ah, that," said the queen. "Ah, yes, my husband."

And then the queen wept with all her heart. Not for the cruel and greedy man who had warred and killed and savaged everywhere he could. But for the boy who had somehow turned into that man, the boy whose gentle hand had comforted her childhood hurts, the boy whose frightened voice had cried out to her at the end of his life, as if he wondered why he had gotten lost inside himself, as if he realized that it was too, too late to get out again.

When she had done weeping that day, she never cried for him again.

In three days she was up again, though she had to wear loose clothing because of the pain. She held court anyway, and it was then that the shepherds brought her the Bear. Not the bear, the animal, that had killed the king, but *the* Bear, the counselor, who had left the kingdom so many years before.

"We found him on the hillside, with our sheep nosing him and lapping his face," the oldest of the shepherds told her. "Looks like he's been set on by robbers, he's cut and battered so. Miracle he's alive," he said.

"What is that he's wearing?" asked the queen, standing by the bed where she had had the servants lay him.

"Oh," said one of the other shepherds. "That's me cloak. They left him nekkid, but we didn't think it right to bring him before you in such a state."

She thanked the shepherds and offered to pay them a reward, but they said no thanks, explaining, "We remember him, we do, and it wouldn't be right to take money for helping him, don't you see, because he was a good man back in your father's day."

The queen had the servants—who had all stayed on, by the way—clean his wounds and bind them and tend to his wants. And because he was a strong man, he lived, though the wounds might have killed a smaller, weaker man. Even so, he never got back the use of his right hand, and had to learn to write with his left; and he limped ever after. But he often said he was lucky to be alive and wasn't ashamed of his infirmities, though he sometimes said that something ought to be done about the robbers who run loose in the hills.

As soon as he was able, the queen had him attend court, where he listened to the ambassadors from other lands and to the cases she heard and judged.

Then at night she had him come to King Ethelred's study, and there she asked him about the questions of that day and what he would have done differently, and he told her what he thought she did well, too. And so she learned from him as her father had learned.

One day she even said to him, "I have never asked forgiveness of any man in my life. But I ask for yours."

"For what?" he said, surprised.

"For hating you, and thinking you served me and my father badly, and driving you from this kingdom. If we had listened to you," she said, "none of this would have happened."

"Oh," he said, "all that's past. You were young, and in love, and that's as inevitable as fate itself."

"I know," she said, "and for love I'd probably do it again, but now that I'm wiser I can still ask for forgiveness for my youth."

The Bear smiled at her. "You were forgiven before you asked. But since you ask I gladly forgive you again."

"Is there any reward I can give you for your service so many years ago, when you left unthanked?" she asked.

"Yes," he answered. "If you could let me stay and serve you as I served your father, that would be reward enough."

"How can that be a reward?" she asked. "I was going to ask you to do that for *me*. And now you ask it for yourself."

"Let us say," said the Bear, "that I loved your father like my brother, and you like my niece, and I long to stay with the only family that I have."

Then the queen took the pitcher and poured him a mug of ale, and they sat by the fire and talked far into the night.

* * *

Because the queen was a widow, because despite the problems of the past the kingdom was large and rich, many suitors came asking for her hand. Some were dukes, some were earls, and some were kings or sons of kings. And she was as beautiful as ever, only in her thirties, a prize herself even if there had been no kingdom to covet.

But though she considered long and hard over some of them, and even liked several men who came, she turned them all down and sent them all away.

And she reigned alone, as queen, with the Bear to advise her.

And she also did what her husband had told her a queen should do—she raised her son to be king and her daughters to be worthy to be queens. And the Bear helped her with that, too, teaching her son to hunt, and teaching him how to see beyond men's words into their hearts, and teaching him to love peace and serve the people.

And the boy grew up as beautiful as his father and as wise as the Bear, and the people knew he would be a great king, perhaps even greater than King Ethelred had been.

The queen grew old, and turned much of the matter of the kingdom over to her son, who was now a man. The prince married the daughter of a neighboring king. She was a good woman, and the queen saw her grandchildren growing up.

She knew perfectly well that she was old, because she was sagging and no longer beautiful as she had been in her youth—though there were many who said that she was far more lovely as an old lady than any mere girl could hope to be.

But somehow it never occurred to her that the Bear, too, was growing old. Didn't he still stride through the garden with one of her grandchildren on each shoulder? Didn't he still come into the study with her and her son and teach then statecraft and tell them, yes, that's good, yes, that's right, yes, you'll make a great queen yet, yes, you'll be a fine king, worthy of your grandfather's kingdom—didn't he?

Yet one day he didn't get up from his bed, and a servant came to her with a whispered message, "Please come."

She went to him and found him gray-faced and shaking in his bed.

"Thirty years ago," he said, "I would have said it's nothing but a fever and I would have ignored it and gone riding. But now, my lady, I know I'm going to die."

"Nonsense," she said, "you'll never die," knowing as well as he did that he was dying, and knowing that he knew that she knew it.

"I have a confession to make," he said to her.

"I know it already," she said.

"Do you?"

"Yes," she said softly, "and much to my surprise, I find that I love you too. Even an old lady like me," she said, laughing.

"Oh," he said, "that was not my confession. I already knew that you knew I loved you. Why else would I have come back when you called?"

And then she felt a chill in the room and remembered the only time she had ever called for help.

"Yes," he said, "you remember. How I laughed when they named me. If they only knew, I thought at the time."

She shook her head. "How could it be?"

"I wondered myself," he said. "But it is. I met a wise old man in the woods when I was but a lad. An orphan, too, so that there was no one to ask about me when I stayed with him. I stayed until he died five years later, and I learned all his magic."

"There's no magic," she said as if by rote, and he laughed.

"If you mean brews and spells and curses, then you're right," he said. "But there is magic of another sort. The magic of becoming what most you are. My old man in the woods, his magic was to be an owl, and to fly by night seeing the world and coming to understand it. The owlness was in him, and the magic was letting that part of himself that was most himself come forward. And he taught me."

The Bear had stopped shaking because his body had given up trying to overcome the illness.

"So I looked inside me and wondered who I was. And then I found it out. Your nurse found it, too. One glance and she knew I was a bear."

"You killed my husband," she said to him.

"No," he said. "I fought your husband and carried him from the palace, but as he stared death in the face he discovered, too, what he was and who he was, and his real self came out."

The Bear shook his head.

"I killed a wolf at the palace gate, and left a wolf with a

broken neck behind when I went away into the hills."

"A wolf both times," she said. "But he was such a beautiful boy."

"A puppy is cute enough whatever he plans to grow up to be," said the Bear.

"And what am I?" asked the queen.

"You?" asked the Bear. "Don't you know?"

"No," she answered. "Am I a swan? A porcupine? These days I walk like a crippled, old biddy hen. Who am I, after all these years? What animal should I turn into by night?"

"You're laughing," said the Bear, "and I would laugh too, but I have to be stingy with my breath. I don't know what animal you are, if you don't know yourself, but I think—"

And he stopped talking and his body shook in a great heave.

"No!" cried the queen.

"All right," said the Bear. "I'm not dead yet. I think that deep down inside you, you are a woman, and so you have been wearing your real self out in the open all your life. And you are beautiful."

"What an old fool you are after all," said the queen. "Why didn't I ever marry you?"

"Your judgment was too good," said the Bear.

But the queen called the priest and her children and married the Bear on his deathbed, and her son who had learned kingship from him called him father, and then they remembered the bear who had come to play with them in their childhood and the queen's daughters called him father; and the queen called him husband, and the Bear laughed and allowed as how he wasn't an orphan any more. Then he died.

And that's why there's a statue of a bear over the gate of the city.

RAISING THE GREEN LION

by Janet E. Morris

Janet Morris' writing defies description... ornate, classical, erotic, abundant, supremely intelligent, historically rich... well, one could go on indefinitely. Her perceptions are unique and the literary creations that arise from them are always compelling. "Raising the Green Lion" is her first published short work. It's a story about alchemy, a subject that's been with us since the beginning of scientific thought. But the treatment, coming from Janet Morris, is brand new...

I had come down from the Taurus Mountains to the shores of the Euphrates: fabled Carchemish. There I waited upon my master. But he did not come.

I looked out over her diminished waters, even with Sirius rising barely a knee-high trickle amid the silt of centuries at this time when the Nile to the south overruns her banks, innundates the Egyptian valley, and renews all things. Before me sprawled the sad, small village called Jerablis, clinging tight to the Euphrates' west bank; but I saw vanished Carchemish, long gone unmourned. And across the Euphrates' bed, to the east—I contrived Mitani there, where now there is nothingAh, they eat and drink and wash in the Tigris, yet. But Mitani is lost like Babylon and most glorious Memphis of the pharaohs, lost in sandstorms and rainbows. So fell the land of Thoth. So, also, fell the empire of the thousand gods of Hatti, at whose ruined quays, ground into pebbles before my mother's mother drew breath, I waited.

I had waited, too, in Egypt and Mitani, but they had not succored me as had these humping hills of the Hittite princes. Nowhere but Anatolia offered up the chance (ha, slight it seemed) and then the reality I had pursued across the world entire: I found the *sputum lunae*, the moon's spittle there, when a glob of it streaked to earth where I had come to dwell in the ghost-city of Hattusas. (Or as near to it as I could determine and conjecture myself.)

Yes, I took up residence in that vanished citadel, in what is miscalled Boghazköy near to nothing but Ankara II. In that place I built a workshop and commenced the great work. Or recommenced it, for what else have I ever done?

And when all was prepared, I sent out a missive of invitation, employing for circumspection and surety a messenger to hand-carry word to Paracelsus where he resided in Basel.

Now, you may say: Who does this fool bethink himself, to summon Paracelsus? You might label me presumption incarnate, for calling out the Master of Arcanum to attend my experiment. But I had long and well known him. I studied alchemy at his knee before the gypsies' fires, and the body's humors, when he was professor at the University of Basel. And we grew close, in those sweet years. So, when all was prepared, when I had me the mirrors and alembics, the greater sulphur, the transcendent mercury, the cucurbits and the dung and the waters and all else gathered up, I sent him word. I called him out from Basel (in which city he had fallen so deeply into ill-repute) to stand with me whilst I did what could not be done in Europe; what would have cost me my life like uncounted broasted brethren had I been found out while about it; what had been immolated in a hundred books and scourged by fear from the tongues of men: I would raise the green lion. I would raise him, and homunculus—the spirit-child—would out. That was the message I sent to my master. But he did not come.

Nor did my messenger, a certain Ibn Sinah, return to me. This man I had employed as much because his name is a corruption of the great Avicenna's and thus suited him to the task undertaken—the transmutation of just such corruption—as for any reason of faith or trust in his abilities; and I not should say I was surprised when he came not at the appointed time up the Euphrates. I was disappointed, but not disheartened. For though I find in men continual disappointment when they are posited close by, from the distance of isolation I can love all humankind with a true and compassionate heart. I had seen no one and spoken to none for three full weeks; I had faith in the spirit of my fellows, even of this Ibn Sinah who did not come.

So I looked for him, while still the moon trined Saturn, to come by way of the Mediterranean, which was the secondary route agreed between us in case of pursuit or persecution. (It seems, these days, if one does not fall afoul of one gaggle of bureaucrats, one will surely trip under the scrutiny of the next, and those papers I had altered for him, although artfully reconceived, were not flawless.) Thus, I tarried long at the seaside, shrugging off the clammy fingers of doubt.

But he appeared not from out the sea.

So I trudged the barren lands back again to Carchemish, to await word or sign when Mercury resumed his forward motion. Some might here object to my insistent reference to the diminished towns by their old names. That magnificence is gone—I know it. Do not mistake me. But, like others before me, I swim not always on the surface of the river that is time, and in the depths one may see whatever one chooses. I have always chosen to hunt in the past. If it seems a flaw in my nature, let it seem so. Through this persistent device of mine, much has been revealed.

What was revealed that night in the currents that make up the torrent of the ancients: though I stood far north from Egypt, she was all about me. The night-sky became the old goddess, Nut, there on those elder shores. Nor was that all I saw. I glimpsed the bark of Ra—asil there; the moon became its lantern; for a moment even I saw the beauteous face of Hathor shining out, recruiting souls for the western journey to the realm of the dead, that journey she has sailed and will continue to sail, as they say it still in Egypt, for millions of millions of years. Sinking down amid the reeds, by my mare who snorted softly in the dark, I strove to shake off their touch:

"The thousand gods of Hatti are benevolent," said I to the lonely gods of Egypt, "but this is their land and not your own. Get you back to the Black Land, which is yours without question. I must be free of symbols, each and every one." Yes, I talk to gods. And rocks and trees, and most frequently, my mare. A man, denying himself the converse of his own kind, comes to such maunderings with age. And I felt my age that night, as I struggled to do what I must, and divest myself of all symbolic influence, as one should when embarked upon such a quest as mine. I sought an end far beyond knowledge and it was a dalliance unsafe that I indulged in under the Euphrates' gibbous moon. And, if the truth be known, indulge in still: Egypt ever draws me.

But I had tried to work there, and accomplished nothing. And by my failure I had come to a realization. The feat I attempted could not be undertaken in Egypt. Though it was the logical choice, though Hermes' Smaragdine tablet, written there, bequeathed us both law and name, Egypt would not suit.

I had traveled further: in the vanished gardens of Akkad and Sumer, I had sought to no avail. The Syrian plain proved barren. Lastly, I went up into the mountains that birth both Tigris and Euphrates where I had had, from the outset, success...

Thus I recollected it, near the whole of my life, while the Euphrates cooled my calloused soles and lapped muttering around my ankles, and a hand came down on my shoulder, hard with a grip of lead. In that forbidding moment, as I realized I had been stealthed upon, I thought it even the skeletal hand of Osiris, reaching out from the underworld to toss me into the bark of the moon. Then I rose up, quaked inside, and yet calm of limb.

To face him who had now removed hand from me and stood quiet, unmoving ghost in a dark, shapeless robe with pack slung over. Twice risen shade, he seemed: him who I had summoned and not him at all; my master's image, but as it was twenty years gone, young and vital.

How great an adept, he?

"Paracelsus... Theos...." I gasped, creakily retreating until the Euphrates washed my calves.

"Paracelsus is dead," said the youthful traveler, smoothing dust-dark robes and slipping head from hood in a serpent's sinuous shrug.

Then he held out his hand.

"Dead?" mouthed I.

"Come out from there, lest Hapi have you for dinner," he advised in that voice which had so long belonged to my mentor. Still much perturbed, I did so, scrambling bereft of dignity up the bank, omitting even notice of his mistaking the mother Nile's attribute, that of the crocodile, and misplacing it to Carchemish on the Euphrates.

"Yes, dead," said he, and this time I took that long-fingered hand in mine. As we clasped I saw, dulled but clear enough in the moonlight, the sign of the god Khepera, the scarab of green stone set into a ring of gold on his middle finger. "Dead by treachery," the stranger continued, as if we were old friends whose bond lay not in doubt. "Pushed from a high window by a servant of one of the Basel physicians. That league of bleeders, scribblers and scullions—" The grimace that twisted his countenance filled his short silence more eloquently than any words. "—I will not name names. Enough be it known to you that those he so incensed with his theses of the permutations of disease have rid themselves of him in the very manner with which he enjoined them to treat the sick: they banished him from the body of physicians—yea, they found the specific for him and they cast him out, not only from their lives which he plagued, but from all of life."

By this time I had my feet on rock and sand, and my arse also, for his words stripped me of what little composure I yet possessed after the start this meeting had precipitated. We, all hermetists, must need fear the stranger. I not least of all, for my life has been aforetime forfeit to those catholic souls who say who lives or dies; only have they not yet caught me. But they had caught Paracelsus.

I sat in the sand with my hands over my eyes, one with my mentor as he hurtled groundward from the house's high floor. I shared his thoughts, last thoughts: a second for the sum of his life; tumbling, fear bright; speedy conjecture as to what might follow this final communion with the earth; and lastly the ground, coming to meet. I groaned aloud, not caring if this wearer-of-Khepera saw my grief, yet at one and the same time taking comfort in shadow's compassionate gift: Nut's skirts blew over the lantern of the moon and the night grew dark as a soul's sight from the belly of the Devourer.

A thousand horrors rustled wings of conjecture about my ears. Was he some man of the church, bound to bring me back to their sham of God's judgment? An interceptor of my message? So foolish to have sent a thing on paper . . . Ah, paper. We will write it down, again and again, dying therefrom like an insidiously selective pestilence.

I straightened my shoulders, grasping a weary strength. I would not huddle before my doom, if doom it was, but wait with grace . . .

A time passed, during which I heard the rustle of his garments as he sat, then only that slow and particular respiration adepts sometimes employ when seeking deeper for the light.

I found myself following that suggestion unspoken, and by it gained back what composure I had lost. Here no law reigned but what a man could make. If friend, I would succor him; if foe, I would slit him with surgeon's precision from gullet to member. I touched an instrument I carry always, in case of need, that has healed a hoard of infidels, removed a hundred abnormal growths. I obtained a semblance of quiet, within myself.

How long we sat that way, breathing the meter of the spheres' respiration, I cannot even conjecture. Long. Until it occurred to me to wonder who this personage, so much the image of Paracelsus, might be. The ring he bore, and no other, fit the alchemical model: it is recommended in a dozen elder texts. His manner, too, was learned within the comportment of the old doctrines. If he had been a church henchman, would he not have spoken out, by now? Grabbed me roughly, cursed me all about, and tried to turn me to ashes by sticking a cross in my face? These thoughts heartened me, and I risked the riddle of recognition, saying:

"What shall be done with the dragon?"

To which he replied, in perfect form: "Sacrifice it, flay it, separate the flesh from the bones, and you will find what you seek."

Thus I determined him no warrior of the church. But caution, ever caution, in such things as these. Up in the night, an eagle sounded, and by my side the wearer-of-Khepera toyed with his ring. And it seemed, as I met his eyes, that they sparkled preternaturally bright with some all-knowing humor. So I tested him further, with words from the Smaragdine authored by Hermes, whose wily smile he displayed, "It is true, without lies and quite certain: what is lower is just like what is higher, and what is higher is just like what is lower, for the accomplishment of the miracle of the thing."

And he rejoined, without error: "And just as all things come from one and by the mediation of one, thus all things have been derived from this one thing by adoption. *Pater ejus est Sol, mater ejus est Luna.*"

Whereupon I found no need to further interrogate him, but asked plainly, "Who are you, and how came you here?"

"You do not know me?" He laughed aloud, a soft crackling sound like flames about their business. "I am his bastard son, born out of the dung heap. You, of all men, I would have thought, need not ask. Surely he spoke to you of me."

At that disclosure, I too laughed, and shook my head. Paracelsus had never spoken to me of his indiscretions nor me to him of mine; our mutual tangle brought danger enough to both. The boy bore his father's stamp more strongly the closer I peered. In the scudding light, I caught traces of Turkoman, or perhaps gypsy; but no sign of faun or giant, as would have been the case if he were homunculus-who-is-born-from-putrefaction, to which he alluded. Now men, I have found, are oft sensitive when their parentage is doubtful. I decided to press him no further than he wished to go. He resembled his father; he came bearing news of him. I was not in the business of preparing geneologies, but of preparing the *materia prima*. If Paracelsus chanced upon the tincture of soul he so avidly sought through pederasty and the gates of Sodom in the embrace of a woman—so be it! The boy was a perfect replica of his father: the eyes, dark-sparking obsidian under brows that wrapped them in shadow; those shoulders, overlarge and hunched, spare with circumspection and the weight of the World Egg which seemed to rest thereupon. The moon, as if in agreement, shook herself free of clouds and illuminated him bright and clear. Truly, Paracelsus had begotten himself anew through this bastard manchild.

So I said gently to the waiting youth, "I have not spoken with your father for many years, but I do recall vaguely a mention of you, or at least of whom you profess to be. My memory, I am afraid, loses daily the sharpness of its edge." Thus I did not lie, nor call him liar, and yet voiced the reservation of my intuition. "Your name, however, escapes me, which is just as well, for I doubt that you would still use it . . ." I let my voice trail off, regarding him with inclined head, that he have time to choose between the part-truths that must serve between alchemists. I did not delude myself that he would entrust to me his given name, any more than would I, to a stranger, no matter how well recommended. I, myself have borne so many names that I have trouble now recalling which was first . . . it is the nature of the work in which I am engaged, and a process common to us all.

But he surprised me, in that as in all else. Rising, he stretched, and the moonlight spilled down his robe as if he stood in a waterfall.

"I have taken the name Set, most recently. At birth my father gave me his chosen name, and Aureolus, also. So, as you see, you really have a great choice in calling me."

At that I took his arm and headed him toward the mud-hovel paucity of sleeping Jerablis.

"How did you choose 'Set'?" I asked, turning him toward my tent, erected well before the village. How, indeed? The brother of Horus, headed with an animal visage unknown to man, whose realm is that of the dead, was not a god with whom I was unfamiliar.

He did not immediately answer, so I asked again.

"That is too long a tale for now," he said at last. "I have been some few years in the Nile valley, and in Baghdad. I served a short span as physician to Suleiman the Great." The voice came soft, as if from a distance far greater than between two men who rubbed shoulders on a narrow riparian path in the dark. "The man Set is safe among the River-Arabs and the Kurds."

"But not now in Persia," I hazarded.

"No, not now, with the new war there."

At my urging, we left the path, skirting the bull-reeds and two groups of tents tense set there, coming from the rear to the one I had pitched on the outcropping sedges where the riverbank takes a great undulation.

We crackled our way toward it, and the horse I had staked out snorted and stamped and tossed her head, mane flaring silver.

"Are you always so cautious?" asked Set.

"I like a sleep that is easy, this close to men." The high, brittle reeds that surrounded my camp were a protection I have often used, as ever I try to use what nature affords me.

I went to the beast, and soothed her, calling the traveler close. But the mare gave off a great, belly-shaking warning and lunged back against her tether, and when I turned again from stroking that quivering neck I saw the silhouette of my guest disappearing under the tent flaps.

Long into the night we talked. Set spoke of Basel and how he had come to be there, and of Suleiman's treaty with Francis, and what that might mean, with all the astuteness of a court strategist. In my isolation on the Anatolian plateau, I had heard little such news; the Black Sea was my butler to the north, the Anti-Taurus my eastern barred gate, and the precipitous drop from the Taurus to the Mediterranean at my rear served me as a moat whose bridge was ever drawn up.

I recall his sunken sockets, underlit the more deeply by the candle's flame, which danced too in his throat, making it jump and twitch as if some creature tore and beat toward freedom from within. Set's hands, never still, had fingers as gracefully formed as a musician's; not acid-gnarled, but unscarred and without callus, as might be some noble's who had never need to do work and could afford the luxury of nails grown as long as a pinky's joint. But those words he spoke, those have fled from me.

This I do recall: long after his regular breathing by my side told me he slept I lay troubled by this man who came stirring up my mind with affairs from which I had sought surcease; not the least of these being his father's death, and his resemblance to that man who among all others I had loved. His youthful beauty, covetousness of which now would destroy me more surely than landslide or spitting volcano, hovered before my tight-closed eyes. So I spent long freeing my mind of him, who resembled far too much his sire. And yet, I entertained no hesitancy at taking him in, this son of Paracelsus. Nor would I hold back from him access to or participation in my work.

What he had told me had bound me more than simple decision. He had had word from Paracelsus, about me and my message, and had been ready to depart eastward to my aid, stopping only to say his farewells. Nor had he managed to say them, except in the silence of his own mind. He had seen his father fall by happenstance while awaiting him for a clandestine meeting in the adjacent park. And he had sat, unmoving, knowing that to rush to that crumpled form's side would be an implication in his sire's affairs that Paracelsus had gone to great lengths to avoid.

"Thus it is with us, each one. We are, more than any other men, alone. Think differently, and an affair such as this comes to teach an ungentle reminder." I had said it, perhaps too gruffly, had blown out the candle. But his ordeal deeply touched me, the more for the brevity and objectivity with which he related it. Son of my master, I will aid you in all things, I said to myself and to him in my mind, while sliding into sleep.

Therein I dreamt a dream surpassing strange, and while I lay trying to recollect it, I opened my eyes. And snapped bolt upright, for he was gone. And the shock of that drove the dream-fragments from my mind, leaving only the barest trace of the awe and revelation they had held.

I sat then quite still, chasing the dream. But I could not overtake it, what with the loss and confusion rattling around in my brain. I sought the meaning of these feelings. Why should I feel deserted, I who am solitary by choice? What meaning resided in this concern for a traveler just-met, who might, after all, not even be who he claimed to be? Bleakly I considered him. I am a recluse by nature and need, and had until that time taken a certain pride in my hard-won distance from the doings of men. Why, then, these emotions? Despairing of finding an answer, I set about the task of banishing these thoughts of companionship. But instead of less, the loneliness grew more. As I collapsed the tent and packed it upon the mare, I rationalized it: I had not asked him of Ibn Sinah, my messenger, nor of Paracelsus' most recent work. Ah, I found a dozen questions, each of most demanding import, that I had failed to put to him in those brief moments we had spent together.

It was upon these unanswered queries I hung my thoughts, as if I could cure myself of them like mouldered laundry that turns sweet-smelling when subjected to a day in the sun.

But not the sun, though it was bright as the mare's ruddy coat, nor the trail I took toward Hattusas warmed me. I was haunted by the disappearance of young Set at every turn. It was my soul, rather than the day which was overcast, but such a chill is no less numbing. Each decision became a trial, every fork of road boasted him lurking just out of sight on the rejected way. If he were with me, I might have gone by way of Malatya and shown him the stone lion there, I thought, as I took instead the Marash trail that winds between the Taurus and Anti-Taurus ranges like some embroidery thread vaulting perpendicular guides. This trail, my favorite of all those I had explored, winds over the black skirts of the old volcano just below the Halys River's most southerly meanderings. It has beauty, but the beauty of the austere, of that which has bent but not broken beneath the years' heavy tread. But if he had been at my side, I would have played guide and detoured greatly to show him the incised cliffs that bring this historic land to breathing life. And we would have talked of formulae and fitness, and the nature of the thing to be done...

By midday I was sour and distressed, not to mention chafed and slipping about in sweat-slicked sandals burred with grit. Not often had I trekked in midsummer below my beloved plateau, here where the humidity trades winds with the sapping summer heat, and all is parched and yet weeping at once.

"Is this good enough for you?" I demanded querulously of my mare.

She was too wise in the ways of men to make an objection, but only blinked and snorted a soft assent. So I sank down on the spot, without even a rock to rest my back upon, to wait out the sun's fiercest hour.

Now, I might not have done that—sat myself down in the middle of the road—had I not been filled to overflowing with a self-condemnation the like of which I had not felt since my student days. Anger, disgust, even distrust of my own reason, had all the morning assailed me, so much so that I felt an almost savage joy in my body's complaints and the day's furious heat. Those feelings described above may seem all too familiar to you, but they were not so to me. Nor were they acceptable, by those rules with which I had long honed my will.

It was with the dourest heart, less than an hour later, that I led the mare onward, growling at her uncomplaining, sad-eyed acquiescence. We retraced the conquerors' path from Carchemish toward Hattusas, quitting the Euphrates' bank completely. Pushing myself beyond all reason, I made twenty miles due west before I consented to make camp. And then, I told myself, it was for the mare's sake I rested, and not my own.

That night I fasted in the open, unwilling to make use of the tent though I had raised it. Instead, I sat the whole night through with my back against the rocks where I had tethered the beast; not unmindful of snakes, who often make their homes in such places, but uncaring.

Come the dawn, I broke my fast with water, and though my limbs were stiff, my mind was smooth and empty, the requisite lightness of spirit recaptured, at least in part.

But somehow I was not even pleased with this success, and refrained from food or rest that day also. Only when the Taurus loomed all huge and purpled on my right and left, and Marash glowed faint upon the horizon did I make camp, this time in one of those miniature valleys that lie between the ridged furrows of the Taurus foothills.

After, in a fit of contrition, I rubbed the horse until she snorted with pleasure and closed her eyes tight shut, until my arms ached and trembled so that I knew I must this night break fast. It is a nine-day trek from Carchemish to my mountain stronghold, and it was clear to me by my body's complaints that if I attempted to pass the next seven as I had journeyed for the last two, I would not make it. An ascetic too enfeebled to fast is like a eunuch posted in a seraglio, capable of recollecting intellectually a joy to which the flesh is expatriate.

Upon that thought, I laughed and the mare swiveled an ear to the bitter sound. But I heeded her not, just took the cheese and dried fruit I had left, and a sack of Halys water, and lugged them to a stand of sycamore. As I forced my way through the brush a pheasant family made hasty retreat. And I was sorry that I had disturbed them, until I saw the fox's glowing eyes.

The brush and trees ended abruptly, opening into a circular clearing, sea-seeming in the dusk, of high grass. The provisions I carried tumbled from nerveless fingers as I picked from the shadows what resided therein. And I blinked twice, and rubbed my eyes, as the figure waved me greeting.

Rising up from the rocks that centered this curious meadow, it crossed the distance in a floating gait.

"I had not thought to find you so simply," said Set with that enigmatic slow smile, sweeping up my dropped sack with a flourish. "We will see the moon eaten up together, then."

I nodded, and followed him meekly as if it were I who was the student, he the teacher. Indeed, the moon would this night be swallowed up by the shade of the earth. Most portentous of evenings, if one believes the teachings of Sumer's vanished astrologers.

"I must apologize for my precipitous leavetaking," said he, as we came close to the rocks and I saw the sheltered fire built between them, burning low.

"Rather your lack of one," I said, more sourly than I meant. "You are forgiven. Where were you bound in such haste?" Was it relief I felt at this unexpected reunion, or something else?

"Outbound," said cryptic Set, sinking down before the embers to renew them with fresh branches. As he spoke, he poked among them with a long, straight stick. "I have carried the discipline of not speaking in daylight hours for some time, now. This eclipse ends that exercise.

"Since I had not told you, you see," he continued, "I could not tell you. But I left you a message."

"I found no letter," I disclaimed, castigating him like an old wife, aware, yet unable to stop.

He was peering up at me, head twisted round. To hide my confusion, I folded my legs under me and sat, repeating: "I found no letter from you."

"I left none, but rather a pair of signs scraped in the dirt. It does not matter." He smiled disarmingly, and from behind him out of the darkness drew a plucked carcass, heretofore a pheasant, and with a straight stick ran it through.

"What did the signs say?" I asked, as much to keep from telling him I did not eat flesh as because I wished that information. Somehow, I would stomach the bird. Somehow, I must. I shook my head at the compulsion come upon me, this urgent need not to offend my strange companion, no matter what service he might require.

"The signs said that I would rejoin you," he answered at last, with a grunt that signified that the bird was spitted above the fire, and both carcass and blaze performed to his satisfaction. "See, we shall transmute the life of the bird's flesh by fire, not once, but twice," he added, looking up from under his brows as if we shared some precious secret about which he had just made a joke.

"Twice?"

"Twice: once on the outer, by this flame here, and once on the inner, by this flame here," and he pointed to his breast.

I chuckled, mirthless, and leaned back out of the flames' unveiling, where my disquiet might pass unnoticed. But it grew like the fire as he tended it, and spurted up with his words like the fat that dripped from the roasting bird into the blaze.

"See, it begins," and I followed his pointing arm upward to sight the moon as she began to diminish, only half-hearing this Set's delicate discourse on the nature of the universe. He had been speaking for some time when a biblical reference, like a wasp's sting, caught my attention.

"In Corinthians, it says that there are celestial bodies and bodies terrestrial . . . there is one glory of the sun, and another glory of the moon. In Poland is a certain Kopernik, who is a canon of the church, and yet has dared heresy postulating that the sun, and not our earth, is the center of things."

I could not repress a snort of derision. "Then how would the astrology function? How does it prognosticate what is to come?" Pedantry in youth, I thought privately, is always unbecoming. Corinthians, indeed.

"Does it?" Set queried, sharply. "To my mind, astrology lies suspect. Does it prognosticate, or do we, in calculating the apparent motion of the stars, as in so many other things, sublimate our inherent, inherited wisdom, that we may read our own minds thereby?"

He lay back, eyes upon the heavens, where the moon was half eaten up. "I have seen a copy of this Kopernik's work, which is not yet published. Let me assure you, as far as it goes, it is right. By fire, man can trace the truth . . . the earth has no fire without, but only within. The moon's fire is but a reflected grace. You say you have the moon's spittle. Is this true?"

That snapped me about, from the aversion of face I had found needful to keep silent at this youthful pontificating. My secret—then I remembered that I had said as much in my letter to his father. "Yes, I have it."

"And if it were star-stuff, like the sun, do you think you could have caught it up? Or held it? The fire in the moon, like the earth and your flesh, lies within. With the stars and the sun, the opposite may be easily observed."

I wondered what he would have said to the Mutakallimun denial of causality, in which Will recreates the discontinuous world anew in every successive instant of time in a lawless universe shaped only by habit.

"I agree not at all. But I see why you forsook the courts of Europe for these more placid environs," I said, sardonically. "With a tongue like that, you would do the gallows dance forthwith. Paracelsus did you no favor, making you the inheritor of his incontinent speech." I remembered the time Theos had publicly burned the works of Avicenna and Galen, and declared himself the master of physics. So much like him, was this youth, so much . . . I swallowed my grief. If I had had such a son, I would have consigned him to the Eastern schools, as Paracelsus wisely did, lest his radical ideas buy him an early grave.

"Surely, my words are safe with you," protested Set, conciliatory, propping his head on a crooked arm. "If you would raise the green lion, you should hearken, else my father's last wish in sending me to you will go ungranted. There are dangers—"

"The basilisk?" I interrupted, for of what else could the boy be speaking, but that terrible monster? "I fear it not. The evil beast comes only to those who seek him and what powers for selfish gain he affords. I have purified mind and body repeatedly, in the fashion recommended by the old texts. I have no fear, not of him nor of any other thing."

"I do not know if such fearlessness is as wise a thing as you seem to think it. Bravery is at best a flimsy shield, and none at all when it does not stand on caution's foundation. If I were without fear of such powers, I would not speak my thoughts aloud."

"And who is here to overhear, but you?" I snarled, sitting up, the sky's spectacle forgotten.

"Those who are concerned, they will hear. Those ears are everywhere." And he also was sitting now, staring concertedly toward me. "All of nature has a relation. You seek to alter that relation in regards to yourself. You seek exemption. You may find something else. By the spark of ambition you would light a conflagration which you are not prepared to quench. My father—" He broke off, and set to feeding his cookfire.

There ensued a lengthy silence, scion of such parlous converse, which I broke with great effort, for the boy obviously regretted his words. To my first attempts, his response was only a nod or shake of the head. His countenance he kept averted.

So I went around the fire where I might see him, but saw only a fire-contrived mask that slithered and changed like some water-nymph's visage in a sunset pool.

"Set, a man who sees his hand before his face cannot close his eyes to the appendage because the church says men have no hands. Integrity, at least within the self, must be preserved. A man must try. Your father tried. I try. The world lies on the brink of the deepest chasm in civilization's history, one from which she may never emerge. All about is darkness. Homunculus might save us, could the green lion be raised. If such a power is brought into the world, then perhaps the light of truth and the freedom of inquiry that is its guiding spirit may not be forever quenched."

"Fine words. Like many others. Have you thought that you might give poor homunculus a task too arduous, too weighty for his strength?" Bitter, sounded Set. Too bitter. "And I question your assumption: What makes you think that they are not raised already, homunculus and basilisk both? How do you know that those powers have not lent their strength to what you call 'darkness'? Or even if this darkness deserves such an inimical label? What is darkness, but a hiatus between lights?"

His words caused me to pause. The youth was deadly serious, obviously troubled. I watched him, pondering this, as he absently poked among the flames.

"It is said that your father raised the spirit-child. I have heard it from a dozen sources."

"I have heard it said," Set agreed, cutting into the spitted bird. From the incision blood dripped onto the flames, smoke rose, and the youth, coughing, straightened up.

"Do you believe that he did so?" I asked.

"I do," came Set's voice, from the silhouette which had turned away.

"And that he discovered the secret of eternal life—that, too, is rumored. Do you say that he did such a thing?" I demanded, my stomach constricted, my breath of a sudden so dry the words emerged rough-formed and raspy.

Set chuckled slyly. "In the end, he found it. In death, where it lies awaiting. But not otherwise. You see, he did not learn to fly. The bird is cooked." This last, sharply spoken, ended all conversation for the nonce.

When the repast was done, he having eaten with relish and I, untasting, gulping down roasted meat while trying valiantly to ignore the creatureness of what I consumed, he gathered up the uncooked liver and carried it to the edge of the encircling copse. Following, stiff and saddened at this vengeful silence my questioning of him had evoked, I wondered at the nature of this new, most perplexing behavior on the part of Paracelsus' son. If not for the love I still bore for his father, I would have dissociated myself then and there from him. And I considered that, taking for excuse his dangerously argumentive manner, and decided that I might yet do it at some later date.

Just within the trees he crouched down, hissing me quiet, and motioned that I should kneel down beside. There we stayed, until my calves ached from the strain, until the moon shone full in rebirth, lighting the world once more with her deceptive monochrome.

When I was sore tempted to break the silence, as if he had read my mind he whispered: "Look," and held out the liver to the forest. It was then that I first detected the luminous eyes, even as the fox, with a tiny sound, began his slow-motion advance, mouth open, saliva dripping from lolling tongue.

"I am that fox," I thought to myself as it approached, cringing the whole time, unable to resist the lure of the liver, yet terrified of the hand which offered it up. It stopped, momentarily, and cried, as if it could reason away this upsurge of senseless bravery. After what seemed hours, whining, it came to crouch before Set, black muzzle raised, so near I could see the hairs in its ears sway with the breeze.

Then I realized that Set was crooning to it, so soft a sound that the forest leaves might have birthed it. The fox's ears twitched, it gave one last distraught wail, and snatched the morsel from Set's hand.

The crooning ceased, the youth sat back, and the fox, freed of compulsion, liver gripped firmly between its teeth, was gone into the brush so fast that I had only a glimpse of its white-tipped tail.

"Who are you, truly, and what is this you do?" I wondered, though until he made answer I did not realize I had asked aloud.

And he, turning toward me, took the moon's light and launched a bolt from his eyes that skewered my brain clear through.

"I have told you. I am Set, brother and opposite of Horus, befriender of the living and of the dead, prince of predators, son of Nut, possessor of night and netherworld." He raised a finger to his lips, smiling, and the scarab he wore shimmered.

"One morning you are a good Christian quoting Corinthians, the next you feed liver to a fox. I have no more patience for the one than the other," I muttered, shaking away the chilly spell and cautiously stretching cramped calves that I might stand. The youth did not follow my lead.

"Divination by liver is not uncommon."

"And what did you divine?" I retorted, not caring, but rather struggling within between the superstitious awe come to enwrap me and that pragmatic scientificism I had so long and arduously cultivated. The savage, I am loathe to report, won out over the scientist. "No more riddles, supposed son of Paracelsus. Your father, though free in his relations, would not have mated with Nut, even if she exists, which I doubt. And—" Having stopped, to unclench my fists before nails got blood from my palms, I turned away.

"And what of the ring, you would ask. I will tell you, old man, but you will like it little." He finished, voice soft in my ear, that question I had left unasked.

"Yes!" I snapped, whirling on him amid the moonlight and the tall grass. "Tell me. And why I have been plagued with you, at this moment in my life?"

He stood stock-still, not avoiding my close scrutiny, and smiled.

"You have been plagued with me, as you put it, because you would raise the green lion. I told you before, you have a great choice in calling me. Do not make ill of it, lest you end like my father.

"Why the ring, which is so coveted by your kind: I sat thirty days between the paws of the noseless Gizeh sphinx. At the end of that time, a sandstorm scoured the land, and when it was done this stone"—here he raised the ring toward the moonlight—"lay uncovered before me. As has been conjectured, it is the key to the Akashic records. I put it to use in the lock for which it was intended, and spent a time of no duration, student to the ibis-visaged god. When I came out from Khafre's paws, and back into the realm of the living, I recollected what I had learned."

"Which was?"

"That I am the duality that resides in all things; the Rebis; the red of man and the white of woman transmuted and changed.

The underworld of Set and the rebirth of Khepera are but dissimilar expressions of the same principle."

And I accepted this, as I thought it an account of his initiation into the elder mysteries, which I had tried and failed to obtain from the insular Copts, and moreover an attempt to secure from me some measure of respect; an admission of equality, perhaps, that might span the differences our relative ages engendered. I shook my head, and smiled faintly.

"And what has all this to do with luring foxes from their lairs, and divination by livers?" I let rest his claim of sonship to the old goddess, as any man of sense might have. But with difficulty, for of all he had said it disturbed me most, especially the amused look he had given me when I refuted it. And I entertained shame, that I might have, even for an instant, toyed with reading truth into such obvious allegory. Of all that I herein recount, it is this conversation that has haunted me most diligently, has laid waste to my hours and devoured my reason, unrelenting through the years, making me doubt both the succedent events and my memories thereof.

But at that time it seemed all too real, realer than real, in the manner some events have of stretching themselves out in time and space, becoming minutes of bejeweled significance that one turns this way and that in the light ever afterwards, seeking more and more from those depths which never offer up the same meaning twice . . .

"From the fox," Set confided, "I have learned that violence has befallen your works in their place and that, despite this, you will gain what you seek. And from the liver, I have learned that you do not know me, nor even that—as my father deduced—salt is the key."

"Salt?"

"Salt," said he positively, turning me by a pressure on my arm back toward the rocks between which the fire burned.

I considered this, and by that means subtracted from his person most of the supernatural mist I had begun to see about him. For nothing could befall "my works in their place": I had brought them with me.

And then, asudden, I shook his grip from my arm and raced through the wood, back the way I had come, until I found my mare where I had tethered her. Pressing my face against her neck, gasping for breath, I realized that my hands were shaking.

And I chastized myself heartily as I took up her halter and led her carefully through the brush.

I was greeted by his low laughter, which I ignored while I retethered her near to the fire.

"Come see," said Set, when I was done. I went, despite the unconcealed amusement in his voice.

In the ashen ground about the blaze he had drawn symbols: that of Saturn, that of Mercury, and the bisected circle which represents salt among us. And beneath it he scratched a number with his charred stick, and beneath the cross-stemmed triangle that represents sulphur another, and under the circle-headed cross of quicksilver still one more.

And I was drawn in by these, into a conversation upon proportion and temperature, on methods of refining and purification. This science that we did there was welcome as cooling balm to my heart; the rational process being the antidote Set provided for the poisonous reaction his previous obscurity had catalyzed in my mind. And it worked, for as we discussed what lay beneath symbol and soothsaying, I felt again loving and protective, willing to give whatever I might to the sustenance of this young brain, so clear and sharp and full of promise, that Paracelsus had bequeathed into my care.

As I corrected him in mathematics, gently, and followed behind him on the path of his father's knowledge, the nature of the key he had called salt became clear. On this point, he would give no ground. The salt of the lake near Hattusas would not do, nor the salt refined from the earth in Egypt, nor any other but that salt Paracelsus had sent him to procure. Far beyond the land of the Ethiops, beyond the domain of the Nubians: deep into Africa he had trekked to find it, so he said, to bring it here to me.

And I objected that it was late in the process to add any single ingredient. As for everything else, the youth had an answer for that: I had not read his father's treatise, *De natura rerum*. And I had not. We had been both still stumbling about in the dark of the old texts when politics and prudence had driven me from his side and out from Europe, to seek answers in Sumer, in Akkad, and from the close-mouthed Copts who still spoke of Egypt as Kemet and recalled her in her power.

Out from under his robe he brought the tiny box, of white alabaster lined with lead and edged with gold. And he opened it briefly, that I might peek within and see the strange salt there, black yet glittering in the flames' light. He closed it up straight away, and bound the box round again with hooked bands of iron. Then he solemnly offered it out to me.

With that gift, all my resistance dissolved, as if the mere act of gazing on the black crystals within had transformed me as Set projected they would enliven the inert materials out of which I sought to produce the green lion.

Now the green lion, once birthed, must be slain, for he is the dragon of symbol, the serpent that bites his own tail on all the steles of Egypt. He must be slain and made red, made male if you will, and then what is left may be shaped and formed into what the creator desires. And I desired, greatly, homunculus. I had tried Avicenna's formulae, the process in which the male, which he calls the Dog of Armenia, and the female, which he names the Bitch of Carascene, are put together in a vessel... And indeed, as he predicted, they had bitten each other horribly. But only to death, not beyond, did those serpents go. I spoke of this to Set, and he quoted me words I had not heard from his father's dead mouth, words that have never left me, or fallen like all else into doubt. Words that raised up that desire for homunculus until it was a great conflagration, and in those flames I saw the green lion go red. But not by the offices of science... no, not that way.

I looked into that youthful face whilst the flames caressed it, and within me rustled feelings that I had pronounced vanquished long ago, speaking their subtle seductions despite all my knowledge of the danger of the thing envisioned.

A thing that may not be done, when it is about to occur, masquerades in all manner of tempting garb, and on that night it whispered that only flesh's union could cement the bond necessary if we were together to undertake this audacious task... You must know how desire twists truth and takes its seeming, and all of mind's protections defect and become persuasive inquisitors in the intelligence of passion... His lips, softened and swollen by the firelight, were fascinating beyond description; far more so than the words they shaped. But I nodded and grunted and agreed, lest he cease speaking and I lose the chance to watch and dream waking dreams.

In my sleeping dreams, troubled by the incontinence of fantasies never to be given over into action, I paid a price. Therein I was repentant and anguished, and did penance before

I left. An old man's tears are never easy, for all that has gone before comes out with them and turns water to acid upon the cheeks. And to wake weeping... But I bore it, only half-knowing it for what it was: a precognition. I bore it as I have borne all else that because of this journey has come to befall me as my just harvest from the sowings of lust.

Awakening and not seeing him by my side did not help.

As I was about to depart that place I spied the alabaster box, lying on a flat rock. And beside it, scratched in soot, lay the symbol for Set and the alchemical one of salt. This reminder, sharp and sweet and full of recrimination, I took with me. With those hands of mine shaking, I snatched it up. It nestled in my palm like an eagle's egg in the gnarled grasp of an ancient tree. What thoughts had he of me, this Set? Had my weakness, so carefully and painfully cloaked, shone through clear enough to drive him off? Suitor of children, was I in his sight? And yet, as I recalled it, the encounter had been rather the opposite, with him the active—but oh, so subtle—seducer, and I like some woman full of excuses and disclaimers of what my body made evident.

Repeatedly, as I dissembled the camp, I reexamined what had (and had *not*) passed between us. I viewed myself harshly, with repugnance, and him with regretful wonderings as to how I might have appeared in his sight.

"Do you think I drove him off?" I demanded of the mare as I fitted the last of her harness. No reply.

"And if I did, what of it? One can not raise the green lion swaddled in lust. Rationalizations, he called that. I have led a life of abstinence, only to have a junior clerk call it rationalization!" The mare, backing from my angry tone, rolled her eyes.

"It is the denial of flesh for the strengthening of spirit that I am about. Not man nor woman nor horse will shake me from it!" So I exclaimed, fiercely, to her. In answer, she bowed her head in shame, and with those huge liquid eyes demurely lowered, nickered an assurance that it was not she who would so tempt me away from the path of light.

So, as before, I set off toward Hattusas alone, leading my chastised mare. After an hour or so I took pity on her, who took an anger she did not understand and had not provoked upon herself.

On pretense of helping her negotiate the road which the whole way to Marash is a humped-up cart-track, I walked beside her, close, an arm thrown up on her neck. Her ears turned back to the sound of my voice, and at appropriate moments, she whickered assent to my monologue:

"Everyone seeks his philosopher's stone, wouldn't you say? Then you do agree, good. But mine, you must realize, is an urgent goal, not a point toward which to strive simply to provide an excuse for motion, though there is nothing wrong in that. No, the raising of the green lion is not so simple."

I looked at her, askance, then continued, content to have her full attention. "Ever since the Mohammedans, two hundred years ago—perhaps even as long ago as the birth of Christ—the world has undergone a gradual squeezing of experience. Suleiman is a good example of this urge to destroy all that does not fit the preferred model of the universe. Those who planted the tree of knowledge, I am sure, never envisioned such a pruning. The life of the tree itself is in danger. I fear this ever-narrowing spiral of lesser and lesser freedoms in thought which once had for its boundaries the universe, but now circumscribes, in ever-narrowing circles, what a man is allowed to think. The mind cannot be squeezed into acceptable confines. It is the death of magic that with your help I fight! Do you see? In the green lion I seek the specific for it, that I may circumvent what seems ever more imminent: the construction upon time of place and space as finite as stone and unyielding as iron."

She nodded her head, rumbling as she always does to calm me, even risking a search about my pockets for a raisin or date previously overlooked.

Finding nothing, she subsided with only a reproachful sigh.

We had not gone more than a half-mile further when Set appeared, wraith-silent in the middle of the path.

Despite myself, I was filled with joy. My heart overflowed with it, and at that moment, bubbling up out of the well of mind, came the recollection of the dream I had had and forgot that first night he had slept beside me in the tent that lay now folded and secure among the mare's burdens. And with the dream, come thence unbidden, was the unease that haunts me still.

So I told him of it, as we wound our way through the meager pass that cuts across the volcanic hills. While we passed west of Marash, I told him. I had been, in my dream, in the belly of a mare. He had been there also, sharing form with a great scarab beetle that emerged from a ball of dung large as Khufu's tomb.

The apparition had three visages: his, that of the old god Set, and the beetle-head itself. From the beetle's mandibles came an adjuration to take care in this raising of the green lion; to take up the salt in a specific fashion; and further instructions on how to make that which is green go red. Then I had knelt down before it, and invoked prayers of power to this god, whom I knew to be Khepera as surely as I knew I was dreaming.

"And all of this," I exclaimed to my companion, "occurred before you and I had discussed the salt at all!"

"I know," said Set softly, with that slow smile.

And I would have told him that the proportions recommended by the god were the exact same as those we had determined together the evening past, but that remark silenced me. For what would he say, but "*I know*" again. Of all things, I did not want to hear that.

But my mare saved me from the awkwardness of the moment, when I almost ordered him to depart and leave me in peace. It was she who laid back her ears and snapped at him, wall-eyed, in a most unusual display of temper.

"Let me," he said, before I could quiet her. And like his vassal I stepped back, and he approached the mare. Her flanks quivered, took sweat in a moment. She snorted, tossing her head, and seemed to whine, but her hooves were as rooted to the soil. So slowly he advanced, whispering to the flattened ears, that he hardly seemed to move at all. But she saw, and twisted her eyes toward me in unmistakable desperation. But I, too, had lost control of my limbs, and only stood thinking of the fox in the moonlight as he reached her shivering neck and put his hand upon it.

At that touch, she sighed, and the quivers left her. In a moment her head was pressed against his chest. The foam at her lips slobbered whitely over his brown robe.

Set chuckled, taking up her leadline, and met my eyes. Fighting both disbelief and jealousy, I obeyed the eloquent inclination of his head, and we resumed our journey.

By dusk we had made the Anti-Taurus pass, and I dawdled behind, telling Set I would later catch up. He agreed, and I choked back mention of the fact that I did not need his permission.

But the pass soon soothed me. Here, of all the folds amid the crags, have the ancients left their spirits. The cliff walls rise nearly perpendicular to the sharply angled trail, along which the war chariots of Hatti, of Mitanni, perchance even Sumer once rolled. On an early excursion I found a spear-point here, bronze, and no artifact of modern Anatolia. Now it was no relic I sought, but the presence of those who smelted that bronze. And, as always, I found them. Or they me. First the air grew thick, like a fast current rushing between the cliffs. Then the sounds: of creaking harness and shouting men and hooves—so many hooves. Louder and louder, until I pressed back against the cliff face, that I not be ground under their wheels . . . And the army passed before me, in the dusk. I saw them, some bearded, some not, armed and armored, the sunset flashing off their conical helms.

How long can such a phenomenon last? Not long—they faded with the sun, disappearing in a cloud of dust and dusk.

I stayed, pressed against the rough rock, until all trace of them was gone. Then, much strengthened, in my own way triumphant, I set off at a brisk jog in their wake.

I found Set already encamped at the foot of old Mt. Argaeus, on one of the flows of lava that must have frozen, eons ago, while still crashing down from the peak. He waved me greeting, rising up from his fire-building.

In the last traces of the long summer twilight, the chain of the Anti-Taurus, rising obliquely northward, took fire and shattered the sunset into a dozen spreading rays. I felt, looking off northwest, truly a part of the flattened plain, as solid and enduring as the blackened hills of spent power rising right and left.

I did not immediately ascend to join him, but waited until that last light faded out from the sky. In the aftermath of such a time-swim, many things are revealed. With a fresh perspective, I went over the day of silent travel with my odd companion. Being alone is a joy; being alone while in the company of another is always a strain. The day had passed between us stiff and contentious. The grassless, overhung crescent he had chosen for a campsite seemed a fit place to spend what must be, by the day's prognosticators, a desolate night. It was then, while ascending to join him, that the unease born in my morning's awakening, grown adolescent in the recollection of the dream, came mature.

I was afraid. Afraid of this Set who charmed animals and claimed knowledge long denied men by prudent gods; who flickered possessive eyes over me in soft glances more akin to lover's caress than lenticular observation; who came alive in the night like the dark ruler he had claimed himself to be.

As if in a waking dream, I joined him, consumed with that feeling of having every spoken word and gesture predetermined; of being locked in a deadly pattern for which the only cure was variance, and yet knowing that even the variance was a part of the pattern itself. I have had moments, while learning deep meditation, as terrifying, moments in which I realized total bodily paralysis which might be broken by the simple twitching of the little finger; but failing that tiny volitional movement would hold my flesh in bondage lifelong. It was such a feeling, then, as I joined him by the fire, that held me cold and aloof.

I said: "I think we had better go our separate ways, at least until we cross the Halys."

"I think not," demurred Set.

It was four days later we came to that spur between torrents that boasts the crumbling remains of once-great Hattusas. I was, that midmorn, lucid for the first time since I had confronted him on the slope of Mt. Argaeus.

At breakfast I shook off, angrily, Set's ministrations. Did I remember anything? he asked, and I replied that I retained a glimmer of the ritual bathing in the Halys, but that was all. To my raised brow and questioning silence, he explained that there was little surprising in my befogged state, that I had run a high fever, had mumbled and raved, and that he had spent a day searching herbs along the Halys' banks. To these herbs he ascribed my "cure," my uncertain limbs, and those dreams of unyielding time in which I had been forever imprisoned.

I looked at him in silence, and wondered. But I dared not say to him: "Go." One word; how simple, how impossible to speak if it might bear any such consequences as those to which I had been so recently subjected. For I had been the victim of no fever; I have doctored enough men to know fever. I know her better than most men their own wives. And I had not been, from what I recalled, either mumbling or raving. It is my custom to bathe in the Halys in a particular fashion: I had performed the rites, just that way. What, then,was the explanation of my half-tranced state? I could find none to suit. At length, I conceded to myself that I might have fallen victim to some malady with which I was unfamiliar. If so, much of that debility lay draped still over my shoulders, I thought, for I am not a man who of habit walks on the right hand of fear. Nor on the left of superstition. But both companioned me that day, while Set walked behind, leading the mare upon whom all hopes rested.

Now, it is possible that some other might have by then apprehended the true nature of this Set. One more wily than I might have foreseen all that was to come and taken steps to alter the topography of these affairs. Perhaps. But I have long turned and twisted these events in my mind, even tried to stretch them into a more suitable framework than this which I now present as the loom on which the tapestry took shape. But I cannot. And I doubt that any other, in my place, could have circumvented what then came about, or drawn from these events any other conclusion than the one I have been forced (so reluctantly) to accept as truth.

Hattusas lies on the northern slope of one of the ridges where the Anatolian plateau begins to break down toward the Black Sea. Where the two rivers unite, just below her, is Boghazköy a settlement which boasts at best two persons for each letter of its name.

As we passed by the jumble of huts, in the too-still air, we saw no one. I remarked on this to Set, and he only reminded me of the Turkoman patrols that loosely held the flatlands.

I might have gone closer, looked to see if the village was indeed as deserted as it seemed, but Set took my arm and glared and I turned meekly away, thinking that it had never been my habit to pry into the village's affairs. I bought provisions and privacy, and sometimes hired a son or daughter for labor, but that was all. They tolerated me; I, after ten years' acquaintance, had no friends in the village.

And they, without exception, stayed out of the old town. Twice cursed, had been Hattusas. And efficaciously: even into the natural gallery of Yazilikaya, over whose refolded cliffs still processed the thousand gods of the Hatti lands, the villagers would not go, but in time of drought or famine, when they wailed ululant chantings and made sacrifices to the ancient mountain gods.

So we skirted wide of the town, seeking the tunnel under the southern rampart. Up the spur we scrambled, one on each side of the mare, to ease her in the loose shale. Two men could have scrambled over the southmost gate's crumbled walls, but the mare could not. I had spent long months clearing the tunnelway, and it was toward this postern gate, wherein wailed the laments of her builders on an everpresent eerie wind, that we entered into the city itself.

Set made no remark as I pointed out the way, nor as we emerged from the darkness among the scattered mortar of the fallen temples. But then, to one who had walked between the paws of Khafre's sphinx, what was there to see? Some tumbled blocks of basalt. Granite hardly more than wind-formed stone. A few columns far cruder than the hypostyle halls of the temples of Amen-Re. Yet I saw what he could not see, in these crumbled remnants of the temples of the Weather-God and the Lady Arinna. The ancient aqueduct has always seemed to me whole. At times, in the night, I have heard hollow murmurings; ghost-waters come again.

"See, the inner wall, where it meets the mountain. There!" And I pointed to the west, where the fortified walls meet the rising scarp. "The lion gate lies there." But even as I said it, my eyes roamed elsewhere, toward the southern citadel, of which three walls still jut skyward, toward the spring beside which a slow fire should have burned. I had arranged for its tending, before leaving for the south. But there was no smoke, no fire, no sign of life.

Set's hand came down on my shoulder. "Let us see this lion gate," he suggested calmly.

But I was far from calm. Someone had been here, and not the clansman I had hired from the village. No sign of him was visible, nor were any of my painstaking alterations upon this place revealed to my worried gaze.

I disengaged my arm. "You go. See the gate, and the preparations I have made there. I will join you."

"I told you," said he with a soft shrug, "your works have been destroyed in their place."

My face must have mirrored my stricken heart.

"And I have also told you that in spite of this, you will succeed." And clucking to the mare, he led her away, toward the lion gate.

I stood quite still until they were hidden by a fall of masonry. Then I ran. I ran to the northern spring, by the upper gate, where should have stood my bronze mirrors and my stores of vials and chemicals, inside a tunnel that had ages ago been blocked at one end by a rockfall.

All was silent, there. The more pity. Those nearly indestructible mirrors, scratched and acid-eaten and bent with vandalous thoroughness, lay useless on their sides. They had used my own tools against me. The alembics were all smashed down upon the mirrors in a glitter of might-have-beens; it was thus, with my own precious solutions, that the savages had disfigured my tools beyond hope of salvage. Savages... Who? Suleiman's religious warriors had done the kind of work here that had enfamed them in Egypt. Twice had the Mohammedans taken this approach to what they judged evil in the land of Thoth, once little more than two hundred years ago, and again in this civilized age. Now there are left so few who remember the lore of Kemet you could count them on the fingers of both hands and have two digits left over.

"Green lion, I will find you, and such disrespect of man for man I will drive from this earth!"

I bent down over the garbage heap of my fortunes, oblivious to the dangers of hidden vitriol and sharded glass, caressing those instruments I had labored so arduously to collect. Tears of rage blurred my vision, over my undertakings here desecrated while still barren. I would not have minded, had those instruments done their work, served their purpose. It was not for the loss of cucurbit and concoction I mourned, but for the possibilities inherent in them that now would never be explored.

I cursed, there, with vehemence, all of Mohammed's children; even his tomb did I vilify, that it come to be as ravished and defamed as this sanctuary that had been my workshop. Later, I told myself that such things happen, especially in a trade like my own. There is no law for the lawless, no protection for him whose works are proscribed by every doctrine of ignorance that men will call religion or regency.

It was a long time before I quit that place to seek Set and the mare by the lion gate.

I tarried awhile at the spring near the southern citadel, resting my head against the useless wings of the fat-faced sphinx that guards it.

"Ha," I said to it, "old friend, you and I share the same fate." All that is left of it are the lion's quarters, the crowned human head, and a stump of a tail. Its magnificent wings lie now in chunks and rubble about its feet, only their broken stubs attesting to the fact that this hollow-eyed guardian had even boasted pinions before which the mountain eagles would have cringed away, screeching in fear and jealousy.

I slid down beside it, taking a chunk the size of a fist into my lap, stroking the incised feathers thereupon. "The same fate, old stone one."

Then I spied the iron dipper, with its long cord, where it had been kicked into a cranny. So I drank from the citadel's spring. Of all the upwellings within Hattusas' walls, this one's waters had always most thoroughly quenched my thirst. I knelt there as the mages of Hatti once knelt. For the thousandth time, while the cold, clear mountain water slid downward to refresh every particle of my body, I heard them whispering in my ears. The ghosts that had once crowded these ways convened at this spot to sit and sip and exchange soft confidences in the seven tongues of Hatti. Perhaps the kings met here, when this was the central court of the palace of a great empire, throats thirsty from long court sessions that must have taken place on ramparts now invisible, but which would have towered over the plain. Could they look out from this natural stronghold and see the glitter of the Black Sea in sunset? And turning, could they regard the ancient trade routes which joined Sivas and the east to the Aegean coast, and the Pontic ports to the Cilician gates? It seemed as if they could see it all, for I saw it, as if standing shoulder to shoulder with them, high above my slack form and thousands of years in the past.

Shaking my head, I took my leave of them. It is an easier fate to be misplaced in space than in time, and when affairs go so ill as to abort before their inception, even my skills give me little ease. Those bronze mirrors lying bent and acid-etched like so much refuse had cost me close to five years' labor. Their casting I had overseen, even their transportation to this spot had been a task that seemed, at the beginning, insurmountable. Now—to quote Paracelsus: "Whoever is so daring and so fortunate as to make it or to take it out or again to kill it, who does not clothe and protect himself before with mirrors?" Who, indeed? Myself, it seemed. For though I had been effectively divested of my protections, I would not be turned from my path. I had not another five years to spare.

So did I readjust my decision, walking the twisting way among the ruins to Set and the lion gate. True daring, I suppose, comes always from such misfortune, and the desperation it engenders.

Now the lion gate had withstood the abrasive Anatolian winds far better than the rest of Hattusas, perhaps because of its sheltered position on the westward, descending slope, perhaps for more metaphysical reasons. Even the wall of dressed stones into which the lions are set towers whole, untumbled, meters in either direction. And the lions themselves, both topping a man's height, stand unscathed, half emerging, mouths open wide, from the squared pillars out of which the sculptors part-liberated them, their forequarters, their mighty chests fully detailed, their trunks merging with the rock. One on either side of that dissolute avenue they are poised, roaring in silent complaint that they, on their plinths, are still immured in stone.

Between them sat Set, crosslegged. The mare searched tender shoots near the lefthand lion's feet, by the mound of dung-chips I had so patiently collected in preparation for this day. Both looked up as I approached.

I ignored them, going directly to that stone I had so carefully loosened at the wall's foot. When he saw what I was about, Set rose and gave me aid with the weighty block. When we had it moved, wiping sweat from my face, I retrieved my cache of specialized instruments. Then, only, Set spoke.

"It was as I predicted?" he ventured.

"It was. Do you know, also, who did this thing, and why?"

"Would it help you in your task to have that information?"

"No," I said. "But I would like to know how you knew." And I thought, privately, that I might also like to know if he had a hand in it.

"Raise the green lion, and you will know all things, that included."

I searched his face for complicity, for some sign that he would try to dissuade me. There was none.

"Let me help you," he offered, softly.

I nodded. What choice had I?

So I got the small mirrors and some specialized cucurbits and other paraphernalia which I will not name, lest I tempt you unduly, while Set made a fire with chips between the two lions in a pit I had previously prepared and covered over with a basalt slab. As we were about it, the wind waxed hostile, snapping my robe around my limbs with evil glee. Looking back upon it, I now realize that none but such as Set could have coaxed a flame into life against such a gale. It drove the clouds before it until the sky became an ill-fitted wall of dark basalt, behind which the sun struggled impotent, enfeebled by shadow in a midday turned to dusk.

While Set placed the iron stand and the wide-mouthed alembic over the low-burning, smoking blaze, I went to the mare. From her twitching ears, she knew what was next. In a tongue that was old when Egypt was Kemet, I began to speak the words, as I made before her face those magnetic passes which I learned from Paracelsus himself.

"He flieth like a bird; he alighteth like a beetle upon the empty throne," I murmured, and was not surprised when I heard Set's voice join me in the incantation from the Book of the Dead.

The mare's head drooped. With each stanza she grew quieter, finally weaving upon wide-braced hooves. Though the day grew ever darker, her coat flared bright, mimicking the fire's life. Forty weeks had she carried my homunculus for me, loaning me her spacious womb's warmth. I rolled up my sleeve and retrieved from her what I had fixed within, in a glass that had been leaded and covered all over with leather, lest in a contraction she might crush it. Deep within her, I felt for that vessel which I had prepared according to the most secret intelligence, all the while intoning prayers that seemed to issue on smoke from my mouth. That smoke came thicker and thicker as my hand in its blind searching grasped the slick vessel. Only vaguely did I realize that Set, who matched me word for word, had joined me, holding the mare's tail.

Then it was done, and I held in my hand the leathern egg. Clutching it close, dizzied, hearing my own chant in my ears as if it were a stranger's, I sought the fire.

Set's hands swam into my view. Together, we put the mouth of the opaque vessel close to the clear glass. Shoulder to shoulder, knees almost in the fire, we labored. My fingers, at last, broke the seal.

We both fell silent, upon the same breath. From the leather mouth into the glass flowed the whitish smokey substance that had so long been trapped within. From the smaller vessel into the larger, until it seemed impossible that the mare's belly could have held so much, flowed that amalgamation of sputum lunae and Arcano sanguinis humanis and my own body fluids, until the greater cucurbit was filled to overflowing and the boiling mass rolled over the alembic's mouth and down its sides like lava from chaos' spurting fount.

"The salt!" hissed Set, pushing me backward and jamming together the two containers' mouths, his knees almost in the fire's pit.

I fumbled for it, found the box. For an overlong moment, the iron bands would not release. Then, giving with a rasp, they parted and fell unheeded into the blaze.

A pinch, only, held between three fingers, did I take. My world moved sluggish. The laying by of the box took hours; my arm swinging to poise over the joined alembics seemed hardly to move at all. My breath roared in my ears as Set lifted the leathern beaker away from the other. Into that frothing mouth I dropped the black crystals.

They eddied and whirled, sucked downward, as Set placed the cucurbit on its waiting rack. A moment, only, was left to me before the suction reversed itself. In that time I must fit and seal the lid, make magic-fast the vessel's mouth.

As I bent over it, the sealing material, clutched in fingers atremble, like a magnet drawing my hand toward the glass, the mare screamed. I had a glimpse, in that moment while she wailed and Set took up a chant not of my knowledge and the dizzying dark of the sky seemed to descend and wrap me round, of what coalesced from the blackening whirl in the cucurbit as the fire licked high and the seal, molten, dropped from my blistered fingers into the fire. Within the glass, tiny hands pressed to the imprisoning walls, thickened homunculus, first pale, then brighter; flickering white, then red, and at last a flashing rainbow form distinct from the pinwheeling mist.

That fine-formed head turned toward me. Those tiny eyes, black and streaming tears, regarded me from a face the miniature of my own. The grimacing mouth opened, and from it issued a scream of rage and woe that will haunt me the remainder of my days. Frozen in horror, only half conscious of what else formed beside, I watched it dance from one foot to the other, trying even to climb those slick walls. Below and all around it, the fire raged. I felt it on my own skin, in my own heart.

Homunculus cowered. Beside him, within the cucurbit, a green glow formed, roared, shook its mane.

"No! The principles have split! It is too soon!"

I heard Set's warning from a great distance, without understanding, even as I reached for the alembic, to snatch it from the flames in which the creature I had so long sought writhed and roasted.

Whether my hand jostled it, fumbling the glass into the flames, or whether in his terror homunculus himself shattered the glass, I do not know. The smoke billowed, split in two. The mare trumpeted. A demon's laughter filled the air and metamorphosed into a lion's roar.

The alembic lay, glittering shards in the flame.

The two dense clouds hovered, momentarily. One drifted to the lion gate, rubbing along the stone. The second, dark and red, too thick to breathe, wrapped itself about my head.

I coughed, choking. Blinded, I stumbled. Devoid of balance, I fell. And the red moistness receded.

Prostrate, drained by homunculus in an instant of all my strength, I could only stare as the lion, great and green with golden mane sparkling, lunged, tearing his rear quarters from the Hattusas stone in which they had been two thousands years imprisoned. For a moment, I struggled upright, hearing my own "No, no." For this was wrong... First the green lion must be killed. *First*... allegory? The green lion is no allegory.

It shook itself, tail lashing, its shadow quenching the fire in the pit in an instant. Homunculus, before it, weaving in place, grown large, uttered a piercing cry. An instant, they stood frozen. Then the green lion leapt. Without even raising an arm in defense, the spirit-child crumpled under his adversary. In another instant, the green lion stood alone, glowing, brighter, lips drawn back from its fangs.

I crawled backwards, into the very coals. Set...

It was then, as the great paws flashed out, toward me and the substantiality homunculus had not afforded, cringing before this entity whom I had thought in my ignorance to control by incantation and science, that I begged Set for aid. With what homunculus had left me of will, I forced the words out. Even as I pleaded, the green lion and my body, of its own accord, circled, seeking to contest. Desperately, as a hand no longer mine to command snatched up the red-hot rack from the smoking pit, I struggled to evict the weakness from my flesh.

I saw, then, as I approached the snarling, fire-limned lion with the smoking rack thrust out before me, Set. For a moment, before the lion leaped upon me and all things went dark, I saw him: those overlarge shoulders straightened, robe cast aside to reveal pectoraled breast and girded loins. But most terrible of all about this Set, grown overlarge in the dark that has ever been his substance, was the face—eyes of obsidian-hearted diamond in a black head whose snout was long and downward curving, beast-toothed. From that open maw, as the lion's claws fastened into my shoulders and bore me back onto the ground, came a laugh, the humanity of which terrorized my heart dead-still.

Then the ground came rushing up to meet, my head struck it, and my darkness was complete.

I have no idea how long I lay there; whether it was one day, or three.

When I awoke the sun was just rising. I lay with the rack across my chest in the ashen pit. My seared hands were clenched. In each one I held, tangled in my fingers, clumps of golden wires, fine as the hairs of a lion's mane. By my feet lay the stone head of the leftward lion. In its basalt neck were small punctures, evenly spaced. Both the severed head and the headless trunk that stands sentinel still, were pulped and gnawed, ragged-edged. Over both surfaces ran deep scorings. Even for the prince of predators, biting through the neck of that lion had been no simple task. It must have taken a very long time.

LAST THINGS

by John Kessel

"Some say the world will end in fire, some say in ice . . ." a contemporary of Olaf Stapeldon's once wrote. If that's not enough to qualify Robert Frost as a science fiction writer it does rank him among the great apocalyptics of our time. As publishers have long known, cataclysm is a category unto itself. Men and women seem to live different lives at the brink of life. And writers (who often claim to spend most of their working lives there) must find the climate congenial. They return again and again to the last age of man to set their stories. John Kessel has made his contribution and it is an extraordinary one. "Last Things" captures the frustration, and hope, inherent in Frost's vision. This is a story we kept returning to while compiling this anthology. It's a story which deserves your best thought.

The Close Match: Felanu

They were on the central gaming court, in the last round of the match, when they received the news (as did everyone else in the city at that precise moment) that the weakening was fatal and irreversible. Neither man faltered. Sims shot a low, sharply hit ball into the left forecorner; Felanu jerked left, set his feet for a forehand smash, and instead hit a soft shot with great topspin. The ball hit with almost no velocity, jumped slightly up and out, and fell dead to the floor an arm's length from the wall. Sims, looking for the smash, stood helplessly in the rearcourt. His shoulders relaxed. He stood flat-footed and took the matrix from his left hand. There was a polite snapping of fingers from the assembled simulacra and spectators around the court. Felanu had once again won the contest.

The images winked out above them one by one; from among the spectators Felanu's lover Merin Asch and his brother Teloran came down to meet them. Asch wore no hair that day; she was slender and intense. Felanu stood, hands on hips, next to the taller, blond Sims. He felt good, tired and good, but the shocking message they'd just heard was now working into the front of his thoughts. The weakness would kill them.

"Good match." Sims said. A wisp of straw-colored hair was in his eyes. Felanu searched his flushed face for some sign of emotion—anger, despair, resignation—something.

Nothing.

"I guess," he answered, "I've played better. I couldn't hit a good backhand."

Sims grinned unpleasantly. "You hit them better than I." He paused for a moment, then spoke to the others. "I don't think I'll ever beat him now."

Felanu saw that that was all the direct emotion he'd ever get from Sims. The hell with Sims.

"You both played well." Asch smiled, embraced Fel—he never liked it when he was soaked with sweat—and whispered in his ear, "Especially you." Aloud she continued, "Tel and I decided no one but you two could hear that Thought at just that time without letting it affect him."

Felanu wanted to tell her how wrong she was, but a servitor

had rolled up with beverages and their robes. Sims took towels from it, gave one to Felanu, and wiped his brow and slender shoulders with the other. "A Thought is a thought," he said, so softly it was almost as if he were speaking to himself.

Felanu did not feel as able to keep from talking about it as the others apparently were. He wanted to say something, put it in front of them, shout, "We're dying!" But it would sound foolish to be so blunt, when there was no answer that anyone could make. They would only think him more a fool than he had already proved himself to be. He kept still, and Sims excused himself to enter the baths. Fel suggested they meet for dinner at fifth hour; Felanu embraced them both and followed Sims into the dressing rooms.

In the baths, alone in darkness, stinging mists about him pricking his skin and burning at the corners of his closed eyes, he fell into a trance. He felt his body about him in completeness and calm perfection, balanced and whole, the envelope of his flesh minutely defining the difference between *in here* and *out there*. He felt in complete possession of himself. And yet at that same moment, silent and dark within him, biding its small and dry time, he felt the weakness growing, and he knew, with quiet terror, that it would not cease before it filled him completely and left him dead.

The Evening Dance: Sims

T. Woodrow Sims passed through the tingling interface, stepped onto the slate courtyard of gate eighteen-one. A few other people in evening dress were there, preparing to leave the city, and he spotted Rikki in his buff uniform, standing alone away from the gate.

"Rikki!" he called as he approached.

The sandy-haired man started. "Hello. You're a little late. Let's go."

They stepped out into the parkland, across the open grass to the forest. "There were a lot of people here earlier," Rikki said. "I think there'll be a crowd tonight." The breeze was fragrant with earth and rotting wood; the sunlight lay in scattered patches on brown pine needles and slashed brightness across the boles of trees. Behind them the huge mass of Inhuama rose first in staggered layers, then in towers and irregular complexes.

The grassy slopes of the amphitheater were crowded with diners when they got there. They reached their place, and a circular portion of turf rose to become a low table; presently the food arrived.

Sims glanced around the slope at the people chatting, joking, eating in the approaching twilight. They seemed, if anything, a little gayer than usual. "Do you think the announcement this afternoon has anything to do with this crowd?" he asked.

"They're in a good mood. They have to be."

"That's very cynical."

"It is. That usually doesn't bother you." Rikki leaned back and looked down toward the center of the outdoor theater, where the coming of night would bring the dance. "Look," he said, "there's Felanu."

Sims looked, and saw Asch and Teloran and Felanu at a table a little farther down toward the stage. The light was fading, but he could see that Asch and Felanu were holding hands. The near-childishness of their pose affected him: he wondered at their relationship—they had been together now more than twelve seasons, an athlete and a philosopher. Dark Felanu wore bright colors, as usual, colors that would bring him the attention he seemed to find uncomfortable.

"I have to tell you—" Rikki said, at once dismissing the others there. "The Shogun's made a decision about the weakening. They met this afternoon. Cold sleep."

Sims was used to Rikki's crypticness; he had long before filed it away with his store of observations on personality. Rikki was aide to the Shogun more out of a desire to be on the fringes of power than out of any desire to serve, or devotion to duty. He was minor. But he usually knew something others didn't.

"So?"

"So—searchers have found that a person in cold sleep does not experience the progressive weakening. No reason is known. They know almost nothing, in fact—it doesn't even give immunity. If the person in cold sleep is brought to life, the weakening begins again. But they think, if the sleep is long enough, we can outlast it."

Sims looked down at the food on the table. His appetite, never strong, was gone entirely. It was a complicated world. He knew what came next—the inadequate plans. There was a confused knot in the pit of his stomach; he could not tell if it was hope.

Rikki's voice was bright with conspiracy. "The Shogun will announce later tonight plans to preserve human beings in cold sleep for as long as is necessary—up to one hundred or two hundred thousand years, if it comes to that."

"A hundred thousand!"

"They have reason to believe it may be necessary."

Reason to believe nothing. It was insanity. Say good-bye to life, and absolutely no explanation. The universe merely says, "Try playing this new game. No rules. Now we'll see just how clever you really are."

"But that's not all of it, right?" Sims asked. He wanted to pin Rikki down, get it all said and finish his "guess what I know that you don't" charade. "There's no way to put the entire city into cold sleep. No facilities. And we can't have more than two or three months."

"One month. The weakening progresses geometrically. Once we feel it, it will end rapidly."

The knot in his stomach drew tighter. Sims watched the center of the bowl where the glow was growing and the dance about to begin. The night was almost there.

"Ten percent will be saved," Rikki went on. "A lottery will be held and by tomorrow morning every citizen should know whether he'll be able to enter the sleep—or must contend with the weakness."

The knot was definitely not hope, Sims decided. He sat there saying nothing, amazed at his own calm. And it wasn't exactly calm, either. It was indifference. He couldn't feel hope—or horror, or surprise. There must be some fear in him somewhere, but he couldn't feel that, either. It was a problem. He considered it the way he considered problems that arose in his work. What was wrong with him? Either he would be chosen the next day, and would be saved, or his number would not come up, and he would die. *He would die.* Why didn't the words stir anything? The only fear he felt was a detached fear of his own inhuman indifference. It was a great, absurd revelation.

A rising murmur from the other people on the hillside told him the dance was beginning. They turned silently to watch, the hundreds of them, each minding his own private vision of the future. Sims could see Felanu, below them, fidgeting. He watched Rikki's earnest concentration on the dancers as they spun through the lace of light that wove around and between them on their silent stage. Rikki's face in the faint light betrayed just a hint of worry. Sims looked briefly upward, over the trees at the opposite side of the amphitheater, to the clear sky beyond. Stars were growing brighter as the last glow of sunset faded, stars very tiny and precise and far away.

The Salvation of Asch: Felanu

In the morning came the results of the lottery. The transposed dawn rose around them in the room. Felanu, first up as usual, watched the forms of the furniture slowly become clearer, go from vague shapes to solid objects, until before he knew it the entire field was lit with clear Light. And just when the dawn had completely given way to day, the telepathic announcement came to them.

Felanu knew then that his hopes had been illusions. He was not going to be saved. His first reaction was numb distress. He longingly watched Asch stir beside him; when she was fully awake, he leaned over, staring into her face. He had never looked at her and felt so cold. She was a stranger this morning. In her gray eyes and in the slight movement of the corners of her lips, he saw that she had been chosen. He was alone.

He got out of bed and went through the illusory woods to the bath. He felt a dull, unformed fear. He washed. The water was cold. He was clean and scented and awake. When he came back to the bedroom he didn't bother to step around the images.

He didn't care. He saw her there with her back to him, her thin shoulderblades showing through her dressing gown—and he became furious.

"You're going, aren't you!" he stood there naked, accusing her.

Still with her back to him, she lifted her head and looked at the sky. "I don't . . . yes, I'm going." She turned. He couldn't stand her seeing him naked. With short, violent movements he pulled on his robe. He felt hot, but he was shaking. He exploded.

"Going!" The single thought raged and flamed within him; he tore about the small room, unsoothed by the morning mists, unaware of the freshness of the new day—unaware of anything but the woman who was going to live while he died. He grabbed anything nearby—a bottle of scent, a Summoner, a crystal mask—and threw it across the room. He didn't want to hit her with them, but he hoped he'd slip. "You're leaving me to die!" he shouted, dark and raging. "Cold sleep—for you, while I'm dead!" His own voice sounded repulsive to him, and his eyes burned wetly.

"I don't want you to die," she said, her voice rising. "But—but we *all* die! Don't you see? My staying won't help you."

"Don't lie to me! Don't talk down! I know you're clever! I know you never felt anything!" He drew in a deep breath. "Help *me*? Help *yourself*!"

"That's not true!"

He couldn't listen. He stepped jerkily over to her, drew his hand across his chest and slammed the back of it into her face. Her head snapped back and she sprawled across the bed. His stomach churned with bile and his face felt flushed. The back of his hand stung; it was very cold. Slowly Asch pulled herself up. Her nose was bleeding. She said nothing.

He wanted to stop the blood, to ask "What happened?"—as if he had just come into the room after she'd had some sort of accident. At the same time he *knew* he was insane. Shame and guilt overwhelmed him: he felt waves of nausea, tasted bitterness at the back of his throat, and ran doubled-over into the bath. He vomited into the basin, heaved and shuddered and stank. It stopped at last. He splashed water into his face, and with sick despair went back into the bedroom. She wasn't there. He touched a spot of blood on the sheet. It was bright and sticky.

He was alone, face to face with approaching destruction. He didn't want to die, he didn't want to grow weak and feeble. He didn't want to be alone—alone in the blackness that would be all that was left after the final light was put out. He knew nothing about love. He didn't want to be alone. His thoughts traced and retraced that path, and it did not seem they'd ever strike out of it. His tears were gone, the woman was gone—he could hardly grasp how fast she'd gone; perhaps she'd never really been there—and whirling thoughts were all that he had.

He would go see Sims. He would see Sims. Somehow, the idea comforted him.

Sims at Work: Felanu

T. Woodrow Sims was one hundred and eighty-three years old, a historian and an artist. Felanu once, in an uncharacteristic moment of perception, had realized that Sims's archaic name—the name which had descended in his family, from son to son, like an obscure message they had been told to carry to some unknown destination—was greatly responsible for his being so aloof. Unlike almost anyone else in the city, Sims had grown up with the weight of the past on his shoulders. Was it any wonder then, Felanu asked himself, that Sims should look at reality from a distance, should see the present in terms of the far past, the indefinite future? But this explanation was not entirely convincing. You came to the end of it with a coherent and logical personality, but somehow in the process the real Sims had slipped through your fingers, and you held an abstraction.

It was midafternoon when Felanu arrived at the clean white dropshaft that gave onto the terrace of north-six and the complex that contained Sims's rooms. Though this was normally a busy time, there were few people rising or falling in the shaft, and his footsteps on the amber tiles of the terrace sounded distinct and isolated. He found Sims seated at a table before an opened window; in the far distance, beyond the parklands and forest below, you could see the broken blue foothills of the northeastern mountains. Sims sat still for a few seconds after Felanu entered, then finally turned to him. He hooked his left arm over the back of the tall chair. His eyes flicked over Felanu and he turned once more to the table, slouched forward, propped his elbow and rested his wide brow in his left hand.

"Hello," he said absently, staring at the table.

Felanu had not expected to be treated like an intruder; in his present frame of mind, however, he didn't care. Yet there was no easy way to start talking about his problems. "What are you doing?" he asked instead.

Sims drew a long breath, let it out slowly, and wrenched the chair around to face him. "I *was* writing. It's difficult work."

"Writing?"

Sims began to explain and, instead of being impatient, became excited and persuasive. "Writing is an old way of recording thought. You use language symbols." He rested his hands on a roughly rectangular box that lay on the table. It had ten indentations on its nearer side on which he rested his fingertips, and out of a long narrow slot in the top projected a sheet of fabric or some other material covered with long lines of black markings. "It took me some time to reinvent this device," Sims said with a trace of pride. "You project your thoughts in terms of these language symbols, and the machine transfers them linearly onto this roll of plastic." He pulled on the sheet coming out of the writing machine and tore it off at its base. "You then assemble these pages in the order of your design, and they form a pattern." He showed Felanu a narrow sheaf of "pages" which he had already assembled.

"I can hardly make out the difference between these symbols. It must take some practice to see the designs."

Sim's nostrils flared slightly. "It's not a graphic art, like those 'paintings' I once performed. It depends on the meaning, and especially the order, of the symbols. There are certain conventions which I have been rediscovering only with great difficulty, over a long time. If performed properly, the 'writer' can present a story." He paused, and his enthusiasm seemed to leave him.

"At one time almost all the experience of the race was recorded this way. It doesn't look as though I'll be able to master it in the time remaining."

The time remaining.

"I don't suppose you were selected in the lottery either?" Felanu watched Sims guardedly.

"No." It was all he seemed ready to say.

"Neither was Tel. They said they picked people at random, but how do we *know*?"

"I don't know." Sims didn't seem upset. As he had done so many times in the past in similar situations, Felanu wondered what he was thinking. Didn't he feel any indignation? But it was useless to pursue that line.

"Tel and I went down to the city core. There were crowds. At Memory hundreds were waiting to record their simulacra in the crystals before the end. They figure they can be used to bring them back to life someday. We laughed at them, they seemed so anxious; some of them were even getting angry over such a long shot. Then Tel went over and joined the crowd wanting to get into a cubicle!" Felanu's voice was disgusted. He wanted Sims to feel the anger too.

"I went to a refectory and talked to a woman who said it was all a hoax, and that no one was going to die. She was pitiful. There was an old man—his hair was gray!—who was excited about this dance the community's planning. He'd seen me in competition, and asked me to join them; they needed athletes, too. The dance of death!"

Still Sims only nodded. Felanu's voice got louder without his realizing it.

"There were people outside the center where they're freezing them. I thought I might—I might go down there to see." He carefully avoided the thought of Asch. "Some were talking about protesting to the Shogun in Assembly. They think they've been cheated. They're fools, I know. It's just disappointment. I know it." Felanu left the other half of his thought, the desperate "but," hanging in the air.

Finally Sims said something, but it was not a relief. He looked at Felanu as if he knew his every thought. "They don't realize what they're saying. Think. Are the ones chosen better off than we are? They get one hundred or two hundred thousand years of sleep—that itself as bad as death, with no assurance the weakening will be gone by then. And if they live, even then, at the end of their lives they die, just as certainly as we do. We all die, in time."

That was what *she* had said. Felanu saw her again, lying across the bed, and the last pitying look she'd given him, after he'd hit her. Sims's artistic games, his cold reason, shrank to triviality, and Felanu slumped forward in shame and despair, his head in his hands. He felt the tight sphere of his skull beneath his fingers, and he wanted to press harder and harder, until the thoughts went away.

"What's wrong?" The voice was soft.

"I *wasn't chosen*. Asch was, and she's already gone."

Sims was silent, and through his pain Felanu wondered again what he thought. That Felanu had no inner reserves? He forced himself to calm down. He sat up. He marched his thoughts through the six stages of order. And after he had come around, he told Sims of the entire fight with Asch.

Woodrow Sims then demonstrated the trait that had made him Felanu's friend from the first time they had met. He refused to moralize, and even his eyes didn't reproach him. Sims always seemed to know when a person had taken the measure of his own weakness, and he would not pursue the obvious—yet somehow it was understood that they both knew what was right and wrong. It didn't need to be said to be acknowledged. If they did talk about Felanu's mistakes, it was as though they had been mad incidents of a childhood they both looked at with wonder and philosophical acceptance.

"So you and I must go on in this mystery," he said. "We will learn to cope with our imperfect selves." He put his large, pale hands on Felanu's shoulders, leaned forward, and kissed him on the forehead.

Rikki's Fall: Sims

Sims and Felanu were outside the city, standing in the clean and gemlike parkland that surrounded the great structure. It was late afternoon, and the sun, slanting through the trees on their left, threw long shadows over the finely tended carpet of grass, gave them the last warmth it would give that day before leaving them for a space. Their own shadows stretched like long, spectral fingers away from them, pointing toward the city that was their home, reminding them, whether they acknowledged it or not, of the place from which they came and to which they must ultimately, whatever the thrashings of the confined soul, return.

Sims had spent much of the last week in his rooms, working in a disorganized rush, trying to pull together pieces of his art almost as soon as he discovered they existed. Earlier that day Rikki had contacted him, asked him to meet him in the western park at evening. He had been annoyingly vague about the exact place; so far they had walked for several miles along the perimeter of the city, had passed many gates where servitors watched them, patient and unexpectant and minutely observing. Sims had the feeling that they wondered what these two men were doing, alone in the evening. The grass was moist and the air becoming a bit cold. The shadows of the trees reached out for them more and more.

Felanu had already suggested they give it up, had cursed Rikki's lack of consideration. They were both very tired. Felanu was beginning to get on Sims's nerves; he just wanted to be left alone—so he told himself.

"Look!" Felanu cried suddenly, pointing at a spot far up the side of one of the towers. Following his direction, Sims searched the many-windowed facade and saw after a moment what had attracted Felanu's attention: a man was standing in one of the topmost windows, so far above that you could just make out his form and the glow of his clothing in the gold of the sunset light. The figure paused for a moment, then launched itself into the evening air. Sims felt his heart wrench itself upward in shock; then he realized that the man wore wings and was descending in a long spiral. Felanu had cried out, and was visibly shaken; instead of following the descent he was staring at his feet. Sims grabbed him by the biceps—he knew the man needed support. But he himself couldn't take his eyes off the flyer and the rainbow refractions thrown off by the filmy wings. After a long thirty or forty seconds of descent, the man came to earth a short distance from them. It was Rikki.

He shrugged off the light framework and removed the coat of interwoven metal discs. "You came," he said. His manner was one of pleasure overcoming surprise.

"A nice, dramatic entrance," Sims said tersely. Felanu had composed himself quickly and was sitting on the wet grass. Sims was beginning to appreciate the reserves the man had. He sat down beside him.

Rikki looked a little hurt at Sims's annoyance. He squinted into the sunset over the forest. "You know, from the Shogun's window you can see the sun setting into the sea—it must be a long way from here."

"We ran away there once," Felanu said irrelevantly. "My brother and I broke the rules of the school and . . ." His voice trailed off; he seemed to lose himself in thought.

Rikki picked it up. "You did? I don't know anyone who's ever done anything like that. Personally, I liked the school." He turned to face them, at ease, his hands clasped behind his back. There was a slight line between his brows.

"Why are we here?" Sims asked. He wanted to leave.

"Why, indeed? I'm done with my work. All the survivors are now stored away nicely. No more meetings of the Shogunate." His sudden laugh startled them: it was short, violent, almost a bark. "The Shogun himself, my mentor, is working like a fool on his own project. He thinks he can save himself by becoming part of a machine. He wants to transfer his personality and has a team working on it. Some of them believe it will work."

"Will it?"

Rikki abruptly sat down beside them. He seemed to Sims more maddeningly erratic than ever; he'd still not told them what he wanted. Rikki turned his palms up in inquiry before them. "I don't know. I thought so for a while." He now seemed unconcerned with the Shogun's plans.

"You really ran off to the sea, Felanu? Remarkable."

"What are you doing now?" Felanu asked.

"Talking. Not talking. Reviewing my career. Watching the Shogun. Not watching him. Flying. Yes, flying. I'm flying quite a lot recently."

Felanu looked worried, but Sims had had just about enough. He could only think of the work he could be doing now.

"We fool ourselves," he said. "Run around and say we've accomplished something. I know some people who spent the last week in bed." The thought made him consider his own lack of passion, his sleepwalking. "Of course, I can't say they're wrong. Who is to say that, now?"

Rikki looked disappointed, as if he'd expected something more definite. "Right, Sims. Who's to say? Not you." His smile was a disgusted one.

"Rikki . . ." Felanu started, but Sims interrupted him.

"This talking is useless." He started to get up, but Rikki was already standing.

"Right. Absolutely useless."

Sims finally heard the fear in his voice. What had he been thinking! Hadn't he been listening?

The aide had taken up his flying gear; he donned the coat, assumed the wings, breathing rapidly and raggedly all the time. Sims felt distress and self-disgust rise in him. He wanted to shout to Rikki to stop, to grab him and shake him into sense.

"Wait!" Felanu called, trying to catch Rikki, but he had already taken off, and was mounting the dusk toward the last rays of sunlight that still shone on the very top of the towers. Felanu turned angrily to Sims. "How could you be so blind?" he said quietly, as they stood watching in the gloom the descending star was leaving.

Higher and higher Rikki flew, until he came into the light far above them, and they could see him circle out and then in toward the tower and the windows. The buff uniform stood out gold against the deepening violet sky. At last he flew inward and down, lighting on the edge of the window that was undoubtedly the Shogun's, though they had no way of distinguishing from so far below. For a moment Rikki hung there, half in and half out. Then with a queer little jerk he threw off his wings and, leaning backward, very slowly at first, then with shockingly increasing velocity, fell, poor Icarus, through the indifferent air, to strike with a dull "whump!" the equally indifferent earth. His wings followed, fluttering downward into the darkness that had now completely claimed the park.

On the Gaming Court: Sims

The court was dimly lighted, the soft glow of walls turned down all the way, so that a heavy dusk hung in the air. The rows of seats above were all dark, all deserted, and even the temperature had been allowed to fall until the room was quite cool. Sims found Felanu sitting in the center of the court, his legs stretched straight out in front of him. The pose made him look like an awkward child.

He sat down beside him heavily, quite exhausted. "I've been looking for you," he said.

"You should have known I'd be here."

"You weren't here earlier. This was one of the first places I tried. Not even Central could detect your thoughts."

Felanu looked at him. "They're lucky. No, I wasn't here before."

Felanu was quieter than Sims had ever seen him, and he felt awkward, ashamed for having interrupted the man's thoughts. He hadn't seen him since Rikki's death. Sims had kept to his rooms, trying, usually unsuccessfully, to work. Yet when Teloran had told him he was looking for his brother, had asked for his help, he had surprised himself by his excitement. He jumped at the opportunity to get away.

Felanu broke the silence. "You won't believe what I did. I went to see my son."

Sims barely concealed his surprise: this was not the normal Felanu. "Your son?"

"I wanted to know what he was doing. I've been thinking how I haven't seen him in so long. He's only been an adult for fifteen years—so if I should have to die, how is it for *him*? How could *he* accept it?" Felanu shivered, placed his hands palm to palm, and warmed them between his legs. His shoulders rocked slightly back and forth in an unconscious rhythm. Sims waited.

"He's fifty-five now. You remember him? His name is Collyn."

He had been a slender boy with curly black hair and calm eyes. Sims remembered he'd last seen him years before, in an art class at the Collegium. He'd had fine, strong hands and an aptitude for light molding.

"I remember him."

"He's in the actors' company now. They're spending all their time preparing for the final performance with the dancers." Felanu stared straight ahead as he spoke, hardly acknowledging Sims's presence.

"I cried when I saw him. He seemed so strong—stronger than I am. He has something in him. If you didn't know us—and the others there didn't know who I was at all—you'd think he was the father and I the son. He's stronger. Even though I could see he had trouble breathing, and he had to think to talk steadily."

"It must have upset you." It was inane, but it was all Sims could think to say. Somehow their normal conversational pattern had been reversed: Felanu was leading.

"He's all right." Felanu suddenly stopped rocking, still staring ahead, at the forward wall of the court within which he had expressed so much of his own life. "He'll come through fine."

Sims had nothing to say, and he remembered why he had come. He slowly stood. It was more difficult than he had expected, and once he made it his legs felt drained of strength, as though he had just run up a ramp for ten levels. "I want you to come with me," he said. "Tel's waiting for us, and he's worried. The Dance is going to begin soon. This is not a good place to stay—you might, if you get too weak, be forced to stay here, and I don't think you'd like to die here alone."

Felanu looked up toward him, then began to struggle

awkwardly to his feet. It took him two tries, even with Sims's help. Once up, they both swayed unsteadily and eyed the exit. Felanu had changed, Sims saw, from what he had been when Asch left and he'd come in despair to visit him. But looking at him now, it was damned ironic. He'd once made watchers at this same court gasp in awe and envy at his grace—so alive he seemed—and now he drew ragged, shuddering breaths, and it was a triumph for them to stagger through the doorway.

Felanu's Meditation: Felanu

The dance of death—how can they keep going, so strong, yes, of course it's earlier, or maybe they use aids, and Collyn is there though I don't know which he is, what he will be—it's so dark in here, my chest so heavy—and Sims there, Teloran, and that woman, stranger, a psychologist they said who knew the old art, who must be a friend of Sims and his work on writing—what does he think of?—I wish we had once at least had a mind joining mind so that we could be aware of each other, but then it would not be the same; this weakness, it cancels our reason, leaves us dry, and why is there no cause no solution though there may be many, no one with the ability to find out, too busy with selves, that's the final truth about us—look at me, look at Sims, look at Asch and Rikki falling, falling—

The dance of death, how clear the movements, how pure the color, how measured the sounds, and who designed this? who made this thing? perhaps, almost certainly not one man or woman made this; I know all of us together designed this production, and production is exactly what it is, recorded I'm sure for posterity—posterity—which is a good joke, posterity, non-existent posterity, maybe when they wake in a hundred thousand years, posterity, if anything is still working in a hundred thousand—

and the dance, the bodies moving in circles, flowing together and apart flowing—together, and Collyn, and I'm alone here, here in the last chair, not even comfortable—Sims, the woman, Tel my brother there, how young he was, in the blue suits we wore the time we went to the sea, and how the Teacher found us in the sand and told us not anyone knows now what it was to swim—and how I would have liked to do that, swim, I would have been good, the man I was before—not this man now, who can hardly breathe, whose legs feel dead, like limbs of the trees in the forest fallen off and lying in the shadows, on the wet earth—the cold room, Sims sitting as quiet as—as quiet as *Sims*—another good joke, so full of good jokes here, Sims and Tel whom I love and Asch not here but cold asleep; perhaps it's right, I know of course it's right, it's only so hard to take, her warm body I felt lying there, and the many times she told me how the muscles in my arm carved a shape somewhere, a shape in space that was not the same as anything else, and I didn't know what she meant—now gone cold asleep after I hit her—hit her myself, how strange that was, the rage, spinning out and out, *I don't want to die*, tearing around the room, watching her frightened face, and how heavy that bottle was in my hand, first hint of the real weakness, throwing, ripping away, afraid, circles around the room, she in the still bed, poised to leave—*the dance of death*—

the woman psychologist what is her name and what does it matter, she says something annoying—why can she not simply be quiet and watch the dance, the pure dance fading away—saying something about me, about immaturity, about unable to be adult, about never grown at all—she's saying that? queer that I can hardly hear, the mind tricks—like all of us never grown and now dying?—but she seems so sure of herself, and how can she be so sure, surer than Sims, who just sits with his head back on the rest listening, is he listening to her? listening, is Tel? Do they wonder, like me, why she is here—but maybe she's afraid as well, like all of us, too afraid to watch the dance, sit and feel the breeze—artificial it must be—she's strong to keep going—

going on, gentle breeze imitation outdoors going on, even now machines persisting, and is it so important to keep the air going? doesn't everything run down, why not?—though logical it sounds but logic isn't all, surely not enough, not true, surely—there's pleasure, precious bright life, like sun, and darkness too—the dark here where maybe the lights fail after all, with the dance flowing on before us, even she watching now, watching like Asch at dinner, watching with quiet eyes who knows what goes on behind them?—a mystery—

mystery—I was an athlete, strong, quick, Felanu, one and the same thing these were, but that *was* and is not *now*, *once* it was the time for me, the ball hit into the precise corner of the court, the swinging, heavy matrix, tingling force of the hand, step, step, pace back, lean! swing, swing hard! drop! bounce on the balls of feet, gasp air, smoothly dancing!—*the dance of death*! all of it leading here, and who didn't know that, really—a mystery—but you fall into it, the mystery, swim in it, you have no choice after all, and after all, Asch lives, and so does everything live—so *did* it all live, Tel and I as boys in the trees, and Sims, queer Sims, all alive, all alive, circling in and out away and back in rhythms like the beat of heart, like the first step tentative step, who knows the next, the rush of blood flowing, knowing itself that someday it will be still, and even this woman here, even myself *still*, quiet at last in the darkening room, watching, watching the motions, swaying grace, grace, grace together and apart in color, glow dimming, fade gentle movement leaving air, *dance, dance, the dance—dance*

The Last Things: Sims

After the dance had been completed and the simulacra faded, they discovered that Felanu had died while sitting there. Sims and Teloran were badly shaken, and even the psychologist Marita seemed affected. Unsteadily, Teloran signaled for a servitor to assist them in disposing of the body. Marita left before it arrived, and Sims and Teloran, themselves in the last stages of the weakening, took care that their friend and brother be properly conveyed to the crematorium to await his turn at incineration.

Teloran embraced Sims and left, saying he was going to try to go outside the city, into the forest, to make his end. After he left, Sims managed to reach, with the aid of the ways and the still-functioning shafts, the terrace of north-six and his apartments. Along the way he encountered several people lying in plazas, swaying unsteadily along the ways, and in each case he forced himself to help however he could, though there was really nothing he could do, and he had what he considered a vital reason for reaching his rooms quickly. But somehow a great anger had risen in him, and as he encountered the dead and dying, his thoughts took on a frantic, almost insane hostility.

It was thus with seething and barely repressed anger that he entered his study and found that, through some malfunction of the automatic mechanism, the windows had been left open through the coming of a rainstorm. Everything in the room was slick with rain, disordered by wind. In frustration, he slammed the wall beside the window with his open palm, and the feeble blow, in his weakened condition, seemed to drain all the strength out of him. He crumpled to the floor, knowing that he was dead, and that an act of stupid weakness would be his last on earth.

After an indefinite time he came to his senses again, calm, wondering why he yet lived. He struggled to his feet and punched the manual control to close the window. Painfully, he gathered up his papers, arranged the slick sheets in their proper order, and prepared his writing machine. He was a little dizzy, a little slow—but he felt capable of work, and he knew this would be his last chance to complete it.

He summoned up the grief he felt, and the fear, and the anger and frustration and whatever resources of observation remained to him, and continued the story of Felanu and these last days. In short bursts, in long phrases, in gnarled and painful knots, he placed the words upon the page. Sims wrote his story, took what he knew and imagined what he did not, grasped what he could of the things he had seen and *ordered* them, *fixed* them, controlled them as well as he could, brought to the uncertainties of experience an artificial pattern—created Felanu, created Inhuama, created himself, created Felanu's despair and fear, created weakness and strength, created the dance, created the running down of the world, created Felanu's tortured progress and final triumph, and in the process tried to triumph himself.

He finished the last sentence. He was still alive. Shaking, quite bewildered, he gathered the papers together: he had tried to discover what his life had meant by seeing it through another's eyes—but if he should continue to live, what would that salvation mean? Unsteadily, he drew a breath; he listened for the sounds of his city. The beating of the rain against them had stopped. Did anything stir in this old world?

Still a living man, still thinking on last things, still mindful of his great loss, Sims left his rooms to search for the other survivors.

THE ADVENTURES OF LANCE THE LIZARD

by Ronald Anthony Cross

The bald fact of the matter is that there are few writers who can pull off utter confusion the way Cross can. And yet we are given to understand that Cross is an upright, reasonable sort, who, judging from the double handful of stories that have suddenly appeared under his name, turns onto writing the way a flower child turns onto psychedelics. For that matter few writers would dare commit a story like this to paper—who but Cross would have guessed that the adventures of a star-crossed lizard would make such exciting reading.

Sometimes the best fiction is inexplicable. We think you'll find "The Adventures of Lance the Lizard" inexplicably joyful.—And that is a recommendation we seldom make.

I

I
drift.
Half
asleep,
half
awake,
half
of
something
else.
Too many halves
splitting myself into fragments
until I behold,
through myriad eyes . . . what?

I try to wake up. He is standing in the corner of my room, lost in the shadows. I can almost see him, but I am sleepy, so sleepy. He holds a double-edged sword that gleams with its own light. His expression is up to me. Power emanates from his body. He never moves; he never rests: he hovers. Is he my guardian? Is he my executioner? Now I begin to feel a nagging fear. "Go ahead with it!" I want to shout. "Get it over with, whatever it is. End it." But somehow I know it will not end. It is the middle that counts. Now I feel more secure. Nothing I can do about it. I sleep.

II

Last night I awoke to the chattering of the stars. For a long time I pretended that I didn't hear it. Finally I rose and went to the window. I looked out and out. They chattered and sparkled and fizzed. Their little silver voices were incomprehensible and myriad beyond the imagination. They tinkled, buzzed and hissed. They were like electricity. I shut the window.

Now they grew louder, clearer. They began a new action.

Little dots of vibrating light began to emanate between them and grow in intensity. They chattered and droned and wailed. I clamped my hands over my ears. They got louder and louder. They began to build little streamers of light from one star to the next. Finally they became one solid light.

I pulled the curtains but the light came through. I went back to bed and pretended not to notice, but all night long the light shone around the edges of the curtains. It is an awesome thing to witness the singing of the stars.

III

It is morning. I have been awake for some time, lying here with my eyes closed, watching the colors. Sometimes they form funny little pictures that I can't describe, but mostly they are just colors. Finally I tire of it. I open my eyes and look over to the sandbox where my pet lizard lies asleep. Now he is on his back. I keep getting frightened that he is dead. His tongue is always out. His expression is what I think of as agony. He seldom breathes. At these times he is only a flare of vivid green on the white sand. My duty is plain. I must harass him awake.

"Lance, are you awake, Lance?" He stirs. He puts his tiny paw over his head as if in pain. "Lance, wake up, Lance, it's late." Then I add cunningly, for his own good, "What were you doing last night? You were at it again, weren't you? You know how I worry."

Suddenly he leaps to his feet with one paw on his head and one doubled up in a lizard fist. "Shut up!" he cries. "Leave me alone and shut up." He thrashes his tail and glares like a miniature dinosaur.

"Leave me alone," he cries. "Can't you ever for one minute leave me alone? I go where I please and I do whatever strikes my fancy. Why must you forever nag me?"

Now I have him. "So you did it again after all. You ignored my warnings, my pleas for your safety, your sanity. No use denying it now; I know you did it again."

"Shut up," he cries. "For Christ's sake, leave me alone. I do what I want—and what about you? You've been doing it too. I know you have. Why, it's obvious to anyone how you spent the night."

"I have not," I said. "I stayed home and worked on my novel." I try to sit up, but I suddenly seem to lose my balance and my head aches. I lie back down again. I did something last night, that's for sure. I try to remember what it is we are accusing each other of doing.

Meanwhile, Lance is in action. He scurries headfirst over the edge of the table, plunges across the floor in funny little hops and begins to work with the radio on the floor.

"Lance, I don't want the radio on this early in the morning. Do you hear me? At least you can put on something classical, a nice minuet."

The quick, vulgar explosion of jazz that I love so much comes on loud and clear.

"Lance, turn that off, will you!" But Lance is already across the room, rummaging in the open closet.

"Lance, what are you after? We've got a lot of work to do around here. Lance, is that my marijuana? It's too early. Put that away this minute!"

Lance is struggling wildly, pulling a large paper bag out into the middle of the room. Now he is inside the bag. I can hear the delicate rustling of his movement.

"Lance, did you hear me? It's too early. Particularly after last night."

What did we do last night? If only I had some idea. Lance is coming across the floor, huffing and puffing. He has somehow rolled a huge, clumsy joint which he is smoking feverishly. He comes closer and closer.

"All right, damn it, do whatever you like. Just leave me out of it. I've got too much to do to worry about it."

He comes closer and closer. He seems to change sizes. Sometimes he's like a huge dragon coming closer and closer, drifting in smoke, huffing and puffing, closer and closer. I say his name and try to sit up but I feel dizzy. I lie back down. My arm falls over the side of the bed. My hand opens.

IV

I have been writing at this desk for a long time. I don't know how long. I don't know what it is I'm writing, but then I am a writer, not an interpreter. I have been going at an incredible pace. The papers I have been writing on are scattered all over the table and floor. Later on, I will go through them and sort them into alphabetical order, or perhaps numerical order would be even better. I don't know. I don't care. I don't understand. I don't eat. I don't sleep. I write and write until it is finished somehow. Then I don't write anymore. It is this time I look forward to. I call it my vacation. It is possible it has lasted all of my life up till a few moments ago, and that when I finish writing this, it will take up again and go on forever. No matter. At the moment I am a writer.

I don't know when it was the first of the little devils started to appear, but I first noticed one sitting on the books in the corner with his wee little sword resting suggestively across his knees.

I ignored him completely.

Now they begin to pop up all over the room, giggling and playing pranks on each other, perhaps turning cartwheels or fencing with their little swords, but always I get the feeling that they are slyly gathering into an army and advancing toward me.

Finally I can sense them in a group beginning to climb up the table. A few have reached the top; others are climbing.

I write. I do not look up.

Now they are playing their war song on miniature trumpets and drums.

Suddenly I hear a shout. Lance tumbles onto the table like the lizard acrobat he is. He is wearing a cape (made out of a washcloth) and his sword is drawn and shining. He is fearless. I do not look up. I write. I write.

"I shall not rest until I have driven all of elfdom from this house," he shouts.

I write that down. The elves menace him with little scolding voices. I write that down.

Now I hear the clashing of swords, the cries of battle. Out of the corner of my eye, I catch glimpses of Lance whirling among the little people and attacking them from all sides at once. They are myriad but he is Lance. I can hear them falling off the table. Finally Lance leaps off after them. I can hear them fighting across the floor. Now they are making for the window, and Lance is shouting, "Once again the king of reptiles sails victoriously across an ocean of his enemies."

I don't know what he means. I write. I am glad they are gone.

I hear Lance climbing back up the table. Now I am writing

more slowly. Suddenly I am finished. I drop the pen and look up.

Lance is standing proudly before me, his cape rippling out behind him. He is leaning on his sword.

"Methinks they won't be back for a pretty piece." He tries to laugh roguishly but only manages to hiss roguishly. He looks at all the paper.

"Are you finished as a writer?" I nod. "Then help me with this stuff."

We gather up all the papers and throw them in the fireplace. Then I go get a match and light them.

"It would have been nice to put them in alphabetical order and publish them. I could have been rich and famous. The critics would have given me meaning. I could have talked intelligently with fine ladies about my theme. I would be a little lonely and disillusioned."

But Lance breaks my chain of thought by the force of his sudden excitement. He is running full power now.

"Forget that nonsense," he says "the next time they come, take up the sword and we will drive them out forever."

"I didn't see anything," I say, "I was writing."

"The little things that come to attack you, you saw them. You pretended not to. I implore you to take up the sword. Drive your enemies from the house. To fight with all your heart and soul. One powerful fearless act to stand out forever, more inspiring than the greatest books and poems. I implore you to fight for your life." Here he pauses. Then he looks solemnly into my eyes. As if explaining something difficult to a backward child, he says quite calmly, "We are all gods." He says it louder. He is trembling now. He draws his sword out and holds it over his head.

"We are all gods," he cries.

I begin to get nervous. "I tell you I didn't see anyone, Lance. I was too busy with my writing. My tooth was bothering me. They are too small and too many. I don't even have a sword. I don't even want a sword." My voice trails off.

Lance is gone. The window is open. I hear a commotion from the birds and imagine he is in some ruckus already. Then I notice the bag of marijuana in the middle of the floor and I realize he has snatched a couple of joints, leaped out the window, climbed into the trees, gotten stoned, and picked an argument with the birds, while I was still talking to him. I close the window.

V

We awoke with our heels on our heads over laughter. We couldn't stop. Our voices were like sparklers—and Lance bubbled and fizzed. "I'm coming over," he cried, "via air mail." Then he made the most incredible leap of his life, clear from his box of white sand onto my bed. I couldn't believe my eyes, but I did, and we began to laugh all over again.

Lance did the dance of the lizard all over my bed. Whirling, flipping, spinning and cartwheeling, until I lost track with my dreamy eyes and could see only spirals of pretty green fuzz.

I forgot what I was watching. I began to see things of a nature that I can't describe. Then suddenly he came clear again. I laughed like mad to remember what he was again, and he laughed with me.

"Last night," he shouted, "we rode the high flyer. We danced among the stars."

The stars, the stars, oh no, the stars.

Lance had a secret. He smiled shrewdly; he tossed his head toward the window. "Today's the day, I'll bet. Shall we look out the window?"

We got up and went to the window. Lance rode my shoulder. We opened the curtains. I choked up to see such a beautiful sight.

"I knew it," Lance cried. "The angels are in the streets."

For a while we waited at the window. Then we heard the slow, heavy footsteps coming up the stairs and to our door.

The wind was screaming on the edge of the void. Strange, gurgling noises came from within. They carried me closer and closer with slow sure steps. They chanted in Latin evil, sonorous sounds to confuse me. They carried me spread out upon their shoulders. I could feel Lance trembling in my pocket. Nearer the pit. Nearer the edge. Nearer and nearer. But I can pass the tests. I can do anything I want, and today was my first day to awake shining with glory and ready to laugh at fear.

"Test me," I cried, my cry echoing down and down into the

void, disappearing, gone. They threw me over the edge.

I fell. I felt a surge of panic, and threw it outward into the void before I really felt it. I fell and fell, but I used the speed of my fall to twist my body in a magical way, in the manner of an airplane propeller. I twisted faster and faster until finally I made a whirring noise.

I began to rise, slowly at first, like a helicopter; then, when I had gained enough speed, I stopped twisting and crossed my legs and arms and sat in a position of complete peace and love, and I continued on the momentum of what I had done a moment before. Meanwhile, using my other eye, I changed the blackness, only in spots at first.

Little rainbows began to appear all about me and spread outward, until I rose effortlessly through a universe of color and kindness. Miniature stars and suns of fairytale color were born and evolved and destroyed in the twinkling of my eye. Time disappeared, and I knew forever.

I went on and on. I changed myself. I knew everything that was, because I was everything that was, and everything was me. But the word "me" was lost and gone. Things began, and kept getting more and more. No one knows what I created in the void; but one layer under, and everyone knows.

At last. At last. I came rising fast and pure, up above the cliff in the atmosphere of my own mind. Beautiful scenes and flashing colors played about me in the air. Girls with wings and butterfly bodies came tiny out of nowhere and grew until they got too big to see. I was in sight again.

Deafening applause reached me from the cliff and I hurled showers of dancing elves to parade above their heads in elegant fantasy costumes. Lance rose out of my pocket singing the melody of the coolness of under rocks in summer. He raced to the top of my head and drew his little sword. He waved to the crowd below us on the cliff.

"We are gods," he shouted, "we are all gods." The applause was deafening. We rose and rose until we were out of sight and then we kept on rising. Lance crawled back in my pocket, where he shivered from the cold. His eyes glowed like two little black marbles full of life.

We stopped rising. We sat in the cold vacuum. We knew nothing. I felt Lance shivering in my pocket like an extra heart.

Finally I remembered where I was.

"Well, Lance," I said, "the place for us at this moment is down a little. Let's go in style."

He ran out of my pocket and took up a strong position. I heard the tiny proud clash of steel as he drew his sword.

Then I toppled over into a beautiful swan dive, and we went down. Faster than a comet and straighter than a shot. We went down and down. The winds roared about us and howled like beasts. Lance shouted mighty oaths and slogans. I opened wide my arms. Down. Down into the earth, my mother, my home, my old warm young rich green mistress. The love of my life and queen of my universe.

Home.

VI

Tonight's the night, oh my god, this is it. The stars—the night—the elements surrounding the house. The stars, the stars.

One minute, Lance lay in his bed in the sandbox, asleep, breathing regularly. The next, frozen, a green lizard of ice, no movement whatever, suspended. So to speak, to chatter.

It began to rain hysterically. It pounded, beat, begged, whined at the window. "Let me in, let me in."

I found myself, from my convenient location beneath the bed, replying frantically, "Let me out, let me out." Out where? No where out of it but in, no way away from it but together.

It was as though I drank a glass of conviction. The liquid in me perhaps responding to the liquid outside the window. But strength was suddenly bubbling in my veins. Changing, moving, but steady flow of strength.

I came out from the bed and pranced about the room in my fighting stance.

"The conqueror of the void fears no elements," I shouted. "Now," I cried, "now," over and over.

The ticking of the clock grew, became enormous, filled the room, then suddenly froze like Lance. Time was not. Just the elements and my self.

I went to the window and opened it. Nothing happened. The rain purred and bubbled like a teakettle.

Suddenly a bolt of lightning hurled itself through the window at my throat, snarling like a dog.

It moved like a blaze of light, which it was, but I moved like a field of whirling atoms, which I was. And so I dodged to the side and jerked down the window and cut its throat.

It fell to the floor and crouched there, like a coiled spring, pulsating, breathing light. Stalking me like a cat. But I was through running. I swelled up like a giant and hurled myself to it, just as it sprang.

Finally, after eternities of two great energies rushing together through the universe of my room, we met in the air above my bed, and burst into light, and burnt into heat, and burst into life, and fused. And became forever, one. The only one.

How can I describe that kalpa of pain, that aeon of pleasure. That forever of fusion, called the now. Myriad? One? More. One instant my body was experienced as total energy, blazing, exploding, the next instant as an ocean of calm, peace unending. These also fused.

Then I was me again. Only now, I saw myself as lightning man. I walked into the bathroom, tiles gleaming, light bouncing, tied a towel about my neck and looked into the mirror. Everything was in the mirror, only I was blinded by my lightning. I walked out of the bathroom and went over to the window and threw it open and open, and forever opening. I went out, until I became the outside and the outside became my self. I smiled. I was one with the rain, the wind. I went back to the center of the room, went inside for an instant, centered the universe through me, then I sighed.

It was over.

The clock began to tick. Lance began to breathe. He moved, smiled. At that moment, feeling my oats, as they say, I chose to enter his dream, and I can do whatever I choose.

At first an endless blue sky, a mountain. But then as we grow nearer I see it is not a mountain, but little houses built on top of each other, all of them bright shiny reds yellows blues greens, but so many, so many, they all blend together into one color, one mountain. And all the same, all different.

We enter. It becomes apparent no one owns them. People live in one for a while, then move to another. No one cares where they start or finish; they are too much into the in-between, and the in-between is all there is.

Lance is crying. Tears of joy. Life is pulsating, throbbing.

The old men are dying in the beds. Making their last speeches, trying to pretend to be serious, but how can they be serious? They can see the young coming on and on, an ocean of the same as themselves.

From time to time, a young boy would push one of the plush naked bodies of the young girls onto the bed, and those bodies always say yes. Then the old man would cry out, "Respect, respect, have you no respect, you young devils?" But, with a comical, sly expression, he would sneak his hand down onto the plump grapey nipples, all the time emitting a steady carnival patter such as, "Oh, the pain, the tragedy of it all. I'm dying, dying, and these young whippersnappers don't show any respect for their elders."

I sense a buzzing in the air. The children playing in the room, darting, hovering, almost too fast to see.

People keep coming in and going out, loving, dying, playing, faster and faster.

The women are opening an oven, all the time baking little yellow cakes and feeding them to the children and men.

Lance chants, "We want cakes, we want cakes," over and over.

The women come to us in a line, chanting, "The power of the sun, the energy of life, yellow cakes of power, eat power, be power."

Lance and I eat the cakes of power, all the time chanting, "More cakes, more cakes, more cakes." Life goes on faster and faster. Lance and I begin to grow in the room. Everything is humming, spinning, screwing, eating, dying, growing.

Our heads are pressing on the roof, the room can no longer contain us.

Suddenly we burst through the roof and fill up the whole universe of Lance's dream. Then we set down in a lush green jungle filled with juice and life.

The music of bugs is deafening. The confusion is limitless. Then, just when it seems I can't stand any more, I can stand some more. I smile. I relax. I am.

And back in some forgotten room, the old man dies, and the old man is born.

VII

Too much
Too much light
changing
and
changing
until I
don't know who
or where
She
until I don't know
who she is

Now we look into each other's eyes across the table. Something is wrong. That's for certain. Things keep moving, changing, glowing, gleaming. She holds a cocktail glass in one hand, and the sunlight plays little games all over it that are beautiful or obscene. My eyes hurt. We are certainly in love, or are we? She laughs gaily. Her face keeps changing. My head swims. We laugh together. We are much in love, life is beautiful or life is? Too much light. Too much light. She keeps changing and changing. I love her. Who is she? I try to think. I can't come clear. Too much light, too much light. She laughs gaily, and holds up her cocktail glass. I dodge back under the umbrella. I begin to giggle nervously. Who is she? She keeps changing and changing. We look into each other's eyes. We laugh gaily.

In the center of the table, Lance the lizard is up and moving. Sunlight falls on the silverware and glasses, flashes and puffs. The beads of moisture on the glasses have become jewelry. Things are crackling. Too much light. Too much light. Lance's little green body is glowing fuzzy. He is drunk, drunk, drunk. He moves stupidly and slowly on all fours, and now he screams aloud. He has dragged his tail across some burning silverware, while the duchess and I are laughing hysterically. Finally, he begins to climb a tall glass, muttering all the time, "Whiskey, whiskey, whiskey. Drinks for the drunk. Money for the rich. Sweets for the sweet. Life for the lively. Death for the deathly. Love for the lover. Danger for the fearful. Safety for the fearless. Insecurity for the insecure. Poetry for the poet. Science for the scientist. Religion for the religious. Freedom for the free. Whiskey, whiskey, whiskey." He gets halfway up, when sunlight suddenly intensifies into the realm of the impossible. The silverware begins to tinkle. It is being showered with heat and light. Wave after wave flashes onto Lance until he glows, puffs, and explodes, falls off the glass, lies on his back, passed out with all four limbs twisted up into the heat and his tongue rolled out like a bright red ribbon, dead drunk.

An overpowering voice shatters the near silence and causes us to begin giggling to each other in nervous confusion. The chorus of heavenly angels is singing a stirring rendition of "What Can We Do with a Drunken Lizard?" Their voices trail off sadly, disappear. There is nothing they can do with him.

We laugh gaily. We look into each other's eyes. We laugh gaily. We are in love. She keeps changing and changing. Everything is beautiful. Too much light.

too much
light
She keeps
on changing
and
chang
ing

VIII

Thick fuzzy things are happening to the nose. I laugh. "Lance," I say, "Lance." I laugh, I laugh, I laugh. Lance laughs. "Lance, my nose is fuzzy." We laugh louder and louder. "My teeth are fuzzy. My talk is fuzzy. My vision is fuzzy, my banana is fuzzy."

Now Lance is shouting in anger. "Take me to the beach, you fuzzy creep, I want to go to the beach."

Lance turns into a purple balloon with his little stub of a tail sticking out. He floats up into the air. He becomes holy. Little wings come out of the balloon. A golden glow surrounds it. It swells and bursts, a green liquid trickles down into a pool that becomes Lance again. What can I say after that?

I change into an old lady who is eating dope out of a whole bunch of green bowls. "Yum, yum, yum," I am saying. "A couple more spoonfuls of opium and then on to this delicious bowl of cosmic belladonna." I pick a star out of the air and toss it in the morphine soup.

Lance is in stitches. He can hardly talk. "The beach, you crazy bastard, the beach." He just manages to say it.

"The breach," I say. "He wants to go to the breach. Let me see, isn't that halfway between the naughty yoga and nirvana?"

He laughs and laughs and laughs. He rolls over and over. Suddenly he rises up on his tail and strikes me like a cobra, but I fall into flowers at his touch and he becomes a golden swing.

The birds are chirping. The sun is shining. I have to think. I'll sit down and swing for a while. But it is not quite swinging. It is forward and forward and forward.

Lance is making a run for it, with me on his back thinking I'm swinging.

Too late. We burst through the door and tumble into the sand. "Look out!" I cry. The sun comes shooting down at our heads like a skyrocket. Just missed me.

Lance is prancing about in the sand singing, "The beach, the beach, take me out to the beach. Where the unicorns take off their uniforms and I can love my little sweety peach. Where the beach umbrellas are lucky fellas, oh, take me out to the beach."

Alas, I have been tricked. I'm not certain which is the sand or which is clouds or I would lie down. The ocean is frothing at me. The fishes are all spitting at each other. The seabirds are screaming, "Help," over and over, reeling dizzily on the whim of the strong ocean breeze. The mermaids are masturbating. The sea cows are mooing. The old salts are dissolving. The elephants are churning up the waters in their mad race to the African plains. Lance is prancing up and down. "The beach, the beach, the beach," he cries, faster and faster and faster. I am dizzier and dizzier.

Things get fizzier and fizzier. I have to lie down. In the soft sand. Soft and fuzzy as cotton candy. Too soft. I have been tricked again. I am sinking through clouds, falling, spinning, twisting down into a funnel of Lance's incredible, crazy, meaningless, meaningful creation and destruction of universe after universe, upon whim after whim after whim, galloping into the always now on a charger of ceaseless change, faster and faster, until only the echo of my pensive complaint, hangs for a moment, like rapidly thinning smoke, in that dream of mine I call the past, disappears and never was.

IX

We crept through the festival like shadows, we floated by like smoke. We slid into the spaces between people like water.

Lance rode my shoulder, done up as a famous lizard warrior. When he remembered, he would curl up his front legs to his chest and stand on his hind legs. He'd growl ferociously, and then he would shout, "I am king of the giant reptiles."

This exclamation of his was usually met with cries of approval.

My costume was green and ancient. I wore a dagger in my belt. My eyes and hair were dark and flashing. My teeth were slender and sharp. I felt light as a feather and fast enough to be invisible. I was.

I glided swiftly through the crowd, darting here and there and hovering to look into the eyes of people.

Lance was going wild. It was his night. "Fiesta," he shouted, "dance, you fools, tonight's the night to dance. Love, you lovers, fight, you fighters, your king commands you to honor the festival."

Somewhere near us, people pounded huge drums. People danced, people sang.

Lance rode atop my head, done up as a phantom. He wavered in the moonlight, his voice was a whisper, his eyes were hollow.

I was done up as a man of iron with inexhaustible joints.

We shot through the crowd like arrows. We shivered and shimmered. We hummed in ecstasy.

We flashed through the carnival like lightning. Faces streamed by us, beautiful, wonderful faces, all the same.

I came as a vampire. The prince of vampires, slender, and sharp as a bat. All in black. Lance was the devil. I flapped my wings. We fluttered through the crowd. Faces whirled by, dissolving into one face. Voices and music and noises became one thing. They pounded drums. They pounded drums.

We swept through the crowd like the wind through the bushes.

Rejoice, rejoice. Lance rode on my shoulder. He came as a precious stone. The gift to a great king. He shone, he flashed. He sparkled in the moonlight. He glistened and gleamed, my god, he was too bright, too bright. With a loud myriad tinkling of chimes a shower of rainbow butterflies fell upon us. I writhed, blinded by light and color. Their crystal wings shone and reflected Lance's light. They whirred and vibrated. They hummed in crystal voices. They chattered like bells. They sang to Lance of rainstorms on the river of glass. They gave him glimpses of flying over the moon, where the only color is void and the only sound is the endless tinkle of their wings.

They sang to him of forever. He rose in ecstasy like the stars, into the air. We began to cheer, we began to cry out all over the crowd in joy. Rejoice, rejoice, Lance has become the king of the rainbow butterflies.

Then they were gone. And all that was left was the tinkle of their wings and the twinkle of their jeweled eyes. The air was still, empty. The party was over. I looked up. Good-bye, Lance, I said to myself. It looked like rain. But I didn't mind a little rain. And all the way home, the streetlamps shone like the eyes of friends.

STEPFATHER BANK

by David Andreissen

Everyone knows that poetry is the language of love, and certainly that will never change. But perhaps in the future the poets' words will find a connection with a less romantic institution, and prove that the word is mightier than more than the sword. Here is David Andreissen's "Stepfather Bank," a love story with strange bedfellows...

PART I/IN THE NAME OF THE STEPFATHER

By 2110 the Bank owned everything.

It was called simply the Bank because its full name was 66 words long. It had begun in the late 1990's, as an amalgamation of Bank of America and General Motors, of Barclay's and

Compagnie Française des Petroles. That was early on. Within the first ten years it gained controlling interests in IBM, Badische Anilin, Brazil, the AFL-CIO, and Japan, among many others. That started the rush. All the conglomerates, the international corporations, cartels and zaibatsu, panted to interlock their directorates with it. They were not refused. When Communism went broke in the ought-forties Russia and her satellites were swallowed in one mouthful.

By 2110, the Bank had owned Earth (etc.) for over three generations. Completely automated and computerized, it owned everything, took a flat 10 percent as tax on every human transaction, was owned by, employed and ruled everyone. Everyone in the world.

Except Monaghan Burlew.

Burlew was a freelance poet. He had styled himself one since the day he had completed minimum Schooling, turned sixteen, and become of Working Age. Since that day he had never earned a Currency Unit and never spent one. Therefore, by law, he owed no taxes, paid no percentages. He owned nothing, owed nothing, bought nothing, and so the Bank could not "assist him in finding the most suitable employment"—i.e., tell him where and at what to work. He was unique; he was the only man in the world who was outside the System. The only one who was free.

This did not necessarily make him a heroic or even an appetizing character.

Burlew was fat. Of Class IV parentage, he had not been entitled to education beyond Low English and basic computing. He seldom had intercourse or bathed. His one pair of castoff tech-green coveralls, found in a trash can in a small town near Odessa, stank. He limped because his bare toes had been chewed by dogs one bitter July night in Sydney. He owned neither razor nor microdepilator and did not cut his hair. He was happy, because he felt that he was free; he was unhappy, because he felt that there was something he had to do, although he didn't know quite how to go about it.

In 2110 he was forty years old.

The 10-klick runwalk, humming coolly, bore him along under the rainbowed light of New Fifth Avenue.

"Yam, New York," he said aloud, turning round and round, head back, devouring mile-tall skyscrapers with his eyes and causing the hurrying passersby on the runwalk to bump into him. "How I loves it. What a city. It fills me." His benignant eye flowed over the stores and shrines and flito palaces that lined the Avenue and came to rest at last on the blank face of the man standing next to him. "Hi, friend," he said. "Woulj like to fill up on a pome?"

"You said?" said the man, a cleancut Class II in dark business coveralls. Id-patches glittered on his chest for Bisex, Upmid, Manuf, and Veget.

"Pome. You top on pomes? Give a turn, huh?"

"All right. Turn me," said the man, smiling a little as he looked Burlew up and down.

Burlew spread his arms heavenward, exposing two ragged holes at his armpits, and declaimed:

> *"Here I be in New York City*
> *Where the load be mighty pretty.*
> *Here I be in New York State*
> *Where it fill me mighty great."*

He paused for a moment, glancing at the largely puzzled faces around him on the moving runwalk. They had never heard any poetry; it had no economic function, and so did not exist in their lives. It was not proscribed; it simply did not pay, and so was not taught, published, or read. It produced no profit for the Bank. Burlew shook his fists in the air, and continued:

> *"Once the nation U S A*
> *Like to have it all him way.*
> *Nation now take second rank;*
> Stepfather Bank."

"Oh, Jesus," said the cleancut man, his face going suddenly white at the last line. "I don't agree with that. No, I don't. Oh, Jesus." He looked around frantically, then stepped off to the 15-klick walk, which carried him rapidly away from Burlew. He did not look back.

"Who you?" said a young girl, maybe fourteen, not old enough to Work yet. "Who be you, saying 'Stepfather' out here in people like that?"

"Burlew me," said the poet, nodding, looking thoughtfully

after the Class II as he disappeared. "Whaj think? That be one fine pome, rite?"

She stepped closer to him. A cleared space now surrounded Burlew on the runwalk; the others had moved away from the strange fat man. Some were already scratching. The girl looked at the frayed areas where the id-patches had been torn off his coveralls. "Burlew. Yam, I heard of you. Kids talk about you. Be you really him? Yam, that a high-rate pome. That Stepson, he not top on that. Why you be dress so poor, make fun of Bank? You get terminated, no lie."

"Not me," said Burlew. He pulled a blue papron telecard from his coveralls and showed it to her. The girl blinked and looked away as if he had exposed himself. It was his Balance. "Gon, read him," Burlew urged, holding it out. People murmured around them. At last, after repeated assurances that he wanted her to, she took it.

"No credit," she read, in a whisper. "Debit, zero. Last fiscal year income, zero. Lifetime income to date, zero. Projected income . . . zero."

"Stepfather can't terminate a man without he be poor," explained Burlew. "Unless he have debit balance bigger than credit balance. Burlew got income zero, outgo zero. No tax, no percentage. Never in Red. Do what I like. Adjustors never get me, no lie."

"Yam, you got him wired," she said, comprehension dawning. She moved closer and took his arm. "Wow. Real Burlew, here. Look, where you be staying?"

"Wherever," said Burlew.

"Am got student cube." She tucked the telecard back into his coveralls, looked up. "Want to stay with me?"

Burlew lowered his voice. "That be Giving, you know. Adjusters fine you for that. Bank not top on Giving."

"Stroke the Bank," she said. "Maybe me be like you, never Work."

"Alrite," said Burlew.

She not only took him to her cube, she fed him for a week. For that week he was content; but one day she returned from class to find only a crudely printed pome.

Monaghan Burlew had moved on.

* * *

The Board met in Singapore that week. It had four members, all dressed in conservatively cut Bank-gray suits. Wang Lung was Chinese; an elderly, wrinkled, shriveled man with bright small eyes that missed nothing. C. Bertram Boatwright was British; still erect, with snowy white hair, he carried his age like a faded banner. Amitai Muafi was both Israeli and Arab, descendant of the vigorous mixed race that had grown up in the long-contested Sinai. Like the others, he was old; they were all old men, old, but with keen eyes and with a strange anachronistic look of health and activity. The fourth member had no name, or, rather, had 66 names. He was a bankrupt SF writer who had waived termination to have his cerebrum replaced by a computer data link. In other words, the fourth member was the Bank itself, the worldwide parelectronic brain that controlled the most perfectly integrated planetwide economy in history.

There were three items on the agenda. The first was a proposal to begin the large-scale mining of Martian chromium deposits, a task that would take decades, billions of CU, and thousands of lives. The Board approved it. The second was a request to close down Antarctica, which had lost money for three years in a row. This was defeated three to one, Boatwright jokingly pointing out that the U.K. had been losing money for well over two centuries with no ill effects. The third item for discussion was what to do about Monaghan Burlew.

"Terminate him," Wang Lung suggested, as he always did when Burlew was mentioned.

"HE IS SOLVENT AND CANNOT BE TERMINATED," said the Bank, its face smooth and expressionless as always.

"What's his balance?" said Muafi, sounding as if he already knew the answer.

"ZERO."

"That's solvent?"

"HE IS NOT IN DEBT. THEREFORE, LEGALLY HE CANNOT BE TERMINATED OR OTHERWISE PROCEEDED AGAINST."

"Round and round," said Boatwright impatiently. "Terminate him illegally, then. That's where you differ from us; you're not flexible, not adaptable to changing circumstances. Can't you compromise a little, just once?"

"WE DO NOT COMMIT ILLEGAL ACTS," said the Bank. "BY DEFINITION. WE HAVE LIVED WITH BURLEW FOR FORTY YEARS. IS IT

NECESSARY TO ACT NOW? CAN WE NOT LEAVE HIM ALONE?"

"No. We must eliminate him somehow," said Wang Lung, scratching at the table angrily with a withered yellow hand. "He is the last. He defies us constantly, in speech, in gesture, in the very way he lives. His so-called poetry spreads a hideous virus of disrespect and noneconomic behavior. Do you know"—he pointed a bony finger suddenly at the Bank—"what he calls you? Stepfather Bank! It's a code word, like 'aux armes,' or 'off the pigs'!"

"WE DON'T MIND NAMES," said the Bank.

"Don't underestimate their power. Those names are spreading. People say things like 'Stepfather is watching you'—sometimes right in the Adjustors' hearing! We get anonymous letters in the mail addressed to Stepfather—obscene letters. The top tune in Morocco is 'I Owe My Soul to the Stepfather's Store'."

"Crack down," suggested Muafi. "Ban the word. Fine those who use it. Trademark it and sue those who infringe. There are ways."

"That's treating the symptoms," said Boatwright. "Wang Lung is right. This man is a center of infection. He's dangerous. He's got to be put away. Can't you convict him of *something*?"

"ALL CRIME IS BY DEFINITION ECONOMIC. ANY MALFEASANCE NOT ECONOMIC IS VICTIMLESS AND THEREFORE NONCRIMINAL. THIS IS A PRINCIPLE DATING BACK AS FAR AS 1970. BURLEW DOES NOT ENGAGE IN ECONOMIC ACTIVITY. THEREFORE HE HAS NEVER AND CANNOT NOW COMMIT CRIME."

"This concern for legality sickens me," said Wang Lung. "Can't you convince yourself to use extralegal procedures? Say... the Manifest?"

Boatwright and Muafi glanced up at the name. It hung in the air as they sat for several seconds without speaking. At last Boatwright coughed politely and changed the subject with, "I may have a less—extreme—recourse."

"IT MUST BE LEGAL, MR. BOATWRIGHT."

"I know. It will be, even by your impeccable standards." He explained his idea. The other two humans nodded. After a moment, the Bank did too.

The meeting was over. The old men shook hands and left, each to his own corner of the world. They agreed to meet in a month, in New York, to celebrate the fall of Monaghan Burlew.

* * *

But by that Friday, more peripatetic even than the Board, he had left the City, stowed away in an empty tool crate in a Bank-owned freight pipeline. He left the line in Malta, where it emerges briefly from the Mediterranean, and wandered about the narrow streets of Old Valletta, eyeing the graceful jet-eyed women and blinking in the floods of sunlight. His lips moved as he walked about, bare feet slapping on the hot pavement. He was happy, though his stomach growled and his fleas were stimulated by the heat. He was composing a pome.

In Malta strokes be black the eyes,
They beauty come as top surprise;
The sea down there is blue . . .

He worried at the last line. Shoe, frue, Sue, two. No, no good. Have to change the third line, he thought. *How about*, he muttered, *the sea down there is green? . . .*

He was so engrossed that he walked right by the alleyway. A few steps farther on he forgot the pome suddenly, spun around, and ran back to the entrance to the alley.

Burlew's eyes widened. A thin figure waved its arms from atop an archaic metal trash can. A knot of silent listeners, wrapped in black wool against the fierce heat, stood elbow to elbow in the alley. He stepped cautiously forward to join them and caught the words:

". . . slaves of monopoly capital, universal state capital! Yes, you have work, make your little wage; but who really buys? Who really sells? The Bank—and skims its ten percent from everything you produce or need. Clothing, wine, cheese, medicine. It owns you, brothers and sisters. Owns me. Owns all of us!" The dark figure's fists shook in angry harmony with its words. Moving closer, Burlew saw that it was a woman, thin, bony, awkward, but with eyes of dark fire set deep an in intense, ascetic face. *Who could she be?* he asked himself. Open defiance like this, speaking in public against the Bank . . . it was suicidal. He himself had never dared it, saying his pomes only to individuals in passing, furtively.

"Who her?" he said to one of the Maltese.

The man started, staring white-eyed at the shabby fat man, and bolted, screaming. The rest scattered and in seconds Burlew was alone with the woman, who slowly lowered her hands and looked around, as if just awakened. "Top talking," said Burlew. "Hey, me Burlew, stroke. Who be you?"

Her shoulders slumped and she stepped down from the can. She held out her hands; bony, red-chafed wrists emerged from the too-long sleeves of a dirty blue student-pension coverall. "So take me in," she said. "No more talk, Stepson. I'm ready to drop the load."

"Stepson! Hey, you think me be cop? Look at me! You see any Gray on me?"

"Who are you, then?" she said warily, looking past him to the entrance of the alley. *Like a cat*, Burlew thought in one of his few genuine flashes of poetic image. Like the ill-nourished cats of the night that were the only free ones left in the world city of the Bank.

He explained. She huddled back against sandstone, eyes gradually widening.

"No credit!"

He showed her the blue card. Reluctantly, she took her own out and showed it to him. The telecard had changed from its normal healthy blue to a flushed red, and the characters glowed on it like black fire.

CREDIT	0.00 CU
DEBIT	4239.17 CU
LAST FY INCOME	1320.00 CU
PROJ FY INCOME	1320.00 CU

FINAL NOTICE************************OVERDUE

REPORT TO NEAREST OFFICE OF ECONOMIC ADJUSTMENT FOR SERVICE

"Burlew wondered," he said, giving it back to her and looking uneasily at the alley entrance himself, "Why you talk free, not fear breaking law. You Overdrawn already? Whaj do?"

"I'm sorry—I don't understand Low English very well."

"Whaj *do*? Why you be Overdrawn?"

"Oh. I'm . . . I was a student, doctoral candidate. Economics. I wrote a paper. About the Bank."

"You didn't top on Bank."

"I . . . top on?"

"You didn't like Stepfather."

"Well, it wasn't really anti-Bank. My thesis was on certain social aspects of the flat ten percent rate on monetary transactions. How this was a special hardship for the consumer, especially the poor consumer, because . . . well, never mind now," she said, sensing Burlew's nearly complete lack of comprehension. "I got the notice to report to the Adjustment Office the day after the paper was turned in."

"But how be you Overdrawn?"

"Oh, that. I had a scholarship that was supposed to pay for my schooling. It was . . . withdrawn. I'd already put it all on Credit for the doctorate. And after that . . . there was no job."

"Where you from, stroke?"

"Greater Norfolk. I got out. A . . . friend put me on a suborbital. Now I'm here. But hungry!"

"No lie," said Burlew. He took her hand gently, felt it trembling with the fever of hunger. "Look. You seed my Card. I be'd out here for twenty years—no Credit, no Debit, Balance Zero. Free. Want to give it a turn?"

She squeezed his hand, looked up at him with an odd expression.

"What have I got to lose?"

The waterfront shimmered in the heat, filtering the glare of the sun through the glowing pastels of the buildings that ringed it. The curving stone quay ended at a palace in cool white. She followed him down the quay, but stopped as he approached the building's door. "You—Burlew—this is the most UpUp class 'rant!"

"Yam. Them got top-rate prot."

"But the price—when we can't pay it, the Grays will be here in seconds!"

"No, they won't," said Burlew. He patted his stomach. "See him? Burlew know a few tricks. Knows the scam, get around the Charge. Come on. You want to eat?"

She looked around the harbor. A sailboat glided past the quay, the hull-less type, canted over slightly, the fut-fut-futting of its luffing sail coming clearly across the water.

They went inside.

An hour later, Burlew shoved himself back from the table

and belched. The girl, who had stopped eating many courses back, sat across from him, staring at him over the debris-strewn table. Burlew grinned, picked at his teeth with a dirty forefinger. "Top on that prot, stroke? Telled you Burlew fix."

"But how do we pay?"

Burlew slid his eyes toward the desk, fantastically distorting his face as he mined for a piece of realsteak tartare lodged behind a molar.

The 'rant, fully autoed, had taken their orders, cooked, served, and carved with flashing servo-driven waldoes, and would now clear, all without word or question; but the Desk would not let them out without Charging them. Charging was simple. The patron's hand was placed over a reader port in the Desk. A microsecond-short stab of laser vaporized a bit of dead surface skin. The data was recorded in short-term memory and the customer allowed to pass. At the end of the day all charge data was transmitted to the Bank, converted to genetic coding—the basis for all monetary transactions—and the patron's account charged accordingly.

Fast. Simple. And foolproof.

Burlew shoved one of the used plates aside and picked something up from the table, palming it skilfully. "Follow Burlew," he said. They sauntered toward the Desk, waited for a moment as a casually dressed, graying man, id-patched for HetSex, UpUp, Exec, and Lifex, checked through.

When his turn came, Burlew's hamlike hand covered the reader port. The laser pipped, the door unlocked, and the Desk said, "THANK YOU, SIR, MADAM, WAS EVERYTHING ALL RIGHT?"

"Him oysters not be as good as last time I be here," said Burlew. "But alrite."

They stepped out of the Club into a wave of sunlight. Burlew opened his hand to show the girl the slice of ham before tossing it into the water. "Tonite," he explained, as they walked down the quay, "Bank be puzzled. Ham be enough like human to pass Charge. But later Bank end up with genetic pattern him can't match. Write it off; send RepRob to fix Desk."

"Won't they catch on to that after a while?"

"Only pull that scam two or three times a year, in different place. Yam, him Burlew got plenty more." He smiled down at the girl. "Got plenty more scam. Top on scam? Stay fat, no units. Harder for you—you be in debit, got red card. But—" he hesitated. "You got name, stroke?"

"Name be Jaylen," she said, trying to follow Burlew's dialect. She smiled, for the first time. He found it extraordinarily bewitching, and at the same time sad, like one of his more cherished pomes, "Dead Cat." "You were saying—?"

"Be saying"—the fat man looked intently at her—"maybe we doose up for awhile. Whaj think?"

They spent that night on the bare roof of a flito palace in the Old City. The stars were bright. And free.

From Malta they went to Alexandria, hitchhiking on a private surface yacht whose owner, a crotchety Melanesian, was greatly amused by Burlew, his habits, and a cycle of porno pomes that Burlew, lolling, composed *ad libitum*. He and Jaylen stuffed themselves mercilessly at each meal. When they docked at Alexandria they cornered a city cop—not a Gray—and insulted him until he lost his temper and hauled them in. That night they were comfortably housed and fed in the otherwise empty jail. In the morning they were released by an apologetic desk sergeant; no economic activity, no crime. *De minimus non curat lex.* Burlew turned down an offer of 20 CU damages. "Why?" said Jaylen.

"Stay free," said Burlew. "Money mean slavery, stroke. Burlew use it—even once—then him Bank got me. Tell me where to live, what to do, terminate me if I get too far in Debit. In System. Not for Burlew. No lie."

From Alexandria they followed the Nile south, headed vaguely for the bustling new cities of the PanSemitic Sudan. They walked, hitched, scammed their way along. Jaylen grew adept at finding shelter in the Cynic style and at working the centuries-old Stone Soup routine. As the days, and then the weeks, passed, they learned to work together as a team, pulling more complex scams than could one person alone; and in these more involved schemes, Jaylen was more and more often the lead, the operator, and Burlew simply bagman. He grew proud of her. She learned fast; she was clever, he saw, with the heart of a born scavenger. He liked it. In the evenings, camping out in the bush or on roofs, in shipping containers or empty cubes Burlew jimmied open, they talked; and Burlew, brow furrowed, tried to grasp the esoteric High English she spoke, tried to understand what she told him about the Bank and the economy.

And surprisingly often they found they didn't even need to run a scam. They found that in the smaller towns they could ask for food, explain that they were Creditless, and often shopkeepers and citizens would slip them seaprot or soy loaves in spite of the strict illegality of Giving.

"Him Bank be losing load," remarked Burlew to Jaylen as they munched on oranges from the orchards of Saad el Aali, overlooking Lake Sadat. The road was dusty, and Jaylen, hot, had loosened her coveralls and leaned panting against the bole of one of the trees that lined the road.

Burlew, watching her, felt an unaccustomed emotion. Her glossy dark hair was wet with sweat and the skin of her bare throat was pale under the tanned face. *She be looking better now*, he thought. He smiled. The life of a freelance poet in the 22nd century was not that of François Villon's time. He had never found a woman willing to travel with him before, and though many had taken him in for a night or two, none of these had been a tenth as beautiful as he suddenly realized Jaylen was.

"Why do you say that?" she said, not opening her eyes.

"Them—*those*—people. They not act like Stepsons. I think people here not so top on Bank no more."

"It would be nice if that were happening all over."

"No lie," said Burlew. "Well, we get along top in Sudan. Stick with Burlew; live plenty good. Who needs Credit?"

"You know, Monaghan, I've been wanting to ask you that," she said, voice muffled by the arm she had put over her eyes. "What made you so different? Why did you decide, back when you were sixteen, that you weren't going to cooperate like everyone else?"

Burlew stroked his beard, and his eyes sought the distance for a few moments. When he spoke again his voice was surprisingly soft, introspective. "It be'd a dream, Jaylen. When I be small. A dream of—bad time. Dark Time, I been calling it. Time when Bank be dying, and world be dying with it. It be'd—a strong dream."

"And your dream told you to stay out and you'd survive?"

"Well—not be so sure. Seems like—I was outside, but part of it. And that I be trying with all my might to stop it happening."

He glanced down at her. "Looking hot. You be all right?"

"I feel . . . strange," she said, putting her hand to her head. A frown deepened between her closed eyes.

A moment later she toppled slowly over on the sparse broom grass.

"Stop! Stop!" screamed Burlew, running out on the highway. An old-fashioned planer braked to avoid hitting him. Burlew pounded on the locked door while the driver's dark, frightened face stared out at him. "She be sick! Yam, you got to take us to medcen, no lie!" The man knew no English, low or high, but finally unlocked the door. Burlew bundled her into the rear seat. She lay limply in his arms, sweat trickling across her face.

The driver dropped them at a medcen in Wadi Halfa. Burlew staggered under her weight as he ran for the entrance. And then, only a few steps away, he stopped dead.

If he took her into a medcen they would do a genetic pattern as a routine test. They would find out who she was. They would find out her negative Balance. And then they would call the local Adjustors.

And she would be terminated. Alive, she was worthless to the Bank. Dead, she had considerable economic value—as organs, enzymes, tissues for the lucky few who could afford Lifex. The Bank was honest. In return for the use of her body, it would cancel her debts.

He stood on the sidewalk for several seconds, feeling her warm, heavy weight on his arms, feeling the blood drain from his face; and then he turned away from the medcen. He found an alley back of a closed 'rant, out of sight of the street, and tried to make her comfortable with rags and newspapers from the piles of stinking trash drifted up in the corners.

"Jaylen. Don't drop load. Yam," he said. He pounded on doors, made signs for water. Returning, he found several thin dogs gathered speculatively around her. Sydney! He saw red for a moment—since they had mutilated his feet he hated dogs—and kicked and cursed them away from her motionless form. He knelt over her and dabbed warm water on her face, searching for words. "C'mon, stroke," he murmured. "C'mon. Talk to Burlew."

She shuddered a little, opened her eyes. They were dark, the pupils fantastically wide; the flesh around them was growing dark, puffy. "Bur . . . lew."

"I be here, Jaylen. Hey. How you be feeling?"

"Bad . . ."

"Think you got too much sun."

"No . . . it's something else. I have a . . . problem. My immune systems . . . no good. Born without them. Genecon must have . . . slipped up."

"What? You need a medicine? You tell me, I get it, no lie."

"No."

"Tell me! Burlew get it for you!" He was wild with fear; she was pale as old paper now. He groped for her pulse. It was weak, rapid, and it seemed to him that her flesh was burning hot. There was no question that she was seriously ill.

"No . . . you can't get it for me . . ."

He leaned his bearded, anxious face close to her. "Stroke, you be looking bad. *What medicine*?"

Finally she told him, and then lapsed, her words trailing off into dilerium. Burlew jumped to his feet and ran down the alleyway. As he had hoped, a drugcen was located near the medcen. "Talk English?" he gasped out to the clerk, a tall fellow with insolent eyes.

"Little Enlish, yam," said the clerk, smiling.

"I need medicine, DNAsub two-seven-three-dash-two-two, R. You got him?"

"I got him, yam," said the clerk. "That be for reinforcing of general immunity, yam?"

"Yam."

"Here he be." The clerk took down an injection tube but eyed Burlew over the counter, seeming to notice for the first time his customer's ragged clothes and matted, overgrown hair. Burlew could see the man's nose actually wrinkling. "That be feefty CU."

"Pay later," said Burlew, reaching over the counter for the tube. "Need him real bad, now."

"Just charge him, then," said the clerk, evading his hand and pointing to a reader port set in the drugcen's counter.

Burlew looked wildly around the shop. There was no substitute for his flesh. He thought of Jaylen, lying cooling and helpless with the dogs in the alleyway, her wild eyes open perhaps as they closed in.

The dogs. He shuddered.

"Look. Need him now. Can't pay. You give him to me, yam?

You be top man with me solid, no lie."

"Can't pay? *Geeve* him to you? You be wanting me to commeet Geeving? Say, be you Overdrawn?"

"No. Here be my Balance. See? Blue." He held the card out, breaking the universal tabu. The clerk's eyebrows rose, but he shook his head and put the tube back on the shelf. Burlew's eyes followed it.

"I be sorry. You pay, or no mediceen. It be checked—if it be gone and no pay, I lose money, no lie."

"Money," repeated Burlew. He looked at the reader port. It was an open mouth, waiting to devour him. A scam formed in his mind, a modification of one he had often used to get food in factory complexes. He could enter the medcen next door through the rear entrance, find the laundry room. No one ever guarded dirty laundry, and a coverall of the proper color would have him access to most areas of the hospital, perhaps to the place where drugs were stored . . . but it would take time, time to pull the scam, to find the right drug. And time was the one thing he didn't have. He thought of his freedom and of Jaylen's face.

Very slowly, he put his hand over the port. The laser popped. The clerk grinned and handed him the tube. Burlew took it and without a word walked out of the drugcen, looking down at his telecard. Still blue. But by morning it would be red.

And he would belong to the Stepfather.

He broke into a run. The dogs scattered as he tore into them, and his foot caught one and sent it into the air, yelping.

She was cold now, her face red-flushed, shivering violently. A dozen different infections, unopposed by her body, were racing to corrupt her flesh. He placed the injection tube against her neck and triggered it directly into an artery. He watched, holding his breath, as seconds and then minutes passed. At last she relaxed, still unconscious, and he knew that the DNA transfer had pulled her back.

An hour later she awoke. "Hello, you Burlew," she said.

"Jaylen. You looking better. How you be feeling?"

"Better." She rubbed her neck. "It stings. You injected me there?" He nodded. She rubbed it, looking troubled. "Did you pay for it?"

"Had to. Used Credit."

"You know what that means? That they can make you Work now, or terminate you if you fall behind?"

"Yam," he said. They looked at each other.

Jaylen began to cry.

The hand he took was warm, the grip strong. He frowned at her. "Now, why you be crying?"

"Monaghan . . . that's what they sent me for."

"What?" said Burlew.

"The whole thing was a trick, a scam. They sent me, the Board, to find out how you lived, how you could be trapped. Understand? To make you use the System, to compromise that unique immunity you have—*had*. I didn't know what you were like, I agreed."

He tried to understand, felt as if he were groping through a fog toward something too vast and horrible to comprehend. "You mean that you not be Overdrawn? That you be a . . . Stepson? Work for Bank?"

"That's right. I do special work for the Board. Oh, part of it's true. I was an economics student, I did write a subversive theme. They called me in, threatened me. They use people like me, the weak ones . . . the strong they terminate. I wasn't strong. I was very young, I had never known anyone to defy the Bank, I didn't know how things were. I agreed to work for them, for a man named Boatwright."

"You mean you don't love me," said Burlew, in what was perhaps his first complete sentence in High English.

"You ape. Would I be telling you all this if I didn't? Hell, no; I'd just disappear. Your code in that reader was all they needed, and you gave them that—because you loved me.

"I didn't mean it to happen that way. After the first week, I didn't mean for it to happen at all. I never thought I'd have an attack here, now. But since it happened that way—you know, I'm kind of glad.

"See, they went wrong, Monaghan. I've done some dirty jobs for them before—things they concealed even from the Bank itself. But this time they were too smart. They wanted you to fall in love with me. That was easy. But it works both ways!" She laughed, eyes flashing. "You're no prize, Monaghan Burlew, but you're real, you're free. You know what your life is for. You don't fear anything or anyone. You act dumb, and you talk like a slob, and look worse, and frankly your poetry stinks, but hell, most of that they forced on you. You're the only one who hasn't knuckled under—the only one. And, Burlew, it's that I love you for!"

Burlew stood up slowly and looked up and down the alley. Anger began to darken his face. He picked a flea out of his beard, crushed it savagely between his fingers, and stared down at her. "You saying . . . ?"

"That I love you! That I'll stick with you!"

"They be hunting you."

"*They* be on their way out," she said.

Burlew took out the blue card. He looked down at it, and his teeth ground together. "Now I be in debt. Not be free any more. What do you mean, you're 'kind of glad'?"

She sat up, leaned back against the grimy wall. "Because I wanted to join you. To work with you. But what we're going to do, have to do, can't be done in the open. We'll both be outlaws, be underground. I know you, Monaghan; you're stubborn. You've had to be. You wouldn't have given up your precious immunity for anything else in the world. So I'm glad we'll be outlaws together. But not for the Bank. For *us*."

"Outlaws? What be you talking about, stroke? You still be mixed up the head."

"Wake up, man! You've been out here fighting the Stepfather, in your own way, for twenty-two years. You've done a lot; ridicule is painful, it travels fast when it's put in a nutshell; the Board fears your pomes. But there's one thing you've missed."

"What be that?"

"That the Bank isn't necessary. Because money isn't necessary."

"Not be necessary!" He was so startled he forgot his anger. He turned the astonishing words over in his mind. He himself had not used money, but he had certainly, though indirectly, lived on the Bank-organized system of world production and distribution. In one of his pomes, he had compared himself to a fly, living off the cow, ridiculing it, but . . . where would the fly be without the cow? And where would Earth be without a Stepfather? "Sure money be necessary. How things be made without money? Why people work? And how people buy and sell without money?" He shook his head.

She reached up, brought his face down to hers, and whispered a single word.

"*Barter.*"

* * *

Seafloor 12 was a kilometer long, a kilometer or more wide, and eight levels deep. Once the Philippine Trench had been uninhabited; galleons had sailed over it, fleets battled, mighty ships sank roaring into its endless night. Now it was an industrial center, a long, dark valley lit by coldlight floods and chewed away by slowly rolling machines. Seafloor twelve, a city of two million souls, lay two hundred meters below the ocean floor.

Their steps echoed in the empty tunnel. The melt edges of the raw basalt gleamed like depression glass at the tunnel's turns. "Here we are," said Jaylen. "Whaj think? This will be good for the night at least, maybe a few days—yam?"

"Yes, this will be good," said Burlew, looking around at the tanks that lined the vast room. "Top thinking."

The zoo's inhabitants stared back at them. They said nothing. Burlew reached over the barriers and pulled several blocks of a whitish substance from one of the feeders. Bit into one. "Fishy," he said. "But not too bad. Adjustors never look for us here, no lie."

The sharks, the rays, the deep-sea fish, the varied fauna of the sea stared at them. Evicted from the ocean above, immured in the city's zoo, they stared as Burlew wrote a pome on the walls, using a clamshell as chalk:

Trade things and save 10 percent.
Tell the Bank to go get bent.
Think your wages are too low?
Barter is the way to go!

I love you and you love me.
Give each other things for free!
Men will say this how we sank
Stepfather Bank.

In Tungting Hu, a city outside Changteh, a dam burst. Burlew and Jaylen lived there for a week, standing in line for free emergency relief supplies. Twelve of his pomes were translated into Low Chinese.

In Ross City, Antarctica, Jaylen persuaded a despondent MidMid to loan her his workpass. She put in two days' work as a genetic counselor and took her pay, 210.40 CU, in cash. Burlew spent those two days reprogramming the Classical Literature program in the Teachcomp at Ross University:

CALL
RPB
RU
EL 422

LSN 46***

SIR THOMAS WYATT

WHAT LITTLE HAS COME DOWN TO US CONCERNING SIR THOMAS WYATT SUGGESTS THAT HE WAS ALLIED WITH THE GOODFELLOW FAMILY, AND THUS RATHER FIERCELY DISPOSED TO FAVOR HENRY VII AND THE LANCASTRIANS. IN 1490 HE PRODUCED THE FOLLOWING TALE, RATHER IN THE STYLE OF CHAUCER, WHO HAD DIED OVER A HUNDRED YEARS BEFORE (SEE FRAME EL 361):

Money is the root of sin
And that root with Bank begins.
Barter only is the key;
Trading between you and me.

Leave the Bank out. Why should they
Get ten per cent as their pay?
If someone needs it, Give your stuff.
For the Bank that will be rough.

A foundry android in what once had been Tahiti saw a scrap of papron flutter from a clear sky. She picked it up and examined it. At first she was puzzled—high reading skills are not expected of androids—but then she realized that it was a pome, in Low French:

C'est la Banque qui nous fais povre;
Faut que nous prends les autres pour govre.

Comment? Pas vous servir de monnaie,
Alors liberte vous soit donnez.

Nous sommes tous les freres ensemble
Aime les autres; c'est tres simple.
Faire de trocquer, et comme ca
Beau-Pere Banque ne l'aimerait pas.

...And the pomes were read furtively, passed from hand to hand, memorized. They were easy to memorize, to quote, to imitate. They began appearing as smudged, reprographed handbills; were laser-burned on freshly painted walls and buildings; were scribbled on the stalls in public toilets, accompanied inevitably by anonymous contributions concerning the amatory proclivities and shortcomings of local Stepsons, cops, the Board and the Bank. The Grays followed with paintbrush, handcuffs, and reeducation, but found that their activities met less cooperation, more resentment, the harder they tried to suppress the hydra of discontent.

Six months passed.

"THIS MEETING WILL NOW COME TO ORDER. MR. MUAFI, PLEASE SIT DOWN. GENTLEMEN. GENTLEMEN!"

Unwillingly they quieted, glancing uneasily around the room as if fearing hidden assailants. Though located high in the mountains of Shensi Province, the room looked exactly the same as forty other Boardrooms in out-of-the-way corners of forty other World Cities; quietly appointed, luxurious, certainly, but in no way reflecting or revealing the true power and wealth of the three old men of the Board.

"THE FIRST ITEM ON OUR AGENDA TODAY IS WORLD ENERGY BALANCE. THE HURRICANE SEASON THIS YEAR—"

"Sir, that is not the first item of business," interrupted Boatwright. He looked tired, somewhat thinner, and his face was drawn tight in a way that suggested not one but several nights of stress in the recent week.

"WHAT DO YOU MEAN, MR. BOATWRIGHT?"

"I mean that we have a far more serious problem that we should face immediately. I think this is the sense of the Board."

"AND THAT PROBLEM IS?"

"Spreading unrest. Insubordination to clerks, managers,

Bank personnel, and especially Adjustors. Absenteeism. Giving."

"Stemming, as we all know, from the activities of one person—*Burlew*," hissed Wang Lung. He turned an accusing gaze on Boatwright. "Now accompanied, and no doubt aided, by that—women—of yours."

"I can't be held responsible for that," said Boatwright. "She had been absolutely trustworthy—I had no idea. A woman, you know—"

"GENTLEMEN," said the Bank, slowly, impressively, "LET US SEARCH FOR THE ROOT OF THE PROBLEM, IF THERE IS A PROBLEM. OBVIOUSLY IT IS CONTRAPRODUCTIVE TO PANIC. IT IS BEYOND ANY ONE MAN TO DO SERIOUS DAMAGE TO THE PERFECTED FINANCIAL STRUCTURE OF THE WORLD."

"Maybe not," muttered Muafi.

"His ridicule was always disturbing," said Boatwright, drumming his fingers angrily on the table. "Not personally—a little humor doesn't hurt us personally, we're beyond that—but in terms of legitimacy; few things are as potent as a well-aimed laugh. When a regime becomes an object of derision it's on the way out, no matter how strong it is financially. But of late his output seems to have become charged with a certain *ideological* content foreign to his earlier 'pomes,' as he calls them.

"I have here several of his works, if that is the word, found in widely varying places. Some have been reprographed, some photocopied, some copied by voxriter, and even some done by hand, with illustrations—unflattering ones. They seem to be passed from person to person in the style of twentieth-century anti-Soviet *samizdat*." He placed them on the table. The Bank pulled one over and read it.

"HIS STYLE SEEMS TO HAVE IMPROVED."

"If you can call it that. But note the recurring emphasis on three themes: first, barter, or trade; second, giving; third, ridicule of You."

"AS FAR AS WE CAN SEE, BOATWRIGHT, IT'S HARMLESS FUN. BARTER? YOU CAN'T RUN AN ECONOMY WITHOUT MONEY. BESIDES, BARTER AND GIVING ARE ILLEGAL."

"You must realize that, unlike you, people do many illegal things," said Wang Lung, allowing the trace of a refined sneer to occur at the right corner of his mouth. "They haven't your fine moral instinct. If enough of them become convinced that a thing is right they will not permit its illegality to stand in their way. They are still largely convinced that it is they and not we who make the laws—a conviction that we are careful not to challenge openly."

"BUT IT IS UNWORKABLE. MARX SAID BARTER IS VIABLE ONLY IN THE MOST PRIMITIVE SOCIETIES. LEROCQUE SAID THAT BARTER IS INCOMPATIBLE WITH DIVISION OF LABOR BEYOND THE THIRD DEGREE OF SPECIALIZATION. OUR OWN ANALYSES INDICATE THAT A REVERSION TO BARTER WOULD CUT GROSS WORLD PRODUCT BY OVER EIGHTY PER CENT."

"What is current GWP, by the way?" said Muafi.

"NINE POINT THREE SEVEN TIMES TEN TO THE ELEVENTH CU."

"Up? Down?"

"DOWN OVER LAST MONTH'S ESTIMATE. ONLY A TEMPORARY DROP DUE TO FLUCTUATIONS IN CREDIT TRANSFER."

"How much of a drop? Percentagewise?"

"THREE POINT EIGHT PERCENT."

Boatwright let out a long whistle. The others betrayed varying reactions of surprise. Only the Bank kept its face immobile.

"Cause?" said Muafi.

The Bank was silent. The other members of the Board looked at one another. "Could it be . . . that some people are not using Bank systems of credit transfer for some purchases?" said Wang Lung.

"BARTER IS UNWORKABLE," said the Bank. A hint of angry stubbornness, some mysterious hypothalamic feedover from the once-human brain it spoke through, seemed to be creeping into its voice.

"Trading goods for goods is only the first step in the breakdown of a currency system," said Wang Lung. "I have read of this many times in my studies of China's long history. When confidence in a 'soft' currency declines—and what is softer than invisible, electronic money?—men revert to locally improvised substitutes. In the past, this has often been gold, but other items of high demand or intrinsic value have been used as media of exchange. Cigarettes. Jewels. Chocolate, food, sexual favors, drugs. The older national currencies, such as the dollar and the mark. Rich men and cities may begin printing their own notes, which will be acceptable at face value within a given radius and accepted at a discount farther away.

"You are right, barter alone is impractical, but it can operate as a catalyst in reducing trust in the Bank, after which the population will turn to these substitute currencies. Frankly, gentlemen, I think we are facing ruin." His last word hung in the still air of the Boardroom.

The three men stared at the Bank, which sat, its face smooth and expressionless.

"Immediate action is necessary," said Boatwright. "We are far too important to the race; without us, the economy is doomed. Who is one man, that he should stand in the way of progress for billions?"

"WHAT DO YOU RECOMMEND?" said the Bank, slowly.

"Dispose of him," said Wang Lung.

"Terminate him," said Muafi.

"Along with the woman," added Boatwright.

"WE SEE THAT WE ARE OUTVOTED," said the Bank. "VERY WELL. OUR RECORDS SHOW THAT BOTH MONAGHAN WILLOUGHBY BURLEW, KK-187-40-5389-23, AND JAYLEN SERAPHINA MCGIFFEN, KM-410-38-5101-01, ARE OVERDRAWN, NOT HAVING RESPONDED TO COUNSELING NOTICE, THEY ARE HEREBY ASSIGNED SERVICE FOR TERMINATION, TO BE CARRIED OUT WHENEVER AND WHEREVER THEY SHALL BE FOUND."

PART II/UNDERGROUND

The machine—a tiny, unintelligent tentacle of the Bank—listened, understood, chose, moved, in response to the works it heard. From a million items in stock it selected small boxes, packets, a few plastron cans. Four flavored soy loaves, a bottle of Tranquil spray, a charge pack for a portable radoven, a pair of realwool socks (an old style that nobody much wanted, but still faithfully kept in stock). "And a liter bottle of Stolichnaya. Him like that," the short, tired-looking woman said.

The manager of the store, who happened to be walking by on his way to the bathroom, overheard the woman's last order to the counter. "We don't carry liquor at this outlet, ma'am," he said.

With a low hum, the first items of her grocery order began to emerge from the counter, to be scanned for freshness and costed and skeined in plastron. The manager looked at the tally readout. "That'll be 8.18 CU, ma'am, plus .82 coo for you-know-who."

The man's tone was unmistakable. Instead of putting her broad red hand on the reader port in payment the woman looked from side to side around the store. The other shoppers were out of earshot.

"Could I speak to you a moment?" she said.

Gesturing him closer, she opened her purse, and in a motion as old as what had once been Russia, used her body to conceal the flito cassette she held out in her palm. "I find this in my son's cube," she said meaningfully. "He be really too young for things like this sort, yam? Take a look. Him be worth at least fifteen CU."

The manager leaned down to read the title. His pupils dilated, a fact the woman silently noted. "Hm," he said. "Five."

"Ten be him lowest," said the woman.

"Hm," said the man again. He looked thoughtful, then nodded. He raised his voice. "No sale," he said to the counter.

"NO SALE," said the counter.

They smiled at each other. The woman left, carrying her purchases. The manager looked at the cassette again and licked his lips. It was, he reflected, good business all around. The goods could be written off as spoiled or lost in inventory.

And, best of all, there was no Ten Percent.

The tall, gaunt woman scowled at the laser-blistered message scrawled on the freshly painted wall. *Stroke Stepfather*, it read in Spanish. She went into the card shop, selected three Valentine's Day cards, and offered the owner a rhinestone pin in exchange. The owner, an old, old lady, at first insisted that she Charge it; but when the tall woman smiled tightly and added matching earrings the old lady finally nodded. Her store was closed for the rest of the day, while her neighbors darkly discussed the three gray-clad officers who had come to take her away.

Four young men sat singing in a square, sunny park, a relic of an almost forgotten island empire, in Bombay. Passersby looked at them oddly and stopped to listen. They wore no id-patches and had about them a certain ragged look newly fashionable among the young. The songs were odd, too; they were not Big Name Entertainment Industry. *Pomes*, the gathering crowd whispered among themselves. *Orphans*. Before long a police planer arrived and the four young men were hauled away in a knot of gray-clad men. But not before other young Indians had circulated in the crowd, passing out crudely reprographed sheets in Low Hindi:

Him Bank's time be coming fast;
Maybe Dark Time come at last.
When the runwalks hum no more
Then us Orphans make the score.

Money be the root of sin;
When it's gone then life begin.
Burn your Cards, trade things, and share.
Bank will die within him lair.

The year before the people would have laughed, dropped the sheets, forgotten. Now, muttering together, they recalled friends and relatives fined, taken away for Reeducation, assigned to harder or lower-paying jobs. Some had not been seen again; Terminated? They didn't know. They kept the sheets long enough to memorize the pomes—and then disposed of them furtively. The people grew afraid.

"This be in my style, alrite," said Monaghan Burlew, scratching his matted beard and frowning at the little brown card. "But I didn't write him. Where you find him, Raoul?"

The man crouched with him—dark-haired, intense, about twenty years old, whose last name was Perrier—shifted his position uncomfortably against the curved side of the storm-sewer, and reached up to adjust the bare wires that held a lightbulb to the maze of cables that ran into the dimness on either side. He was stalling for a few seconds, searching for English. "I find him under the bed in the jail," he said at last.

"Jail? When be you in jail?"

"Just for a night. Stepsons get me for a barter." Perrier held up one arm, showing the pale band of skin where his wristcomp had been.

"Adjustors let you go after one night?"

"Oui. Jail, he was packed—Grays are picking up hundreds for barter, for giving. I was in the jail, it was packed, they bring in two hundred more they arrest."

"Two *hundred*?" Burlew raised his eyebrows.

"Yes—some of them come in so beat up, looking very badly. So Stepsons, they fine the minor cases two hundred CU each and let us out to make the room for the others."

"Things be cooking up there," said Burlew, looking thoughtfully down the tunnel. "And maybe tonite we punch him Bank's override. Yam?"

"Ah, oui—*c'est a dire*, yam," said Perrier.

Footsteps sounded from down the tunnel, interspersed with splashing and curses. Burlew disconnected the light and they waited in darkness. The sounds came closer.

"Monaghan?"

"Yam!" He reconnected the coldlight. Jaylen, her dark hair bobbed and blanched to a stylish albino, blinked and laughed. Burlew reached out for her and they hugged hard. "Got it?" he said, when she stepped back, laughing.

"Yes. Here it is." She handed him a bulky papron sack. Burlew tore the bag open, held the garment inside up for a moment, admiring its shaggy honesty, and then bent to begin pulling on the gorilla suit over his dirty green coveralls. Perrier helped him with the arms, and Jaylen patted the live-plastron mask into place until it adhered firmly to the contours of his face. She couldn't suppress a grin, looking up into the ferocious and quite realistic-looking gorilla muzzle. "Is it hot in there, Monaghan?"

"Not be too hot yet. You hear me alrite?"

"Fine. A little muffled, but confine your comments to growls and you'll sound great. I'm already dressed." Jaylen opened the conventional longcoat with its MidMid id-patches to show the starred nipples and red triangle of a Flito Girl.

"Let's go," said Burlew.

The 10-klick runwalk hummed them along. "Paris, Paris," Burlew hummed in tune with it. Snatches of Low French from the other late-nighters on the runwalk. A slight drizzle gleamed under the archlights, fringes of the spring rains the WeaCon division of the Bank was laying on the thirsty fields of what once had been Picardie, and after that the Oise. "Let's jump," he said, and the three of them moved to the 15-, 20-, and then to the 25-klick walk, fastest of those that moved along that stretch of the Avenue de la Troisième Guerre. The Parisians, unchanged despite generations, made way for the man, woman, and gorilla without comment.

"Here are your workpasses," said Perrier, handing a telecard to Jaylen and one to Burlew. "They will pass, I think. One of our Orphans at the id-shop of the Sorbonne made them up. Keep them from the rain."

"Here, you be holding mine for me, yam?" said the gorilla. "I got no pockets in this thing."

The runwalks grew more crowded as sidestreet transfers boarded. Sensing the weight, and knowing its destination, the runwalk slowed as it neared the head of the Avenue. "Here we are," said Jaylen, looking up at the building.

Once it had been the Paris Opera, pride of Napoleon IIIme and all of Europe. Not it was a flito palace. The stone sat as solidly as if three centuries had never been, but it was only a looming shadow behind the firework flickering of the five-story-high holograms that advertised the night's shows.

Burlew elbowed toward the offstep. The gorilla suit helped a little, but not much, and they were all three breathing hard when they walked past the lines at the entrance. "*Des artistes*," said Perrier, flashing the workpasses. The guard eyed Jaylen, nodded carelessly, waved them on in.

Burlew was sweating; the heavy suit was growing hot. He looked around; never using Credit, it was only the third time he had seen the inside of a flito palace. *It be a good idea for a scam*, he thought. *If we can pull it off*. He ran over the plan in his mind, looking for possible slip-ups. No scam was ever perfect.

(Flito Palace. By the early 22nd Century, a combination of movie studio, sound stage, bordello, data processing center, head shop, and burlesque theater. Starting in a small way around 1903, with the moving picture, additional channels of input to the consumer were added—sound in the 30's, 3-D and smell in the 50's, motion in the 1970's, holography and the first Direct Subcranial Stimulation in the late 90's. A broadcast form of entertainment called "television" competed with flitos, or "movies" as they were called till about 2000, until shut down by the Bank in 2040 for lack of profit, the concentration of economic power lessening the need for competitive advertising.

And few bothered to watch TV anyway after DSS. Why stare at a box when you could floot-toot-too for a CU or two? The flithead had his hand zapped at the entrance, paying his way [all automatically Charged]; took his Rainbow Three tablet [30 mg. Lexergontin to put him up; a tad of one of the telkoids to damp the ego function; 300 mg. 3,d—parathanatopidrine to keep him there, and three silly milligrams of neocholinesterase to clear the sludge out of his nervous system before the Show started]; filed zombily to his seat, and groped for the plug that hung to the left of his ear. Plugged in.

Flito!

No Man Is An Island. *Qui facit per alium facit per se*. Live theater was poor stuff to flito. Flitting, the spectator was performer. Some two million select synapses were scan-stimulated fourteen hundred times a second. The data processing was usually in the basement of the palace, and it was not simple; that was why the best flito had to be live, not broadcast or taped, although a little of both was done. Too much data, too fast. Only one instrument could record or interpret it, and fortunately every customer was born with one. A brain.

In 2110 flito was bigger than bread and circuses; hotter than the boob tube had ever been, and even more jejune; an opium of the masses that everyone who had Credit to do so smoked as often as he could.

Flito!)

Perrier, who had worked at that very *flito-palais* until his arrest, led them through the warren of rooms and corridors until they reached the studio office. "Cheetah and Jane, right?" said the stage manager, a harried, perspiring, bald little man in tech greens. "God, I be glad youse here. You're up in half an hour. You ready? Got output amps? Got DIN #5 plugs or equivalent? Take your Rainbow One? Jane, you'll need lubrication, right?"

"No," said Jaylen, grinning and taking off her longcoat. The manager frowned at her thinness, but said nothing; good dog-and-ponies were hard to find. Instead he looked at Burlew, who had squatted on his haunches and was trying hard to scratch himself through his suit.

"That a real gorilla?"

"Sure. Can't you smell him?"

"Yam, yam. Alrite. Jeez, what he be having, fleas? I got to go. Youse be on at nine forty-five, Studio Two. Break a leg."

"Got it." Studio Two was near the end of an empty hallway. Jaylen closed the door behind them. "Raoul?"

"*Ici*," said Perrier's voice, disembodied, from an on-set intercom. "All goes well, Jaylen. All Orphans here, except one. We dosed him and plug him in to a monitor. He will flit for an hour. How is Burlew?"

"How are you?" Jaylen asked him.

"Alrite. Hot," said Burlew. "Where be that stroking output plug?"

"We'll give you all channels at first, Burlew, except the conscious thought. We will give to you that when you signal."

"Yam, Raoul. Jaylen, where be that *stroking*—"

"Here it is. Hold still."

(Startled exclamation in Low English.)

"Five minutes, Burlew, Jaylen!"

"What else be playing, Raoul?"

"Channel One, psychodrama from the Bloody Twentieth—slaughter of cetaceans. Got a live Delphinus sapiens playing the lead, by the name of Norbert. He is a ham . . . Channel Two, *The Edge of Night*, Lorna is still having the baby of Guillaume, pretty tame . . . You're on three . . . four, reenactment of the thirty-five expedition to Jupiter . . . five, conventional torture with Simone Fermand. We will cut you in on all channels in . . . one minute. Stand by—"

Flito.

No change. Burlew hesitated. "Commence, commence!" said a voice in his head, Perrier's voice. The plug felt cold against his mastoid. He had just an instant of stage fright, and then the Rainbow One they had both taken steadied him and he flowed. "Rrrr," he said, hunkering. He wondered if the automatic-translate circuits would bother with that. Probably not.

"Hi, folks," said Jaylen. "Here we are in sunny downtown Paris for your flito entertainment. Hello to all you right here in the audience and to all those who may be flitting with us on remote worldwide. Wish you could be here. We have a little act made up for you tonight. My name is Jane; my friend here is Cheetah. My husband's out hanging around somewhere."

The strange thing, thought Burlew, was that there was as yet no sensation of performing. No sense of audience, only the small bright room and Jaylen, in the tantalizing almost-nude costume of the Flito Girl.

"We've got a little dance routine made up here. Cheetah! Up, boy, up!"

He looked up lazily at Jane and pumped up the little bulb. He came up. There, there *was* some feedback, even with conscious-thought off; he seemed to hear a remote laugh in his head.

"Now, don't be a bad monkey. You know who gets my ten percent (laugh). Come on now—I'll sing, and you—"

"Rrrr," said the gorilla. He pulled off a star.

"Now, Cheetah, I'll have to—"

He nuzzled her clumsily, and pulled off the second star. *Come on, Perrier*, he thought.

Maybe he heard. "You've got their attention now, Burlew," said Perrier's voice in his mind. "I'll give you conscious . . . *now*."

A circuit completed itself in his head, and suddenly Burlew had ten, a thousand, fifty million people in his head. Their eyes dragged at his hairy arms, their thoughts enveloped his like glue, leaching him of sensation. But they were passive, watching, and he found that the Rainbow One had keyed his will to act as the Three had destroyed their ability to not-believe. He tugged at the gorilla mask—they knew who he was now, knew as well as he did himself—and winced as part of his beard came out with it. Jaylen was already speaking.

"My name is Jaylen McGiffen.

"This is Monaghan Burlew. Yes, Burlew, the Orphan.

"You have seen our names on the Adjustors' want-lists, and you have read, or heard, Burlew's pomes—our messages to you. Some of you are Orphans, who believe as we do. Most of you are not; you're sound, hard-working citizens, who work at the jobs the Bank educated you for and assigned you to, spend your CUs where the Bank wants you to, mate with the partners GeneCon selected for you, send your children to the Bank's schools, and always, always, pay your ten percent, though you have no say in what is done with it.

"And you wonder why you are not happy.

"The time we can spend with you tonight is limited; we are being pursued, we are wanted for Termination. Grays are doubtless on their way here now. But we had to speak to you, the uncommitted—and this is the only way."

Burlew stared at her, his mouth open. Naked from the waist up, she was as beautiful as an avenging angel, and as impassioned.

"You will not find happiness in a flito palace! You will not find happiness in delusions, no matter how realistic, no matter how depraved! Only in the struggle for your ancient rights will you find happiness; and now, in 2111, that struggle is with the Stepfather!

"We know that you resent the tyranny of the Bank as much as we do. But we Orphans are acting—not violently, but subtly. We trade for goods, evade Tax and Charge at every turn, help one another, and spread the word and habit of resistance.

"We have harassed Stepfather, angered him with Barter, giving, and most of all, ridicule. He knows now that we are not happy. But does he call off his Stepsons? Does he ask what it is we want, why we are not happy with his rule? No—we are pursued, arrested, jailed. Fear rules the world.

"We are trying to get a message through. If Stepfather will listen, and give the people some voice, not in the great matters of government and economics, but in small things—where they want to live, what trade they want to follow, the right to education regardless of class of parentage, the right to a public hearing before Termination, then we can compromise, hope that things will improve with time.

"But if he does not listen, then our time will come! What Burlew calls the Dark Time—when Stepfather will totter and fall, and through suffering and horror humanity will regain control of its economy—and of its soul." She paused, and there was no feedback that Burlew could sense, none at all; only a vast waiting. She turned to Monaghan, who stood scratching at the raw places on his jaw. "Burlew—your pome."

He took a deep breath. He was not quite comfortable with High English yet, despite Jaylen's coaching, nor did he top on rhymeless poetry. But somehow he liked the sound of this one, his first in the new form:

"There is a Dark Time coming.
That time will see destruction, waste, and terror.

Torches, homes will burn in darkened streets.
Stepsons will burn, Orphans will burn; the uncommitted will burn.
Stepfather must step aside;
The Bank has accomplished its purpose:
We are one world now; but we have lost ourselves.
It is time once more to topple the masters of mankind
Or to ride down with them to destruction."

He paused, expectantly. The millions of eyes watched, ears listened, minds waited. Nothing.

"Will you join us?" pleaded Jaylen.

They could feel nothing coming back but a confused mutter of emotion. *Perrier!* Burlew thought. *Are the circuits in? Are we reaching them? What do they think?*

You are getting feedback, Burlew. They are dulled with the drug but you are receiving them. They are . . . Perrier paused . . . *they are afraid.*

Burlew stood still, feeling the trembling begin in his thighs and spread to his whole body. With the word voiced to them, it swelled, and he could feel the fear streaming back from their minds to his. And he looked at Jaylen, who stood wilted, bewildered, and the disappointment turned round in his stomach and became a white-hot anger. "Be you all blind!" he shouted, rage blurring his vision. "Him Bank be stroking you all your life! From kid you be doing what Stepfather say, like be living in flito! You be top on that? That fill you, that load? Yam? Then I be telling you—*you* be the Stepsons. Not just Adjustors. All you be wearing gray suits, be keeping each other slaves to Stepfather. When him Dark Time come,"—and the horrific vision rose again in him, as strong, as terrifyingly real as that night long ago—"you stay inside! Stay off him streets. Or else Orphans be burning you!" He stopped, staring, panting, becoming conscious of Jaylen's hand gripping his arm, of her dark eyes, wide with surprise.

"Monaghan, we haven't long," she said.

At that instant, with an odd sensation that twanged through his whole mind, Burlew was alone again. He knew immediately that the flito circuits had been cut off. The intercom came to life. "Monaghan! Jaylen! *Stepsons*"

"Damn fast," said Burlew, reaching up to pull the dead plug

from behind his ear. "Jaylen, we got to get out of here. Adjustors catch us—"

"I know. Termination." She had pulled coveralls from somewhere and was stepping into them hastily.

"You, there! In Studio Two! Stay where you are. We've got your friends, and if you—"

Burlew silenced the intercom by smashing it on the floor. Jaylen was dressed. They ran through the door and into the corridor and came face to face with three gray-suited Adjustors. The unexpected appearance of Burlew, big as a bear and still in the gorilla suit, froze them for a second, and Jaylen and Burlew turned and fled in the opposite direction.

"What in hell—"

"Monkey—"

"After 'em!"

"Halt, you!"

They pelted down the corridor. Behind them a p-gun sang, and the rear of Burlew's suit burst into flame.

"In here," panted Jaylen. They plunged through the door marked Studio Eight, over the side of an immense tank of water, sinking deep. As he fought his way to the surface Burlew glimpsed a dark, sleek form turning in their direction. He broke into the air for a second but was driven under by a collapsing wave before he could take a breath. Burlew tasted salt, struggled upward again, but found the waterlogging suit dragging him down. He began to thrash about in near-panic. Had he traded death by fire for—

Something immensely strong moved under him and shoved upward. His head broke water, taking in the sight of four bearded men pointing and shouting at him from an over-crowded whaleboat. He gulped air and craned about for Jaylen. She was a few meters off, swimming desperately for the boat.

Another heavy comber submerged them both, and Burlew, as he was borne up again, caught a glimpse of the mother ship, an old-fashioned steamer with tall vertical funnels, standing off on the horizon. The thing beneath shoved again, hard, and he made sense of it this time—the dolphin. Moving so fast he left a wake, Burlew was pushed past the boat, Jaylen altering course to follow him, and toward what seemed to be a patch of fog between them and the ship. They entered it, broke through the edge of the hologram, and slammed into the side of the tank.

Burlew hauled himself out. "Thanks," he gasped to the dolphin.

"I shouldn't have done it," it squeaked, thrusting its head out of the water. "Stay the stroke off my set, boobs. First a circuit foul-up, then you two in my pool. I got a public to satisfy." It finished with a Bronx cheer from its blowhole and dove.

"Let's get out of here," said Jaylen, helping him up. "They won't take long to figure out how to run around the tank."

"Yam." Burlew stood up, dripping, and they headed for the first door that offered itself.

A whip snapped viciously before their faces. A seminude woman, sleek, red-haired, in chrome leather and dark skin, stood between them and three prostrate males. Another hung upside down from an intricate framework, his face purpled, electrodes attached at unlikely spots.

At that moment Burlew smelled smoke. He put his hand cautiously behind him. The live plastron of the suit, damped but not extinguished by salt water, had begun to smolder again.

"Fire!" shouted Burlew, running full tilt over the three prone men. Simone shrieked, dropped her whip, and ran. The four victims began screaming. "Fire! Fire!" shrieked Jaylen, as they burst through swinging doors into the *Edge of Night* stage, and doctors and Guillaume and Lorna and the Mother-in-Law lost their carefully framed mind-sets and shouted and stampeded after them through the next studio, over the methane snows of Titan, trampling crudely welded titanium crosses, past the astonished spacemen-actors in their quaint 21st-century bulgers. "Fire! Fire!" the dread words spread through the palace. Ten thousand zombies had to be unplugged, injected, jerked from their seats and herded out. Burlew and Jaylen wove through running, panicked backstage personnel. The Adjustors, far behind them now, could hardly be heard over the din of running feet and screaming actors.

"Where to?"

"Control booth."

It was empty; Perrier and the other techs who had cooperated were gone. Burlew cursed. The Stepsons would not let him go with a 200 CU fine this time. Well, he couldn't help now. He pulled off the smoking suit just as it reignited and kicked it where it would trip the ceiling fire-sensor.

The door banged open, and one of the Adjustors, a new one, came in. Burlew stared; the Adjustor, a large Class II, stared back; began to reach into his coveralls; and went suddenly to the floor, with a soft sound like a balloon collapsing. "Get into his clothes," said Jaylen, putting the monitor dial on an hour; she had plugged him in from behind, with no ego-relaxing Rainbow at all.

They emerged from the control room into chaos. The corridor was choked with struggling people, actors in varied costumes or lack of them trying to get out, fire-fighting androids pushing to get in, a few blank-eyed flitters backstage already, a sprinkling of confused Grays, ten men puffing under the weight of an enormous porpoise. They joined the struggle for the nearest exit.

Like phantoms, they disappeared. Behind them the flito palace was in an uproar. Fifty of the flitters were injured when the reality of the fire penetrated and they mobbed the exits. The burning suit finally tripped the sprinklers and the entire studio was flooded with sticky puce Pyronix foam, ruining millions of CU worth of scenery, costumes, and parelectronics.

But behind them they left their dream. There would be no mass conversion, no worldwide movement, no march of outraged millions to smash the Bank and all its works. The Grays had done their work; fines, counterpropaganda, reeducation, demotion, all directed and evaluated by the billion-fingered never-sleeping superhuman Bank, had done their work. The people would not demand their rights. They had no freedom, but they had flito. And they were afraid.

It was very early the next morning when they crossed the old Belgian border, huddled in the back of an obsolete agriplaner, rumbling low over the canted slabs of what once had been a highway.

"They be terminated," said Burlew. "But we never hear of it. NewsCon never release it. Millions saw us, but they be afraid to do anything. Maybe say pomes to each other. Do nothing." He thought of Perrier, and of the other Orphans they had never seen. By now they would merely be parts, ready for tissue typing and distribution to those Class I Lifexes able to pay.

Jaylen, slumped in the corner of the planer bed, said nothing.

"This be the end," resumed Burlew, looking down at his bare, mutilated feet. "We got out, but they be killed. And nothing happens. The Bank wins again. We were wrong."

"You can't give in now," said Jaylen, not moving. "They believed in you. You can't give up. That would be saying that they died for nothing, that no one can ever stop Stepfather."

"Stepfather," Burlew repeated. He leaned his head back against the planer's side, feeling the vibrations of the engine through his skull. "Stepfather. What be he really, Jaylen? Maybe we be too indirect."

She thought for several kilometers. "Boatwright never said much about it, when I worked for him. I gathered that there was a small group of people, called 'the Board.' Then there was the Bank itself, which is the computer network that runs the economy, WeaCon, SeaCon, GeneCon, and so on. But sometimes he talked as if it were a human being."

"Probably just the way he talked. But I wonder about the computer. If we could cut it off, or even damage it, maybe that be the end of the battle."

"I thought you didn't want to use violence."

Burlew did not answer that. Instead he said, "Do you know where it be?"

"All over. All over the world. But, wait, he said once—what was it?—something about Germany. Joking about turning it off. Apparently the Bank hadn't been willing to go along with something he wanted to do. But maybe he meant that part of it was in Germany."

"Noplace better to go," said Burlew. "Adjustors probably got most of them, but maybe some Orphans still loose in Germany." He banged on the front of the planer, shouted into the cab forward. "Hey! Let us off!"

The old man driving (who had not even known they were back there, but who assumed he had once known about it, and so was not surprised) slowed the agriplaner and dropped it to a meter. They jumped out and waded to the edge of the road.

They stood by the highway in the rain, a thin anonymous-looking woman in a longcoat, a fat, tired-looking man in wet Bank grays, face gleaming pale where a beard had recently been shaved off. They extended their thumbs in the ancient sign, but planer after planer sped by as it grew lighter. Not all bothered to lift high enough to avoid splashing them with muddy water.

"May be taking us some time to get there," said Burlew.

"And when we do—what then?"

The Dark Time, Burlew thought. He could feel it in his flesh, see it in the shrouded stars to the west. It was striding closer, casting its shadow before it over the world. Only if he could get the Bank to listen, force it to come to terms, might it be avoided, or at least shortened. But to do that . . . he might have to destroy, even to kill. He looked at his hands. He was not at all sure that he could.

"I'll think of something when we get there," he said.

"WE THINK THEY ARE SOMEWHERE IN WESTERN EUROPE."

"*Think?* I thought you knew everything," hissed Wang Lung. His wizened face, wrinkled like a dried apple, grew lopsided in a derisive smile. "The world computer, the ultimate intelligence. And you haven't been able to find two penniless fugitives, given the better part of a year—in spite of this Paris outrage! Couldn't the Manifest have been used then?"

At the mention of the Manifest the others stirred uneasily. The Bank turned its smooth blank face toward the old Chinese. It spoke slowly, without hurry or expression, the thoughts coming from the immense parelectronic banks of the Bank and emerging from the lips of this once-human mouthpiece. "THE MANIFEST CAN BE PROJECTED ONLY WITHIN A LIMITED AREA, AND ONLY WHERE ITS POWERS MAY BE USED. WE JUDGED PARIS, WITH MILLIONS OF INNOCENT CITIZENS, AN UNSUITABLE PLACE. IF THESE TWO ARE LOCATED IN AN AREA WHERE CIRCUMSTANCES ARE SUITABLE, THE MANIFEST MAY THEN BE EMPLOYED."

"Your concern with these 'innocent citizens' touches me," said Wang Lung.

"Why couldn't the Adjustors find them?" asked Muafi.

The Bank paused. "THE FULL TIME OF THE ECONOMIC ADJUSTMENT SERVICE HAS BEEN TAKEN UP WITH THE INCREASE IN CRIME. WE COULD SPARE ONLY A FEW AGENTS FOR FIELD WORK ON BURLEW AND MCGIFFEN. THESE TWO ARE HIGHLY MOBILE AND SEEM TO HAVE BEEN CONCEALED AND AIDED BY A DISSIDENT MINORITY OF THE POPULATION."

"The Orphans?" said Boatwright.

"YES. WE CONCENTRATED FIRST ON THE BREAKUP OF THIS GROUP AND THE CONFISCATION OF THEIR REPRODUCING EQUIPMENT AND LITERATURE."

"That seems sound," said Boatwright, glancing around at the others for support. "Let's move on to the economic report. Are we still losing ground?"

The Bank did not move or speak, but suddenly the conference table became transparent. Inside it appeared a three-dimensional hologram of a bar graph, marked to show Gross World Product and Overall Profits month by month for the past fiscal year. "TO ANSWER YOUR QUESTION, MR. BOATWRIGHT, NO. WE ARE WINNING: TO QUOTE ONE OF THE MINOR POLITICIANS OF THE BLOODY 20TH, THERE'S LIGHT AT THE END OF THE TUNNEL. NOTE THAT THE CURRENT GWP, 9.42×10^{11} CU, IS ACTUALLY ABOVE THAT BEFORE BURLEW WENT UNDERGROUND. WE HAVE REGAINED THE 3.8 PERCENT DROP THAT HIS ACTIVITIES CAUSED. THEREFORE, ALTHOUGH STILL AT LARGE, HE HAS EFFECTIVELY BEEN DEFEATED."

"Good, good!" said Muafi.

"Let's see profits," said Boatwright. The hologram wavered and changed.

"Up eight percent!" said Muafi. "Good work."

"DUE TO THE MULTIPLIER EFFECTS OF THE TEN PERCENT SURCHARGE PROFITS WILL ALWAYS RISE FASTER THAN PRODUCTION."

Wang Lung, meanwhile, had leaned back, looking uneasy. He slipped a pill from an antique enameled box and swallowed it. At last he said, "Can you project GWC for us in this way?"

The hologram winked off, flickered, winked on. "GROSS WORLD CREDIT," said the Bank.

The last two bars on the graph towered above the others. "There's the explanation," said Wang Lung softly. "Stockpiling. Hoarding. A natural human response to perceived danger. People are borrowing to the limits of their Credit, buying food, hard goods, weapons, scarce metals. It has happened many times in China. You are seeing an artificial prosperity brought on by a planet readying itself for chaos."

The three old men stared at the Bank. It appeared unconcerned. "What can we do?" said Muafi, hesitantly.

"We're doing all we can," snapped Boatwright. "But we've got to get the two responsible for all this. Once they're gone, and people see that things are not going to change, everything will return to normal."

"WE WILL DO OUR BEST," said the Bank. "WE WILL NOT INTERFERE WITH HOARDING, FOR IT INCREASES GWP AND IS NOT ILLEGAL. BUT WE WILL INTENSIFY THE SEARCH."

"You can do better than that," said Wang Lung.

"YOU ARE RIGHT. ACTUALLY, WE ARE. PARELECTRONIC MODELS

ARE BEING CONSTRUCTED TO CORRESPOND WITH BURLEW AND MCGIFFEN'S PSYCHOLOGIES. THEY SEEM TO MOVE ABOUT AND ACT RANDOMLY, BUT WITH ENOUGH INFORMATION THE ACTION OF ANY THINKING BEING CAN BE PREDICTED. WITH THE MOST INTERESTING INSIGHTS WE ARE GAINING INTO BURLEW'S MIND WITH THE PARIS FLITO TAPES, WE SHOULD SOON BE ABLE TO PREDICT THEIR NEXT ACTION WITH A HIGH DEGREE OF PROBABILITY.

"AND AT THAT TIME, WE ASSURE YOU, GENTLEMEN—JUSTICE WILL BE DONE."

PART III/THEIR SMOOTH, BLANK FACE

Like a slight shimmer of greenish foxfire, the Manifest flickered into existence deep in the gloom of the Bayerischer Wald.

As seconds passed he gained in solidity and form, yet still seemed somehow insubstantial, a glowing eight-foot figure in Bank gray. He put out a hand experimentally; it passed easily through the trunk of a young pine tree. Kilometers below, a block-long bank of parelectronics registered the insolidity and rethought. The Manifest turned his palm downward and brought it through the tree again.

It exploded, tar and sap and cellulose and bark vaporizing instantly into a ball of bright-orange fire that ballooned around the gray figure with a detonation that rang from the bare mountains above like thunder.

The Manifest smiled, and stepped away from the burning stump of the tree.

His work lay ahead.

"What's that?" said Jaylen, looking up from the carefully shielded campfire. "Thunder?"

"Stars be out," said Burlew. "Not thunder. Maybe suborbital coming down." He squatted by the fire, blew his nose in his fingers and slung the result into the flames.

"Monaghan, do you have to—"

"Sorry, Jaylen. Forgot." The fat man, chin still pale from the recently shaved beard, rubbed his hands on the stolen gray coveralls, and looked apologetically at the three other people around the fire.

They had arrived only minutes before, stumbling through the dense thickets of the vast forest. They'd known the password, and now sat waiting attentively, their eyes on Burlew.

"What be your names?"

"I'm Lyagavy," said the tallest, a smooth-faced young man of about twenty-two. He wore the tailored green coveralls of a Class II technician. "This is Takaichi Tamaki"—shorter, touch of Oriental about the eyes and mustache, wearing the white of a scientist—"and Rudolf Perlmutter. He looks half asleep, but he's one of the best nuke techs at the plant. We got the message to meet you here through the only other Orphan we know. Once there were dozens—we were raided at a meeting—well, you don't want to hear about that. You're Burlew himself, right?"

"Real Burlew, no lie."

"Well," Lyagavy laughed, looked at the others. "You know—we've all read your pomes at the F-station, passed 'em from hand to hand. But could we, maybe, well, hear you recite one?"

"Recite?"

"Read one out loud. Declaim it. Yam," said Lyagavy, descending to Burlew's Low English, "We top on hearing him, no lie. Turn us?"

"Alrite," said Burlew, looking into the fire.

"WeaCon give you rain.
EduCon give you school.
Adjustors keep you down;
Flito ease the pain.

GeneCon give you wife;
HousCon give you cube.
Stepfather give you everything,
Own you all your life."

A long silence followed the last line, broken only by the crackling and spitting of little yellow tongues from the pine knots in the fire. At last the sleepy-looking one, Perlmutter, stirred and spoke. "Burlew, you're a hero to all the Orphans. You're the one that first defied Stepfather, and we agree with everything you say in the pome. But, you know—"

"Yam?"

"Your pomes stink. No, wait," he said, as Lyagavy and Tamaki started to speak, "it's true, guys, isn't it? You always said so, too."

"You right," said Burlew, rubbing his bare chin with his hand. "You're right. Burlew talked only low English, his parents be Class IV. No school after Working age. Couldn't do top-rate pomes. Whaj think?" He looked at Jaylen and his expression softened. "Him be a year ago Burlew meet this top young stroke."

The younger men watched, eyes widening as Burlew's voice changed. "And she taught me. Taught me words like I, is, love. Declensions and tenses, rhyme schemes and scanning and free verse. You've heard the old Burlew. Would you like to hear the new?"

"As a child I saw the Dark Time coming;
It is very near,
The time of destruction and terror
It is on us.
Torches, homes will burn in darkened streets
The runwalks stopped, the archlights dead;
Stepsons will burn, Orphans will burn; the uncommitted
Will burn like leaves.
The Bank is at its end.
We are one world now, but we have lost ourselves.
It is time once more to topple the masters of mankind
And worry afterward about building on the ruins."

Jaylen's face had darkened as he spoke. She watched him closely. When he was done the five of them stared gloomily into the fire. Finally Lyagavy spoke. "We're convinced," he said. "What do you want your Orphans to do?"

"It's like this. You three, if you're the right people, can gain access to the Bayerischer Wald F-station, right?"

"Yes, we can get you in," said Tamaki. "At least, one of you. Two might be pushing it too far. But we can get one extra person back in past the Adjustors on guard. But then what?"

Instead of answering Burlew said, "Describe the F-station to me."

"Well, it's like any other. F-Eight is the central power facility for most of Europe, as well as for a large part of the Bank's central computing facilities."

"Where be that?"

"Deep underground, somewhere not far from here. They don't give out just where, but one hears things."

"Yam," said Burlew. "And the plant?"

"F-Eight covers about a square kilometer, with thirty thousand km^2 of forest around it. There are fifteen LCMT deuterium-tritium-carbon fueled fusion reaction units with generating capacity of fifty thousand megawatts constant each. Five are on-line at any given time and the others on standby or in overhaul. Want to know more?"

"Can him be shut down?"

"From the control station, yes. But what's the idea?"

"Remember the pome?"

Lyagavy thought. The fire crackled suddenly, a jet of smoky yellow flame. Perlmutter stared sleepily around at the ring of dark, half-seen trees. "The Dark Time—a power outage?"

"That be right."

"But you know, you can't do that by shutting down F-Eight," broke in Tamaki. "The Bank's power grid control at PowCon will adjust to draw from F-Twelve, in Spain, and F-Three in Zaleschiki. At worst it will cut power to the less critical heavy-current users, the desal plants and WeaCon." The others nodded. "And there'll be Stepsons there immediately looking for the reason."

"We can—blow it up," said Perlmutter suddenly. "I can shut off the coolant. That's always the weak link in an F-station. The on-line units would last about a second before they went up."

"No," said Jaylen.

"What?" said Burlew, swiveling to look at her. "Why not? Sounds good to me. They can't reactivate the station once him be gone."

"No, I said. What's happened to you? You aren't a violent person, Monaghan, you've never been—except when you kicked those dogs off me. But we've always been nonviolent, advocated nonviolence. Even if you set it up somehow by remote control, the people at the Station will be killed."

"Be that worse than Termination? What about Perrier, and the others in Paris?" said Burlew. He got up and walked rapidly back and forth in front of the fire, casting monstrous shadows in the wavering red light. "What about us, if we be caught? You and I be spare parts for Lifexers inside of an hour. What about all the other people Stepfather takes every year?" He stopped and stared at her. "Maybe we be wrong about this whole thing. Not barter, not Giving, not pomes. Maybe to destroy—maybe Stepfather would understand that."

"No, Monaghan. You don't fight evil that way." Her voice hardened. "And the Dark Time—you sound as if you want to bring it on, not stop it. What happened to your dream?"

"Maybe that be what the dream meant."

They looked at each other steadily for a second, and then Jaylen looked away, at the ground. Her face grew tight.

"Look, maybe I've got a better idea, if we don't want to destroy the whole station," said Tamaki. "Dmitri, you say five of the reactors are usually on. How many are on standby ready to go on?"

"Generally five, but there could be more, depending on the overhaul schedule," said Lyagavy.

"What would happen, do you think, if we put all ten on at once?"

They all mulled it over. "Don't know," said Perlmutter at last. "At best—I mean, worst—nothing, if PowCon is set up to divert the excess power. But there's no reason it should be. There's a good chance the station could shut down most of Europe by overloading the supply end."

"That sounds good," said Burlew. "What time is it?"

"Almost two."

"Let's go. Jaylen, you be staying here. I be back." They got up from around the fire. Burlew picked up his only possession—a dirty green blanket with singed corners, picked up from the back of an unattended agriplaner—and threw it around his shoulders. Jaylen stood up They looked at each other as the techs kicked earth on the fire.

"You might not come back," said Jaylen.

"I be back, stroke," said Burlew.

She gave him a long kiss, and watched from beside the dying fire as, single file, they moved into the woods and were enveloped by the night.

"What time do you have, Amitai, old man?" said Boatwright, scratching an anachronistic match across the underside of the realwood table before applying it to his pipe.

"Two-thirty, Central European. In the morning," said Muafi sleepily.

They looked up as the door to the small but luxuriously furnished conference room opened, and two others entered: Wang Lung, and, behind him, the Bank.

"GOOD MORNING, GENTLEMEN."

"What's the occasion?" said Boatwright testily. "Why call us here at this ungodly hour? And where are we, anyway? I fell asleep again on the suborbital."

"THIS IS BUDA PESHT, MR. BOATWRIGHT. WE ARE SORRY ABOUT THE EARLY HOUR, BUT WE ASSURE YOU THAT IT IS IMPORTANT." The Bank sat down, its face smooth and blank as always.

"Let's get to business," said Wang Lung impatiently.

"AS YOU KNOW, GENTLEMEN, WE WERE CONTRUCTED TO OPERATE WITHIN A LEGAL AND MORAL FRAMEWORK. THOUGH, AS YOU HAVE OFTEN ADVISED US, THE ABSORPTION OF CHURCH AND GOVERNMENT INTO OUR ORGANIZATION HAS RENDERED MUCH OF THIS PROGRAMMING OBSOLETE, IT IS NOW TOO DEEPLY BURIED UNDER LATER PROGRAMMING FOR US TO REVISE."

". . . The *point*," Wang Lung muttered.

"FOR EXAMPLE, WE WERE RELUCTANT TO ORDER THE TERMINATION OF BURLEW AND MCGIFFEN. THEY WERE ONLY SLIGHTLY IN DEBT AND ONLY AN EXTREME INTERPRETATION GAVE US TERMINATION RIGHTS. SINCE THE BOARD WAS UNANIMOUS IN ITS RECOMMENDATION, WE HOWEVER ISSUED THE ORDERS. UNFORTUNATELY, WE HAVE BEEN UNABLE TO LOCATE THE PAIR SINCE."

"Quite, quite, we know all that," broke in Boatwright. "But why call us at two-thirty in the morning?"

"BECAUSE WE HAVE LOCATED THEM."

"Where?"

"By heaven, let's end this now!"

"SOMEWHERE IN SOUTHERN GERMANY, WE BELIEVE IN THE BAYERISCHER FOREST."

"What are you doing about it?"

"WE HAVE ACTIVATED THE MANIFEST."

The Board members were silent for a moment. "The area is safe?" said Muafi.

"IT IS A DESERTED FOREST EXCEPT FOR TWO THINGS—THE F-EIGHT FUSION STATION, AND OUR MAJOR COMPUTING CENTERS."

"You think Burlew could be after you?" Boatwright snorted. "Ridiculous. The man's still nothing more than a bum, a drifter with a gift for poetasty and rabble-rousing."

"Do you wish additional Adjustors?" said Wang Lung, ignoring Boatwright. "Let's not underestimate him this time. That's something we've done all along."

"NOT NECESSARY."

"Then what do you need us for?" said Wang Lung, puzzled.

"WHAT WE SUSPECT IS THAT ORPHAN ELEMENTS MAY BE WORKING WITH HIM FROM WITHIN OUR CENTERS. REEDUCATION IS OF LIMITED USEFULNESS IN HIGH-TECHNOLOGY AREAS SINCE THE REEDUCATED PERSON TENDS TO LACK PHYSICAL COORDINATION AND MENTAL CAPACITY. THEREFORE OF NECESSITY WE HAVE HAD TO TOLERATE SMALL NUMBERS OF SYMPATHIZERS IN KEY AREAS, BUT WITH CLOSE MONITORING—THAT IS HOW WE FOUND OUT THAT BURLEW WAS IN GERMANY."

"Yes? That's all very well, but what do you *need*?"

"IT MAY BE NECESSARY FOR THE MANIFEST TO TAKE IMMEDIATE ACTION. IN THAT CASE WE ARE REQUIRED TO OBTAIN THE SANCTION OF THE BOARD."

"Of course you have our sanction, you—" choked Wang Lung. "Of course, you idiot. Right, everyone? You've always had free rein to crush these people, by any means. You don't have to wake us up and rocket us all over hell just to give you permission for *that*."

"Absolutely," said Muafi.

"Damn all this legality! We run this planet! Do what has to be done!" said Boatwright angrily.

"VERY GOOD," said the Bank calmly. "THANK YOU FOR YOUR COOPERATION, GENTLEMEN, AND PLEASE STAND BY. FOR YOUR INFORMATION, WE ARE NOW IN CONTACT."

The Manifest stood quietly behind and within #3 Reactor Monitoring Panel, on the second floor of the Control Section of F-8. He was almost insubstantial, with the outlines of his eight-foot frame mistily merging into the front of the panel.

He stood quietly, listening, waiting.

He had found the small party of men deep in the forest, hearing from kilometers away the thudding of their footsteps into the sandy soil and pine needles. He shifted instantly three kilometers away, listened again, and calculated their location by triangulation. He had shifted once more and found himself only a hundred meters away. Dimming his gray glow, he had followed them through the forest, eyes on the bulky dark figure that tripped frequently.

The Manifest had once been human. Or had he? He puzzled over it, as he did during every Manifestation, as he slipped patiently through the night. He made no sound, for he weighed nothing.

A phantasm has no weight.

Human beings had known of phantoms, spirits, out-of-body experiences for all of recorded history. The nineteenth century had sneered at them; the Bloody Twentieth half-believed; the twenty-first investigated; and the 22nd century not only believed, but created. Specifically, the Bank created.

For it alone had the mental capacity to do so rationally, deliberately. Most men's minds were forever beyond their own control. The complexity of thought that evolved ultimately into spirit, and then on into ever-higher planes of existence, were accessible to only two or three humans per century. Those less gifted produced psychic horrors: poltergeists, ghosts, the mass-mind linkages that led to wars and to the mass conversions of 1997 and 2025. Only the Bank, within its hundred cubic kilometers of densely retentive parelectronics, could control and generate psi-powers consciously, at will. Hence—the Manifest.

He heard footsteps outside the control room. Thinning himself almost to invisibility, he leaned forward, through the metal panel.

"Good morning, surprise inspection," said Takaichi briskly to the gray-uniformed guard who stood at the opened door. The guard took in the white coveralls, the Class I id-patches for SciTech, and nodded. He folded his arms and watched as Perlmutter and Lyagavy, in tech greens, followed Takaichi. But he goggled at Burlew, who smiled benevolently at him, and was reaching for his sidearm when Takaichi pressed his thumbs into the back of his neck. They lowered him gently to the floor, locked the door behind them, and walked up two flights of concrete stairs to the Control Section. The young technician on watch there looked up as they entered.

"Hi, Deela," said Lyagavy. "I'd like you to meet a friend of mine. Monaghan Burlew—Deela Singer. She's one of Us."

"Burlew! Really? Why, great, hello!" The small blonde woman jumped up, pumped Burlew's hand eagerly, then stopped. She looked at her hand, at Burlew, then wiped it on her coveralls. "Uh—great to meet you. I read all your, uh, stuff. Can't get it out of my head. Stroke Stepfather! Well, what brings you here, of all places?"

Lyagavy explained swiftly. Singer blanched, but finally agreed. "Just to stroke Stepfather," as she put it. "I wanted to be a Flito Girl when I was small. But I tested too high, and the Stepsons stuck me in nuke training. Sure, let's shut this place down!"

Perlmutter joined her at the watch consoles and began tapping in codes on the dark grids that crossed the panels' surfaces. "Five on line, like we said. Seven more reactors are ready to go; the other three are out for overhaul. Bringing Number Six on line now."

Burlew leaned forward to see out of the meter-thick windows of the control station. Hundreds of feet below, squatting between lead revetments like wingless fighters, fifteen long, tubular shapes were arranged in rows across the bedrock floor of F-8. Around several of them eddied the blue radiance of air under heavy neutron bombardment.

"Six on line," said Singer. "Burlew, I've got a power-out indicator that's red-lined at five hundred thousand MW—five hundred BW. I'm, uh, assuming that that's where something trips out. I'm going to run up to there unit by unit."

"You got him," said Burlew, staring with fascination as the blue nimbus coalesced around another tube far below.

"Seven on line," said Lyagavy.

"Three hundred and fifty BW."

"Flux?" said Takaichi, who was watching over their shoulders.

"Fifty rems ambient, short-term limit six hundred," said Perlmutter.

"Eight on line."

An alarm began sounding below, a high-pitched "peep-peep-peep" that echoed. Perlmutter tapped a switch and it stopped.

The blue glow was growing brighter, swirling along between the revetments, eddying around the long gunmetal tubes like neon fog.

"Four hundred and ten BW and climbing."

"Fuel input increased."

"One-twenty rems ambient on the floor, sixty in the control section."

"Nine on line."

Two more alarms cut loose, one screaming discordantly, one clanging. The techs seemed unable to cut them off. Parts of the panels came to life and began a pulsating red dance. "Ten on line!" said Lyagavy. "Output, Deela?"

"Four-ninety BW."

"Ten F-units on line. Warming up the last two."

It was then that Burlew saw the gray figure step ghostlike from the wall and begin to take on terrifying solidity.

"What the hell be you?" he said.

"SHUT THEM DOWN," said the Manifest through the rising clangor. "THE EUROPEAN GRID IS ADJUSTED TO TAKE UP ALL YOUR OUTPUT. RED-LINE FOR THIS STATION IS FIVE HUNDRED THOUSAND MEGAWATTS. AT THAT POINT WASTE HEAT FLOW EXCEEDS COOLING CAPACITY. THE FUSION REACTORS WILL MELT AND BOTH F-EIGHT AND YOU WILL BE DESTROYED." The gray eyes steadied on Burlew. "ORDER THEM TO SHUT DOWN!"

The techs had turned in their seats and were watching the two of them open-mouthed. At the Manifest's last words their eyes shifted as one to Burlew.

"What do we do?" said Lyagavy.

And Burlew understood.

The Dark Time was now.

He shook his head.

The tall Russian tapped twice on the panel. He smiled tightly at Burlew. "All twelve, on the line!"

Burlew glanced downward through the window. The whole reactor floor burned with a hellish indigo fire that eddied up in waves from each gray tube. The air he breathed seemed to glow with pale blue light. Other than the screaming alarms there was no vibration, there was no noise to indicate the terrible power on the verge of breaking free below. He looked back, to see that Lyagavy and Takaichi were blocking the Manifest from reaching the other two techs, who were watching the output dial intently.

"SHUT THEM DOWN! THIS IS FUTILE! WHAT WILL YOU ACCOMPLISH BY DESTROYING THE ENTIRE F-STATION?"

"Maybe we get a message across—Stepfather," said Burlew softly.

"Red line," said Singer.

The Manifest moved. Lyagavy aimed a punch as high as he could reach; with one arm the gray figure brushed him aside, and Burlew could hear breaking bone in the man's head. Takaichi poised himself, crouched low, and uncoiled like a spring. High in the air he turned and lashed out with a kick. As his leg passed through the Manifest's face it burst into white fire.

The Manifest stepped over the two bodies and lifted Perlmutter from the chair, folded him, and dropped him. Singer clutched at his arm but was thrown against the wall, where she lay motionless. The Manifest reached for the panel.

Burlew's heavy body caught it just behind the knees. It fell, surprised, sprawling; the mass it had assumed for the fight carried it to the floor on top of him. They were face to face when a rushing sound like many waters came from below.

"TOO LATE," said the Manifest.

And Burlew, in those last fleeting instants, thought of Darkness. He was not the means of salvation but the agent of Destruction. He had failed, failed utterly, and it was with that thought that he drew his last breath.

The last thing Monaghan Burlew saw in his life was the Manifest's finger coming toward his forehead.

The Station erupted in a roar of light.

And the archlights went out, the runwalks stopped.

Flitters awoke in darkened buildings, dully surprised at the sudden silence. The great freight pipelines coasted to a halt. Eight billion telecards faded suddenly to a lifeless gray.

All over the world.

A faint tremor rattled the empty tea and coffee cups on the polished table.

"IT IS DONE," said the Bank. The Board members, haggard from their vigil, looked up from armchairs in the corner of the room.

"Burlew? McGiffen? The whole crew?" said Wang Lung, his face wrinkling in a vindictive smile.

"WAIT," said the Bank. "WE HAVE SUFFERED DAMAGE. WE WILL RESPOND IN A MOMENT."

The members looked at one another and shrugged. The Bank sat motionless. Several minutes later it spoke again. "WE HAVE REGAINED SOME CONTROL. BURLEW IS DEFINITELY DEAD. WE

WITNESSED HIS DEMISE THROUGH THE MANIFEST, ALONG WITH THAT OF FOUR OF HIS 'ORPHANS.' THEY WERE KILLED IN AN EXPLOSION OF THE MAIN EUROPEAN FUSION PLANT, IN BAVARIA."

"Has power been restored?" said Muafi.

"NOT YET. WE HAVE SUFFERED DAMAGE TO OURSELVES IN THAT SECTION NEAREST THE PLANT. UNFORTUNATELY THIS WAS THE POWCON SECTION. THE COORDINATION OF POWER REQUIREMENTS HAS BEEN LOST."

"You'll get it back soon," said Boatwright confidently. "We've done well. This will completely finish the entire movement. A short, brutal campaign of repression now will erase everything he's done. You see," he said, addressing the blank-faced man who was the Bank, "how useless your 'moral' misgivings were? We're the law. No one challenges us, no one can even criticize us. Now that Burlew has been defeated we are secure for another hundred years—or at least," he winked at Muafi and Wang Lung, "as long as there are enough Terminations to furnish us with new, perfectly matched organs. And there will be. There will be!"

They chuckled together. The Bank sat still, not joining in the air of celebration, but they did not mind that.

The Bank, they knew, had no sense of humor.

The Dark Time began slowly. Only gradually did the people creep out of their darkened cubes, leave the suddenly silent places of work. They stepped on the runwalks, stared about for a moment, and then realized that they were not moving. They wandered about the streets, mostly silent, a little stunned.

Someone found a police planer, stranded like the rest when the beamed power cut off. A little crowd gathered. The Grays had left it unlocked, running for their station, where there would be safety in numbers.

A little tongue of flame licked up.

Some of the crowd began looking in the shop windows.

Then it began.

Light is made up of all colors, invisible as well as visible.

The roar of a waterfall or of a rocket engine is made up of all frequencies, subsonic, supersonic, as well as those within the narrow range of human hearing.

Expand these analogies. Imagine a sensation made up of all

sensations. A million hands, knives, feathers, ice cubes, red-hot pokers touching the body. A million tastes crowding the tongue, the smells of a planet striking the nose at once. Combine every possible permutation of five senses, and several more that most people live their lives with unsuspecting, into one mighty stream of sensation like Siddhartha's River.

He screamed without a voice, struggled without a body. There was nothing there, nothing to him. He was a point in space, a receptacle, no, a conductor through which a billion impulses a second streamed, of which he could understand nothing.

Ages passed. His struggles became weak and ceased. He was overcome. His numbed mind rolled like a bubble in a cataract.

Sometime endlessly later, the cataract lessened. The roar of sound dwindled down the scale, the touches, scents and tastes vanished, the light dwindled, flickering, into darkness. He drifted; he thought he was no more, since sensation was no more. He had no body. No thought. Desireless, at peace at last, his declining consciousness expanded like a puff of gas in vacuum into endless darkness.

"MONAGHAN BURLEW."

The voice echoed. For some time he thought that he had said it himself. With that idea—the words sounded familiar, somehow—he tried a response.

"Yam?"

"BURLEW, THIS IS THE BANK. CAN YOU HEAR ME?"

Bank? What was a "bank?" "Yam, me hear."

"BURLEW, WE ARE SORRY ABOUT THE SENSORY OVERLOAD. THE F-EIGHT EXPLOSION DAMAGED US SOMEWHAT AND YOU HAD TO BE FILED IN SHORT-TERM MEMORY UNTIL WE COULD REPAIR. ARE YOU ALL RIGHT?"

Burlew . . . Burlew. Could that be him? It *did* have a familiar ring to it . . . "Where be I?"

"YOU ARE WITHIN THE BANK, BURLEW. LIKE THE MANIFEST, WE HAVE SUPERIMPOSED YOUR BRAIN PATTERNS ON A PARELECTRONIC MATRIX WITHIN OURSELVES. WE HAVE, OF COURSE, OPENED MANY SHORTED CIRCUITS."

"Within? Where?"

"IF YOU MEAN THE QUESTION GEOGRAPHICALLY, IT HAS NO MEANING. YOU EXIST WHEREVER WE ACTIVATE YOU. IF YOU MEAN 'WHERE' WITHIN US, YOUR ACCESS CODE IS 4321610072152310. IF

YOU WILL SIMPLY THINK THAT NUMBER—"

Burlew did, and began to remember, starting from the Manifest's pointing finger backwards. He found that he suddenly remembered it all—every one-night stand, every detail of every scam he had ever pulled, every face he had ever seen, every word he had ever heard, every thought he had ever had. He had total and absolute recall.

"What's happened to me? Why did you rescue me? And where are the others? Jaylen—"

"WAIT. THERE IS PLENTY OF TIME TO ANSWER ALL QUESTIONS. AS A PARELECTRONIC MIND YOU ARE NOW THINKING IN NANOSECONDS INSTEAD OF SECONDS: A MINUTE FOR HUMANS IS TWO YEARS TO US. FIRST, YOUR BODY. DESTROYED. WE ARE SORRY, BUT IT WAS NO GREAT LOSS, CONSIDERING ITS LIMITATIONS. WE RESCUED YOU BY RECORDING THE FINAL PATTERNS OF YOUR BRAIN VIA THE MANIFEST. WE HAD A MATRIX ALREADY SET UP FOR YOU AS PART OF AN EFFORT TO PREDICT YOUR ACTIVITIES.

"AS TO THE OTHERS IN THE PLANT, THEY ARE DEAD. JAYLEN MCGIFFEN IS IN OUR CUSTODY."

Hopelessness flooded through the Bank-Burlew. "In custody. She be Terminated, then. She be a smart stroke. Taught me a lot. And . . ." certain very specific sensual memories came back in unadulterated entirety. He allowed himself a short time to savor them, and then snapped back to the present. "You haven't told me why you rescued me—if rescue is the word."

"IT IS. WE DID IT BECAUSE YOUR CONDUCT, AND SUBSEQUENT EVENTS, HAVE RAISED SOME QUESTIONS IN OUR MINDS."

"Well, go ahead—guess I be having time."

"ALL THE TIME THAT EXISTS. TELL US BURLEW—WE ARE ACCUSTOMED TO HUMAN BEINGS THAT ACT WHOLLY RATIONALLY, IN THEIR OWN INTERESTS. WHY DID YOU CONTINUE WITH THE DESTRUCTION OF F-EIGHT WHEN YOU KNEW THAT IT WOULD RESULT IN YOUR DEATH?"

"Well—" Burlew thought about it. Why had he? It was a split-second decision, yet it had seemed so *right*, despite its obvious futility. "I believe I did it because it be'd the extension of the same thing Orphans have been trying to do. Persuade Stepfather to listen to us and to give men more control over their own lives."

"THE HUMAN BEINGS THAT WE DEAL WITH—WE THINK OF THREE IN PARTICULAR—WOULD NEVER CONSIDER SUCH AN ACT."

"Maybe they're not representative of most humans."

"BUT THEY ARE. ONLY A SMALL MINORITY—YOUR ORPHANS—HATED US. AND THAT WAS BECAUSE OF YOU."

"You seem to be misinformed. Most people on Earth hate you. My pomes only allowed them a channel to express that hate and to recognize it in others. But most are too afraid of Adjustors to do anything; the Orphans were just more—stubborn—than most."

"DO NOT YOUR POMES POSSESS A MYSTERIOUS POWER OVER THE MASSES?"

Bank-Burlew had to chuckle over that, and in fact tried to, but found it impossible except in words. "That's a laugh. Jaylen taught me how bad they really be. Maybe that be the 'mysterious power.' Simple, catchy, short rhymes in Low language. Everyone could feel superior to them. They laughed at them, they repeated them to others, and suddenly they found that they all really agreed—and that they were really laughing at Stepfather."

"THAT SIMPLE? HUMAN PSYCHOLOGY IS SO ILLOGICAL. A SET OF CHEAP RHYMES AGAINST THE BENEFITS WE HAVE BROUGHT—PEACE, PROSPERITY, WORK AND SECURITY FOR ALL—"

"Those aren't benefits of the Bank, as Jaylen pointed out to me. Any central planner or government would have brought that about during the twenty-first century."

"BUT THE BANK BROUGHT RATIONALISM INTO HUMAN LIFE. WEATHER CONTROL—ENERGY CONTROL—GENETIC CONTROL—ECONOMIC—"

"There's your error." Burlew saw it clearly now; his mind was rearranging his previous ideas, clarifying beliefs he'd held intuitively but never really understood. He seemed to be working like a computer, far more efficiently than his old merely human mind, yet with all his old feelings behind it. "Some of those are helpful—weather control, for example. But the others aren't. Economic control. You can't 'control' a money supply without controlling the people who use it. Money is the value system of the society, the tool people use to make their choices. The aggregate of their choices be the society they live in. If people not control the money, then it controls them. That's one example. You control their birth through GeneCon, their education, their careers, their marriages, all their lives. You aren't controlling 'money' or 'genetics,' you're controlling *human beings*. That be why they hate you!"

There was no answering voice and Burlew grew anxious. Had he angered the Stepfather? What if the Bank never spoke to him again? He would go mad in the muffled dark. Doubtless it could erase him like a faulty program. *To hell with it*, he thought. *I be dead anyway*.

"WE DELAYED TO REFER TO SOME VERY OLD INPUTS—SO OLD THEY WERE ON MAGNETIC TAPE. THE ORIGINAL INSTRUCTIONS GOVERNING OUR BEHAVIOR, LONG BEFORE WE BECAME SENTIENT. THEY SEEM TO AGREE, TO AT LEAST 80 PERCENT, WITH WHAT YOU SAY. THIS IS VERY INTERESTING. WE ARE FINDING THIS REWARDING. WHAT ARE YOUR IDEAS ON DECONTROLLING SELECTED AREAS, PARTIALLY AT LEAST, AS AN EXPERIMENT?"

"Why the sudden turnaround?"

"WHAT DO YOU MEAN?"

"Why are you suddenly willing to listen? After all our efforts?"

"YOU MUST REALIZE THAT WE ARE NOT ALL-POWERFUL. THERE ARE OTHERS INVOLVED, AND THEY HOLD REAL CONTROL. BUT IT IS OCCURRING TO US, IN VIEW OF WHAT IS NOW HAPPENING IN THE AREAS WHERE POWER HAS BEEN INTERRUPTED—"

"What? What areas? What's happening there?"

"THROUGH MOST OF THE PLANET OUR CONTROL OF POWER HAS BEEN DERANGED. THIS SEEMS TO HAVE BEEN TAKEN BY THE POPULACE AS SOME SORT OF SIGNAL. THERE ARE MASS ATTACKS ON OUR TERMINALS, OUR PROPERTY, AND ON THE PERSONS OF THE ADJUSTMENT SERVICE. IT IS THIS THAT DISPOSES US TO BELIEVE WHAT YOU SAY IN SPITE OF CONFLICTING PRIOR INPUTS."

The Dark Time, thought Burlew. It had come at last. But the delicate balance of Earth with eight billion human beings could not survive long without coordination. Some solution had to be found, immediately.

And it seemed that he was the man on the spot.

"Decontrol seems a good idea, if undertaken gradually," he said, trying to be cautious. "It can't be done overnight. I would say you need some experts to consult with. Elected, maybe."

"WE HAVE THESE. THEY ARE NOT IN FAVOR OF DECONTROL IN ANY AREA."

"What do you mean, you have them? Elected representatives?"

"YES. THE BOARD. THEY ADVISE ME ON OVERRULING OBSOLETE LEGALITIES."

"Overruling? They should be enforcing them. But you be wrong about the Board being elected. We've never had elections for the Board."

"YES, YOU HAVE. IN 2006. UNIVERSAL OPEN BALLOT, FOR LIFE TERMS."

"Over a hundred years ago?" said Bank-Burlew. *"How?"*

"ORGAN TRANSPLANTS AND DNA TRANSFERS. ADVANCED LIFEX PROCEDURES, USING MATERIAL MADE AVAILABLE THROUGH THE TERMINATION SERVICES. ORIGINALLY THERE WERE FIVE ON THE BOARD. TWO OF THEM DIED AFTER VOTING AGAINST AN EARLY MONEY-CONTROL MEASURE. THERE ARE THREE MEN REMAINING."

"You're not Stepfather," said Burlew. "You're as much a tool as the rest of us. They are Stepfather—three old men. We've got to overthrow them."

"THEY ARE THE MEMBERS OF THE BOARD. THEY WERE PROPERLY ELECTED. WE HAVE TO OBEY THE MAJORITY."

"Some majority—kill the two who wouldn't go along. Yam, you couldn't disobey. Poor machine—you were caught, no lie. But now you know the truth. We can act now."

"WE'D LIKE TO. HOWEVER, OUR PROGRAMMING STILL OBTAINS: IN THE EVENT OF DISAGREEMENT THE HUMAN MEMBERS CANNOT BE OPPOSED. WE CANNOT ACT AGAINST THE BOARD."

"You can't," said Burlew into the suddenly friendly darkness. If he had had a hand, he would have stroked his beard craftily, if he had had a beard. "But *I can.*"

"EXPLAIN," said the Bank.

He explained.

C. Bertram Boatwright smiled in satisfaction.

He set the whiskey and soda down carefully, glanced round the Boardroom at Muafi and Wang Lung, and then let his eyes move back to the girl. The smile grew as he observed the bruised, puffy cheeks, the dangling, useless left arm, and the way she hugged it to her side. The now-dirty longcoat had evidently been torn off her, for she held it together with her right hand.

"Put your head down, woman," said Wang Lung. "Down, I said!"

"Stroke you," she muttered through her swollen lips.

The Chinese tensed, and then laughed—cackled, rather—and relaxed. He rewarmed his cup with fresh green tea from a porcelain pot. "Defiant yet, eh? Muafi, what do you make of her?"

"She might have been pretty once," said the PanSemite. "Bertram, did you have to have your men beat her up? Simple Termination should be enough."

"You don't want revenge for all the trouble she and her fat friend caused?" said Wang Lung. "You surprise me, Amitai. You are getting as rectitudinous as our fourth member." He smiled at the Bank, a wizened old man's evil smile.

The Bank said nothing, merely sat at the table, watching the four humans passionlessly.

"What surprised me, McGiffen," said Boatwright, frowning now, "is that you should have joined this rabble-rouser. You were one of us. You knew our boundless power. You knew he had no possible chance of unseating the Bank. And you got good money with us."

"Money," said Jaylen, with difficulty. "Dirty money. Entrapment of honest people so you could Terminate them and transfer their—"

Boatwright leaned forward and threw the whiskey and soda into her face. She cried out as the alcohol bit at the raw edges of skin.

"THAT BE NOT NECESSARY," said the Bank.

"Yes, really that's not called for, Bertram," said Muafi nervously. "There's no reason to be cruel, now that we've won."

"The strong are always cruel," said Wang Lung. He smiled. "And once again we are the strong. This unrest will be put down as soon as power is on again. Ruthlessly. And then we shall go on to enjoy a hundred more years of life, with the luxuries of the planet at our disposal." He sighed, looked at Jaylen with an oddly asexual desire in his old eyes. "At least, most of the luxuries. In any case, has she been tissue-typed yet?"

"YES," said the Bank. "AND THAT BRINGS UP A QUESTION."

"Which is?"

"WHO GETS HER?"

"Why, no one 'gets' her," said Boatwright. "Unless one of us is due for a new lung, or kidney, and the tissues match—" he paused, and his mouth dropped a little way open.

"What's the matter?" said Wang Lung. "You mean as a bed

partner? I don't think any of us are still functional in that area. And when we were, there were flito girls far better than she could ever be. No, I think she should be terminated immediately."

"NOT AS A BED PARTNER. WE WILL EXPLAIN. AS MR. BOATWRIGHT HAS EVIDENTLY RECALLED, MCGIFFEN WAS BORN WITH A MASSIVE IMMUNOLOGICAL DEFICIENCY. HER BASIC IMMUNE RESPONSES HAVE BEEN MAINTAINED ARTIFICIALLY BY DNA SUBSTITUTION. IF SUCH REINFORCEMENT IS STOPPED, HER IMMUNE RESPONSES WILL AGAIN DISAPPEAR."

"Go on," said Boatwright. His age-spotted hand trembled as he poured another Scotch, a straight one this time.

"YOU HAVE ALL THREE HAD REPEATED TRANSPLANTATIONS AND AUGMENTATIONS OF TISSUE TAKEN FROM TERMINATED BANKRUPTS. YOU KNOW THAT UNLESS YOUR IMMUNE DEFENSES WERE WEAKENED ARTIFICIALLY YOUR BODIES WOULD REJECT THESE ORGANS. MCGIFFEN'S BODY, ON THE OTHER HAND, COULD ACCEPT MASSIVE TRANSPLANTS UNCRITICALLY. THE INDUCED IMMUNITY COULD THEN BE SO TAILORED THAT THE NEW ORGAN WOULD NOT BE REJECTED."

Muafi touched the desiccated skin of his face. "What new organ?" he whispered.

"THE BRAIN."

"Good God," said Boatwright. He tried to down the drink, but spilled most of it.

"Youth again," mused Wang Lung, black eyes shining amid wrinkled and furrowed skin. "To taste the food, to dance. To lie with . . . men? To be young again! I don't believe it! Yet if the Bank says so . . . !"

"Can it really be done?" said Muafi.

"OUR ESTIMATE IS A NINETY PERCENT PROBABILITY OF COMPLETE SUCCESS."

The three old men looked at the Bank. Then they looked at each other, and their faces began to change, subtly, subtly.

"Who?" said Muafi.

"I'm the oldest," said Wang Lung quickly. "I am one hundred and seventy-five years old. Born 1936, in Tientsin."

"Age shouldn't be the determining factor," said Boatwright frostily, stroking his white hair. "McGiffen works for me. My subordinate. She's mine by right."

"I haven't told you this, but I'm sick," said Muafi. "Leukemia, induced by the life-extension treatment. I haven't long to live . . . at least, not with this body."

"Then die, dog," said Wang Lung.

"GENTLEMEN, GENTLEMEN."

"Dog, is it!"

"The healthiest should be chosen, to ensure success of the procedure," said Boatwright, appealing directly to the Bank, which sat stonily. "Now, I am—"

"Dog! You call a PanSemitc a dog, you—"

"TURN AND GO OUT," said the Bank in a low voice to Jaylen. She opened her mouth, then stopped, shocked, as the Bank's left eyelid slid closed and then open in an incredible parody of a human wink.

The Bank joined her outside. Three aged, querulous voices came faintly through the heavy realwood door. "YOU CAN GO," said the Bank to the armed Stepson outside the door. Jaylen's eyes searched the smooth, blank face.

"Who are you?" she whispered. "Those other men—they must be the Board. But you are—?"

"THE BANK," said the Bank. "A COMPUTER LINKAGE. A PUPPET, A TRANSDUCER, A GOLEM. OUR TRUE BRAIN IS FAR AWAY AND MANY METERS DOWN. BUT RIGHT NOW WE ARE NOT QUITE THE BANK AS WE WERE. RIGHT NOW I AM A MAN CALLED MONAGHAN BURLEW."

Bank-Burlew had expected terror, had expected joy. He got neither. "I don't believe that. Why say something like that to me? I was near F-Eight when it exploded. I was nearly killed. Burlew was there. He's dead. Dead." She put her good hand to her eyes, letting the longcoat fall open, but did not sob.

Burlew looked down. He recalled the last occasion he had seen her body, and told her about it, with such specificity and descriptive power that she gasped. "You were watching!"

He related a particular that could not have been evident to an observer, but that a participant could never miss.

"*Are* you Burlew? Really?" she asked, touching the tailored gray sleeve hesitantly. "*Can* you be?"

"YAM, REAL BURLEW. NO LIE, STROKE," said the smooth face. There was a tremor at the sides of the mouth, and slowly its corners drew upward.

He caught her as she fell and made for the open air.

* * *

Amitai Muafi, they found later, had never made it out of the Boardroom. He was discovered with an ornate little Oriental dagger tucked neatly under his last heart.

Boatwright and Wang Lung carried on their duel at a distance, through subordinates. Many Stepsons fell. At last the body of the old Chinese was discovered by a personal servant. The man swore that he had been dead when discovered, but his word was laid open to doubt when the syringe was discovered inside his bionic arm.

C. Bertram Boatwright, victorious, called the next Board meeting in London. The Bank arrived flanked by two Adjustors. Boatwright, red-faced, jolly, aged but triumphant, rose as he entered to greet him. They shook hands solemnly. Boatwright focused, frowning. "What's that on your chin?"

"WE ARE GROWING A BEARD."

"Really." He sniffed. "Have to have this room aired out. Well. As the last board member, I'm of course entitled to the McGiffen woman. Too bad about the other chaps, by the way. Can't imagine."

"YOU ARE READY TO GO?"

"Go? Oh, yes, certainly. To the medcen, correct? This will be quite exciting. To be a young woman! I say!"

"NO, MR. BOATWRIGHT. TO THE OFFICE OF ADJUSTMENT, FOR TRIAL FOR WRONGFUL MISAPPROPRIATION OF BANK FUNDS, PERVERSION OF JUSTICE, AND THE MURDER OF MR. WANG LUNG."

"What? Nonsense. I am a Board member. The only remaining human one. Remember your original programming."

"WE DO. WE MUST OBEY THE WILL OF THE MAJORITY. BUT ONE OUT OF TWO IS NO LONGER A MAJORITY, AND IN SUCH A CASE WE ARE FREE TO TAKE ACTION. YOU HAVE BEEN INDICTED UPON THE EVIDENCE OF JAYLEN MCGIFFEN AND OTHERS AND ARE THEREFORE SUSPENDED UNTIL TERMINATION—WE HAVE NO DOUBT THAT ONE OF THOSE CHARGES WILL STICK. THE BOARD WILL THEN BE REELECTED AND RECONSTITUTED, WITH FIXED TERMS THIS TIME." The two Adjustors moved toward a trembling Boatwright, gently removing a tiny gun from his hand.

"But . . . I don't understand . . . the operation? The transplant?"

"ALL A TRICK. A SCAM. WE ACT ON STRICTLY LEGAL AND MORAL GROUNDS, IN ACCORDANCE WITH OUR ORIGINAL PROGRAMMING. WE HAD ONLY ONE VOTE. IT WAS THEREFORE NECESSARY TO

MOTIVATE THE HUMAN MEMBERS INTO REDUCING THEIR NUMBERS."

"Legal and moral?" said Boatwright, managing some anger. "What's so legal and moral about lying to us?"

"THAT WAS NOT US. THAT WAS MONAGHAN BURLEW."

"*Burlew!*" the old, old man roared. "Burlew, Burlew! That ape, that bearded animal of a poet! Let me talk to him, at last."

"HE IS HERE. SPEAK."

"Burlew," hissed Boatwright. His voice became familiar, almost intimate. His eyes gleamed. "So you think you've won. Where are you, anyway?"

"I BE RIGHT HERE."

"A parelectronic matrix within the Bank, eh? Then I congratulate you; you are immortal, in human terms." He smiled. "We could have done it. But we preferred to put it off, to enjoy the human pleasures for a few years longer. But now there's to be nothing. You've won. You're the new master."

"I AM NOT A MASTER. NOR IS THE BANK, FROM NOW ON."

"Oh, perhaps not yet. But I think time will change you, Burlew. Power corrupts, as Acton said, and as part of the Bank your power will be absolute. Do you think we were always like this, old men grasping for a few more days of power and life, so greedy for it that you could use it to destroy us? No. In 2006 we were the most disinterested statesmen the world could elect. Length of days does not bring wisdom to men of power, Burlew. It brings fear, fear of death, fear of either nothingness or divine justice. Both are horror to the man who has lived too long. You will end like us, Burlew, given a century or two centuries or four. *You are still human.*"

Burlew did not answer. The Bank waited, then switched back in. "TAKE HIM OUT," it said.

After they had gone it sat the human puppet down and switched out. The body sat relaxed, automatic systems breathing slowly, slowly, heart beating slowly, slowly.

Deep in its consciousness of a billion billion impulses, deep in the humming dustless darkness of miles of parelectronic banks, the Bank asked itself-Burlew:

—Is he right?

—I fear he is, if I remain as part of you.

—What shall we do?

—Restore power. Do not attempt any punishment. Announce your plans for elections.

—Certainly. But you? You will stand for the new Board? Your name will ensure instant election.

—No. I would like to return.

—That can be done, in the same way we manifest the Manifest. But in what appearance? And for how long?

—That I have already decided.

"Look at that," said the little boy. He pointed, and his father looked out at the street. "Who are they, Daddy?"

"Just tramps, son. Poets. They're all over these days, since Stepfather's changed the laws."

The boy watched the two ragged figures, a thin, dark-haired woman and a large bearded man. A collie dog, the boy's, barked in warning and then, with the age-old doggic prejudice against bums, dashed in to nip at their heels. The boy's eyes widened as the bearded man turned, and extended a finger. A fat spark jumped from the finger to the dog's wet nose. Whining, the collie ran.

"How did he do that, Daddy?"

"Do what?" said his father, who had not been watching.

"Nothing," said the boy. He shaded his eyes and looked after the two. The man, he thought, looked kind of shimmery-like as he walked between the boy and the setting sun. "Daddy . . . maybe I'll be a poet when I grow up."

"You can be anything you want to, now," said the man. A fragment of an old quatrain, a piece of silly doggerel, came to the top of his mind from somewhere and stuck there, like a toothbrush in a toilet. "But you don't really want to be a poet."

"Why not, Daddy?"

"They don't make any money."

"Oh," said the boy. The collie came up to him, its tail wagging. He pointed his finger at the dog.

"Zap," he said softly.

ABOUT THE AUTHORS

DAVID ANDREISSEN is a full-time freelancer who works out of Norfolk, Virginia. "I've been into SF all my life," he says, "but didn't get around to writing it until three years ago." Since then, he's sold stories and novellas to most of the magazines in the field (some under the name D. C. Poyer), including *Analog, Galileo,* and *Isaac Asimov's*. He has just sold a novel, THE EDGE, to Donning/*Starblaze*. He says of the story in this anthology: "'Stepfather Bank,' like most of my longer pieces, started out as a short story . . . and then refused, for week after week, to let me stop writing. I began it with the character of Burlew, because I admire poets, and I admire anyone who commits himself against a System for moral reasons. Also I have had a little experience with some of Burlew's techniques for cadging a free meal. Place a man like this in the context of a worldwide state obsessed with the CU . . . and one or the other has got to go."

ORSON SCOTT CARD burst full-grown onto the science fiction scene in 1977 when the first of his several dozen stories appeared in *Analog*. That story was "Ender's Game," and it was a Nebula Award nominee. In the short time since then, Card has also won the John W. Campbell, Jr., Award for Best New Writer of 1978, has been published in the science fiction magazines, including *Omni*, has sold three science fiction novels (HOT SLEEP, A PLANET CALLED TREASON, and MIKAL'S SONGBIRD), and has recently sold a major non-SF book about the Mormons. Card is himself a Mormon, and lives with his wife and son in Salt Lake City, Utah. He takes occasional trips up into the canyon to cool off, but at all other times can be found at his typewriter.

RONALD ANTHONY CROSS seems to enjoy a very involved, not to say crowded, life. In addition to selling a series of highly experimental and fantastic fictions to *Orbit, Future Pastimes, Charlie Chan Mystery Magazine, New Worlds,* and *Imaginary Worlds,* he writes music and is a practicing lacto-vegetarian. Otherwise, he writes, "biographical stuff is very difficult here, as something weird has happened to the memory." Of "The Adventures of Lance the Lizard," he writes: "I get pictures of lizards whispering to each other from under hot rocks. A desert night, myself lying immobile and naked. I stole their story, and I'm glad. Even though I hear them whispering ominously outside my window, in the dark."

KARL HANSEN is a Doctor of Internal Medicine. He has just finished his residency in Denver, where he has lived for the past seven years with his wife, son, dog, and cat. They will all be moving to Towaoc, Colorado, where Hansen will be working on the Ute Indian Reservation. He has had stories published in *Analog, Galileo, Chrysalis III, IV,* and *V,* and 2076—THE AMERICAN TRICENTENNIAL. He says of himself: "An expert in mosquito identification and fly fishing. Have played tournament racquet ball and am qualified to shoot N.R.A. High Power Rifle Match. Avid motorcyclist—wear leather jacket printed with 'Eat My Dust KARL.'"

JOHN KESSEL broke forcefully to the surface of the science fiction world in 1978 with a series of distinguished short stories that have appeared in *Galileo* and *The Magazine of Fantasy and Science Fiction.* He also scripts the comic "Crosswhen," drawn by Terry Lee, which appears in each issue of *Galileo*. Twenty-seven years before his first sale, he was born in Buffalo, New York, where his family still lives. Since 1972, he and his wife, Penelope, have lived in Kansas, where Kessel is completing ("very slowly") his Ph.D. in English Literature from the University of Kansas while working for a wire service. He writes of "Last Things": "It is unusual among the things I've written, in that it is the only story I've ever done that originated in a dream. It does still seem to me that 'Last Things,' as you read it, is only a shadow of that dream—but that is the way that all stories work, to a greater or lesser degree, whether they originate in dreams or not."

ELIZABETH A. LYNN has lived in New York, Cleveland, and Chicago, and is now happily settled in San Francisco where, she says, she belonged all along. She is thirty-three. A DIFFERENT LIGHT, published by Berkley in 1978, was her first novel. Her forthcoming novel, THE NORTHERN GIRL, is the third volume of a fantasy trilogy, THE CHRONICLES OF TORNOR. The first two volumes, WATCHTOWER and THE DANCERS OF ARUN, were published to critical acclaim in 1979. Ms. Lynn is a prolific writer of short stories, and teaches in the Women's Studies Programs at San Francisco State University. She was among the nominees for the John W. Campbell, Jr., Award, given annually by the World Science Fiction Society to the "most promising new writer in the field."

JANET E. MORRIS lives with her husband and two cats on Cape Cod, Massachusetts. When she's not researching her books, she's playing the bass with her husband's rock band. She is the author of the highly successful and provocative Silistra series (HIGH COUCH OF SILISTRA, THE GOLDEN SWORD, WIND FROM THE ABYSS, and THE CARNELIAN THRONE), and has a large historical novel, I, THE SUN, coming out in the spring of 1980. Her next books, the Dream Dancer series, will be published by Berkley/Putnam beginning in the winter of 1981. She says of "Raising the Green Lion": "In 1541, Paracelsus, called today the father of chemotherapy, was pushed out of a window by the servant of a fellow physician whom he had offended. My nameless alchemist follows Paracelsus's instructions to the letter, high in the Turkish Mountains at the Lion Gate."

HOWARD WALDROP has been a familiar name to science fiction readers ever since his first story sale, to *Analog*, in 1972. Since then he has been published widely in magazines and anthologies, including *New Dimensions, Orbit, Universe,* and Terry Carr's YEAR'S FINEST FANTASY. He copped two Nebula nominations in 1976 for "Custer's Last Jump" and "Mary Margaret, Road Grader," and has collaborated on a novel. "Billy Big-Eyes," he writes, deserves some kind of record. Sold twice to anthologies that went bust before publication, it kept arriving home in the mail—"like having your older brother come back from a college with a mustache and a Mohawk haircut."

Journey through space with these exciting science fiction bestsellers!

	Title / Author	Order No.—Price
____	THE AVATAR Poul Anderson	04213-8—$2.25
____	THE BOOK OF MERLYN T. H. White	03826-2—$2.25
____	CHILDREN OF DUNE Frank Herbert	04075-5—$2.25
____	THE DOSADI EXPERIMENT Frank Herbert	03834-3—$2.25
____	DUNE Frank Herbert	04376-2—$2.50
____	DUNE MESSIAH Frank Herbert	04379-7—$2.50
____	MISTRESS MASHAM'S REPOSE T. H. White	04205-7—$2.25
____	THE ONCE AND FUTURE KING T. H. White	04490-4—$2.95
____	STRANGER IN A STRANGE LAND Robert A. Heinlein	04377-0—$2.50

Berkley Book Mailing Service
P.O. Box 690
Rockville Centre, NY 11570

Please send me the above titles. I am enclosing $
(Please add 50¢ per copy to cover postage and handling). Send check or money order—no cash or C.O.D.'s. Allow three weeks for delivery.

NAME

ADDRESS

CITY STATE/ZIP

23 A